# MISS VIRGINIA

## AND THE SWEET SISTERS

A NOVEL

## DONNA LAWRENCE

**Crescent Hill Press**

Published by Crescent Hill Press
Visit the author's website at: donnamarielawrence.com
Copyright © 2023 by Donna Lawrence



Cover Art:
Jenny Quinlan at historicalfictionbookcovers.com

Editors:
Jessica Cale, Developmental Editor at www.historicaleditorial.com
Nikki Busch, Copyeditor at www.nikkibuschediting.com
Proofread by Linda at www.victoryediting.com
Formatted by Tami at www.victoryediting.com

Paperback print book ISBN: 979-8-9872168-1-1
Copyright: TXu 2-327-323

Disclaimer:

# DEDICATION

*This book is dedicated to the men in my life who have gone on before. I love and miss you greatly.*

*My father, Thomas Euclid Lawrence Jr., my uncle Harry Lee Harris, and my nephew Gary Kenneth (Scootie) Lawrence.*

*Also, a special dedication to Mrs. Kenney Roseberry.*

*All have helped me realize that hopes and dreams are worth pursuing. Thank you.*

# Table of Contents

# TABLE OF CONTENTS

# PREFACE

This story has spent some time renting space in my head. Its development slowly taking shape on the page. Then I placed it back on the shelf for a while and pulled it back out again. Reason? I wasn't sure I could deliver the subject with authentic honesty, sensitivity, and purpose. But timing and recent social events have compelled me to complete this work. Of the many issues our nation has had to face, the issue of racism refuses to lie dormant. The divisions this can cause seem to arise when we least expect it. Sometimes explosively so.

One of the lesser-known aspects of this issue is intraracial racism. I decided to explore this from the perspective of a mixed-race thirteen-year-old girl. I wanted to examine how this issue impacts her life and affects her self-esteem, sense of worth, and self, particularly when racism and bullying come from her own social circle and race. How does one grapple with ostracism when puberty starts to manifest or when hormones create changes in the body and mind?

Heady prospect, to be sure, but I didn't shy away. I let the story develop on its own, taking me along for the ride. Racism is committed regardless of color or social status. I do not sugarcoat it here. The added burden of intraracial racism makes the struggle for acceptance among racist ideologies seem unilaterally unfair. With the added element of good versus evil permeating this story, the stakes are high indeed for the main character.

As already mentioned in the disclaimer, I must remind the reader that this is a work of fiction. Although I have drawn on a few of my own experiences, I have no knowledge of the events depicted here as factual. They are purely from my imagination. My muses have been many. I have tried to authenticate the characters' interactions through raw and honest regional expressions indicative of the time depicted. Even though I have been sensitive to racial slurs and gratuitous generalizations, any slurs used are per the vernacular of the period to give authenticity to the story. They are not meant to be offensive to today's reader but to provide context to events as to time and place.

This novel pays homage to so much, but especially to relationships, complicated and simple. It reminds us that people are not so different from ourselves; our neighbors are just like us. It is also a labor of love that pays homage to a small town—a township of people who came together to make a better future in which we can all live. And I hope this story teaches lessons we can still live by today.

*The Author*

# INTRODUCTION

*An Introduction to Local Color*

Paris, Kentucky, is the setting for the events unfolding in this story. The focus is on the intricate relationships within Paris's Black community. We read how their lives intersect with Whites and come together when a crisis strikes, impacting the main character and those central to her story. As someone who came of age in small-town Kentucky during the civil rights era of the 1960s, I offer a brief history of Paris and Kentucky as a whole, so an understanding of the land and its people is clear.

Kentucky is bathed in beauty and surrounded by a dense canopy of many trees such as hickory, beech, dogwood, sugar and red maple, oak, black walnut, ash, cherry, poplar, and the occasional blue spruce pine. Autumn in Kentucky is a marvelous place to be when the explosions of color occur in the fall, and the hot air of summer cools to a level of enjoyment. Spring and summer rains are warm, while winters can be harsh, mainly when the water-filled air turns bitter cold. In winter, ice storms are a common occurrence. When the occasional snow blankets the surrounding hills, it is a rare treat for children to delight in using their sleds or snow boots that wouldn't get used otherwise.

Kentucky is known for its Thoroughbred horse racing. It is home to champions such as Citation, Man o' War, American Pharoah, and Bourbon County's Bold Ruler, who sired Triple Crown winner—Secretariat. Secretariat now rests at Claiborne

Farms near Paris, where Seabiscuit grew up and was trained. Kentucky is also known for tobacco, supplemented by corn and corn's by-product, whiskey. Kentucky Bourbon, to be exact, and distilled with the best waters limestone aquifers can provide. The rich soil from which corn and tobacco grow produces beautiful flowers such as roses, begonias, and impatiens, to name a few. The Bluegrass region of Kentucky gets its name from this fertile soil, which produces grass so green that it can appear blue in color. If allowed to grow to its natural height, this variety of grass, *poa pratensis*, even produces a blue flower head. The Blue Ridge Mountains, far to the east, which make up the Ridge and Valley province that borders Eastern Kentucky, get their name from the color released by the many trees in the area.

In the early-morning light, evaporated dew rises from condensed cold air, creating a fog that hugs the ground around the hilly knolls called the Appalachian Mountains, giving them a smoky appearance. The beautiful "dark and bloody ground" of the Shawnee, Cherokee, and Chickasaw Indian nations, to name a few, is also the land of President Abraham Lincoln, the Kentucky senator and abolitionist Cassius Marcellus Clay, pioneer Daniel Boone, and the legendary boxer Muhammad Ali.

Kentucky is composed of many geographic regions. Paris is the county seat of Bourbon County, right in the middle of the Bluegrass region, settled by British, German, Ulster Scots-Irish, and their descendants. Approximately fifteen minutes northeast of Lexington, Paris is also never far from the hustle and bustle of its faraway western city on the Ohio River, Louisville. Somehow Paris, situated on the Licking River and Stoner Creek's cross tributaries, never feels isolated but more nestled, as quaint small towns are often known. Surrounded by Lexington to the south, Cincinnati to the north, Georgetown and Frankfort to the northwest, and Winchester to the east, Paris seems the center of everything.

Kentucky has a storied history. Like many Southern states, Kentucky was known for its slave trade. Still, its abolitionist participation caused Kentucky to be viewed as fickle in its allegiance to the Southern cause, especially during the conflict which sparked the Civil War. Indeed, Kentucky was a slave state and a pathway to freedom for enslaved people seeking refuge in Ohio. The book *Uncle Tom's Cabin* by Harriett Beecher Stowe is inspired by the true story of Josiah Henson, a Maryland enslaved person who was also enslaved in Kentucky. He eventually traveled to Ohio to win his freedom.

The Bluegrass region is full of historical relics of slavery. The beautiful rolling hills of green grass are reminiscent of the Old South's landed gentry, with the black fences framing fields for horses to roam. The vast meadows and majestic mansions set on hilltops offset this conspicuous wealth and animal husbandry with miles of fenced stone walls. The walls began construction in the early 1800s by Scots-Irish stonemasons, who later taught this craft to "helpers" or enslaved people and indentured servants. Laid without mortar, the stone walls line many of the region's roads. They remain a testament to a long-lost skill of engineering and architecture completed by slave labor.

The most celebrated of these roads is between Lexington and Paris. On this scenic parkway, one can gaze upon the languid sights of the many horse farms, with some barns still painted in their riding silk colors. Farms such as Runnymede, Indian Creek, and Claiborne are in Bourbon County, with Calumet and Lane's End in Lexington and Versailles, Kentucky.

However, the wealth for which Bourbon County is known is diametrically opposed to people of color who are full of pride and part of the fabric of Paris. Although descendants from enslaved people, mixed-race mulattos, and beautiful "fancy girls" from New Orleans, the divisions of "race" are evident during the time depicted in this story. Still, this was not a cause of dissension among those who lived and worked in the county but rather a conscious need to develop and cultivate tolerance and harmony among its citizens. This was no more apparent than in Paris, where the wealthy mixed with the nonwealthy. Many residents can recount the names of leaders who emerged from Kentucky and became renowned, but few know Garrett Morgan, the inventor of the tri-color traffic light, a Black man born and raised in Paris. The races understood "place" but, for the most part, ignored it at the same time.

By 1967, the Civil Rights Act was in its infancy but never rose to high importance in Paris because equal rights had already begun to ease itself into a way of life. Some say this was due to school sports. A sports culture that intertwined when the schools were fully integrated in 1964. Others say it was due to the civility that came naturally to its citizens. It was not always easy. There were the occasional skirmishes but nothing the city and school administrators, with the influence of Mr. William (Bill) Reed—or "Chief Reed" as he was fondly called—could not squelch with respect and compromise.

According to rumors, a nervous city council waited for the NAACP officials to arrive in Paris, escorted by the principal of Western High, Mr. Reed; they were astonished to see him appear alone. Per the rumor, Mr. Reed stopped the NAACP officials at the county line from entering Paris because, in his opinion, this would rile the populace and make matters worse. He told the NAACP representatives to go back home because the citizens of Paris could handle their own racial problems. If the NAACP was needed, he would contact them, not the other way around. This ever-prescient nature propelled Mr. Reed to become one of the most revered leaders as the era of race relations pushed toward harmony, not dissonance and anarchy.

This is no more evident than in the 1960s when communities were ripped apart on the verge of civil rights reform. More and more cities accepted and/or grappled with the decision of integration in schools and businesses. Like today, social justice was the mindset that shaped young people's lives during this time. Music also had its influences, as demonstrated by rhythm and blues, rock and roll, and socially conscious folk.

This land. This Kentucky. Once the soil seeps into your soul, it's hard to shake loose. As shown in its landscape, cultivation, cultural interaction, and contradiction of values, rules, and social mores, Kentucky is a land full of diversity. Citizens are proud of their heritage, upheld religious beliefs, love of land, country, and legacy. They display pride through dignity and respectful interactions with each other. Most of the time. With Paris's diversity and sense of community, its long history helps weave together an intricate tapestry. It paints a portrait of the struggles and successes of mankind and the acceptance, compassion, and tolerance embedded in its bluegrass soil.

Thus, as I look back on the civil rights era of the 1960s, it proved to be a time of growth and connectedness. Although some may argue, I believe those vestiges are still felt and shared today. Through my research, I've come to understand the collective: a collective of people wanting positive change and whose stories need to be told. This story is one.

I've chosen to showcase how events beginning in the summer of 1967 affected and shaped our main character, a young girl on the cusp of young adulthood in the small town of Paris, Kentucky.

# PROLOGUE

## *Murder in 1953*

JIMMY NEVER LOST at craps. Never. But tonight, he was losing and didn't like it, no sir, not one little bit. He squinted, thinking this guy, Calvin, had to be cheating or something, which was easy to do playing a simple back-alley game. What was he missing? Then Jimmy thought he saw a shift to the left of Calvin's hand that held the dice, but he couldn't be sure in the weak light from overhead. One bulb shining down the bowels of the alley behind Jason's corner bar was barely bright enough to draw moths. He told himself he should have thought twice about coming to this backwater town, a twenty-minute drive, give or take, from his home in Winchester. But Lylesville Street in Paris, Kentucky, was *the* place to be. And tonight the street was hopping.

Just moments earlier, Jimmy had joined the throng of patrons spilling outside the crowded bar to escape the trapped heat accumulating inside. Jason's Bar & Jazz, which stood on the corner of Lylesville and Eighth, was a juke joint Jimmy liked to visit on occasion. It held its own against the larger American Legion Dance Hall, located a few blocks farther down Lylesville. It was jam-packed and hopping just as loudly as Jason's, but he didn't care for it as much.

The sun had gone down long ago. The late evening heat of August made the night air muggy. The pressing heat always set

Jimmy on edge, making it easy to lose mental control. He wiped his brow as he walked out of the Eighth Street entrance of Jason's, grateful to feel whatever coolness the humid air could offer. There was no escape from the heat. The yelps and squeals of women and the chatter of local prostitutes wanting to be picked up irritated him more than usual. The searing trumpet sounds from Miles Davis's and Dizzy Gillespie's horns didn't soothe him as usual; instead, this set him more on edge than he was already. The noisome smell of stale beer, piss, and puke made matters worse, adding to the building ache in his head.

As he turned the corner onto Lylesville to grab a smoke, a group of men walked into the alley behind the bar where a game of craps was taking place. This was the usual late-night activity, so to pass the time, Jimmy decided to join. As he made his way to the alley, he mentally located where his car was parked in case the game went sideways and he needed a quick getaway. Jimmy gave the car a satisfied nod as it sat on the other side of the street next to a vast field of tall grass once used for farming.

No one knew Jimmy, which suited him just fine. He didn't like people in general and liked to lie low. Now very late in the hour, Jimmy had better things to do than waste more of his time playing with these country Negroes whose clothes hung limp and tattered about their bodies. But the lure of winning money, which had alluded him thus far, was more important for the moment.

Jimmy idly wondered if the noise and heat contributed to throwing off his game. The thing was, Jimmy couldn't afford to keep losing throw after throw, not if he was to propose to his lady that night and impress her with his winnings. But Calvin's dumb luck was getting in the way of that plan.

Calvin Manning didn't look very lucky, thought Jimmy. He was young and, like his friends, appeared as if he hadn't eaten a meal in a while. He was well-liked, judging by how he joked around with the other fellows. Jimmy really couldn't blame him for feeling cocky. After all, his luck seemed too good to be true.

This thought alone accounted for why Jimmy couldn't shake the feeling that something wasn't quite right with *this* particular game or with Calvin. Which was why Jimmy kept watching him. Very closely, watching.

For a Black man, it wasn't cool to sweat like a pig during a back-alley game of craps. Each time Jimmy bent down, droplets of the stuff trickled from his forehead and hit the dirt, indicating where he had stood, giving away his lucky spot if he won. This was another irritation Jimmy could do without.

After placing their bets, five of them tossed money in the middle of a circle drawn on the ground. When all the bets were placed, Calvin picked up the dice and shook the pair in his hand. Jimmy watched as Calvin felt the rough edges of the dice. "This gotta happen for me, fellas. These greenbacks'll come in real handy for little sis when her baby gets here. Damn, if it won't." Calvin slowly licked his lips, blew on the dice for good luck, and looked up at Jimmy.

"Seven come eleven, come on, baby, come on!" Calvin yelled as he snapped his wrist and threw the dice against the back wall of the building. Sure as shit, the dice fell, with one showing six black dots and the other showing five black dots, totaling eleven. Calvin had won again and shouted, "*God* bless America!"

*What the fuck!* Jimmy said to himself. *This son of a bitch's cheating.* The standard roll on a call is seven to win in a simple game, but Calvin previously called eight and won. Now, winning eleven was too much luck for one man. Jimmy's jaw tightened.

"Pay up, suckers!" Calvin exclaimed.

Calvin was patted on the back because of the win, with everyone saying his sister would be proud. He picked up the remaining bet money from the ground, then held out his hand to collect two more dollars from each man who had placed extra bets, but Jimmy held his back.

"How 'bout it, man?" Calvin asked.

"Let me see the dice," Jimmy said.

"What? You holding out?"

"No. *You* holding back. Let me see 'em."

"Look, man, I can't help you keep crapping out!" Still excited, Calvin said this with a shrug. "Not your night or somethin'!"

"Let me see the fucking dice, man." Jimmy held out his hand, expectant. "I ain't paying until I see them things."

"Fuck you. Pay up!" Calvin feigned insult.

With a quick move, Jimmy had Calvin in a chokehold from the back with his left arm, while all around him, the other men yelled at Jimmy to chill out. But by then, Jimmy had the dice and felt the unevenness of the weight.

"You switched the dice! You got these weighted, man? What the fuck, motherfucker?"

Sucking air to breathe, Calvin tried to tell Jimmy that he had him all wrong. Others moved to either break up the fight or check the dice themselves. But Jimmy pulled out a switchblade with his free right hand and pointed it at those daring to come closer. Jimmy never loosened his hold on Calvin as he switched the blade from his right hand to his left. Then he deftly reached into Calvin's right side pocket and removed all the money inside. He released Calvin, who breathlessly turned to face Jimmy, still pleading his case.

"You got it wrong, man. Ain't nothin' wrong with them bones."

"Yeah, like nothing wrong with you winning every throw, asshole?"

"Look, man, I need that money, okay? Not your night is all!"

"Maybe not, but I know a cheat when I see one. I'm taking this and to hell with y'all," Jimmy said, thinking these country jigaboos had a lot to learn. Calvin was a stupid fucker who needed to get up a lot earlier if he thought he could get over on ole Jimmy.

Then *It* started to come on, raising its ugly head. Jimmy thought, *I'm about to lose control, and it's all Calvin's fault.* Jimmy could feel himself slipping a gear, as they say. When this happened, events occurred as if in a thick fog of confusion. He even spoke in a different voice, not his own. Jimmy couldn't let *It* take him, so he shook his head to clear the fog creeping up and closing in. He had no name for *It*. It just was. He had taken a few steps to leave when he felt a hand forcefully turn him around.

"Where the fuck you goin'?" Calvin asked.

The right cross to Jimmy's chin was weak. But it caught him flat-footed, so he fell backward onto the ground as loose dirt flew up and around him. Calvin's inexperience at fighting showed. He threw himself on top of Jimmy, swinging and flailing wildly, throwing jabs at Jimmy's head and sides. The other men gathered around, egging Calvin on, some shouting, "Get his blade!" "Get his blade!" Jimmy was unconcerned because he was good with switchblades—in fact, better than most.

In a breathtaking move, Jimmy twisted around and regained his footing, then swiveled, cutting Calvin across the left side of his chest as he rose. Calvin seemed stunned and rose slowly from the dirt to gaze in awe at the deep cut. Jimmy came from behind with an animalistic growl and stabbed upward under Calvin's right arm, severing tendons and a vital artery. Blood spurted everywhere. The person known as Jimmy was no longer there. *This* Jimmy enjoyed being bathed in blood.

Jimmy let *It* take him and change him; he gave *It* full control, becoming that other person who loved mayhem and death. He knocked Calvin's feet from under him and straddled his body. *Calvin's making me do this,* Jimmy thought as he savagely stabbed the man repeatedly, swooning at every thrust. Calvin begged him for mercy, but he had none. Others fled the scene. *Cowards.* Tears rolled down Calvin's face as the last breath left his body. Fascination seized Jimmy as the blood fanned out in a pattern of angel wings behind Calvin's body. This drove him on.

When the frenzied attack ended, he slowly rose from the lifeless form of Calvin Manning and, with a confused and disconnected stare, looked down at the young man. Then he thought he saw Calvin smile! He couldn't quite make this out for a second because he was soaked in Calvin's blood, and Calvin didn't look so good. As the dirt claimed the blood spilling out of Calvin's body, the fog in Jimmy's head started to clear—but just.

He casually bent down and wiped his blade on Calvin's tattered clothes. Feeling invisible, his car an afterthought, Jimmy ran into the field of tall grasses on the other side of Lylesville Street. The feel of sharp blades of uncut grass tickled him, and he laughed maniacally. The laughter rose above the din of the nightlife noise as Jimmy faded into the grasses amid the humid night air.

# CHAPTER 1

## *Get on with It*



*Thirteen years later—1967*

I KEPT TELLING myself to get up and do what Mom asked of me, but it felt like the heat was melting my brain. Everyone complained about Kentucky's hot summers, but this day was a scorcher. It took forever to get cool by fanning myself with the paper fan from church. With the face of Jesus pictured on the front of the fan, it seemed He was saying, "Linney, now you should know better."

Reluctantly, I got up and again inspected the zit in the center of my forehead for the hundredth time, knowing it wouldn't do as an excuse for not doing what Mom asked of me. The big Wally, which we called these monsters, was the last thing I needed to deal with. Especially on the day Mom expected me to visit the two ladies across the street. I at least wanted to look decent. Of course, I was stalling because visiting strange old women wasn't cool. But I was stuck. I taking a deep breath, I told myself it was now or never, so I might as well get it over with and, yes, *get on with it.*

I would never live this down if my friends found out. Doreen and her friends teased me enough already, mostly because of my almost-white skin. I could just hear Doreen now. "You so weird! Reading books all day and now you visiting old people? That ain't cool! You're such a White girl. Don't you know *we* don't *do* things like that?" Words like these always made me feel stupid and different. I suppose my two good friends, Carolyn and Angie, whose families had long-standing ties in Paris, wouldn't mind so much. But not Doreen Elizabeth Munro. She was my mother's conceited younger sister, and aside from Angela and Carolyn, I considered her my best friend.

Because I was part of the Munro family, Doreen and I were known as the Munro girls. I was called Linney, short for Lindsey Anne Hollis. I hated the name. The only child of Janie Mae and Laurant Hollis, I looked White compared to other light-skinned Blacks in Paris. Slightly singed, as they say, and with no freckles, because of my so-called Creole blood, I always felt "other than." I inherited the physical traits of my Creole father and knew only a few words of Louisiana Creole French, which Mom learned after she married Daddy. Aside from the food and some words in Creole, this was all I ever knew about my heritage. When Mom referred to me as her little Creole girl, it painfully reminded me that I was different from everyone else. I accepted that even though I had never been to Louisiana and only knew where it was on a map, I was Black—not Creole.

However, I was so light-skinned that most Blacks jokingly referred to the coloring as "light, bright, and damn near white" or "high yellow." I stood a little taller than most of my friends. My thick wavy dark brown hair had to be kept in braids because it never stayed straight for long, and in Kentucky's humidity, it frizzed every time I stepped outside. My looks were the bane of my existence.

Because of these shortcomings, Doreen and *her* friends, Brenda and Karen, were relentless in teasing me. They showed no mercy. I used to think they were joking or simply having fun, but their jokes were not so funny anymore. It hurt my feelings when Doreen called me "White girl" or asked me to unbraid my hair to see how big it would get, saying, "Why's your hair so frizzy when you look so White?" Trying to hide tears each time she did something like this was harder to do. I'd do just about anything to stop the teasing. But it never worked.

"Doreen's a spoiled, selfish, and reckless little brat," Mom said. "I don't like you spending so much time with her and her wild ways. She's too loud and pushy for her own good, and I don't like you traipsing across beams in that old rock quarry or swimming in that creek water either. Always climbing trees and playing in that strip of woods across the street. What do you call that place, the Jungle?"

"Yes, ma'am, but it's not like we—"

"Well, I don't like it. It's not right for young ladies to behave like you two."

"Yes, ma'am."

Whenever Mom talked like this, I'd slowly put my hands to my ears because the truth was hard to hear. How could I get her to understand that it was hard *not* to do what Doreen said? Because Mom was studying to be a nurse and attended night classes in Lexington, I never wanted to be a bother. But, these days, her studies made it difficult to speak to her about anything.

Yep! This summer was turning out to be a doozy, all right. Such was my introduction to a summer of adult responsibility and my teenage lot in life in the small town of Paris, Kentucky.

It's easy to fall in love with Paris, which is north of Lexington. It's horse country where summer's long hot sticky days give way to autumn's coolness. In summer, most days, you had to bathe at least twice just to stay cool! However, the trees provided shade for endless wandering and exploring through dense blue-green grass and clover fields that opened to vast meadows for thinking and reading.

Winter brought ice storms and bitter cold. Snow fell on rare occasions, and when it did, we got permission to sled down Mr. Sauerkraut's hill. He was a cranky old farmer, and I'm not sure if this was his real name or a nickname given to him by the neighbors because he was from Germany, but we liked him all the same. We didn't think the name might be considered a slur at that time. We thought it was funny and fit his outward demeanor. Even though he was mean during the tobacco-growing season, he was always kind to us in the winter and ensured we were properly dressed for sledding. He usually had warm apple cider—or wassail, as he called it—at the ready after a sleigh ride down his steep hill. He knew all our names and woe to anyone who wasn't careful not to hurt themselves. Yes, winters could be harsh, fall was the best, but summers were worse.

On the other side of the hill from Whites, we lived in Paris proper in a new subdivision called Greenfield. Our house was one of ten single-story, three-bedroom duplexes lined up to form a string of units that created a neighborhood of twenty-family homes with yards in front and back. The first four duplex buildings were on our street. We lived in the third building, right-hand side. Our set of duplexes sat on a slight rise that, from the backyard, overlooked the remaining six duplex buildings below. There was a convenient shortcut to those units through a descending set of steps. The backyards shared a common grassy area, where cookouts were held, and kids played softball on a bare spot at the far end using a red rubber ball. Laundry hung on clotheslines that stretched down the back of each duplex unit. However, it wasn't uncommon for a wayward dusty ball to get caught in a neighbor's set of drying sheets, much to the dismay of whoever hung them. It was a tight-knit neighborhood where everyone knew one another. Neighbors were close, and gossip was plenty!

Daddy was a military man who lived in California, and for reasons I was not allowed to know, he and my mother were separated. All I knew was Mom would be sad for days. Sometimes, I could hear her cry long into the night. Daddy called once a week, though, and I couldn't wait to hear him say, "Hi honey!" I felt Daddy was as miserable as Mom, just by what he said. I begged him to come home, but he never did. Sometimes, in the middle of the day and out of nowhere, Mom would reach out and hold me close, saying how much she loved me. I loved her too but knew I could never erase the sadness she felt for missing Daddy.

My mother was a well-known and respected lady who worked as a front desk secretary and receptionist in Dr. Roberts's office along with Miss Sandy Beaumont. She cared about everyone and *everything*. I'd even heard some say she was like a Girl Scout, but I didn't care. I thought she was the most beautiful person I had ever seen, and I often wondered if I would ever be as pretty, wise, or as kind when I grew up. My friends referred to her as Miss Janie. The "Miss" is how we addressed older women in the South, such as Miss Anne, Miss Pearl, Miss Loren, Miss Julie Ann, Miss Tally, and Miss Edna Allen, whom no one liked.

To hear Mom tell it, Miss Edna was a terrible gossip who could be petty and mean. Rumor had it she spied on us with binoculars and could be seen peeking out her window or around the corner of any house. The lies she told had some truth, but lies were lies just the same. She was a nuisance we put up with and someone I dreaded facing as the days of summer unfolded.

Many would describe me as a timid and quiet girl, so getting a reputation for being stuck-up and a Goody Two-shoes was easy. But what most didn't know was that I could be impetuous at times and stubborn. I tried to avoid teasing by reading books, studying hard, and doing crafting projects, but it didn't help. The highlight of my day was going for long walks to my favorite secret spot under a shady sugar maple tree high on a hill overlooking a small portion of our neighborhood. There I could escape the stings of teasing and plop down to daydream or read one of the many books from the local library. Losing myself within the plot of books such as *Little Women, Lord of the Flies, Anne of Green Gables,* or one of a series of Nancy Drew mysteries was pure heaven. I would visualize myself as every heroine rising triumphantly and vanquishing every foe. However, when the courthouse clock tower chimed the lateness of the hour, it was my signal to return and face the real world.

Most kids attended Vacation Bible School in the summer, a camp for studying the Bible and living in its teachings for a solid three weeks. There wasn't much in the way of camping activities. After reading verses and reciting the books of the Bible all day, it soon became boring. I hated Vacation Bible School and, after begging Mom constantly, was thrilled not to have to go that summer. Without much to occupy my time, though, boredom set in quickly. Then one day it happened. As Mom hurried to leave for work, we talked about how I should spend the rest of my summer.

"Okay, young lady, since you begged not to go to Bible school, can you at least do something productive instead of reading all day?" Mom asked. "I don't like worrying about you getting into mischief while I'm at work."

"But I like to read! What else is there besides reading?" I pouted. "I'm tired of knitting and crocheting. I could macramé some more, I guess?"

"I can't have you lying around all summer, Linney. I won't have it. You need something to keep you busy, and I don't mean hanging out with Doreen all day either."

"I can run errands for the neighbors or something. I know! We can paint my room pink."

"That's not what I mean, honey." Mom was thoughtful as she weighed her words carefully before hurrying out the door. "You've been quieter these days. I don't mind the reading, and crafting's fine, but you need more rounding. I'm glad to see some of that tomboyishness start to fade. You're growing up so fast. I'll come up with something."

Unfortunately, I didn't have to wait long. Mom had decided I should visit the Sweet sisters to occupy my time while she was at work. There were many Misses so-and-so's, but I couldn't think of a single Miss Sweet. I was confused for a second, and then I couldn't think of anything worse.

"You mean those weird old ladies across the street? Mom! Why?"

"Watch your mouth, young lady! It won't be *that* bad."

"But Mom—"

"You need to recognize the benefit of befriending others older than yourself. Anyway, they're not that old, about sixty or so, I think.

"Sixty! That's older than Grandma!"

"Don't fight me on this now. Besides, young lady, it's only for the summer, and it'll do you good."

Whatever she meant, I didn't like it. To me, they were just two old ladies who walked through town or in front of our house, one walking in front of the other, single file. The one in front walked with her head held high, shoulders back, and moving forward, full of purpose. The other had an unusual way of walking and used a cane while dragging one foot. She always looked down at the ground and followed slowly behind her sister. They were shrouded in mystery with rumors of practicing voodoo and witchery. They never smiled or said a word to anyone. Although I didn't know their names, I was mildly curious about these ladies whom we avoided because we thought they'd put a curse on us. *Are they really witches? Who are they anyway?* Mom obviously knew them, but it was annoying she felt I *needed* to visit the sisters, not once a week, but every day! I'd rather go to Vacation Bible School.

"Why do I have to go every day? That's like going to Sunday school *and* church all on the same day," I said. I never saw the benefit of doing both and was glad to say so.

Standing with my arms folded across my chest and pouting usually worked with Mom, but not that day. I had little choice in the matter.

"You'll do as I say, and no more argument." Mom ended the discussion. It was final.

It was June in the summer of 1967 when I first met the Sweet sisters. I was all of thirteen years old.

# CHAPTER 2

## *The Misses Sweet*

THE SISTERS LIVED in a small single-story house diagonally across from us. It was a humble-looking home surrounded by a well-maintained lawn with irises on either side. It was a small two-bedroom bungalow painted dark green with white trim, sitting well back from the street. A worn patch of grass served as a walkway and marked the comings and goings of the sisters. The grassy walkway ended at several steps leading up to a wooden porch that stretched across the front of the house. The front door on the left, not in the center, and the porch were shaded by an overhanging eave. To the right of the front door, as I looked at it, were two windows with flower boxes on the sills. In front of these windows, two empty rocking chairs rocked in the humid breeze. The long narrow tangle of trees we played in, called the Jungle, was far to the left side of the house, leaving an empty lot of green grass between the two.

As I stood studying the house, I wondered why I hadn't noticed it before. The gate to Old Man Sauerkraut's farm was a few paces down the road, and even trudging through the snow to sled down his hill, I never gave this house a second look. It was as if the house magically appeared, invisible until now.

For a hot day in early June, I felt adequately dressed in pink-and-white floral-patterned shorts; a white, sleeveless, straight-hemmed shirt; and dirty white Keds. If it wasn't for the zit in the center of my forehead, I at least was presentable. As I pouted and stared at the front door, Mom's pecan pie, which she'd made for this occasion, was cooling in my hands. Pecan pie was Mom's specialty, and this made me think a doily made from my macramé kit would've been a nice gift for me to bring. But since I knew nothing about the inside of their home, it was probably best I hadn't made one.

An uneasy feeling crept over me merely thinking about the rumors of what went on inside that house. But the talk of voodoo practices and witchery was something I didn't want to dwell on just then. Aside from seeing the sisters walk to and from the store or on errands, no one ever saw them once they'd gone inside. Even Miss Greene, who occasionally threw big parties, never saw them. And she lived almost directly across the street!

This thought added to the puzzle of why my mother insisted I visit ladies we hardly knew. I took a deep breath and walked up to the green-colored screen door. I could see the front door was open on the inside, but before I could knock, a voice from inside said, "Come on in. The door's open."

I stood dumb, then slowly opened the screen door and stepped inside.

━━━◈◈◈━━━

It took time to adjust to the darkened space from the sun's glare. A nice breeze blew through the house to cool the inside. The room had a cozy feel, and the shelves were full of trinkets with beautiful pictures on the walls. I thought a doily or two would've been proper to bring after all. In poorer families that couldn't afford a larger house with an extra bedroom, it wasn't unusual to see a bed smack-dab in the center of the room. With a lot of children, a makeshift bedroom was typical. But this bed was huge and took up almost the entire room. Placed between the bed and the two front windows was a rocking chair, where the slower of the Misses Sweet sat. Because she was on the other side of the windows, she might have seen me standing in front of the house looking like an idiot.

"I-I-I heard you, you come up the stairs. So nice, so nice," she said.

She seemed to look past me as if I wasn't there. Because of this, I thought she was blind, but I couldn't be sure. The way she said stairs in a slow Southern drawl, "sta-uhs" made me smile. Not everyone in Kentucky spoke this way, but to hear her words in a different kind of accent from others was unusual. Some Kentucky accents had long a's or i's, which could sound exaggerated and twangy, but hers were soft and sweet with a lift at the end. I liked it. I thought her stutter might be due to nervousness, so I hurried with introductions to put her at ease. But my mouth went dry. I tried to get more spit but swallowed hard instead. How I got the words out, I'll never know.

"Hi, I'm Lindsey Hollis, Miss Janie's daughter from across the street? Most of my friends call me Linney, though, but you can call me whatever you like. Mom made this pie for you to enjoy. I hope you like it. I didn't make anything to bring because I wasn't sure what you might like, but maybe next time I can bring something if that's okay?"

I was breathless after saying all this, and while catching my breath, she continued to smile without looking at me. I shifted from foot to foot, standing just inside the front door, not knowing what else to do or say. Finally, I smiled, but it wasn't my best because I could feel it mimicking the crazy smile of this lady with the vacant stare.

"That will be quite nice, dear," came a commanding voice from what could be described as the kitchen tucked back and away from view. An imposing figure entered, wiping her hands on a dish towel. "I'm Katherine, and this here is my sister Dorothy or Dottie if you so choose." She had none of the Southern accents like that of her sister. Her accent was more proper and precise, not that I was an expert, but I couldn't quite place it.

This lady didn't seem friendly at all. On the contrary, Miss Katherine stood very proud with an air of self-importance. She was dressed nicely, neat, and pinned up for a hot summer day with an apron tied around her waist. Her hair was done up in a simple twisted braid and pinned behind her head. She wore her hosiery rolled down around thick ankles above tiny feet inside practical shoes.

I trembled slightly as I reached out to shake her hand, but she made no move. In fact, nothing moved, not me, not the Misses Sweet, nor the air in the room, only the blood in my veins. I was being studied. Then Miss Dottie made an ugly grunt and guttural sound, which scared me enough to move back against the screen door. Miss Dottie stared up at me from underneath frowning brows and said, "Them woods… don't go in them woods." I opened my mouth to speak, but no sound came.

"Now, hush up, just hush! It's all right now. Why this child won't know what to think, will you, darlin'?" Miss Katherine's voice seemed to calm her sister because Miss Dottie settled back into her chair and began to rock again, face blank, staring at nothing.

Without missing a beat, Miss Katherine turned her full attention to me. "Now, where are my manners? My, but you are a pretty thing! I've seen you playing over there in that mangle of trees from time to time. Here let me take this pie… while you have a seat."

Miss Katherine motioned me to the other side of the bed, and in this cramped part of the room, she pulled out a chair for me to sit. She said and did this with more kindness and enthusiasm than she'd shown before. It was as if she were a different person, more relaxed than earlier. The change was peculiar. *Maybe she's making up for how her sister behaved?*

As she took the pie into the kitchen, I had a chance to observe her sister closely. She wore a lovely day dress with a small black hat on her head as if ready to go to church or something. Then she began to drool, and her head dipped to the left side. Slowly she reached up to wipe her mouth with a cloth. She seemed sad and different from the welcoming Southern belle I met when I entered, blind or not. By her look, I could tell she must have been pretty in her day. In fact, she was almost

White in appearance; they both were. But Miss Katherine had a slight olive cast to her complexion compared to her sister's rosier tones. Were they Black or White? Up close, I couldn't tell.

Miss Katherine returned, carrying a silver tray and serving plates for a slice of pie. "I apologize for not being prepared for company. We usually entertain upon invitation, but I forgot your mother telling me you would be stopping by today. I do hope you like tea?"

"No'am. I mean, yes, ma'am."

"Well, I do declare."

I wasn't sure what to say because I was captivated by the gleaming silver serving tray; it was so shiny. I had never seen anything like it, and what's more, I had never had hot tea before. Iced tea, yes, but not hot like this. Miss Katherine placed the tray near the folded sideboard table on the far wall, across from the large bed and near a fireplace. From where I sat, I could see clear through the fireplace to the back bedroom and thought how cool it was to use the fireplace on the backside as well. Miss Katherine lifted one edge of the sideboard, creating a half tabletop for us to use.

For me, the sight of the silver service and tea made the visit a formal affair. I didn't know what to do and fidgeted with concern about saying or doing something that might embarrass me. She began to talk as she poured the tea into porcelain teacups.

"Now, Dottie, here is the younger of us by a few minutes. We are fraternal twins born in Chicago." I didn't know what *fraternal* meant, but I considered it rude to ask.

"We were raised by two loving parents and had a wonderful childhood," Miss Katherine said. "We moved to Kentucky late in life without knowing anyone. It's been just the two of us for many years, except on the rare occasion your mother comes to visit. She's a lovely woman who's told us so much about you. I see you're a little shy, so I hope you'll excuse my sister. She has outbursts from time to time. I hope she didn't scare you."

"No'am, she didn't scare me." I lied. I wanted to ask what

her sister suffered from, but asking outright was also considered rude, so I kept my mouth shut.

"I'm glad to hear it, dear. Dottie is easily excited. She's a little slow and doesn't understand things like you and me. When she gets familiar with you, she'll relax more. I'll admit her behavior can be disturbing at times, and I apologize to you for that, especially with this being your first visit." Changing the subject, she said, "This pie is delicious! Did your mother make it from scratch?"

"Yes, ma'am." Now, this was true. I was keeping my lies to a minimum.

"I *thought* so. Please ask her to pass the recipe to me?"

"Yes, ma'am, I will."

She managed the tea service as well as some characters in the many books I'd read, with ease and high-born airs; at least, this is what I imagined. She offered cubes of sugar and asked how many I wanted in my tea, one or two. I didn't know, so I said, "One, please." I also had no idea what to do with the cream and lemon wedges. Because of her manners, my curiosity was getting the better of me. I had so many questions that were killing me not to know! But Mom told me not to be nosy.

"It's not often Dottie and I receive company. Now, you must tell me about yourself."

By now, she had lost some of her proper accent and took on a soft Southern drawl as if she were just getting used to it. I don't know if she did this to make me feel more comfortable, but it was a curious mix of accents. She pronounced each word perfectly, even if she did drop her g's every now and then. She wasn't tall, but sitting up straight on the edge of her chair gave her an appearance of height and more importance than she would have otherwise. As she leaned in slightly to hear every word I said, she never let her smile drop but looked directly at me. She seemed interested in listening to me talk about the books I'd read, blue ribbons won at the fair and the Girl Scouts. I told her my age, what grade I was in, what school I attended, and such. She even listened to what I had to say about my friends and hobbies. I noticed she never raised her pinkie as she drank tea. *Ain't you supposed to? What do I do with the cream and lemons? Am I talking too much?*

After a while, Miss Dottie's rocking increased and became faster. I asked if Miss Dottie would like a slice of pie, but Miss Katherine said it wouldn't be necessary. Then Miss Dottie's rocking began to slow, which is when I decided it was probably a good time to leave. Miss Katherine made my visit pleasant, but Miss Dottie's behavior was creepy. *What did she mean about the woods?*

"Well, I should get back."

"Please come visit us anytime. I always have hot water for tea, so it's no bother. No invitation needed."

"Thank you for the tea, Miss Katherine. It was a pleasure to meet your acquaintance."

After so much formality, I hoped this was the correct way of saying these things when leaving. I didn't bother to say goodbye to Miss Dottie; I simply left their house for the safety of my front porch. When I reached home, I turned to see Miss Katherine standing at her dark green screen door, watching me.

I had never been more afraid, bewildered, and curious, all at the same time. I didn't want to go back and thought about how to tell Mom. Maybe I could stretch the truth a little, but I could never bring myself to lie outright to her. Should I tell her how strange the sisters behaved toward each other? What about Miss Dottie's behavior, how Miss Katherine served hot tea on a warm day, or how white their complexions were? *Are they White and passing for Black?* I couldn't figure it out or get it straight in my head. When Mom got home from work, I had to try and convince her that another visit would be a waste of time.

"I want to hear all about your visit today. How did it go?" Mom asked.

"Can't I do something else, Mom? I can't keep visiting them every day. I just can't! Don't make me go back. Please."

"Yes, you can, and you will." She said, but I was determined and pushed anyway.

"This is ridiculous! They're strange, Mom. Like they have this weird, mysterious thing between them or something. It's spooky!"

"Some people have a lot of secrets to hold on to." This was her only reply.

After many pleadings later, my mother finally gave in. She decided visiting *once* a week would be enough instead of every day. However, I went one step further. I made up other reasons for not going at all, such as being too busy, having other things to do, don't want to. They all sounded reasonable to me.

Unfortunately, as the weeks passed, my curiosity about the Sweets grew. Their mysterious way of life drew me in, and like the latest book of Nancy Drew mysteries, the less I knew, the more I wanted to know. To satisfy my curiosity, I made up stories about their lives. Was theirs like the movie *What Ever Happened to Baby Jane?* where the two sisters were jealous of each other, one a cripple, the other not? Was it a situation of one born 'flicted— a term I'd heard used—and the other had to take care of her? Did they dislike each other but had to stay together because of money? There had to be a reason.

My curiosity was way too much for me to stay away for long.

# CHAPTER 3

## *A Little Neighborhood Gossip*

I T WAS THE Fourth of July, and celebrations were underway, not to mention it was the hottest day on record. In the meantime, the Greenfield neighborhood was full of activity. Everyone was in their backyards and had gathered in the common green space to eat hot dogs, hamburgers, and Miss Loren's potato salad. A few neighborhood men tended the huge barbecue pit in the middle of the green, no doubt visiting and gossiping just as badly as the women. The Tallys set up a badminton net in their front yard for a few games later. Some neighborhood kids played softball in the barren part of the common area using the usual red rubber ball, which was safer and avoided accidentally breaking a window or two. But that didn't prevent it from whizzing past my head when I headed out the back door to join Mom in Miss Tally's backyard.

"Heads up!" I heard someone yell too late.

"Hey, watch where you throwing at!" I said, surprised by the near miss. Some of the players made a few shrugs but said nothing more.

Jess Tally was my mother's best friend. I always called her Miss Tally, which seemed to fit because she and her husband, Mr. Jackson Tally, were like family. Her voice was just loud enough for a Southern lady not to be considered rude. Tall and lean with short-cropped hair, she was a nice no-nonsense lady who didn't accept a lot of foolishness from what she termed "lazy people." Meaning people who lacked the desire to think or do for themselves or lacked the responsibility to obtain gainful employment, or were careless in their regard for others.

Still annoyed at almost being hit with a fast rubber ball, I leaned against a tree nearby and pretended to watch the softball game while eavesdropping on Mom's conversation. Miss Tally sat in a plastic lawn chair sipping iced tea with her long brown legs crossed at the knee. Flanked by my mother and other neighbors, she seemed aware of a change in my behavior.

"So what's going on with Linney, Janie Mae?" Miss Tally asked.

"What do you mean?"

"She's unusual today. Has been for weeks. Seems to be moody and lost in thought."

"Oh, she's just going through a phase. She'll be okay after a while."

"What kinda phase? What's going on?"

"I've given her a summer project, so to speak, of visiting the Sweet sisters."

"Do what? You mean those weird old biddies living together in that house across the street? Have you lost your mind? I wouldn't go within three feet of those women, let alone send any of my kids over there."

"What're you talking about, Jess? They're harmless. I had a long talk with the one who seems older—and goes by the name of Katherine, by the way. They seem to be nice but lonely women. I don't see any harm allowing Linney to visit every once in a while."

"*Really?* You don't? Well, I don't buy that! What'd she say anyway? They don't seem crazy or strange to you?"

"No more than you and me," Mom said. "A little eccentric, I guess, but being alone like that is natural. I didn't get any weird vibe if that's what you mean. I felt sorry for her and thought it would do them good to have a visitor every now and then. You know, Katherine seems cultured in a way I've only read about. She's well-spoken, curious about us—well, me and Linney anyway." Miss Tally peered at Mom from the top of her sunglasses without saying a word as Mom continued, "Oh, I don't *know*. I'd visit more often if I could, but I can't because of my studies. Besides, what harm will it do? It'll keep Linney out of trouble and out from under the influence of my little sister."

"If you say so," Miss Tally said. "Girl, those sisters seem creepy to me. People like that, alone and unsociable, almost always seem to have secrets that would horrify us if we knew… the way they carry on, keeping to themselves and all. You know I heard one of them killed her husband?"

"Naahhh! You don't say?" Mom asked, teasing Miss Tally with this question.

"You *know* how people talk! I wouldn't be surprised if they cut his head off and ate him for breakfast, lunch, *and* dinner."

Miss Tally laughed and slapped her thigh, spilling some of her lemonade, while Mom's mouth hung open at Miss Tally's gossip. Then Mom laughed along with her inside joke. Miss Edna, who sat nearby, too close for comfort if you ask me, chimed in asking what was so funny.

With sunglasses now perched on top of her head, Miss Tally casually told her it wasn't any of her business, but Miss Edna kept it up. "It must be something for you to splash lemonade all over the place and on my legs."

"Oh hush, Edna! Ain't nobody splashed nothing on you. Stop being nosy, plus this conversation's between A and B, so you just C your way out of it."

"Come on now, Jess. What's wrong with a little neighborhood gossip among friends? You ain't got room to talk being nosy about Linney. Pot calling the kettle black?" Mom asked.

"Now you know that's different." Then turning to Miss Edna, Miss Tally said, "If you want to know, it's just *some* gossip we talk about every now and then about *some* people."

"If anybody knows what's going on around here, it's me," Miss Edna said. "So whatever you think you know, I know it first, believe you me." Then she turned to my mother. "I don't pay no mind to Jess. She don't know er' thing."

"I may not know *everything*, but I do know *one* thing: some people need to mind their own damn business before their noses get cut off to spite their own faces. Let that sink in," Miss Tally said.

Miss Edna bristled and shifted in her chair, pretending to look at the game just as the red ball bounced on the hard ground, then rolled out of reach of one player before being picked up by another to tag a runner sliding to third base. Then she tapped Miss Julie Ann on the leg and began discussing something out of earshot of the rest of us.

My mother and Miss Tally exchanged glances and, with knowing smiles, simultaneously drank their lemonade. I enjoyed the conversations, stifling a laugh every now and then, pretending to watch the game, but Miss Tally knew better. Right on time, she squinted at me and asked Mom if I might have heard anything.

"Linney, I know you not watching that game over there," Miss Tally said. "Come on over here and talk to me."

I was caught. I slowly made my way to where my mother and Miss Tally were sitting and prayed no one would ask about my visits to the Sweets, but that prayer was a lost cause.

"You getting all tall and pretty. Look at you," Miss Tally said. The ladies sitting around the group stopped talking to look at me. It was hard to hide my self-consciousness, which got worse when Miss Tally went on. "Ah, look at her blush! Come on now, you got to get used to compliments as pretty as you are, ain't that right, Janie?"

Where was the hole in the ground to swallow me up? As I knelt down on the grass to sit by Mom, I hoped the stares from others would go away soon.

But leave it to Miss Edna to not let an opportunity at gossip go to waste. "I hear tell you're visiting those sisters across the street, those crazy old ladies. How's that going? They put a curse on you yet?"

*How did she hear Miss Tally and Mom? Now everyone'll know.* It was embarrassing, so I stared at her without answering. The smug look on Miss Edna's face was like a cat who had swallowed a bird. Then Miss Tally attacked.

"Now, why you bring that into conversation, Edna?" Miss Tally asked. "If the child wants to speak about it, she's got a tongue. Oh, but you don't know how to hold yours, do you? Last time I checked, I told you to mind your business, thank you very much. But just like a low-life busybody, you don't know how!"

"Jess, calm down," Mom said.

Miss Tally either didn't hear or ignored Mom altogether. "You think you know everything," she said to Miss Edna, "but you don't. Try looking after your own—"

"Jess, that's enough, now! Calm down—" Mom interrupted again.

"No, I'm *not* going to calm down, Janie Mae. I'm tired of this foolishness!" Miss Tally continued, "I can't stand how she meddles and stirs up stuff. It ain't right. Don't like it, Edna? Then take that mess somewhere else outside of me, and I mean just that."

"Well, well, well! Something *is* going on you don't want us to know about, now ain't it?" Miss Edna said. "Otherwise, I wouldn't get this kind of rise out of you." She leaned in. "How come we can't know? Why you getting all upset, Jess?"

"I've heard enough from both y'all!" Mom said. "I plan on enjoying this day. I can use another glass of lemonade. Come on, Linney, let's get you a hot dog or something." Then Mom pulled me up from the grass and walked toward the barbecue pit, with Miss Tally following close behind.

When Miss Edna got up to come along, Miss Tally harrumphed and threatened her to stay seated by saying, "I wish you would!"

Miss Tally apologized to Mom for her behavior. "Girl, I been holding back my temper as long as I could after she lied about my husband. You know Jackson would never cheat on me! Edna's a menace, I swear! The nerve of that woman, lying like she does, gets on my *last* one."

Mom and Miss Tally continued discussing the nature of Miss Edna's lie. I was surprised to hear that Miss Edna could be so underhanded by lying to break up the Tallys' marriage. At the barbecue pit, Miss Tally and her husband hugged each other. Apparently, Miss Edna's plan to separate the Tallys had failed.

I grabbed a paper plate and a hot dog bun. But when I asked for a hot dog with mustard and ketchup, I got an idea. I asked for two extra hamburgers with everything on it and lots of potato salad and grabbed two extra plates and forks.

"Are you all right?" Mom asked.

"Yeah, I'll be right back," I said.

When I turned to leave, Miss Tally tweaked me on the nose with a smile. Then I walked over to visit the Sweet sisters, sure that Miss Edna was watching after me with beady eyes.

# CHAPTER 4

## *Fireworks with Friends*

FTER MISS EDNA'S nosy behavior, leaving the barbecue and visiting the Sweets was a relief. Overhearing how others felt about the sisters caused me to want to prove them wrong. So here I was at their house again, happy to share a picnic lunch.

"I'm so glad you came by to see us. I waited all day, hoping you would. But, my, it's hot today. I thought the heat might keep you away," Miss Katherine said.

Her face seemed to light up when she saw me, making me feel bad about staying away for so long. I had only visited once, but she missed me more than I realized. I couldn't help but smile, pleased with my decision to drop by.

"I wanted to come by and say hello, especially today," I said, telling a white lie. "There's so much food at the barbecue and lots of people too. I kept thinking about y'all and decided to bring over some picnic food. I hope you like it."

"It looks delicious. Don't you think so too, Sister?" Miss Katherine asked Miss Dottie, who said nothing and gazed out the front window. "Well, you'll have to tell me all about what your days have been like lately. Go ahead and start while I get some real forks and plates to put under the paper ones you have there."

Miss Katherine was dressed in a long, loose-fitting chemise wearing her usual practical shoes in her typical old-fashioned way. Miss Dottie was dressed as before, but this time without a hat. Miss Katherine had also baked raisin cookies and had prepared water for tea.

After eating the last of Miss Loren's potato salad plus a few raisin cookies, we spent the rest of the day talking about school and my insecurities. Miss Dottie rocked quietly in her chair and sometimes wiped at her mouth or softly moaned, but she made no strange grunts. Before I knew it, I found myself discussing Doreen and her accomplishments.

"Doreen's so smart; she aces every test. She's very popular at school, not like me. She gets away with everything and breaks every rule, like not coming home when she's supposed to. That's so reckless, but that's Doreen for you. When it comes to boys, I think she has them eating out of the palm of her hand. But that's because she's so funny and tells it like it is most times. We used to share everything when we were little, but lately, she's been keeping secrets. She hurts my feelings whenever she can and makes fun of my skin color all the time and I don't understand why. It's so embarrassing."

Miss Katherine listened and offered a nod or shake of her head when appropriate. When she asked why I chose to follow Doreen's lead, particularly when she was so mean to me, I didn't have an answer.

Instead, I proudly described Doreen as inheriting the physical traits of our family's ancestors. Everyone envied her coloring, which was like that of a bay Thoroughbred. "Sometimes people say she looks like those ladies from India. You know those ones who wear rubies on their foreheads? She's not pale like me." I continued saying that having her creamy light brown complexion and straight, glossy blue-black hair that hung partly down her back would make me so happy. Her eyes were deep-set and expressive, unlike my doe-eyes. The barely noticeable mole on her right cheek didn't hurt her looks either. I looked up to Doreen with the admiration of a starstruck fan.

After a while, Miss Katherine said, "Where has the time gone? I must give Sister her medication before I forget."

"Oh, I'm late for fireworks at Garrard Park! I promise to come back soon, Miss Katherine. Okay?" I said my goodbyes and was off.

⟫◈◈◈⟪

Each day became harder *not* to tell my friends about my visits with the sisters. If I did, they would make fun of me or worse. Doreen's teasing was brutal enough, so I decided my first thoughts were correct. This would be my secret, all my own, and kept to myself.

I liked to think of Doreen and me as the same age, even though she was older by more than a year. Because she was my aunt, Doreen carried a superior attitude toward me, often saying, "I'm your aunt, so you do as I say," and I would.

Doreen was antsy as she stood in front of Miss Tally's house, waiting for me. I knew she hated waiting, but I didn't care so much that day. Her eyes usually sparkled, but this time they flashed.

"Where've you been? I've been waiting forever!"

I shrugged instead, choosing not to answer. Doreen looked at me with suspicion, then said, "We need to play a game of badminton before we go to the park."

"But I don't want to play," I said. "We'll miss the fireworks!"

"You never want to do anything these days," she persisted.

"That's not true—"

"Then here, take this and play." Doreen shoved a racket in my hand and turned toward the direction of the badminton net.

She was forcing me to play, and it annoyed me to no end. Then someone called out, asking, "Hey Doreen, you still up for playing?"

"Yeah. Linney and I are up," Doreen said.

I reluctantly took my place in front of the net to play four-on-four, opposite Doreen on the other side. Anyone playing softball earlier or sitting around to gossip had now gathered in the front yard of Miss Tally's house to watch the game. The birdie went up for the serve, and we volleyed back and forth, scoring each side point for point. Doreen played full-out, eager to get the upper hand for her side. The streetlights had come on in the early gloom of twilight; however, they provided little light on the game. The birdie was becoming harder to see, but I couldn't say the same about the comments I heard.

"Linney's good at badminton, Janie Mae," Miss Tally said. "I don't think she realizes how pretty she is, do you? I hope she never finds out, though. That might be a problem for her later in life."

"I know what you mean," Mom said. "She certainly didn't get those looks from me. It's those Creoles from Larry's side. She's so unconcerned about her looks, though, and that's a good thing." Saying this within earshot of everyone was bad enough, but leave it to Miss Edna to make matters worse.

"But look at that turkey meat on them legs!" Miss Edna said. "Her legs the color of white turkey meat. Ain't no man gonna find that attractive."

The laughter was loud. I was mortified. I was comfortable in my shorts, but now I wished I had worn long pants instead to hide my pale legs. I glanced over at Mom, but she sat there with her arms folded across her chest while Miss Tally leaned to the side of her chair to stare directly at Miss Edna's smug face.

It was my serve, and while all eyes were on me, I'm sure no one saw my tears welling up. I bit my lower lip, blinked them back, and then served the birdie up. It barely made it over the net. The scramble was on to gain control before it hit the ground, and with determination, Doreen spiked it back. Score again, and even. Now it was her turn to serve. It was sudden death. After a few more volleys and a foul, I had to rotate to the front of the net again. As Doreen served, I reached up and over, spiking the birdie directly at her feet. Hard. Game over! A whoop rose from the crowd of onlookers. I was pleased with myself because spiking the birdie to end the game was not easy to do after sucking up Miss Edna's remark. I accepted the pats on the back for my efforts, but Doreen just stood there, glaring at me. Knowing her the way I did, I felt she was angry about losing the game. So just for fun, I did an awkward mini curtsy and walked over to get a soda.

By now, it was full-on dusk, and others started heading for the park. I moved along with them but then held back and looked around for Doreen. She was standing so close behind me with a badminton racket still in her hand that she startled me, and I stumbled. Doreen held the racket as if to strike, but I knew she wouldn't dare go that far even if she did hate losing. She pulled me by the arm to her side and squeezed hard to make her feelings known.

"You think you so cute, don't you?" she said.

"I can't help it if y'all lost the game. You just mad."

"We wouldn't have lost the game if you wasn't showing off in front of everybody."

"What're you talking about?"

"You heard me. All that talk about 'she's so pretty' and stuff. You just ate it up."

"You're crazy. Let go of my arm. That hurts!" I winced and tried to get out of her grasp, but she held tight and got close to my face.

"Just between us, if you think you could ever be as pretty as me, you got another *think* coming. I'm your aunt, so remember that."

Doreen brushed past me, knocking into my shoulder as she went to get a bottle of coke-cola. There she was, surrounded by a lot of friends while I stood watching and alone. I tried to rub the soreness out of my arm from where she'd held it tight, unsure if I should go to the park. Eventually, I followed behind the group, wishing for all the world to have time to change so I could hide my white turkey meat legs.

⇒◦◉◦⇐

The chrysanthemum-shaped burst of red, yellow, and green fireballs overhead didn't have the same effect on me as last year. Absentmindedly biting my cuticle, I stood in the back of a group of people, lost in thought over how Doreen could think such things about me. I was still embarrassed by what Miss Tally had said, and even though it was nice, she shouldn't have said it out loud. What Miss Edna said was worse. What Doreen said and did was just plain mean. I glanced over at her, laughing and enjoying herself with the others. I couldn't help but wonder how she could be a mixture of sweetness and nastiness rolled into one person. How could she get away with being careless with words that could cut like a knife? *She* was the pretty one, *not* me. I shouldn't let Doreen push me around, but she scared me sometimes. When it came to her, I didn't know how to fight back *and* keep her friendship. How was it I could stand my ground with others but not her? Then, just before the tears welled up again, I felt someone tap me on the shoulder.

"Why you standing back here by yourself?" Angela asked.

Angela Theresa Beaumont was the daughter of my mother's high school friend and sometimes enemy, Mrs. Sandra Leland Beaumont. Angie was a terrible gossip, and I liked that about her, but lately, she was pouring it on thick. Complaining about it was no good, though, because I could never find a more fierce and loyal friend. Angela's hazel eyes flashed as if on fire whenever she got angry or annoyed. We all envied her eye color and wished like crazy we hadn't been stuck with plain brown ones.

"Hey, Angie. I don't know."

"Well, I'm here to keep you company," she said. "We sure could've used you earlier in the ballgame, you know. I didn't know you could play badminton like that, but I should've 'cause you're good at most things. We didn't want you to play softball against our side 'cause we *just knew* we would've lost if you played. I hope you don't mind, so don't be mad, okay?"

"That's so mean!" I gave her a light nudge, then continued, "I'm not mad. Besides, I wasn't the only good player at the net today. Doreen scored a lot."

"Doreen played that way to get at you," Angela said. "I could tell. Badminton was an easy *get* for her. If you'd played ball with us, she would've been terrified. She either might not've played or been afraid you'd put one right down her throat. That is if you had half a mind. But you don't, not as far as she's concerned, do you? Why do you let her lead you around and walk all over you? She's so mean and calls you out all the time, just for spite. That ain't right."

"Don't say that. She's my aunt, so stop."

"Well, it's true! Everyone can see it, but they don't say anything 'cause it's *family*. But I don't care. You don't need to take that from her, ever."

"Stop talking like that! It's just the way she is, and whose business is it anyway? You're my friend. She's my aunt. There's a difference." Slapping at mosquitoes, I had the odd urge to slap at Angela instead, just for trashing Doreen.

"The difference I see is a doormat that keeps getting dirty from her feet. She treats you like dirt. Don't be mad, okay? I'm only saying this so you can stand up for yourself sometimes. We'll always be friends, Linney, but Doreen… I don't know."

Irritated and annoyed, I turned away in silence to watch more of the show.

"Hey, y'all! Nice night, huh?" Carolyn said as she moved to sit beside us.

Always studious and careful, Carolyn Susan Avery liked to think things through. She never used swear words or considered herself better because she was the preacher's daughter. Kind and considerate, she was the thoughtful one of my friends.

"I wouldn't know. Numbnuts here is sulking about Auntie's insults again."

"Am not—"

"Are too! But that's okay. We're still friends, right?" Angela asked with a grin.

"Well, I didn't come here to referee," Carolyn said. "Let me know when the dust settles."

Carolyn left us needling each other with elbows until we giggled. Angela's words stayed with me for a long time during and after the bursting colors of chrysanthemum-shaped, arrow-shaped fireworks and exploding bombs faded from the night sky, leaving white ash to fall around us.

# CHAPTER 5
## *The Strange Boogeyman*

AFTER THE FIREWORKS ended, I lost Angela in the crowd and walked alone, which suited me just fine. I passed through the green fields of Garrard Park, then the numerous tennis courts, watching out for lost softballs along the way. The park was supposed to be used by everyone, but we didn't often go because it was located on the White side of town. As I made it to the tree-lined avenue outside the park, I daydreamed about living there. Aside from my favorite spot under the maple tree, this avenue seemed a magical place, especially at night when you could take your time to look at the beautiful houses along the way.

I could only dream of the lives these people led and the types of work they did. But why they left their curtains wide open so that others could see inside at night was a mystery. Maybe they felt secure in showing off what they had versus what others didn't. That was the difference between this part of town and ours; we didn't live this way. On the other side of the hill where we lived, our curtains were closed at night out of privacy and fear of someone wanting to take what we had because they had less. *But we never lock our doors, and I bet they do. Maybe we should too.*

It was then that Doreen came up from behind me, acting like she hadn't been angry with me only a few hours ago. After all, it was the Munro family's way of pretending all was well and forgiven, even if it wasn't.

"How you doing?" she asked.

"One day, I'm going to live like that," I said. "Window curtains open wide, big house, nice yard. Do you think that will happen for us?"

"I don't know about you, but it'll happen to me. I plan on living in Lexington in a big house on a hill. Servants and maids and everything. Yep, that's how it'll be."

"Keep dreaming… I mean, it's good to have dreams."

"Yeah. That was a great show, huh? The fireworks were so big! I had fun. How about you?" Before I could answer, a call came from behind.

"Hey, y'all, wait up!" Carolyn yelled out. She and Angela ran up to walk with us.

"Wow, that was fantastic! I'm so glad we don't have to go to school tomorrow and more months of summer," Angela said.

"Two more months, you mean. We have July and August to go yet," Doreen said.

"Yeah, you're right… as usual." Angela let her disappointment show with a sigh. "Geez, Louise, way to ruin a nice thought, Doreen."

"I'll be glad when it's over. I don't like summer," Carolyn said.

"You can't wait to go back to school?" I asked.

"No, just waiting for something to happen is all. I'm bored and can't wait to vacation this year with my parents," she said.

The fact that *they* chose not to go to Vacation Bible School was not lost on us. And Carolyn was a minister's daughter, for Pete's sake! Maybe making vacation plans was more important.

Just when the road full of people began to thin as they found their way home, I listened to the clack-shuffle-clack sound our shoes made on the sidewalk and how it quieted when we walked in the road. We didn't live far, but the transition from this side of town to ours was dramatic because we had no sidewalks to walk on, only the soft poured asphalt we called "the road."

The talk of summer plans ended when we neared the hilltop where the road met at the three points of William Street and Atlas and Lilleston Avenues. Carolyn waved goodbye and ran to walk with others toward her home on Eighth Street. Located diagonally from Grandma's was Angela's house. A narrow three-story house on the corner of Lilleston and Williams. Few friends visited Angela because her house was next door to her father's funeral home business. They thought it was creepy and scary, but I didn't think so and was the only friend who dared to visit.

After Angie said her goodbyes, I walked with Doreen to where Grandma met us at her front door. In a cheerful voice, she waved hello and then called for me to be careful going home. When the door shut, I was alone. Doreen often said I didn't need anyone to walk me home at night because I had a built-in night-light shining through my almost-white skin. That night, I didn't mind too much, because I enjoyed the quiet and listened to the distant voices of those safely on their way home. Because of the new moon the night was darker than usual, and the cool night air was nice to feel for a change.

Farther away than I cared to think about, our house seemed even more so on that moonless night. I walked in the middle of the road, which was safer than walking close to houses with dark spaces between each one. Why I bothered being so careful when no one even locked their doors at night was out of habit. Mom would say, "You can never be too careful," especially when an awful murder from long ago was still discussed on the tongues of gossipers. Whenever the murder came up, my mother said of the memory "hovering ever so slightly, tickling the minds of those who were there." On dark nights like this, thoughts of the boogeyman were never far from my mind. I wasn't too concerned, though, because I could outrun anyone—all without twisting an ankle. Then I saw or rather *felt* his presence.

I turned around to see a tall figure coming up behind me. The stranger made little noise as he walked with his head bent, moving sideways, slightly zigzagging along. If I didn't know any better, I would've thought he was drunk or something, but no. He seemed intent, moving at a fast and steady pace. My heart pounded as I mentally calculated how far it was to the safety of my front door. *Linney, you're just overreacting.* But when I got nearer to our lighted street corner, the hair on the back of my neck rose. I could hear his heavy breathing! He was close, too close. When I heard him say, "Brand-new penny," and felt a tug on the back of my shirt, I ran.

Where the speed in the sprint came from, I'll never know. I was so frightened I forgot to scream. I didn't stop at the streetlight on the corner. I ran straight across to our neighborhood on legs that felt like jelly. My feet hit the nearest front porch hard, and I skidded to a stop. I turned quickly to see a lone figure standing under the streetlight with shadows across his face, dark and foreboding. Watching me.

Mr. Tally opened his front door, probably to see who or what had landed on his porch. "There's a man following me!" I said before he had a chance to speak. But when I pointed to where the man was standing, he was gone.

"Where child? I don't see no one."

"But he was there! Right *there* under the light!"

"Well, whoever it was, he's gone now. You all right, Linney girl?"

"He was just there! I *swear* it!"

"Yes, yeah, I'm sure." Mr. Tally stepped out on his porch to have a look around. Then he began staring at Mr. Morrison's house on the corner and across the street, and without looking away, he quietly said, sounding more concerned than I was breathless, "You go on home now. I'll keep watch."

Shaken, I ran to our house, two duplexes down from theirs but looked back to make sure Mr. Tally was watching after me. When I got home and safely inside, I told Mom what had happened, the words tumbling and spilling over each other as if I couldn't get them out fast enough. My heart still raced, and I felt myself shaking from the inside out. My visible trembling caused Mom more concern as she tried to calm me down. When she asked for a description of the man, I couldn't tell her much. The dark outline of his body was all I could see. I did tell her what he said and what I felt from the tug of my shirt.

A few minutes later, the Tallys came to our back door, with Mr. Tally holding a sturdy Louisville Slugger and Miss Tally a flashlight. Mr. Tally told us he saw movement in the bushes between Mr. Morrison's and Miss Clay's houses when I was there earlier. He didn't like the uneasy feeling the sight gave him. But looking around now, they hadn't seen anyone or anything out of the ordinary.

"I think we should keep our porch lights on, Mom, front and back," I said.

"I don't know." Mom shook her head. "That'd tell whoever it was exactly where we live. What do you think, Tally?"

"What makes you think he don't know already?" Mr. Tally asked.

"Well, that's a fine answer, Jackson! What're you saying?" Miss Tally said.

"I'm just thinking out loud, baby—." Then, after rubbing his chin, he said, "Sorry, Janie Mae…. We turn our front porch light on from time to time, but I think we should do that most nights anyway. Be a good idea if we all did."

"You should tell everyone too, Mr. Tally." I was grasping at straws, trying to think of how to keep us safe. Judging by how Mr. Tally rubbed his chin, I could tell he was more concerned than he was letting on.

"Oh, for sure," he said almost absentmindedly. "I'll come up with something to tell the neighbors without alarming the whole town. Yeah…. That should be enough." Mr. Tally never looked up at us as he spoke. He just continued to frown, staring at the floor in thought.

"Janie Mae, I don't like the way this feels. I certainly don't like what I'm hearing," Miss Tally said. "This child was scared out of her mind. Who knows what would've happened if Linney wasn't so close to home. We don't even lock our doors, and to think—"

"Can we start locking our doors now?" They stared at me as if I was from outer space, but I didn't care. I didn't feel safe, so I pressed on. "I know it's nothing, but you didn't see him. I did! We never lock our doors, Mom, and I don't know why. Please let's?"

"You know we used to lock our doors after that murder long ago but slacked off into old ways again," Mr. Tally said. "So it only makes sense to do so now." Without saying more, he began checking all our windows and doors to make sure they were closed and locked.

"Now that I think about it, not locking our doors is an old habit that needs to end anyway," Mom said.

After a few minutes, Mr. Tally told us he had secured our house. He had to wrestle with one window lock, which obviously hadn't been used in a long time.

"Okay, now y'all make sure to keep the doors *and* windows locked," Mr. Tally said. "I know the night air cools the house, but better safe than sorry. You know, I've been thinking about that bad time in fifty-three when that boy lost his life. When the news got out, a bunch of us came around to see for ourselves. I never seen anything like it or since. People still can't stop talking about it."

I listened as they continued to talk more about concern and safety in this way until they left. That night, we slept behind locked doors and windows for the first time. Around us, the warm breeze swayed the leaves of the trees in the dark of night.

We didn't know then that the Jungle we played in as kids was a perfect hiding place for evil.

# CHAPTER 6

## *Miss Edna and the Chicken*

EDNA ALLEN CAME to Paris by way of Centerville, Kentucky. Born Edna Louise Craven in 1910 to a poor family who didn't think much of their futures, she had always loved Paris and vowed to become a town citizen before leaving this earth. She succeeded in doing that just shy of her seventeenth birthday, leaving behind an abusive husband and lots of dirt that came in and around her house whenever the wind blew.

Edna was cute and pert in those days but was too loud for her own good, with big eyes and a mouth to match. She joined the Baptist church choir, sang loudly off-key, and became an unwanted member of their prayer circle. She was a frequent patron of the American Legion's Charles Young Post, often referred to as the American Legion Hall or The Hall, where the beer was good and the men were better. There she discovered her skill of frying chicken, which became her sole source of income at that time. She was never blessed with children, so she finagled her way to become a formidable scout leader and member of the Girl Scout Council for Western High School, just as integration laws were passed in 1954. But that was short-lived because her heavy-handedness marked her as a bully, especially to young girls who could not stand up to her behavior. To say she was pushy was an understatement. She was tolerated despite her bossy ways, but what few realized was she desperately wanted to fit in. By trying too hard, her tactics worked, albeit at the expense of her reputation.

Luckily for Edna, she never divorced her husband, and he never remarried. When he died of cirrhosis of the liver fifteen years after World War II, she received a substantial pension for his military service. In time, by the blessed age of fifty-seven, she appointed herself to the position of Greenfield's matriarch and snoop extraordinaire.

Edna Allen never wanted to get caught spying. She was the one person in the neighborhood who knew what was what. However misguided, Edna prided herself on being the neighborhood watch person and a good judge of character. Not only could Edna pinpoint every inch of town and recite her neighbors' business, but she also knew their secrets, follies, and foibles. If not, she'd make up what she didn't know. That way, in the retelling, she would hit the mark of truth.

For instance, she could tell you that the Fishers had been stepping out on each other since the day they got married. Many a night, she saw the mister or missus quietly leave their house, tiptoeing through the yard to get into a vehicle down the road. Full of liquor most days and nights, Mr. Evans beat his wife unmercifully with a rock in a sock. Mrs. Evans thought she was fooling everyone with that story of being clumsy and falling more than usual. There was no way in hell Edna believed that! Then there were the Jameses with their seven children and barely enough food to eat. Each child was as smart as a whip. How they managed was anybody's guess, but you would never know by how they kept up appearances.

There was Stooly and his sister Bess. Bessie was a wild child for sure, and Stooly would certainly break a lot of hearts with his good looks. Edna would bet dollars to doughnuts Bess would be pregnant within the year, yes ma'am. The Johnsons sat in the dark most nights and barbecued most evenings because Mr. Johnson couldn't stay away from the blackjack and bid whist tables. Gambling all his earnings so that nothing was paid, not even the light bills! What a shame. Then there was Mr.

Lonesome, all by himself, and she supposed he liked it that way. If Edna could find the dirt on him, she'd die happy.

Yes, Edna was a font of information. She spent most days watching her soap opera stories, using her binoculars, and frying chicken at The Hall, which she did most nights from six to ten or near midnight, depending. The price of her chicken was considered cheap for home fried, even though she charged whatever she wanted. On slow nights, at ten o'clock on the nose, she would leave one of the other girls to serve up the rest of the chicken and hurry home to spy on the goings-on in Greenfield.

Her latest curiosity would push her further into the lives of her neighbors because the Hollis family had secrets. Secrets she meant to uncover and soon. Edna liked Janie Mae but knew in her heart that her daughter, "Little Missy," considered a goody-goody because of her half-white skin and quiet demeanor, was up to no good.

As Edna looked out from behind her bedroom curtains on the night of July Fourth, she saw Little Missy running across the yard, seemingly in a panic. Edna had no idea what lit a fire in that girl's pants, but she was running as if the hounds of hell were on her heels. Later, the Tallys hurried by her backdoor window on their way to Janie Mae's. *What in the world?* Now she just *had* to get to the bottom of these shenanigans. What with Little Missy visiting those sisters across the street and running for her life? Something was amiss.

To add to Edna's frustrations, she had a weakness for Jackson Tally. She didn't give a whit that he was twenty years her junior. She was a woman determined to get her man, or at least have him for a night or two. She'd tried her best ruse a few weeks earlier, spreading stories about Jackson cheating on his wife, Jessica. But that failed to bring any problems because, according to Jess, they trusted each other. *No way* would Jackson ever cheat on her! Edna prided herself on her appearance. She still had all her hair, and even though she had put on a few pounds, loving potato salad a bit too much, her figure was still good. Jess Tally was considered pretty in her own right, but how Jackson could resist Edna's charms and ample bosom was beyond her comprehension.

Jackson usually came to The Hall in the middle of the week when it was quiet. After cooking all evening, Edna seldom took time to come out from behind the kitchen pass-through and socialize with the locals. For Edna, cooking was about making money. But on this weeknight, she would have to adjust a bit to lay her trap and get a word in with that little slice of heaven called Jackson Tally. Maybe get him to spill the beans on the previous night's activities to boot.

⚊⚊⚊◦◦◦⚊⚊⚊

When Mom didn't feel like cooking and had to study, she occasionally sent me to The Hall for fried chicken. Miss Edna's delicious chicken was served either inside or outside through a convenient serve-through window. Because of the previous night, Mom made sure I had someone to walk with me. So she decided that Doreen was the perfect person. Doreen was always fascinated by the goings-on at The Hall, so I was glad she wanted to go. I couldn't wait to tell her everything about the strange man.

"Do you think he knew you or who you were?" Doreen asked.

"I don't know. All I know is I was *so* scared. And the way he said those words, you know, drawing it out all syrupy and slow, and the tug at my shirt! Then he stood under the streetlight… just standing there stock-still… looking at me! It was creepy. I swear on a stack of Bibles when I got to Mr. Tally's front porch, he was gone. Vanished! Right into thin air!"

"Ooh-wee! That's scary."

"Yeah! I ran the rest of the way home, and girl, I thought he was going to grab me from behind, right in front of Mr. Tally! I ran so fast it felt like I was flying."

Mom said our neighbors had been told to keep their lights on and lock their doors. What Mr. Tally told them was a mystery, but so far, no complaints. Because of this, I didn't see the harm in telling Doreen to do the same.

"We locked our doors for the first time and turned on the porch lights. It was *my* idea. I think y'all should too. Mom thinks everyone should start doing it all over Paris."

"Linney, I ain't about to let no weird old drunk make me start locking my door. You probably walking like you had no care in the world like you always do. Not paying attention or being careful. No wonder he snuck up on you."

"That's not fair. I was so! I was as careful as anybody. What if it was you? What would you do? If it wasn't for Mr. Tally, I don't know where I'd be today. I'm telling you. You better watch out for your own good. He was *really* scary!" I don't know where the courage came from, but I was glad to have the nerve to say what I did to warn Doreen.

"Well, if *you* say so," she said.

I could tell she didn't take my warning seriously. It was just like her to think she was above it all, thinking nothing could hurt her. Her stuck-up attitude was becoming more annoying with each passing day, but I managed not to let it bother me too much that day as we walked along the streets toward The Hall.

The narrow streets were made for walking in our part of town, especially on lazy Sunday afternoons. Most of the roads were lined with trees, but Williams Street, which weaved through our neighborhood, had a comfortable feel about it. The houses were set back, just enough from the overhanging trees near the road, so that people could easily wave and chat with passersby. This never failed to give me a sense of family being close and watchful. However, Lylesville Street had a different feel altogether. The Hall was located on Lylesville Street.

Mom told me most cities had streets like this where the atmosphere seemed to change and come alive when you entered. She often said nightlife lived on Lylesville Street, and when arguments and knife fights were entertainment, they weren't talked about out loud. The neighborhood itself was filled with families who either liked living among the excitement of Lylesville or hated the chaos it could bring. Some even thought it was the best place to live. All I knew was that living there, you grew up very quickly.

Leaving William Street, we walked across busy Eighth Street and passed Jason's Bar & Jazz on the corner of Eighth and Lylesville. Jason's used to be a busy place long ago, but now it was run-down from disuse, unable to compete with the American Legion Hall. Awful things used to go on at Jason's. At least, so I'd been told. But whenever I asked for details, people said some things were better left unknown.

On the other hand, The Hall was *the* dance center in Paris for adults, and by itself, it had quite a reputation. It was common for Black service veterans to gather for meetings and swap war stories during World War II, Korea, and now Vietnam. Since that time, it didn't look to have changed much. It was known as a place to see and be seen. Mom often talked about the local musicians and out-of-towners who stopped by to test their musical chops. Even Ray Charles had played there once! It was a wild place with questionable characters, a place to socialize, dance to music played on a jukebox or an occasional local band, serving hard liquor, beer, and Miss Edna's fried chicken.

We were first in line at the chicken window, waiting for it to open. Good thing because I didn't want to wait any longer than necessary. I got the heebie-jeebies standing there smelling urine, spilled beer, and whiskey. For all I knew, that man from the other night might be watching us right now; however, Doreen was taking it all in.

She was acting "fast" and sass-mouthed some people who apparently said something she didn't like, such as, "Look at that pretty young thing."

"My, my, *my*, I'd like to take you home," said one man too drunk to stand up well.

"I know you ain't talking to me!" Doreen sassed back.

Another said, along with a chorus of others who questioned what she was doing there, "You Munro girls shouldn't be here. Go on home. This ain't no place for you."

Doreen's general reply was, "We're just getting chicken, so mind your business." At times like these, I was glad to have her around.

Miss Edna opened the window to take orders at seven o'clock

on the nose. Her eyes widened, then narrowed at me. "Well, what do we have here? If it ain't Little Missy and her friend, or auntie if I'm not mistaken."

"Yes, ma'am, I'd like to order—"

"And I would like to know what in the world you're up to this evening?"

"I just want to order chicken for—"

"Yeah, I bet you do! What else you up to besides visiting old folks and running for your life on them white legs of yours? You still ain't learned to cover them things up?"

I was stunned. Was Miss Edna asking about last night, and if so, how did she know about it? Until now, I'd forgotten her comment about my legs when I was playing badminton. I felt embarrassed all over again and cornered. Frantic, I didn't know what to do, so I looked around for Doreen, but she'd stepped farther away and hadn't heard Miss Edna. I wanted to get out of there and go home.

Ignoring the insult, I changed the subject. "Have you heard about keeping your lights on at night from now on? I think Mr. Tally passed the word to everyone in Greenfield today."

"Keep my light on? For what? No one said nothing to me, and I should know. What you trying to get at, girl?"

"I'm just trying to order some chicken. I'm also trying to tell you—"

"You trying to start some trouble is what you trying to do!" Miss Edna said.

Miss Edna was taking it way too far, which didn't seem right. What did I ever do to her? Why was she insulting and referring to me as "Little Missy"? To my relief, Doreen came up to see what was holding up the order.

"What's going on?" Doreen asked.

"I'm *trying* to order, and Miss Edna's asking questions," I said.

Doreen looked up at Miss Edna from underneath her brows and raised one in question. Then, with her hands on her hips, she spoke directly.

"Miss Edna, we trying to buy some chicken. Why you holding up the line? Our money not good enough?"

"Not until I find out why I gotta turn my lights on."

"Linney, you being too nice," Doreen said. Turning back to Miss Edna, she said, "Because someone out there might want to hurt you! I hear you like using binoculars on people. Keep looking, and you just might see someone waiting to *pounce!*"

Others waiting in line laughed at Doreen's sass, while Miss Edna seemed surprised by it, then she gave in. "Ohh…kay! All I know is somebody's got secrets around here and think they too good to share. I'll get to the bottom of it 'fore long."

"Just give us some chicken. Dark meat, three legs, three thighs, and *thank* you!" Doreen said and turned to me, "Is that all you want, Linney?"

I nodded while looking down at my Keds. I didn't want to be a weenie, but I could only listen as Doreen took over. We both had respect for our elders, but of the two of us, Doreen was the only one brave enough to take on Miss Edna that day.

Because her chicken was precooked and ready to serve up for orders, she quickly handed out the legs and thighs in a brown paper bag, then pulled it back, telling us we owed her ten dollars. Most people suspected Miss Edna was sketchy with her home-fried chicken prices. It was common knowledge that Miss Edna's chicken prices were one dollar for white meat and fifty cents for dark. Six pieces of dark meat amounted to three dollars.

"Do what?! Miss Edna, you know you cheating on the price," Doreen said. "We can get a whole bucket of fried for less at Colonel Sanders."

Turning to Doreen, I said, "Yeah, I just have five dollars. I can't pay that much."

"You pay what I say! I got to make a living somehow. Can't give it away for free. Maybe next time you won't come here asking for chicken with that high-and-mighty attitude of yours," Miss Edna said.

Before we could say anything more, Stooly, who had walked up to the entry door of The Hall, overheard what Miss Edna had said. He stopped and asked, "What's the problem here?"

"Miss Edna trying to take Linney and me for chicken, and I don't know why," Doreen said.

"Well, how much you owe?" he asked.

"*Ten whole dollars* is what they owe and not a penny less!" Miss Edna said. Then, she turned to Stooly and sweetly said, "How you doing, baby?"

Stooly chuckled and turned to us. "How much money you got?"

"I only have five dollars. Mamma's studying tonight and doesn't feel like cooking. So she asked me to come here to get chicken for dinner." I don't know why I gave this information to Stooly. He didn't need to hear all that, but I couldn't help myself. I lowered my head out of embarrassment and blushed. He smelled so good, and I knew denying him anything he asked was out of the question. What happened next took us by surprise, but it shouldn't have; after all, this was Stooly.

"Give me your money," Stooly said. When I did, he gave it to Miss Edna while pulling another five dollars from his pocket to make up the difference and handed that to Miss Edna. "There's the money for your delicious chicken." He turned to us again. "Don't worry, you'll owe me one day." Stooly winked, then went inside, and was gone.

Miss Edna squinted at us and called for the next customer in line while we took our sack of expensive fried chicken and hurried away. Swooning with chicken in hand, all Doreen and I could talk about was Stooly. Our hero!

⇒◈◈◈⇐

John Edmond Davies got his nickname from the song "Pink Shoelaces" by Dodie Stevens, but instead of "Dooly," he was called Stooly. It was the perfect name because he lived his life as a lady's man, a sharp dresser living fast and loose. He and his sister Bess lived in our neighborhood. I didn't see him often, but it wasn't unusual to get weak in the knees and all tongue-tied when I did. I avoided him as much as possible.

To say he was good-looking was an understatement. I had a massive crush on him, as did most girls. He was tall and slender with a light tan complexion, jet-black curly hair that appeared soft to the touch, a curvy mouth, and a softly chiseled face. His voice was strong and just deep enough, with honey tones mixed in for maximum effect, which made anyone want to listen to what he had to say. His deep-set eyes were also watchful and playful, as if he was very much aware of his effect on people when he was around. Most found him easy to talk to and friendly. It was not hard to find him because he spent his time with a known woman or two. No one knew his line of work, nor did they care. He was Stooly, and Stooly was cool.

As we walked back to Williams Street again, I found a knotted bare tree branch on the ground, which felt good to swing back and forth with my hand. As I casually swatted at green leaves sticking out between the fences from hedges in front of houses we passed, I sang the song "Pink Shoelaces," messing up the lyrics using Stooly's name instead of Dooly.

"You know those ain't the right words, don't you?" Doreen said.

"I know those ain't the right words, but Stooly fits, and I like singing it that way."

We laughed, and after the fit of giggles passed, we talked about what happened with Stooly, Miss Edna, and her fried chicken.

"Girl, Stooly is so handsome with his fine-looking self," Doreen said.

"Did you see how *smooth* he was talking to Miss Edna? I don't like that woman," I said.

"Ooo-wee, just straight up and took care of *everything*! He *was* smooth, wasn't he?"

"Holy moly. I don't think I'll ever get over it and that wink! He was winking at me, you know."

"No, Linney was winking at me, and you know it."

"He was winking at both of us then."

As soon as I started singing the song again, Doreen suddenly stopped walking and put her hand on my arm. "Do you think we'll ever marry someone like that, good-looking, all smooth and cool?"

"I don't know." I resumed swatting at leaves, then added, "I don't think about stuff like that. I dream about Stooly after I see him, then that's all I can think about. After a while, it goes away, and I'm right back to what I was doing before."

"I want one, Linney. I want to be loved by someone *just* like that."

"Like *him*, Stooly, and his shiny shoes?"

"Well, not exactly *like* Stooly, but someone who doesn't take a lot of stuff off people and can charm the skin off a snake. You know, a handsome guy who dresses nice and will make everyone jealous of me just for having him."

"Charm skin off a snake?" I stopped swatting at leaves and looked at Doreen seriously. "I think Stooly's a dream and all, but I don't know about charm or snakes for that matter. Something about him makes me nervous. I can't think or talk when he's around. You don't get nervous around him, though. How come?"

"I don't look at him that way." Shrugging, she picked up a rock and casually inspected it. "He's good-looking, but geez Louise, he's too old for me, us, right now. I can't be stuck with no *old* man," she said, throwing the rock down for emphasis. "I want someone *like* him, but not him. You just too young to understand."

"Am not! I do too understand. But I don't care 'cause Stooly looks young to me. Anyway, we can keep dreaming, huh?"

"Yeah."

We sighed together and continued our walk home, with Doreen kicking at rocks and stones and me swatting at leaves with a branch. We moved on to other topics and didn't give Miss Edna, Stooly, or the strange man in town a second thought.

But we should have.

# CHAPTER 7

## *Stooly's Patent Leather Shoes*

S TOOLY STOOD JUST inside the door of The Hall, adjusting his vision to the dim light. He liked that they kept the place darkened, giving those inside a chance to size up anyone walking in, temporarily blinded by the brightness from the outside. The American Legion Hall was his spot. He was a frequent visitor, and today was no exception. Stooly knew he had a reputation and didn't give a damn what others thought of him. He liked that too.

"John-nay," was the call, full of bass, which came from the back of the empty room.

Slim was the only person who called him by his given name. It was good to know he was waiting because Stooly had a bone to pick. Slim, born Clarence Jeffries, was as black as tar and hard to see in the inky blackness of The Hall's interior. Before his eyes adjusted, if it weren't for his shiny white teeth, Stooly would not have known he was there. Slim had lived a hard life. Tall and lean with a scar down the side of his face and a scowl to match, he was hard to forget once you saw him. The scar on his face had a history but didn't compare to the deeper scar under his skin. That scar had landed Slim in prison. But the one on his face announced to everyone, without saying a word, that he was not one to mess with. Stooly always smiled when Slim was around. Slim was his best friend, his ace boon coon, as they say.

Stooly greeted his friend in the usual way, high five, handclasp, and a hug. Slim had his long fingers wrapped around a can of beer, cold with sweat and tasty. Relieved of the kitchen's hot stickiness for a while, Luella came over to take Stooly's order.

"Yeah, baby, I'll have what he's having, except for that nasty yard bird he's smacking on," Stooly said. It was no secret that Stooly disliked Edna's chicken. To him, it was as nasty as her disposition. There was no reason to point this out, but how she treated the Munro girls a moment ago irked him. So, he couldn't help saying the obvious out loud.

"Sure thing, Stooly," Luella said. As she sauntered away, Stooly admired her from behind, astonished that her ass always seemed to wave bye-bye as she walked. He chuckled to himself and got right to the point with Slim. Never one to mince words, he began to get in Slim's ass.

"What's going on, Black man? Haven't seen you around. Why not?"

"Not much, man, just hanging around Lexington, then over at Winchester for a spell."

"Missed you yesterday. Expected to see you, but a no-show is a no-go, you dig?" Stooly pulled a Lucky Strike cigarette, their favorite brand, from Slim's pack on the table and lit it. Luella walked over with his beer and set it down in front of Stooly. As he rubbed her firm backside, she didn't object, just smiled and walked away.

"Nah, I got caught up in some things and couldn't make that move, man. What you gonna do when you got shit popping off at home? It won't happen again next time." Slim asked.

"You handle your business and get on with it. I waited all day, but you never showed. I asked around, but no one knew where you were, man. That ain't cool."

"What ain't cool is you riding me about it a whole day after."

"Yeah, I'm gonna ride you until you straighten up and fly right," Stooly said. "This ain't no game, man. I can't let myself get hung out like that again. There might not be no "next time," and not only do I lose, but *you* lose." He sipped his beer and blew smoke from his cigarette, waiting for Slim to respond.

"Yeah, I hear you, man. When's the next shipment?"

"I hope you hear me 'cause if you fuck up again, you won't be able to see, hear or flap your gums. You know I'm good for it," Stooly said.

With that, Slim and Stooly stared at each other with cool understanding. Stooly was a stickler when managing his business and knew Slim understood the consequences of disappointing him. They had been friends for a long time, and what Stooly needed wasn't excuses. However, married life could be a real bitch. Slim's wife was more of a stickler, and the less she knew about their business dealings, the better their lives would be. Between the two, Slim's wife scared him the most, but he'd never let Slim know that.

"*When* is next Friday. You free?" Stooly hoped the sarcasm wasn't lost on Slim.

"Yeah, man. Today's what, Wednesday? That should give me time to get some stuff straight. You my nigga, man. I ain't gonna let you down again," Slim said. Stooly let the silence between them hang in the air. It spoke for itself. Further words were unnecessary.

As Stooly and Slim began to work out the details of their next shipment, the door to The Hall swung open and bright light flooded the dark cavernous room. Stooly and Slim made out a figure of a man they hadn't seen before. The stranger adjusted to the darkened room and took a seat at a table not far from them, within full earshot of their conversation. Stooly didn't like this closeness and leaned back in his chair to study the swarthy, odd-looking fellow. *Not from Paris, that's for sure,* thought Stooly. Stooly glanced over at Slim and opened his palm to question who this man might be. Slim shrugged and proceeded to ask questions of the man.

"Say, fella, what brings you out in this heat?" Slim asked.

The stranger said nothing at all. He fidgeted in his chair a bit, then settled back into it.

"Hey, son, I asked you a question. What brings you out in this heat?" Slim asked again.

"Who wants to know?" the stranger said.

Sound traveled differently in a vast room with a low ceiling, particularly when the jukebox wasn't spinning tunes, so his response was more than audible. Stooly steadied his chair and glared at the stranger.

"I'm trying to be neighborly, man," Slim said. "Not many people here, and I don't recall seeing you around town."

Still, the man said nothing as he fingered the table and began strumming an unknown tune. Now it was Stooly's turn.

"Excuse my buddy's rudeness. My name's John, and this here's my buddy Slim. And you?" Stooly asked as cordially as possible.

"Your name ain't John. It's Johnny Davies, but most folks call you Stooly. Your buddy, there ain't no prince either. Got a long list of troubles to his given name." The stranger said no more.

Stooly thought, *Who the hell is this fool?* Slim must have had the same thought because they both rose from their chairs in unison and walked to where the stranger sat. Luella approached the stranger to take his order, but Stooly waved her away.

Looking closely at the man for study, Stooly noticed an odor that was not pleasing to the nose. His face was unshaven, and his nails were dirty. His clothes were too big for his frame, but what was most disturbing were the man's eyes. They were sunken and feverishly focused, with an animal intensity Stooly had only seen from some prison inmates or, at worst, in an insane asylum.

"Hey, man, I don't know you," Stooly said. "I don't want no trouble. None of us do. I'm trying to be friendly, but I think you might have other plans. If you have a beef with Slim or me, let's talk. Otherwise, stop fucking around."

"Don't have no "plans," *friend,*" the stranger said.

The sarcasm was not lost on Stooly. This situation didn't feel right to him, and although this guy sat quietly, minding his own business, it seemed his *business* included knowing more about them than he was comfortable with. Slim's patience, however, was running thin, and it showed.

"Who the fuck is you, man? What's your name, nigga? You got one, don't you?"

"Name ain't Nigga," the stranger said.

"How about Mr. Smell Bad then, *nigga*?" Slim asked. "Don't know that I like you knowing us and us not knowing you!"

The stranger stood up and adjusted himself, then made a move to leave, but Slim stepped in his path, causing the stranger to stumble into Stooly.

Stooly spun the man around and spit on him. "Find some soap and water before you go bumping into me!"

Just then, Jackson Tally came in for his afternoon libation. He spotted the three men together and immediately made a beeline for the stranger, placing himself between them.

"What's going on, Stooly?" Jackson asked, spreading his arms to further separate the men.

"Son of a bitch step on my patent leather shoes." Stooly threw up his hands in frustration, then bent to wipe at his shoes.

Tally shrugged, unbothered. "Hell, man, he didn't know they were patent leather."

Stooly appreciated Tally's habit of making light of a bad situation. But his witty reply didn't ease the tension in the room and fooled no one.

"Who the fuck is this asshole anyway?" Slim asked.

"He's a friend of mine. Mitch, Mitchell Duncan. He's been staying at the YMCA, working at the A&P here in Paris loading meat part-time. Just got into town," Tally answered.

"Well, why didn't he say so?" Slim said. "Clammed up real tight when we asked. Hey, we tried to be friendly, but he wants to be a jackass acting like he knows us and shit. That's fucked up, man. Fucked up my whole day now. Strange motherfucker!"

Slim pointed his finger in Mitchell's face as he said this, but it didn't change Mitch's disposition. Mitch stood, brooding and steely-eyed, saying nothing more during the exchange. Stooly noticed but was silent. He saw everything, missing nothing as he continued to wipe his shoes.

"Let me apologize for him, then. It takes time to adjust to new people, and I admit he takes some getting used to. Let's sit over here and have a beer, huh?" Tally asked.

"No. I don't think so." Stooly had no intention of sitting down to jaw with this man, Mitchell Duncan. "Let's go." Stooly motioned for Slim to follow and, nodding in Tally's direction, said, "Tally."

There was no point in discussing anything further with Tally. The man gave Stooly the creeps, and he'd known plenty of creepy fellas. Stooly didn't like him and was glad to leave for fresher air outside. The cloying air inside had grown stale. To his way of thinking, Mitchell was on a whole other level of creepy, so much so that Tally couldn't see it. Although Stooly wasn't sure what had just happened, he instinctively knew that trouble had come. And to Paris of all places.

On his way out, Stooly ran into Edna Allen, which was unusual because she never came out from behind the kitchen wall.

"Well, I do declare! You leaving already? I was hoping to have more time to visit with you and your buddy here," Edna said in surprise as the place filled with patrons.

"Now, ain't that a shame. You have work to do before closing, and unfortunately, time is not on our side," he reminded Edna. With that, Stooly let the door open and close on her as he and Slim exited before she could say another word.

⊰◈◈◈⊱

However, the evening was full of surprises. Edna would not be deterred in her quest to wrangle Jackson Tally. She was hell-bent on speaking to him that night and any other night she could. Smoothing down her hair and dress, she approached Tally's table and saw he was not alone. *Damn!* Upon closer inspection, Tally was sitting with a strange man who was dirty and had an odorous smell about him that wafted above the aroma of her fried chicken. *Who the devil is this, spoiling everything for me? Oh my Lord,* she thought, *what is this?* When Edna arrived at their table, Tally and the stranger got up to leave. Edna put a hand to her throat, cleared it, and began to speak.

"I saw you come in and hoped to sit with you while you had your beer, but I see you have company. Are you leaving so soon?"

"Yes, ma'am, I am. I have some business to attend to, but let me introduce you to my friend Mitchell Duncan. Mitch, this is Edna Allen, my neighbor."

The stranger made no move to offer his hand to shake, and Edna did not offer hers. She stared at the man, knowing evil when she saw it. After quickly exclaiming that her chicken must be burning, she excused herself and hurried away.

In the kitchen, breathing hard and still holding a hand to her throat, Edna had the feeling of barely escaping something dreadful. She would surely turn her porch light on that night and, in her prayers, thank God for his mercy.

# CHAPTER 8

## *Very Personally Yours*

—————————◆◇◇◇—————————

I WAS SO full of thoughts about Stooly, and Doreen's idea of having a boyfriend like him, that telling Mom about Miss Edna's behavior never occurred to me. But that night, alone in my room, Miss Edna was all I could think about. Yes, I had secrets. But why Miss Edna thought I had them up to my armpits was too weird for words. It wasn't until I decided to talk with Doreen about it that sleep finally claimed me. As I dozed off, I knew I'd have to fess up about my visits. It might be worth it if I could get a clue about why she so nasty toward me.

Mom and I always rose late and tended to oversleep. Especially when Mom studied late into the night. The following day was no exception, but we got up later than usual. Whenever this happened, it was a rush to get her out the door even before I could put the breakfast dishes away.

"Linney, I've laid out lunch and put it in the fridge for later."

"Is it the same thing again, left over from a few days ago?"

"Don't get sassy, young lady. It's meatloaf sandwiches…left over from last night," she said with a mischievous smile.

"Yes, ma'am. I was just wondering."

"I know." She sighed as if defeated. "Will you sweep and mop the floor in the kitchen? The linoleum feels sticky in spots, and we don't have any cleanser. So, take this list with you to the A&P for groceries. Don't forget cleaner for the floor and cleanser for the sink." Holding me by the shoulders, she said, "You're growing up so fast. Such a good girl. Be careful and lock the door behind me, okay? Remember to take the keys. Gotta go!" She kissed me on the forehead and then was gone.

Ignoring my mother's instructions, I decided to see Doreen first, then do chores after, and maybe visit the Sweets before Mom got home. I hadn't seen Miss Katherine in two days and wanted to bring her up on the latest event, especially about her porch lights and locking her doors.

Out of concern for my safety, I had become a source of constant watching from the neighbors. Seemed like I was now hearing "Lock the door" every day. Lock the door meant I had to carry a key *all* the time. Lock and bolt the door when I came home and lock it anytime I left the house. It was a pain in the neck to lock and unlock, but it *was* my idea. With so much to do, it's a miracle I didn't lose the key! Before I took one step outside, the watchful eyes of the neighbors were on me.

"You looking after yourself, Linney?"

"Yes, Miss Loren."

"Okay, good. You be careful."

"I will.

"Linney, you come back home soon now."

"Yes, Miss Pearl. I see you in your window. You cleaning?"

"Can't let you get lost. I'll be watching for you now these windows are cleaned."

"Okay, thank you."

"Girl, your momma know you out?"

"Yes, Miss Anne."

"Where you off to?"

"Over Grandma's. Then the store."

"All right then. You hurry back before I come after you myself."

"Yes, ma'am, I will. Thank you."

Several people called out to me before I reached Grandma's house. They meant well, but it was embarrassing, just the same. The worst was Miss Tally. She stood on her front porch, telling me she could not let me walk by myself. When I told her it was full daylight and early in the morning, she was still not convinced.

"I don't care if the good Lord's watching from above. You can't be without a chaperone."

"Miss Tally, I'll be fine. You holding me up as it is, and if Mom's okay with me going alone…." I let this hang in the air, holding my arms out in a questioning gesture hoping she got the full meaning.

"I'm gonna be right here by this door until you get back home safe. You got your key?"

"Yes, ma'am, don't worry. Thank you."

The Tallys didn't have children, so they had unofficially adopted me. Some Black women, like Miss Tally, worked either in their own homes doing domestic chores, such as ironing or sewing, or outside their homes as domestic housemaids. Others worked in hospitals, schools, offices, or the local mills. Some even held military positions at Avon Station near Lexington. For all I knew, some of these well-meaning women wouldn't be home or would be too busy to concern themselves about me when I returned.

In summer, the walk to Grandma's house was filled with sights and colors of beautiful flowers, mostly tea roses, with a few impatiens or begonia bushes mixed in that lined the fences and yards. Grandma wasn't into growing flowers like the Sweet sisters. Vegetables and fruit did her just fine, thank you very much. Her large kitchen pantry was always full of canned foods.

If she wasn't in her garden, she could be found in her sewing room. My grandma worked at home as a seamstress. She did alterations for the neighbors when time allowed. Her most frequent clients were White people. She did excellent work, and I just knew she could make a boatload of money if she opened her own business. But she enjoyed working at home and in her garden too much to do that.

Grandma's house was a two-story farmhouse with a garden in the back. Grabbing an apple or pear from the trees on either side of her garden was something I loved to do. The house was fenced on all sides and situated catty-corner from Beaumont Funeral Home. It was a welcoming house that would, if it could, smile and wink at you when looking up at it. Even though it was a chaotic scene when she had two or three projects going at the same time, her house always smelled good and fresh. Not that ours didn't, but Grandma's house felt like a warm hug, always comfy, crisp, and light.

Grandma was born Julia Edith Eadys. A gentle and sweet lady, tiny and petite with a shock of wavy platinum-white hair, she never used the name Julia, so everyone called her Grandma Edith. After she married my grandfather, Ernest Munro, she had five children. My other aunt and two uncles had moved away, except Doreen, who now had the best of everything. I've often heard some people wonder about Grandma's racial makeup, but for me, her German, Scots-Irish, and Black features were clear to see, while Grandpa Ernst brought in the Black and Indian ancestry.

Every month, she couldn't wait to receive a copy of *Reader's Digest*. She loved a good read, and a cup of coffee served in a porcelain cup with a saucer to relax her from a hectic day. I loved my grandma, who was funny and smart. She walked everywhere, saying it was healthy for her lungs. She always had a smile and a huge hug that held me for a long time when I came over. I know she wanted me to visit more often, but the misery I suffered at the hands of Doreen was too much to take sometimes.

Grandpa Ernst didn't like me. I avoided him whenever possible. I never followed up on this feeling, but I felt in my heart that whenever I was around, he wanted me gone. With tied-back, shoulder-length, jet-black hair and a hawk-billed nose, Grandpa never said much but stared at me from under heavy brows with brooding dark eyes. Because of this, I tried to visit Grandma whenever he was not at home. Or Doreen and I would lock ourselves in her room when he arrived home from a hard-working day doing the odd plumbing, electrical, or carpentry job.

Like most days, I timed my visit when Grandpa was out. Dressed in a loose-fitting chemise with a full apron tied loosely around her neck, Grandma motioned me into her enormous white kitchen. A tape measure was draped around her neck, with dressmaker pins sticking out from a pin cushion tucked into one of her apron pockets. Her hair stuck out in all directions from under a scarf used as a headband. Crazy beautiful was her impression, and I loved her for all things "grandma."

The house smelled of bacon and eggs. It was also a mess of chaos and loud noises. Grandma had taken a break from repairing a torn jacket pocket for someone who lived in the Highlands area of Paris and poured herself a cup of coffee. At the same time, she banged away at pots on the stove, preparing to can more of her homegrown fruits and vegetables.

After I helped lift hot jars from boiling water and set them aside to cool before canning, she told me, "I think I can handle the rest of this. Thank you, baby. Doreen's in her room going over a box she received in the mail."

"What kind of box?" I asked.

"Why don't you go on up and see for yourself?"

"Okay." I grabbed an apple before she peeled it for canning and listened while she called to Doreen that I was on my way up. She certainly had a large set of lungs for a tiny lady.

I bounded up the stairs, taking two at a time, and stood gasping at the top of the landing to catch my breath. Doreen poked her head out of her bedroom door and waved me to her room.

At the top of the staircase landing, on the left, was my grandparents' bedroom, which overlooked Lilleston Avenue. The spacious bathroom full of fragrant soap and pristine white walls was between my grandparents' and the blue bedroom. This room was painted a light blue with white trim that overlooked the garden out back. As a child, I loved staying in that room with its blue-and-white quilt on a giant four-poster bed. Doreen's bedroom was on the right of the hallway and across from the delightful bathroom. Like my grandparents, her bedroom window also overlooked Lilleston Avenue. I called it the pink room, all pink and white with plum accents. Her bed had an overhead canopy that matched a fluffy floral-printed comforter, which dressed the whole bed and its skirt. The bedding was slippery and not easy to sit on. I always slid down the sides, but it was great for lying across.

As I slowly walked down the hallway, Doreen popped her head out again and motioned for me to hurry. I stood at the threshold to see her bed littered with pamphlets, papers, strange contraptions, and a lot of other stuff. Doreen pulled me in with a wide grin and hurriedly shut the door. Then she held up a pink-and-white box from Kimberly-Clark that read "Very Personally Yours" inscribed on the front.

"Look what I have. Can you believe it?" Doreen asked. "Mom ordered it for me."

She bounced excitedly up and down on her toes as she said this, probably thinking I would know what she was going on about, but I had no idea.

"Who's Kimberly Clark?" I asked, mildly curious as I bit into my apple and wiped at the juices that ran down my chin.

"It's for when you start to bleed, silly." I had deflated her excitement somewhat, but Doreen continued, "It tells you all about it right here. I never knew this would happen to us when we got older. Did you?"

Confused, I forgot all about Miss Edna *and* the apple. *Do I cut myself, or does something cut me?* The thought of bleeding without knowing why scared me.

"What do you mean bleed? I don't want to bleed. Why do you do that?"

"All girls do it when it's time. Look, it says so right here." She pointed to a booklet, pulling me down on the poofy bedspread next to her as she sat with crossed legs, in a position we called

"Indian-style." In this way, I read along with her, sometimes with my mouth open, not believing what I was reading and listening as she read aloud.

"It says that all girls start to bleed around twelve or thirteen. Latest at fourteen. It says that it doesn't hurt and not to be afraid. It's nothing to be ashamed of, and all women do this once a month. Can you believe that?"

"Holy moly!"

"Look, I got all this in the box too." Doreen held up an elastic band with strange loops and a set of padded strips. My curiosity got the best of me. It was all so mysterious; the box, the contents, and the news of femaleness were bewildering and strange. I wanted to know more and reached for the other reading materials in the box.

We were in Doreen's room for hours, pouring over the information. There was a lot to read with so many instructions, and I think we read the same booklets at least three times over. We were so innocent about these things. How could we know about what we were never told? Neither one of us had boobs yet!

As mysterious as it was, I thought, *This kit is really cool!* I was fascinated. But there was one catch: it was for one person, Doreen. When her time came, she would have all she needed. I wouldn't have anything. So again, in this, Doreen was special while I was not.

"Go tell your mom about this kit so she can buy one for you," Doreen said.

"I guess I could, but money's tight. I don't feel right asking Mom to do that for me."

"Well, I'm glad I have mine, at least. Poor thing, it's a shame you can't have one of your own. It's just as well. I'll probably be a woman before you anyway. Maybe Janie can buy a kit for you by the time you do. See, it'll all work out."

With that smirk on her face, Doreen had slipped back into her usual selfish nature, or maybe she simply didn't know how to express herself without insulting me. In any case, I had already stayed longer than planned and needed to get going and told Doreen so, but she didn't seem to notice.

Leaving her room, I slowly descended the stairs, thinking about what I had seen and learned. I found Grandma in her sewing room, and I told her that I loved Doreen's special kit. I was hoping she would hear the disappointment in my voice that I didn't have one of my own, but no. "I'm so glad you like it. One day, you'll experience all the mysteries of life for yourself. Won't that be nice?"

*Well, I guess,* I thought. "I'm going to the store. Do you need anything, Grandma?" I asked and kissed her gently on the cheek.

"Thank you, honey, but I have everything I need right here." Grandma watched as I walked down the steps of her house and out into the afternoon sun. As she blew kisses and waved goodbye, I walked along in a daze, thinking how unfair life could be.

⇒◦◦◦⇐

The A&P announced itself with huge red "A & P" letters, outlined in white neon, emblazoned on the front of a redbrick building. It was situated on an elevated hill in the middle of town. Most residents shopped there on the weekends, so it was always crowded. But today, there were few people. The sun glinted off the black-and-white-checked linoleum tile, which was sparkling clean, probably mopped with Spic and Span, Mom's favorite brand. The shopping aisles were brightly lit, making it easy to see whatever was needed as shoppers quietly scanned the shelves to make the best choice for the day's purchase. Vegetables were displayed in baskets, fresh from the local farmer's market, and milk kept cold in glass jars could easily be picked up by the red rubber collar around the top. Cool, clean, and orderly, even the meat department displayed fresh cuts of meat so red and mouthwatering you just had to stop and admire.

On this day, instead of enjoying the A&P atmosphere, I kept thinking of the Very Personally Yours kit and what a mystery it all was; but it didn't mention how babies got inside you.

Squinting at a carton of eggs, I couldn't help but wonder why ours were hidden inside and not outside us, like chickens, to hatch. As I absentmindedly shopped for the items on Mom's grocery list, these questions and much more ran through my head. Aside from everything else Doreen had that I didn't, now I resented her more for having something I wanted in the worst way.

As I picked over the yellow chickens, an odor wafted up that wasn't pleasant. The smell was so rotten I thought, *Something must have gone bad in the meat department.* After choosing a good enough chicken for dinner, I hurried away, but it lingered regardless of the aisle I was in. When I picked up a bottle of floor cleaner, I snuck a sniff under my armpits, took a whiff, and was satisfied it wasn't me. Mom always said I had a sensitive nose, so I shrugged it off. Once outside, the odor was gone, and I thought no more of it—that is, until I ran into Miss Tally. Her home was the first of the duplex units and the porch I landed on the night I was followed. Looking head-on, her house was to my right, while Miss Edna's joined on the left.

"Where you been, young lady? I was fixing to call the police after you," Miss Tally said as she smoothed down my hair. "You been at your grandmother's all this time?"

"Yes, ma'am. I mean no, ma'am," I said. "I was there for a while and stayed longer than I should've, sorry." Then I saw a dark shadow dart behind Miss Tally's house. I moved my head and body slightly to the left to see if I could catch the movement again. Miss Tally turned around to see where I was looking and then asked what was wrong.

"Nothing, I thought I saw…." But I didn't know what I had just seen.

"Child, you look like you seen a ghost," Miss Tally said. Studying my face with more scrutiny, she tried to ease any worry I might have over imagining shadows and chuckled. "You know it might be my husband's new friend, just in from work. He's staying down at the Y and joining us for dinner. Jackson'll be home in a little bit." Then she called out, "Mitchell! Hey, Mitch, you in there?" But there was no reply. She shrugged. "He might be washing up for dinner and can't hear. Try not to be so jumpy over everything, okay? Now you go on home, and don't forget to lock the door."

"Yes, ma'am," I said.

As I walked away, I got a whiff of that horrible smell again, which had followed me around at the A&P. *Is it something in my bag of groceries?* I wondered. It was all very strange.

My immediate thought was to bathe when I got home, especially with an offensive odor swirling around my head and body. Plus, it would help to cool off from the day's heat.

Once I got home, I rechecked my armpits and the groceries, and all seemed well. I found nothing rotten. I wondered if it might be coming from inside Miss Tally's house; after all, the windows were wide open, so it was possible. But why did I smell it also at the A&P? Miss Tally said Mr. Mitch just got in from work. If he worked at the A&P, could it be Mr. Mitch? I laughed at the thought, thinking that if the smell belonged to Mr. Mitch, he should bathe in a large tub of water instead of washing up at a sink.

# CHAPTER 9

## Miss Virginia

I COULDN'T WAIT for Mom to come home from work. I finally told her about Miss Edna's behavior at The Hall and the friend at Miss Tally's house that day. Mom didn't seem concerned about Miss Edna and called her a silly, nosy, and petty old woman. On her way home, she said Miss Edna was outside, spraying the air with a can of air freshener. God only knew why Miss Edna would do this, but it showed how ridiculous she could be. However, Mom was curious about the goings-on at the Tallys' house.

"Jess usually tells me everything, but she's never mentioned this new friend of Jackson's," she said. "I need to learn more about this 'friend,' especially after what you experienced a few nights ago. I just might pop over, but not tonight. It's been a long day. I'm tired, and I have studying to do."

Not waiting for the moment to pass, I casually brought up Doreen's Very Personally Yours kit. I told Mom all about it, excited to describe what I had read and learned. I couldn't bring myself to ask outright but made sure to hint that it was *so cool* and all girls should have one of their own. Secretly, I couldn't wait for my body to change and become a woman.

"Mom, do you think I'll get boobs soon?"

"All in good time. Don't be in such a hurry to grow up. Things will start to change when they're supposed to and not before."

"I know, but I can't wait. Were you scared when it happened to you?"

"When it happens, you'll hardly know. I should get some items to prepare for that eventuality, just for you and you alone."

Mom tweaked me on the nose and explained some other issues the kit left out. I was a captive audience of one, and Mom made my day with Doreen seem not so bad after all. After dinner, I had just enough time to visit the Sweet sisters, so I hurried off while Mom went into her study.

⟡

"I thought I heard little feet running up to my door," Miss Katherine said.

Miss Dottie smiled and nodded, rocking in her chair as usual. I was disappointed that the silver tea tray was not out because it was the one object I wanted to ask more about. But she had baked walnut brownies, which I couldn't resist.

"I'm sorry I haven't been by. It's been so busy." I reached for a warm morsel and then picked it apart, savoring every walnutty bite.

"Well, I want to hear all about it," Miss Katherine said. "Help yourself to milk in the fridge."

"Yes, ma'am. Thank you. For one thing, the neighborhood's on alert for a strange man seen around here. We've all started to lock our doors at night and turn the porch lights on. Locking doors was my idea."

"You don't say? I got concerned when I saw the lights on over there. I wondered if it had to do with a new city ordinance of some kind, but now I hear about this man…. I suppose we'll have to do that as well, right, Sister? I don't know if we have a key to lock the door, but I'll look. Sister, do you know what we did with the key?"

It was strange Miss Katherine would ask Miss Dottie anything, let alone about a key. However, Miss Katherine didn't seem concerned about speaking out loud to her at all.

"Have you seen this person?" she continued.

"He followed me home! I didn't get a look at his face because it was dark, but I was *so* scared. I ran to the Tallys' front porch. Mr. Tally heard me and came out to help."

"Well, goodness me! I wonder what he wants around here. Times are changing so fast. It's a shame you can't come and go without concern. I hope you're careful, especially playing around in those trees next door. You never know who or what could be hiding in there."

"Yes, ma'am," I said. My mouth was full of a delicious brownie, so it was hard to speak.

"You know, I used to hear you kids playing in that field from time to time, but I don't hear it much anymore. I guess most of you've outgrown it some. I think the bugs in the garden are coming from those weeds and trees over there. I've asked the city about cutting it back, but they keep ignoring me. Such a nuisance."

"You should see it, though! We call it the Jungle." She waited while I drank the cold and fresh milk to wash down the brownie before I continued, "We have a tree house and flat places laid out for sitting and a fort to hide behind when we play war between girls and boys. I don't go there much anymore."

"I think you ought to stay out of that place until this stranger business is settled. It's not safe and could be dangerous."

Miss Dottie gurgled. She was trying to speak, then said, "The key's in that box by the bed, yes it is. You can't go in there, no." She wiped at her mouth and said no more.

"So what else has been keeping you busy?" Miss Katherine asked quickly, changing the subject and ignoring her sister's comments.

I didn't. It was odd, and even though she was asked about the keys a while ago, what did she mean by "you can't go in there?" The Jungle? Why? Because of this, my excitement to discuss the Very Personally Yours kit faded. But before I could ask about the comment, a knock came at the door.

"Well, hello, my dear Virginia, hello!" Miss Katherine said.

"Hello, ladies. I didn't realize you had company. I hope I'm not intruding. May I come in?" she asked.

"Not at all. Please, come in, come in!" Miss Katherine said.

"I wanted to come by earlier, but I couldn't get away until now," she said to Miss Katherine. She turned to me. "And who is this young lady?"

"Hi, I'm Lindsey Hollis, but you can call me Linney," I said.

"Pleased to meet you. My name is Virginia Morgan."

It was rumored Miss Virginia would be chosen to teach at Paris High this school year. She was a popular and favorite teacher at Western who taught eighth grade English, but no one knew much about her personally. I couldn't wait to be one of her students. She had a pleasant voice with no Southern drawl, was average in height, and had a friendly roundish face and shoulder-length dark brown hair worn in an outward flip.

"I know, ma'am. You'll be the new English teacher at Paris High, huh?"

"Why I suppose that's a possibility, but there's more to consider on that matter. Are you in high school yet or transitioning soon?"

"Yes, ma'am, I'll be in eighth grade this year. I won't be in high school until next year."

"Now, how exciting is that! It must be something to look forward to, going to the *big* school in a year and all? You'll do just fine, I'm sure. Now, how is everyone?" Miss Virginia asked of the sisters.

She seemed sure of herself, direct and polite. She made me feel welcome to be part of her visit, so I didn't feel the need to leave when she arrived. It wasn't long before Miss Virginia told Miss Katherine the reason for her visit.

"I came by to let you know my intentions to leave Paris. I've accepted a position in Chicago and will leave after this coming school term ends."

"Well, I do declare! This is the best news! What finally brought you to this decision?" Miss Katherine asked.

"Well, as you know, I've thought about it for a long time now, but recent events have led me to make this move. Western will be closing its doors due to school integration, and let's face it, not all of us teachers will find positions at Paris High. I don't want to hedge my bets that they'll hire me there; it's been too long a wait. So, I contacted your connections in Chicago, Katherine, and was offered a position at the University of Chicago to teach next year. It was just too good an opportunity to pass up."

"My dear, I am so glad for *you*," Miss Katherine said.

Even though Miss Katherine was jumping for joy at this news, I was disappointed that Miss Virginia wouldn't be teaching at Paris High when I got my chance to attend. At least I would still be her student *this* year at Western, though. However, the fact the sisters still had connections in Chicago was interesting. So I sat with my elbows on my knees, leaning in to hear more in the crowded front room of the house.

"You can certainly stay with my cousin Lucille," Miss Katherine said. "I'll make sure she knows you're coming. Oh, it will be so *nice* for her to have *you*! You'll be a great help to her, I'm sure. Chicago is a wonderful place with so much culture and history. It's a shame that Bronzeville is not as vibrant as it was in my day."

"I don't want to intrude on your cousin, Katherine. I can look after myself. I know Chicago's a big place, but I'm sure I can work it out just fine."

"Nonsense, I won't hear of it, and you know it! A year is not that far away. It'll be here before long. Now, Hyde Park is the best neighborhood to live in, and it's not too far from the University of Chicago. Come to think of it, Cousin Lucy lives not far from the university, so it's perfect. A university position, my, my, my! Teaching English, I suppose?"

"Literature, actually. It's a new position created to expand diversity at the school. I'm already working on my Ph.D. and plan to complete my dissertation, which they'll allow me to do there."

Although this must have been good news for Miss Virginia, why did she look like she was about to cry? She didn't seem particularly sure of her decision, so I decided to speak up to let her know I wanted her to stay.

"Why not take the chance of being hired and stay here, Miss Virginia?" I said. "The word's already out that you'll be chosen this fall. I love to read and can't wait to learn more about poetry and why authors write what they do. Can't you go later?"

"I appreciate you saying that, sweetheart, but unfortunately, I feel the need to do it now."

Miss Virginia fiddled with her skirt and fidgeted in her chair. Then her eyes darted around the room and toward the open front door. She seemed either nervous or maybe hiding something, but what? Her behavior made me think there might be another reason for leaving town.

No sooner did I have these thoughts than she spoke to me again. "You know, if you want, you can come to my house from time to time. That way, I can share some literary knowledge with you before leaving. Although I'll have you for English this year, I'm disappointed I won't have you as a high school literature student. You seem eager to learn, and I don't get that kind of enthusiasm from students these days. I'd really like to get to know you better. How does that sound?"

"That sounds great!" I tried to hide my surprise but couldn't. "I can't wait. Tell me when and I'll be there!"

"Come by anytime." Miss Virginia chuckled. "The invitation's always open. Well, I should be getting on. The sun's past the horizon, and because I didn't drive over, I have a ways to walk."

"I am so glad you came by, Virginia," Miss Katherine said. "You hurry on, and you, Miss Linney, tell your mother to come by, you hear? I haven't seen her in a while and miss her lovely smile. She works so hard. How are her studies coming along?"

"Fine. She has a few more tests to pass before getting her license, at least before Miss Beaumont gets hers." Turning to Miss Virginia, I said, "Mom's studying to be an LPN, a licensed nurse. Isn't that great?"

"Yes, it is," Miss Virginia said.

"I think so too. Well, good night, everybody," I said.

Suddenly Miss Dottie, who hadn't said but a few words the entire time, called out a terrifying warning that froze me in place alongside Miss Virginia.

"Don't go alone, no! Don't let that child go alone! Them woods!" Miss Dottie said.

"Oh, Dottie, it's okay. It's okay, my girl," Miss Virginia said. "I don't live that far, remember? Just near the corner of Hanson and Thomas Avenue."

Miss Dottie rapidly rocked in her chair, staring at nothing while Miss Katherine tried to soothe and calm her, feeling her forehead.

"I think she means Linney, Virginia. Will you walk her home?" Miss Katherine said.

"Of course I will. It's on my way. How does that sound, Dottie girl?" Miss Virginia asked.

Miss Katherine then asked Miss Virginia to get some medications from the bathroom. After Miss Dottie was given her pills, we left the sisters and walked together to my house.

I was lost in thought and didn't say much. This was the second time Miss Dottie had said something odd, and it was almost always directed toward me. What was she trying to say? Walking in the dusk of night, I could barely make out the shapes of the trees when we walked by the Jungle. As we did, I caught that putrid, rancid smell again. Miss Virginia did too. I know because she slowed and turned to look at the Jungle, then moved away from that side of the road. It wasn't until Miss Virginia reached out for my hand, trembling, that I felt dread. Her eyes were wide as she quickened her steps. She didn't say a word but pulled me along.

"Did you smell that? I've smelled it before at the A&P but can't figure where it's coming from or what it is. Do you know?" I asked.

"Yes, I do, sweetie, which is why I have to leave this town."

# CHAPTER 10

## *Not Ladylike at the DQ*

━━◆◦◦◦◆━━

AFTER MISS VIRGINIA made that statement, the stunned look on my face must have been funny because she nervously chuckled. I suppose she had her reasons for saying what she did. But why not tell us the truth about leaving instead of telling us it was because of a new job? As she walked away, I knew for sure she was hiding something. *And I thought the Sweet sisters were mysterious!*

Like people, I quickly learned that mysteries are hard to figure out. It felt like the whole world was spinning around on its head, topsy-turvy. So fast that it made me dizzy. First, there was the smell and Mr. Jackson's new friend. Next, that feeling of dread when Miss Virginia and I passed the Jungle and again when I was followed home the other night. Then there were the Sweet sisters who'd lived in Chicago. Why move to Kentucky? Miss Katherine had obvious ties there and still loved it, so why move to Paris of all places? Finally, there was Miss Edna's meanness toward me, not to mention the personal changes I was supposed to experience soon. It was overwhelming. So many people. So many mysteries.

One way to keep my world from spinning out of control was to talk it out, not with Mom or Grandma, but with Doreen. The Very Personally Yours kit took my focus away from discussing Miss Edna with her a few days before. We shared a closeness that day, so I figured it would be perfect to have Doreen listen and help me unravel so much of what I was going through. *If only I could trust her.* Now with Miss Virginia in the picture, I wasn't sure if I should say anything at all.

The next day, I called Doreen, who was about to meet up with Brenda and Karen for a walk to the Dairy Queen. She asked if I wanted to come along. Brenda Thomas and Karen Benson were friends of Doreen's who didn't like me much. These girls were fast and loud, lived on Lylesville Street, and smoked in secret. In my opinion, growing up like that was just not ladylike. As Grandma said, "You can't buy class. You either have it, or you don't." They didn't. I never understood why Doreen was drawn to them. I guess she thought they made her look cool or something, but she was better off without them if you asked me. With them around, I would have to put off talking to Doreen for another day. However, a Cherry Coke from the Dairy Queen sounded good, so I agreed to go.

Every day the humidity got worse, and this day was no different. I wore my favorite pair of shorts and a sleeveless, straight-hemmed shirt. Staying cool was one way I could walk in my Keds without sweating too much. How I wished Mom could buy me a pair of sandals so the Keds could get a break from the heat of my feet. Doreen had already left to meet Brenda and Karen, so it was a race to catch up with them. When I did, Brenda and Doreen didn't disappoint.

"Girl come on, you so slow!" Doreen yelled.

"You should order a Coke, Linney," Brenda said. "That'd put more color in your skin."

"Geez Louise, why can't you wear something different?" Doreen asked. "Every day, you wear the same old thing. Until you get new clothes, don't walk next to me. It's embarrassing to walk beside you."

That was a blow I wasn't ready for. As they walked ahead, I tried to make my clothes look different, but tucking in a shirt that wasn't meant to be tucked was useless.

I was glad to see Angela and Carolyn when we got to the Dairy Queen. Their presence would make the time with Brenda, Karen, and Doreen bearable. Doreen ordered a chocolate shake; Angela and Karen ordered lemonade. The rest were satisfied with the Cherry Cokes, made with coke-cola and whole or crushed cherries dropped in for extra flavoring. It was new and so delicious.

Gossip was always juicy on a hot summer day, especially when sitting in the shade of a DQ steel umbrella in the middle of a round cement table with benches. I used my straw to break up the cherries, wiped the sweat from my forehead, and listened as they began. Like how Mr. Johnson didn't want anyone to know how broke he was and how his wife recently divorced him and took the kids to live in Indiana. Mr. Fisher caught his wife wild dancing with Mr. Evans at The Hall, and wouldn't Miss Fisher be filing for divorce before long? There were bets taken. The Christian church choir was better than the Baptist choir because Lois Williams had the best singing voice in Paris. Miss Bessie was too hot to trot, and how Mr. Lonesome wasn't all that lonely, according to Miss Clay.

Eventually, our conversation turned to school in the fall. This year I would be left behind at Western while they attended Paris High as ninth graders. Paris was slow to integrate since the 1954 regulations were passed. Paris High and Western High were good schools, so what to do? It was eventually decided to merge them by closing Western, one class at a time. Western High became an elementary school for Blacks until Southside Elementary was ready to receive the younger kids. Paris High was the integrated transitional school every ninth grader looked forward to attending as a rite of passage.

"We'll all be fifteen this year, except you, Linney, so it might be time to think about getting serious with books and stuff. I hear those White boys are really cute," Doreen said.

"I heard the same thing, but it don't beat our fine brown brothers. I hear it's nice there too, nicer than Western," Karen said. She could be a little simpleminded and tended to follow Brenda's lead. But in this, her opinion differed from that of Brenda, who didn't care for the whole idea.

"Girl, speak for yourself," Brenda said. "I can't stand being there with them. They don't like us, and I don't like them. After you around them for long, you start talking funny, and they smell like dirty water."

"No, they *don't!*" Angela said. "That's a horrible thing to say, and you oughta be ashamed, saying things like that. You just looking at it all wrong. Western's closing. They're going to tear it down, and there's nothing we can do about it, so you might as well get used to the idea. Anyway, integration's the law."

"All I know is White people look down their noses at us like we stink, so I don't think it's wrong to say that about them," Brenda said.

"Without knowing the truth?" Carolyn asked. "I hear their houses smell really clean, like lettuce and Clorox. Not like some smelly houses I've been to in this neighborhood. So how bad can they be?"

"Nuh-uh! You lying. Have you seen them with that stringy hair? That should tell you how dirty they are," Brenda said. She looked suspiciously over at Carolyn, I suppose trying to figure out who she was referring to with her smelly house comment. But Angela cleared up any confusion on that score.

"Like your nappy head don't stink?" she asked. "Brenda, you smell like roast beef and greasy cabbage on a *good* day!"

We exploded in laughter. It was uncharacteristic for Angela to say something this bold, and it was made funnier because it was partly true. This caused Karen to spit lemonade through her nose and choke while Doreen coughed on her milkshake, which had gone down the wrong way. We laughed even more at ourselves.

"Oh my God! Does it have to be 'greasy' cabbage!" Carolyn teased back, barely containing herself.

"That's greasy, boiled cabbage!" Doreen said after she got her voice back.

"Uh-huh, see, y'all crazy!" Brenda shook her head. Teasing back, she continued, "Angie, you think you cute. But I tell you what—you won't be laughing when you get there. You'll see. All them honkies and peckerwoods be checking us out, looking at our clothes, thinking we a bunch of stupid dirty niggas, you just wait." Count on Brenda to take the fun out of a moment.

"Stop calling people names!" Carolyn yelled. A little bit of Brenda went a long way, and she was getting under Carolyn's skin. "You wouldn't like it if they called you nigger or worse! That's the problem with this *whole* integration business. Just because we have to go to school with White kids don't mean we have to start calling names. Reminds me of what they might be saying about us, and I don't need those kinds of reminders going into this, thank you all the same. Y'all saw the stories about Little Rock on TV! *That* ain't Paris! So get a grip, okay? Drives me up a wall."

Brenda was an unhappy person, and it showed. When she was this foul, which was most times, I wished she would just go away. This offensive talk was her attempt at being funny. It never was, and what's more, it produced the kind of tension we didn't need on a hot afternoon.

"Ah, that's sticks and stones! That was more than ten years ago, and nothing's changed. I can't see Dr. King coming here to help if they decide to act out," Brenda said.

"I don't care if you get mad, Brenda, but Dr. King's done a lot for civil rights. Otherwise, where'd we be?" Angela was standing her ground and not backing down from Brenda while at the same time sticking up for Carolyn. "We had a few fights happen in Paris, but nothing like what's happened in Lexington or Louisville. A lot's changed, and I think name-calling brings *real* sticks and stones. Do you think of yourself as a low-life nigger?" Brenda didn't answer, so Angela continued, "*I* didn't think so, so don't *act* like one. I don't think *they* think of themselves like the names you call them, and I bet they don't act like it, either. And even if they do think of us as low-life niggas, *so what?* You can't let it affect how you feel about *you.* That's all I gotta say."

Angela finished with a firm headshake. Brenda clapped her hands, but not one to be outdone, she had to do her part to keep it going.

"Damn! Way to go, girl. Y'all all fired up, shit. Since when did you become such a smartass, Angie?" Brenda asked. Then she smirked, getting even more under Angela's skin.

"Hey, who you calling a smartass?" Angela asked. "Did I say I knew everything? Well, I don't. Some things just make sense, so don't go getting mad at me for telling the truth."

I enjoyed watching Angela and Carolyn put Brenda in her place. I didn't often speak up, but I'd had enough of Brenda's bigotry and picking fights. I sucked up the last of my Cherry Coke with a bottom-of-the-cup sucking sound. This got everyone's attention.

"I don't like *any* bad names and don't care who says 'em either. Sounds like cursing. It ain't right, and it makes no sense to do that just because they do it. It's mean. It can't be that way at Paris High, or we would've heard," I said.

"Shut up, White girl, and drink your Coke," Brenda said. "What do you know about anything, anyway?"

I bit my lip, staring down at my Coke.

"That's mean, Brenda!" Carolyn said.

"Yeah, she's done drinking her soda, *Miss* Know-It-All!" Angela said.

"God don't like ugly, and He ain't too fond of cute," Carolyn said. "Or so my father says Sunday mornings when we act up listening to his sermons."

I was glad Angela and Carolyn came to my defense, but at the same time, I was curious as to why Doreen had not. An uncomfortable silence descended on our group. We waited for someone to break the ice that had formed around us, as frosty as the chocolate shake or the ice cubes in our sodas.

At last, Karen decided to wake up and say something.

"*I'm* going to take one day at a time. Yes, ma'am," Karen said. "Seems to me the sports in this town is drawing us together, and that's a good thing, don't y'all think?" This thought made a lot of sense to me.

"That's if Mr. Reed can keep the troublemakers in Lexington," Doreen said. "It was tough at first, back in what, '63? After a while, playing football and basketball together wasn't so bad, and things got easier. Maybe it really was sports that brought us together."

Principal William Reed, or Chief Reed, was also head coach of the football and basketball teams at Western High and had been involved in the smooth integration of our schools. There were rumors he helped keep trouble out of Paris during the early days of civil rights. When faced with racial tension in Paris, his ability to bring people together could always be counted on.

"They started winning games like crazy, y'all," Carolyn added. "If it wasn't for sports, I don't know where we'd be. God bless Chief Reed."

Karen's comment had melted the tension on that day at the DQ. *Is it true that competitive sports really pulled us together?* This question nagged at me as a gentle breeze moved under the steel umbrella. Each side seemed to have tremendous respect for the other on the sports battlefield, where race was of little importance. It did seem that this kind of brotherhood spread to the students, teachers, and the rest of us.

"Do you ever think we'll have a Black Homecoming King or Queen?" Doreen asked.

"Naaahhh!" We all said in unison and laughed at her for thinking of something so ridiculous.

"Girl, are you crazy? Yeah, *all* y'all crazy. Never, no, *never* will you *ever* see a jigaboo crowned king at that school. Might as well forget that!" Brenda said.

"I know! But you know what?" Carolyn asked. "I plan on learning as much as possible, doing the best I can to graduate and get out of Paris. Like I said, I'm not paying those people any mind. How they feel about me won't get in the way of my education."

Always the practical one, Carolyn could be counted on to make sense out of nonsense. On the other hand, Brenda could always be counted on to shock us when we least expected it.

"Girl, I'm going in there high!" Brenda said. "I dare them to tell me I can't bring a joint in there."

"You mean weed?" I asked. But Brenda glared at me without saying a word. We all stared at her for a while until Doreen called her bluff.

"You trying to psych us out? Girl, you ain't got sense God gave a goose. You can't be going in there with one of those. You kidding, right?" Doreen asked.

Brenda wasn't able to contain herself for long. Not when our faces showed the look of awe, suspicion, and oh my goodness!

"Psych! I got y'all. Psych, psych, psych!" As Brenda said this, we shook our heads at her, letting loose a hail of laughter. She laughed along but then got serious. "Nah, I'm just gonna make them think—"

"If you did that, you'd be in so much trouble, Bren-da," Angela said.

"Angela, mind your business!" Brenda said. "Don't tell me what to do. I do as I damn well please. You think I'm stupid? No way am I going in there like that. Fooled y'all good, though."

"Hey! Sorry," Angela said as she held up her hands in surrender. "I was just trying to point out the obvious."

At this point, Doreen turned her attention to me. "Will you stop eating yourself? You been bitin' on those fingers forever and ain't said but a few words since we got here. Say something, White girl, so we know you still breathing. Momma says you busy with a project or something, but you ain't said a word about it. How're those cherries in that Coke?"

"They're fine, not enough of them, though," I said.

"What project?" Angela asked.

"Y'all, it's only been a few weeks. Geez!" I said.

"That Coke's done gone to her head y'all. You high?" Brenda asked.

Everyone laughed at Brenda's pun except Doreen. She stared at me, then shook her head and widened her eyes as if to say, "Come on, tell us."

"Mom asked me to visit the Sweet sisters once in a while," I said, barely whispering the truth. My plan to discuss this privately with Doreen wasn't working out well.

"What? I can't hear you," Doreen asked.

"You mean those old ladies who live across the street from you? You know they say they're witches, right? Girl, why she want you to do that?" Angela asked.

"I don't know. Anyway, they don't live directly across the street, just diagonal from us a ways. I didn't want to tell because I knew y'all would ask a lot of questions or—"

"Why's that secret?" Carolyn asked. "I think it's cool. It's the charitable thing to do, and nothing's wrong with that."

"It's no *secret*. It's just that it's all weird that I have to go in the first place. I didn't want to say anything because I knew y'all would make fun of me." Though Doreen and Brenda had already done that, they never missed an opportunity; today was no exception.

"What're they like? I hear they're *really* strange, and the 'flicted one casts spells causing you a lifetime of misery. I hear they fool you with baked cookies, jam, meat, and stuff, then WHAM! You're dinner. Oh, wait, old witches don't like dark meat. They like white turkey meat!" The dig at me using Miss Edna's comment about my legs wasn't necessary, as the uncomfortable laughter showed. Sometimes I really hated Doreen.

"I see them walking around town, with the weird one dragging her foot behind her," Brenda said. "No one seems to know them at all—"

"Stop it, y'all. They're nice!" I'd had enough of the sniping. "I think they're lonely, and they like me coming by to visit from time to time."

"In what way are they nice?" Brenda asked.

"Yeah, how're they nice?" Karen asked, following Brenda's lead.

"In lots of ways, I don't know, just… nice." I shrugged. "Nosy Miss Edna is bound and determined to find out about my visits. She was mean to me when we went to get chicken the other day, huh, Doreen? I think it's because I won't tell her anything, calling me 'Little Missy' and stuff. She's so mean!" I hoped to get some advice and less teasing. But Doreen said nothing in support until I asked outright, "Doreen, do you think I should tell Miss Edna *something* so she'll get off my back?"

I didn't like asking in front of everyone, but it couldn't be helped. Doreen stared at me and said nothing for a while. But when she did, the words were nothing that I expected to hear.

"Don't be silly," Doreen said, casually dismissing me. "Miss Edna's a mean, nosy old biddy just trying to get information. Let me talk to her and give her the satisfaction of knowing *just enough*, so she'll leave you alone. I'll take care of it."

I didn't like how Doreen said "just enough" slowly, as if there was some hidden intention that, for me, meant she was up to something. I was asking for an *opinion*, not for her to *do* anything.

"I-I-I don't think that's necessary. I can take care of it myself. Why would you say I couldn't?"

"You don't know how to talk to people sometimes," Doreen answered. "Miss Edna needs to be put in her place and stop messing with people's heads. She's just trying to psych you out. Let me deal with her. That way, she'll stop doing or looking into whatever she *thinks* you might or might not be up to."

"Ahh, look at Auntie coming to the rescue," Brenda said. "I know one thing. If anyone can do it, Doreen can. Girl, you don't know what kind of trouble that woman can get started, so let your *Aunt Doreen* handle it."

I never liked it when Doreen talked to me like that. The Sweet sisters and Miss Virginia obviously didn't have a problem with how I spoke. But when they all, including Angela and Carolyn, nodded in agreement, I had no choice but to let Doreen have her way without argument.

Brenda lit a cigarette and blew smoke in my direction as if cementing Doreen's decision. Brenda's smoking was a quick reminder of how much younger I was among this bunch of worldly-wise girls, some of whom were not all that ladylike. They would always know more than me. So I said nothing else and spent the rest of the time listening to the talk of summer shenanigans, all the while coughing and waving smoke out of my face.

# CHAPTER 11

## *The Youth Center*

IT WAS NOW the middle of July, and although Doreen said she would talk to Miss Edna, she never seemed to find the time at the Youth Center. So I welcomed a chance to get together with her and my friends. This way, I might get the opportunity to ask what was taking her so long.

The music we received on the radio was either country and western or a selection of songs from Billboard's Top 40 out of Lexington. The Beatles or anything from Britain topped the charts and swept the radio waves. I secretly loved Dolly Parton, Patsy Cline, and Loretta Lynn, but "Ode to Billy Joe" by Bobbie Gentry was my latest favorite song. When I couldn't find anything interesting to watch on the three channels on our television, I listened to the radio, read outdoors, or did house chores. My daytime hours kept me busy, but my newfound afternoon activity was the Youth Center.

The Center gave Black teenagers a place to hang out, play pool, and dance to the same music enjoyed by adults. It was a single-story building, long and wide, with one front door placed dead center of the building and a back door situated in the room's back-right corner. Near that back door were bathrooms for boys and girls. The interior separated the building into two halves. On the left were the pool tables and a jukebox always keyed up to play loud bass for the best effect. Sometimes the walls pounded with the sound. A pony wall divided the left side from the right, lined with wooden benches on either side of the floor for dancing. We had outgrown the playground in the backyard, but it was still used by the very young. On the left side of the building, outside, was a basketball court that was always full. The night air was much cooler, so some local boys played well after sundown.

Directly across from the Youth Center were a few vacant houses marked by an overgrowth of weeds. Cars crowded both sides of the street, especially at night when the Center became a hive of activity. In summer, the Youth Center opened early or right before the evening sunset. On this particular day, it was open earlier than usual. There wasn't much to the place, but the crowd was thick, and the music was great.

Here, I discovered my favorite type of music: rhythm and blues, also known as R&B or soul music. With artists such as the Supremes, the Temptation, the Four Tops, Stevie Wonder, Smokey Robinson & the Miracles, Jr. Walker & the All-Stars, and Gladys Knight & the Pips, the songs were the best dance music. Sure, songs such as "Dancing in the Street" by Martha Reeves & the Vandellas were fun to sing when we walked the road on hot summer nights. But for dancing, you couldn't beat this song and so many others.

The excitement of being with my friends to go dance was overwhelming. Soon, the idea of asking Doreen about Miss Edna was forgotten. Doreen wore a checked skirt, a sleeveless white blouse, and sandals. I wore the same shorts, sleeveless white blouse, and Keds as when we were at the DQ—still no sandals for me. Doreen's hair was pulled back into a high ponytail, loose and flowing while Angela and Carolyn wore theirs pulled back in clips. I wore the same pigtails as always, feeling very young while they appeared grown-up in skirts and hair ties.

I was amazed at the number of people outside the Center that summer afternoon. If I didn't know any better, I'd have thought the place was completely empty inside, except the noise and music booming from the jukebox told me otherwise. Once inside, I could see the crowded dance floor full of teenagers pranking each other or dancing to the latest tunes. They laughed and talked or looked around to see who was dancing with whom. They also gossiped along the wall of benches or ran in and out of doors.

I had seen a lot of dances performed on *American Bandstand* and could lose myself in the steps. I loved it. I watched and learned from my friends and danced well, but I still couldn't fast dance. Dances like the mashed potato, the monkey, the jerk, the bump, and the swim were easy to do, but fast dancing—or the swing, as Mom called it—was something I was too self-conscious and shy to try. It seemed complicated, *and* I would have to dance with a boy, which only made my shyness worse.

I stood against the wall whenever people were fast dancing and secretly moved my feet, trying to duplicate the dance steps. As the ceiling fans worked hard to keep us cool, I found my usual corner to stand and watch. Couples danced the slow dance, where they held each other tight and moved only their hips. To be held that close, grinding against each other like that, was disgusting to me. If I had to be held, it would be during the fast dance.

Barry Manning was cool and popular. Every girl I knew liked dancing with him and no one ever turned him down. Whenever he looked in my direction or caught my eye, I blushed blue blazes, biting the corner of my lip every time. I liked watching Barry. A lot.

Doreen was always on the dance floor, showing off the latest steps. Doreen and Angela started to dance the monkey, the swim, and then the pony, sometimes mixing these moves together in one song. I joined the group when the floor filled with people, especially when they did the jerk. When the music ended, I quietly moved back to my space by the wall to watch again.

When the song "(I'm a) Road Runner" by Jr. Walker & the All-Stars started to play, the whole place, now full of people, went out to the dance floor. The soaring notes of the trumpet filled the room as the booming bass and drumbeat made the walls pulse. Everyone had a partner. Feeling left out, I turned to go outside but felt a tap on my shoulder. I turned around to see Barry, who surprisingly asked me to dance. My feet felt glued to the floor; I couldn't move. I started to shake my head, but I didn't want to be the first girl to turn him down, so I accepted and joined him on the crowded dance floor. To my horror, he grabbed both my hands in the stance used for fast dancing!

"Just follow me," he said.

I followed his movements and found myself matching his steps. Still holding my right hand, he dropped my left and counted, "One, two, one-two-three, one, two, one-two-three." My God, I was doing it. I was fast dancing! We did this simple shuffle step for a few more minutes, and my heart almost stopped at what he said next.

"Now I'm going to spin you around. Don't be afraid." He lifted my right hand and, without letting go of it, turned me around until we were face-to-face again. I laughed out loud, and he kept on encouraging me. Then he grabbed both hands again, and we continued the shuffle step. With him letting go of my left hand again, he turned me one more time, and we faced each other after the turn without missing a step.

"Not bad, nothing to it, right?" Barry asked. He was right. It was glorious! I was amazed at how well we moved together. I suppose his hand felt hot to the touch because I held it tighter than necessary.

Before I knew it, the song had ended. I thanked him and walked to my spot by the wall in a daze, grinning from ear to ear. As the Miracles' slow song "Ooh Baby, Baby" started to play and partners coupled up on the floor, I thought more about Barry. Doreen and Angela came over to stand beside me, one on each side, with Angela starting to tease.

"Heeeyyyy, you were out there with Barr-ry," Angela said.

"Yeah, you were doing the *fast dance*! About time! So how was it?" Doreen asked.

"It was amazing, y'all!" I said. "I can't believe I finally got a chance to do it! Barry's a good dancer. He really is."

"Cute too! Look at him out there. He never stops dancing," Doreen said. "You know, he's never asked me to do that dance. I've done it lots of times, but never with him."

"You're always out there running around, Doreen. Maybe he hasn't had a chance to grab you." After Angela said this, Doreen went quiet. She just stood there, staring out at the dance floor. It occurred to me that I'd never seen Doreen fast dance with anyone. But then I was not so concerned with the truth of it because I had finally fast danced and was thrilled.

"I don't know why I thought it was so hard to do. Barry made it seem easy. I can't wait to do it again," I said.

We watched, fascinated, as people leaned on their partners in that close-holding slow-dance way with hips moving against each other. When the music stopped, there was a quiet shuffling about, and then I got nervous when "Love Is Like an Itching in My Heart" by the Supremes started to play. I looked around to see if Barry would ask me to dance again because I wanted to so badly. Yes! He was walking toward us, but then Doreen began walking toward him. He stopped, and she motioned him to the dance floor.

My attention was glued to them as they began dancing, not any dance, but the fast dance and they took my breath away. I watched in amazement as she and Barry started off holding hands. Then he let go of one hand and spun her around with the other. He didn't stop there and turned her not once, but twice and a third time! Barry then grabbed both her hands and without letting go, they lifted their arms and wrapped each behind the other's heads while turning together and keeping the steps in sync. He twirled her again to face him, still holding hands, and leaned back on his heels, yet never lost a step.

Doreen was showing off and she knew it. As her skirt spun out from her body and twirled around her legs, she gave the impression of being relaxed and polished. When Barry spun her in a full turn and then a half turn after, it was perfect. I was jealous. I felt the blood rush to my face in embarrassment and humiliation. To think, I had gushed over my feeble attempt at this dance and to none other than her! Angie and I stood in awe at the skill of Doreen and Barry dancing together. Angie's hazel eyes flashed with anger, and I felt the heat coming off her body. Either that, or it was getting very hot inside despite the fans turning overhead and a breeze blowing through both open doors.

When the music stopped, Barry whispered something in Doreen's ear. She put her hand to her chest, laughed loudly, thanked him, and walked back toward us. Standing directly in front of me, with both hands on her hips, she looked at me with dead eyes and uttered a phrase I will never forget.

"Now that's how you fast dance."

I felt the blood leave my face and rush to the bottom of my feet. I said nothing in response but hurried toward the back door, humiliated. I vaguely heard Angie say to Doreen, "You know you can be a...." I didn't hear the rest.

⟞⟝⟞⟝

I ran across the playground out back without crossing in front of the Center. In my mind, the whole world knew my humiliation, which I thought was plain to see on my face. I asked myself a million questions, such as how could Doreen keep secrets like that from me? How could she lie to us? How could she treat me as if I had no feelings? Why would she embarrass me like that and in front of Barry of all people! I didn't think I could ever forgive her.

I wandered alone, thinking, and after a while, found myself not far from Carolyn's house, an old Queen Anne–style inherited by her father, Reverend Avery. To me, it always seemed to need repair or painting. The house served as the rectory for the Averys and contained furnishings my grandmother called aged or vintage, which was another way of saying very expensive. Carolyn always seemed too busy studying scripture to bother with gossip. But she usually saw situations clearly, and I needed someone to help me figure out what Doreen had done and why.

Reverend Avery was leaving when I came up the walk to their house. Elias Avery came from a long line of ministers, well-spoken and respected. We all sang in the church choir, and he often had a word of praise for our singing efforts. Tall and sturdy in stature, he had a warm, friendly face, was soft-spoken, and was a little pudgy around the middle. I always thought of him as the father all girls should have. Carolyn was lucky to have him.

"Hello, my dear, and how're you today?" Reverend Avery asked.

"I'm fine. Just thought I'd come over and visit Carolyn. Is she home?"

"Why yes, she is—in there studying her scriptures. Her mother's out, so she's by herself. I'm heading to the church to prepare, so you go right on in. I'm sure she'll be happy to see you. I must say, I really enjoy hearing the youth choir sing on Sundays. I hope you keep up your attendance. Nice to have our youth give their service to God."

"Thank you, sir, it surely is."

"Well, good day, young lady, and tell Carolyn I look forward to discussing what she's learned when I get back."

"Yes, sir. Thank you, Reverend Avery."

I figured he said this to make sure my visit would not be a long one. I took a deep breath, knocked on the massive door, opened it, and called out to Carolyn. She answered with a hello that echoed off the high ceiling. I stood in the open foyer, staring at the fading wallpaper and stained wood of the Victorian trim around the entry to the living room. I walked in to see Carolyn lying on a lounging couch. It was covered in a material patterned with pink and green flowers scattered throughout. It didn't look comfortable to me.

A rose-colored throw was casually tossed across the couch, which might have covered more stains than the ones I could see firsthand. The wooden floor was covered with thin oriental rugs that crisscrossed across the floor at weird angles. It was hard to make out the pattern or color because they were dusty and dull from wear. This was all in contrast to Carolyn, in capris, a white no-sleeve blouse, and white Keds. She looked like those models I'd seen in one of Doreen's fashion magazines.

"Hey there. Fancy seeing you here. Gosh, it's so hot outside!" Carolyn said.

"You think so? I guess. I thought I'd come by to see you." I tried to sound cheerful while sitting across from her on the edge of a pale green-and-blue Queen Anne chair, whose seat cushion and faded armrest had seen better days.

"I'm trying to brush up on my scripture lessons. I'm so behind," she said. "Lord knows Daddy will expect me to recite the gospel from these verses when he comes back, but I get so distracted. My thoughts are going a mile a minute, and it's hard to concentrate sometimes. Do you ever get like that?"

"I-I guess…" I couldn't say anymore because I broke down in tears. This caught me by surprise and Carolyn off guard. After a while, she brought water in a dirty crystal glass and offered tissues to blow my nose.

"I'm so sorry, Carolyn—"

"What in the world is wrong?"

But I couldn't answer because of the crying. Carolyn knelt by me and rubbed my back until my tears eased up. My thighs hurt from sitting on the edge of the worn-out chair, so I asked if she wanted to walk with me. The window's air conditioner was going full blast, and I wanted to get some fresh air. Carolyn hurriedly put her study books away, saying she needed a reason to get away for a while anyway, and suggested we walk to the Tastee-Freez downtown.

Much to Carolyn's relief, the air had cooled down as we walked toward town with the sun still high in the hazy sky. I told her the whole event of just moments ago, sniffling every now and then. She listened, making the proper sounds of agreeing and feeling sorry for me.

As we entered the Tastee-Freez with its friendly blue-and-white interior, I said, "I was so embarrassed. I can't understand why Doreen would do that to me! She's done a lot to humiliate me before, but this takes the cake."

Unlike the DQ, which had painted red-and-white awnings and outdoor seating, Tastee-Freez was comfortably air-conditioned and had indoor seating. We sat in a section that, until recently, used to be reserved for Blacks only but was now open to everyone.

"There might be something you don't know. Maybe Doreen has secrets she doesn't want to tell you right now," Carolyn said.

"You think?" I asked. "We share everything. Doreen should've told me she knew how to fast dance, especially like that! I always told her I wished I could. But no, she just stood there and told a *bald-faced lie*! Acting like she couldn't, and that's just *mean*!"

"I agree. It was a dirty trick. I wish Doreen wasn't so hateful toward you. I think she needs to tell you what you need to know now you've seen it for yourself."

"What'd you mean?" She was hinting at something I was missing.

"Linney, everyone knows Doreen's dating Barry. They have been for months. I thought you knew. She goes to the Youth Center regularly and dances with him all the time. I'm so sorry."

# CHAPTER 12
## *Words of Wisdom*

B ARRY WAS NOT like Stooly! Definitely not like Stooly. These were the thoughts going through my mind when Carolyn told me about Doreen and Barry. It was hard to concentrate on anything she said, thinking, *Doreen wants someone like Stooly, not Barry Manning!* It was all so confusing and made no sense as Carolyn tried to help me understand what might have happened. I couldn't figure out the attraction Doreen might have for a boy like Barry. I knew of Barry's family. They were nice people, but his uncle's killing was the one no one ever wanted to talk about. They said Barry was a lot like his uncle but not as reckless. He was cool, all right, and loved dancing, but he wasn't *that* handsome. He had a charming smile and bright eyes, but the rest of him was not that appealing, unlike Stooly's curly hair and curvy mouth. In contrast, Barry was just, well, ordinary.

Carolyn did what she could to explain, but I wanted my mom to hear what had happened. If nothing else, just so she knew. By the time I got home, the sun had started to dip below the horizon. Mom stood in her stocking feet at the stove, preparing hot dogs with pork and beans for dinner. I sat at the kitchen table and watched her rush around. Acting this way meant she had to study soon, so I dove right in.

"I have to talk to you about something, Mom."

"What is it, baby?" She grabbed the pot of hot beans without a potholder. "*Got* to be more careful!" Mom yelled out as the pan of beans fell onto the stove with a clang. She had slightly singed her fingers and immediately began running cold water over them. I grabbed butter from the refrigerator to spread on the burn, which she usually did to take the sting away and prevent blistering. The cold running water on her fingers didn't ease the signs of mild agony on her face, so I knew this was not a good time to talk.

"What do you want to talk about, Linney?" she asked.

"Um, I want to tell you what happened at the Youth Center. You won't believe it."

"Oh, did you have fun?" She absentmindedly blotted her fingers on a towel and reached into the freezer for ice cubes, ignoring the butter altogether. Her mind was elsewhere; why else lift a hot pan with bare hands?

"Yeah, I fast danced today! I danced with this boy named Barry—"

"So you had fun then," Mom said in a hurry. "Don't try to eat all the hot dogs, Linney. I need to save some for tomorrow. I have to study, so eat and clean up after, okay? I can't possibly wash dishes in hot water with these hands. Not until the soreness goes away anyway. Thank you, sweetie! Glad you had fun at the Center."

Like the snap of a finger, she was gone. She left with a hot dog in a bun, no beans, no plate, then into the study. I knew she didn't mean to be dismissive. At least, that's what I told myself. Her focus was elsewhere, and she didn't have time to listen to anything I had to say just then. There was no point in distracting her further, so I accepted her dismissal and ate my hot dog in a bun, no beans, and no plate, alone in front of the TV. I tried with all my might to forget everything that happened that day and focus on the shows, but it was a losing battle.

Mom was still studying when I locked the house up for the night. I couldn't sleep, still confused about how Doreen might have been jealous of me for dancing with her boyfriend, Barry.

Boyfriend Barry, that was his new name. Why was she jealous of me? Even Carolyn couldn't explain that away. I could still see them dancing, missing how she looked at him and how they smiled at each other, her ponytail swirling along with her skirt. I could still hear the music and see how their feet moved in time, pausing at the exact moment for effect, in sync with the lyrics. I could never dance like that. Then the tears started again at the reminder of the humiliation, all for thinking I could. I half expected Doreen to call and apologize. But the phone never rang that night, and I cried silently into my pillow until I fell asleep.

<hr>

Mom didn't wake me before she left for work the following day. Still groggy from sleep, I dragged myself from bed and read the note she'd left. She let me know her fingers felt better and thanked me for helping the night before. Because it was a school night, she wouldn't be home until late. It went on to say, "Warm up the hot dogs and beans for lunch, and don't wait up. Be careful to lock up and come home before dark." I missed my mom.

I often entered her room when she was away, and that day I especially needed to feel her presence. Her perfume lingered in the air like a soft invisible mist. I closed my eyes and twirled to inhale the essence of her. The rosewood dresser she usually sat at when getting ready gleamed red in this early daylight hour. I rubbed its surface, hoping to absorb the magic of the light with my fingers. After opening a few of her jars of cream, I inhaled the soft fragrance of rose water and fingered some of her jewelry pieces. So pretty and shiny. Sitting at her dresser, I stared into the mirror and mentally compared myself to her. I didn't have her creamy light brown complexion, soft blue-black hair, or kind, soulful eyes. I didn't think I resembled her at all. I stood up to look at my figure and was disappointed, seeing only a flat chest, no butt or hips, and a few small zits on my cheeks. *When will I ever fill out like Angela and Carolyn?*

Until yesterday, I never thought about how boys felt about girls. I had experienced what grown-ups called "puppy love" for two or three boys, sometimes all at the same time. The rules were that if he was my boyfriend, all I had to do was say so, and it was so. My crush on Stooly couldn't be denied, but I never thought about how a boy might feel about me. Now so much was changing, and I felt lost and confused.

Feeling worse than the day before, I dragged myself into the kitchen to eat a bowl of Frosted Flakes and thought about watching an old rerun of *The Little Rascals*. As I grabbed the refrigerator's door handle to open the door for milk, it felt like holding Barry's hand while fast dancing. Strange. Pretending to hold his hand, I began dancing with the refrigerator door. I practiced fast dancing while holding the handle and even leaned back on my heels like Barry. Before leaving for Michigan, my uncle taught me some hillbilly hard-shoe dances, and I mixed in a couple of shuffle steps. I could've gone on like this for hours, but the thought of food thawing inside the refrigerator caused me to shut the door. It pleased me no end to have found a way to practice the dance, with extra steps thrown in for good measure. If I stayed at it, no one would be able to best me again: not Doreen, not even Barry.

I couldn't wait to tell Miss Katherine. She was a great listener, and I wanted to tell her everything, if nothing else, to help me feel better. But before I could leave, the phone rang. It was Angela asking if I was okay. After I left, she tried to find me but couldn't, so I told her what I had learned about Doreen and Barry from Carolyn.

"I don't know what's gotten into me lately. I just can't keep my mouth shut," Angela said. "But when you left, I told Doreen about herself. She didn't like it, and I didn't care. It was awful what she did! Don't be mad, okay? It's just that she's so sly and slick, thinking she can one-up you anytime she wants. Who does she think she is?"

"Barry's girlfriend. She's my aunt too, and… well, she does it all the time—"

"And that's a crime! We all know you're whiter than most of us light-skinned girls, but that don't give her the right to treat you the way she does. You need to stand up to her and give her what for! Even I didn't know she could dance like that *and* show off with Barry in front of you after you tried so hard. What can I say? Don't be mad. I shot off my mouth, okay? I'm so sorry she hurt you."

"Don't be so silly. I'm not mad. Thanks for sticking up for me, though. I'll tell Doreen off, but only when the time's right. It's a whole day after, now…. What good will it do anyway? Have you heard from her?"

"Nope! I doubt if she'll speak to me anytime soon. Maybe she's with Brenda and Karen, just rubbing it in over what she did to you… or out with Barry somewhere. Who knows?"

"I have to run errands before Mom gets home, Angie. I'll call you later, okay?" Angie meant well, but I didn't want to hear more about Doreen and Barry. I guess telling a white lie to Angie couldn't be helped. I'd rather visit the Misses Sweet than stay on the phone gossiping about Doreen, who *was* family after all. I was proud of myself for ignoring Angela's goading, but as hard as I might, I couldn't dismiss it altogether.

<hr>

The day was what my mother called "close" because the air barely moved and the clouds hung heavy and low in the sky. It was a gray day, with overhead clouds full of water that threatened to become a downpour at any minute. My shirt stuck to the skin on my back almost as soon as I stepped outside. Some neighborhood kids played in the Jungle, squealing and making enough noise to wake the dead, but playing there no longer interested me. I needed to cover myself fast if it started to rain, and the Jungle was a poor substitute for an overhead porch any day. I ran over to the Sweets' house and up the stairs, knocking on the door with more urgency than necessary.

But there was no answer. After three more tries and still no response, I gave up and turned to leave. That was when Miss Virginia pulled up in a light blue Oldsmobile.

"They're not home. I knocked three times already," I said.

"Huh, you don't say? Well, by the looks of that sky, I expect they'll be back soon," she said. "Knowing Miss Katherine, they're probably right around the corner. I think I'll just wait here for them to return. You mind waiting with me?"

"No'am, I don't mind."

"Okay then. Let's grab a seat on the porch and talk awhile."

The two front windows were open enough to allow a slight breeze to blow from inside the house onto the porch. Miss Virginia sighed as she took a seat, stretched her legs, and began to fan herself as we watched the lace curtains blow through the open windows.

"Ah, that breeze feels good," she said. "Well now, how have you been since I saw you last young lady? You promised to come by, but I haven't seen you."

"I know. I'm sorry. I didn't mean to break my promise. There's so much going on. It's hard to keep up."

"How so? Tell me about it."

"Well, too much to figure out, like… I don't know…."

"You *can* talk to me, you know? Really. You can trust that what you tell me will stay between us. So what's on your mind? I have all day."

"It's just that I don't understand people," I said. "One day they're nice; the next, not so much. People have secrets, and they pretend they don't, and when you find *out* they have secrets, it's a sin to know they have them. This year'll be the first time I'll be alone at school because all my friends are going to high school. It's just not fair. I don't know *what* to do and… I'm starting to feel things about boys and stuff. I can't figure out why people get jealous and want to hurt your feelings. Why are they jealous anyway? They hurt my feelings all the time. What did I ever do to them except be born? Sometimes I even get jealous, and I don't know why. I try to be a good girl, but sometimes I get so *mad!* I just want to *hit* someone! Is that wrong?"

"My goodness! You're speaking in riddles," Miss Virginia said as she blew away hair that had fallen onto her forehead. "I can't give an answer or opinion if you won't say right out and be specific."

"It's hard to say," I tried to explain. "People are hard to understand, and I don't know how to see things straight. I guess that's what I'm trying to get out, but the words won't come like I want."

"If there's one thing I know, it's that people will let you down more often than anything. People have secrets. There's no getting around that, and I suspect you have some of your own. Unless they decide to show themselves, leave secrets alone, and don't pry into others' affairs. Take Miss Edna over there. Now, *I* don't believe it's her intention to be nosy. I think she's a lonely woman trying to belong, but meddling in other people's business is not the way. Who knows why, but dredging up old wounds to find out won't help anyone. Understand?"

"I guess. It makes some sense, but at the same time, it doesn't. She's been really mean to me, and I don't understand that at all. If she's so lonely, why's she calling me names?"

"Calling you names?" Miss Virginia asked. "Now that I can't figure. For someone as sweet as you, I suspect she'll come around and stop that nonsense."

"Maybe. But it's still strange. Gosh, so much is happening and all at the same time. I can't even read or think straight anymore because my head's full of questions and stuff. Mom's not around much, so it's mostly up to me to figure things out on my own. Like the other day at the Youth Center—you know where that is, right?" Miss Virginia nodded, and I continued, "So why is it when I dance with a friend's boyfriend, she gets mad?"

"That depends on whether she's a good friend or not. She might be confused about her own feelings and doesn't quite know the intricacies of relationships, especially how it affects those she cares most about. I assume you've been told about the 'birds and bees.'"

I shook my head and frowned. I was confused, which I think showed because she continued explaining.

"Well, if not...." She trailed off and shifted in her seat. "Trust me, all will reveal itself in time."

"But when? When we were little, we used to share all our secrets—that's why she's my best friend—but now she keeps stuff from me. Every year she gets meaner and meaner. She hates me *so* much, and I don't know why. I'm just not very pretty, I guess. I would be, though, if my skin was brown like hers. If it was, I think she would like me more. She thinks I'm stupid, always says mean things, and teases me something awful, mostly because I look so White. It hurts my feelings when she calls me *White girl* all the time. She hurt my feelings yesterday, and I got so mad at her. I'm still mad, and I want to hurt her back. Sometimes I hate her so much!"

"Oh, now hate's a strong word, don't you think?" Miss Virginia said with a surprised look on her face. "I don't think you *hate* her. Disappointed and hurt, maybe, but not hate. Don't ever allow hate to grow in your heart, sweetheart. Always try to see the other person's point of view and look at life through their eyes—"

"But she has everything!"

"Does she? Humm, I wonder—"

"I have to wear the same clothes every day 'cause we can't afford new ones. I don't even have sandals! She told me I embarrass her because of it."

"Okay, stop this now," Miss Virginia said sternly. "I need to address something important. You know, Dr. King's teaching us that it's what's inside a person's heart that matters, not skin color. Your skin color should not define who you are." She leaned close to me, "Your coloring is perfect. God gave that to you, so don't let anyone make you ashamed of it, not even yourself. Who's this *friend* anyway?"

"My Aunt Doreen. She's a year older and always tells me she's *my aunt* and I should do what *she* says. I do, but it doesn't seem to matter no matter how hard I try. If I climb a tree, she climbs higher, making me climb even higher, and when I look down, I get dizzy, and she laughs at me, thinking I'll fall. She walks on these rusty beams in the old quarry building, and it seems awfully high, and then she makes me walk across, and I do, even though

I'm really scared. But she can be nice too, which makes me more confused. Like the other day, Doreen let me in on something she got in the mail, but then she made me feel bad because Mom can't afford one for me. Why did she have to rub it in? And then I danced with her boyfriend when I didn't even know she *had* a boyfriend. Why didn't she tell me? Everyone knew except me, and that's not fair! She's my best friend, and friends are supposed to share things like that, right? I really liked him too. How was I to know he was *her* boyfriend? Maybe she's not my best friend. I don't want to be her friend anymore, but because she's family too…. It's so confusing."

"Sounds like competition exists between you two. It's got to be exhausting trying to live up to her standards, don't you think?" Miss Virginia asked.

"Huh? I don't understand."

"Look at it this way," she said. "Whenever you try to reach for something, she seems to get it first. She forces you to do things and pushes you past your comfort level to see how far you'll go, but you push through and succeed anyway. That's competition, and when you succeed, it can cause some unconscious resentment on her part. Does that make sense?"

"I *think* so. Doreen didn't even call to apologize for showing me up by dancing better than me. It was so embarrassing."

A lump formed in my throat, and I fought to hold back the tears, but too late. They trickled down despite my efforts. She was kind, this Miss Virginia, smiling while lending me her lavender-scented handkerchief so I could blow my nose. I don't know what it was about her that made me feel comfortable enough to share so much on that muggy morning. It might have been the peaceful setting of the front porch or the direct way she asked questions or listened and then put everything in place. But whatever it was, I could say what I wouldn't have dared say an hour earlier, even to my mom, let alone Doreen.

"There now. You go ahead and cry, but first things first," Miss Virginia said. "Pretty is as pretty does, as the saying goes. And you, my dear, are very pretty. If Doreen does something ugly, does that make her pretty? No, it doesn't. It's what's on the inside that makes the beauty shine. In this life, you'll always run into someone smarter than you, prettier than you, wiser than you, and who has more than you. Just be the best *you* can be so none of the other matters. Life is unfair in that way, but what *is* fair is the knowledge you gain in realizing you can pass almost any test she sets before you. Knowledge is power. It evens out the playing field."

"Like grabbing the tree limb out of reach or walking the beams without falling?"

"No, not quite like that. Whatever you try, do it for yourself, not Doreen or anyone else's favor. Life is full of lessons, and we never get too old to learn. It's also full of disappointments, but those disappointments will be easier to overcome if you know who you are deep inside. I bet in time, she will need you more than you need her."

"So you don't think Doreen tried to embarrass me after I danced with Barry?"

"I bet she hurt worse after, which is probably why she hasn't called," Miss Virginia said. "She's impressed you didn't lose your balance and fall off that proverbial beam, metaphorically speaking. You might have slipped a bit but didn't hit the ground. If I had my guess, showing off what she could do was not done intentionally to embarrass you but to impress her boyfriend. You just got in the way. Maybe it's better to look at it that way, huh?"

I liked hearing these words of wisdom, even though I didn't know what "proverbial" or "metaphorically" meant.

"How do you know Miss Katherine and Miss Dottie?"

"Oh, that's a long story. One day, I might share it, but for now, let's just enjoy this breeze." Miss Virginia closed her eyes, leaned back in the rocker, and looked relaxed.

"Have you ever been married?"

"Nope."

"Why not?"

"When you get older, you'll understand."

Then it began to rain. Hard.

# CHAPTER 13

## Devil in a Fast Car

T HE WARM RAIN came down like a white curtain that was difficult to see through. We immediately thought about the sisters, caught in the sheet of water, walking to or from who knew where. Without saying a word, we ran to Miss Virginia's car, thinking of nothing else except to find them. I felt terrible that we hadn't tried to search for them before the rain came, but time had gotten away from us.

Just as I wiped away the condensation building inside the car windows, we saw two figures huddled under a tree at the top of Lilleston Avenue. One stood over the other, whose arms hugged the base of the tree. Miss Dottie was on the ground with her mouth opened in what looked like a scream.

Miss Virginia put the car in park and ran toward the two women. I was close behind, ignoring the running water soaking my Keds, making them slippery and squeaky. Miss Katherine pointed to Miss Dottie, who was terrified for reasons I couldn't make out. The lightning crashed around us, followed by large deafening thunderclaps that boomed overhead. After what seemed like forever, we got Miss Dottie into the vehicle, trembling, wet, and sobbing with fear. I sat in the back seat with Miss Dottie while Miss Katherine sat up front. Breathlessly, Miss Katherine told us what happened and how they were caught in the storm. The rain drumming on the car's roof was so loud she had to shout to be heard.

"My land, I'm so glad you're here! Praise the Lord!" Miss Katherine said. "I thought we were going to drown, which is the last thing I wanted to think about after the fright we had at the A&P!"

"What in the world possessed you to go out on a day like this? You should have called me. You know I would've gathered whatever you needed, Miss Katherine," Miss Virginia said.

"I know, I know, but Dottie wanted to walk, and I couldn't find it within me to deny her this trip," Miss Katherine said. "She's been agitated lately, and I thought the walk would do her good. Lordy me, all was fine until we got to the register at the A&P. Sister can be slow sometimes, you know. It took longer today because of all the specials and things we needed, like Boraxo detergent, special soap for Sister's skin, toiletries of various natures, and things. Well, like I said, we finally got to the register, and suddenly, we got that smell we've been noticing lately around the house. Smells like an animal died, rotting, needing to be buried. Well, sir, Dottie looked up and pointed straight out, yelling, 'It's the man, the devil himself!' I looked to where she was pointing and didn't see a soul. Dottie swore he was there and started pulling at the buggy to leave. She got so confused and agitated that she wanted to take it. I explained we had to pay for our purchases first, but she wouldn't hear of it. God help us!"

Miss Dottie was holding me tightly, wild-eyed and mumbling to herself. For the first time since I saw the strange man, anxiety, fear and concern gripped me, and I felt light-headed. *Could this be the same person?*

When we pulled alongside the sisters' house, the rain showed no signs of letting up. It had been difficult getting Miss Dottie into the car; now it was just as hard to get her out. We had to reassure her it was safe before she finally moved. When Miss Katherine tried to take her from me, she wouldn't let go. Once we got inside the house, the first thing I did was ease Miss Dottie's grip on me and adjust the window sash to allow some air inside, but not enough to chill her. Because of the overhanging eave, the house was undisturbed by the wind and rain.

"My God, has she ever been like this before?" Miss Virginia asked.

"No, no. Dottie has these visions from time to time, but nothing to cause this kind of thing. I just can't make out what she might have seen," Miss Katherine said.

Miss Virginia helped Miss Katherine get blankets and towels to dry ourselves. Miss Dottie never took her eyes off me, which was spooky. After we dried and wrapped her in warm blankets, we dried ourselves as best we could. Miss Katherine readied the house and resumed her story while Miss Virginia put hot water on the stove to brew tea.

"We left the store and all our groceries in that basket," Miss Katherine continued. "I managed to apologize to the clerk and told her I'd come back. She said she'd hold them in the cooler until then. You know, it's funny how that smell came up and then gone once we got outside. Sister managed to calm down but was certainly in a hurry to get home, with me following *her* this time. Can you imagine? I kept thinking over and over, 'How am I going to get the groceries we left behind?' That's when I thought of you, dear Virginia. That is if I could impose on you for assistance?"

"I've already said it's something I could've done for you today. As soon as we get you two warmed and Miss Dottie settled down, I'll do just that," Miss Virginia said.

"That will be lovely, dear. Thank you so much." Miss Katherine continued, "Well, it was at the top of Lilleston when Sister started again. A car drove by as fast as lightning, and Sister screamed, 'The devil! The devil's here with us. He's right there!' Then the sky opened up with so much rain I couldn't see anything but that tree and shadows. We went under it, and do you know, Sister could not bear to remain standing out of fear, yes, fear! She fell, hugging that tree, screaming along with the thunder and lightning. I never got a good look at who was in that car, but Sister saw him and began to have a fit such as I'd never seen. I didn't know what to do, and then you both came along. My God in heaven!"

The whistle from the teapot startled us. Miss Virginia got up to help Miss Katherine prepare tea, leaving me to sit on the floor in front of Miss Dottie, who seemed calmer now. I dried myself with a towel and felt her hands, which were clammy to the touch. She didn't seem to mind my touch and rocked gently with her head cocked to the side. I couldn't imagine the terror she felt by just seeing someone. What I felt a few weeks ago when that strange man followed me home was terrifying. As scary as that was, I never thought of him as the devil. I thought again, *What if it was the same man?* Just the other day, Miss Virginia and I smelled something. Now the sisters did too. What was it? Miss Dottie slowly stopped rocking, and as she did, her gaze was on me again. She was starting to freak me out, but I leaned in close to her anyway. My curiosity was getting the best of me. I couldn't help myself.

"Did you *really* see the devil, Miss Dottie?" I asked.

"Yes. He's coming for you, sweet girl. He wants to do *you* harm. But never you mind. I'll protect you, I will. Danger's in there, it is. It hides. Stay out of them woods," Miss Dottie said.

This was the first time I'd heard her string entire sentences together, and what she said shocked and scared me beyond words. What was going on? Stunned into silence, I watched her continue that vacant stare of hers and rock quietly. She began to drool and absentmindedly wipe at her mouth as if she'd said nothing at all. I reached for a cloth kept nearby on a table, handed it to her for use, and pulled the blanket up around her damp head. She reminded me of pictures I'd seen of the specter of death, not the sweet invalid lady I'd come to know.

What did she see? How was I in danger? Creole legends were full of stories of visions and veils of sight, voodoo, and Santeria curses. Mom said curses could only harm you if you believed in them; otherwise, they had no effect. Sometimes my mother would get premonitions, but that was rare. She told me it was just a woman's intuition when she did. Was this Miss Dottie's way?

Miss Virginia and Miss Katherine came in with oatmeal cookies, carrying teacups on the silver service tray I loved. Their conversation seemed far away as if spoken in whispers. I faintly heard Miss Virginia ask for a favor of some kind. Lost in thought, I didn't hear the details. I tried not to appear visibly shaken as I reached for a cookie.

"Is it true Miss Dottie has the gift of sight? Has she ever been wrong?" I asked.

"No, not once," Miss Katherine said. "Why do you ask something like that, child?" Miss Katherine had become that lady I met on my first visit, stony and cold, pausing her cup before her lips as she peered over its rim at me. I tried to confirm what Miss Dottie had just said but fumbled over my words instead.

"What you told us was crazy. I mean scary," I said. "Finding y'all under the tree with Miss Dottie saying stuff about the devil… well, I-I just wonder if what she said might really be true." I tried to conceal my shaking hands, which could barely hold the cookie.

"There are evils in this world, but not all are in magic and spells. Evil lives deep in the very souls of men, and to a degree, in us all. The spirit guides us, and fate can't be changed, so stay mindful and believe that God will take care," Miss Katherine said.

"What?" I asked.

"It means to be careful!" Miss Katherine said sternly. "Something, or someone, wants to do harm. My sister knows it, and now you both know it too. I've never second-guessed Dottie's visions, except for one regrettable day that I will *never* forget and won't discuss right now. I told myself I'd never draw on that memory again, so take care and heed Dottie's words. I don't mean to scare you, child, but what you've seen and experienced today cannot be discussed outside this house. People think ill of us enough already. As a warning, Linney girl, *do not* go into those woods you call the Jungle for the time being. Dottie saw something today, so come home before dark and watch out for what's around you from now on. That goes for you too, Virginia. Understand?"

Miss Katherine's stony face softened when she asked if I understood. I did understand that she believed in what she was saying. Miss Katherine couldn't have known of her sister's warning to me, but it was enough to make me take it seriously when she warned me also.

"Yes, ma'am," I said.

Miss Katherine noticed my trembling and asked if I was warm enough. I reassured her I was. Then I slowly looked over at Miss Dottie, who hummed softly while rocking in her chair. The rain finally began to ease up, and the soft hissing sound the rain made on the tree leaves was soothing. That gentle sound of Kentucky rain and the serene silence it brought caused me to go deeper into my thoughts. I played with my fingers to steady them, unable to think about anything other than Miss Dottie's premonition; Miss Virginia stared into her teacup. Until that moment, she was full of gab but now was as silent as the room itself. When she decided to speak, her words came out so softly that I had to lean in to hear them.

"Dottie's words are not meant to frighten us, so don't be afraid, Linney," Miss Virginia said. "I know because she protected me when I needed it, and for that, she will always have my loyalty and devotion. The evil she speaks of is real, and it's for that reason I've decided to leave. I'm not asking you to keep this from your mother, but be careful what you tell her. In the meantime, I want you to heed Miss Katherine's advice. They'll watch over you."

"Yes, ma'am. But shouldn't we call the police or something about the man Miss Dottie saw? He sounds dangerous. I don't understand why it should be a secret."

As soon as I asked that question, Miss Virginia's words echoed in my head, reminding me about secrets, prying, and leaving well enough alone. Neither did it help my predicament when they said nothing but stared at me.

Miss Virginia sighed. "I know we're asking a lot of you, and I suppose this is even mysterious in ways you can't possibly comprehend. Because of that, it's only fair to tell you as much as I can about why we feel the way we do. This is my story, my secret, and I hope it helps."

Now wrapped in a blanket for warmth, I listened as Miss Virginia Lee Morgan told her story in a steady and firm voice with a singsong lilt in the right places.

---

"When I was assigned to Western High School, I was a young teacher, fresh out of Kentucky State University in Frankfort. I knew no one, boarded at the YMCA and struggled to make ends meet until my path crossed with the Sweet sisters. After a long day at school, I was offered home-cooked meals, friendship, and lots of conversation and advice. During the summer, I stayed with my family in Frankfort but returned to Paris during the school year. When integration laws were passed, I was immediately placed on the list to be reassigned to Paris High, but that reassignment never came.

"At Western High, I met a friendly night janitor who was funny and charming named James Marx, or Jimmy, who jokingly called himself Ajax because he cleaned so well. Some thought he was just ordinary in appearance, but I thought he was the most handsome man I'd ever met. Piercing brown eyes, smooth complexion, and a wicked smile. Oh, how I loved to hear him talk. I fell in love instantly and dreamed of marrying him one day. Unfortunately, the sisters disapproved because Jimmy had a mean streak. He hit me a few times, and they advised me to steer clear of him. Ah, but it was hard to stay away once in love, especially when he apologized with promises of 'never doing it again.' So I accepted him, warts and all, but I kept it hidden; no one else knew. I discovered he had other unsavory behaviors that I just could not accept. Irresponsible behaviors like his terrible temper, lateness to work, or not showing up without calling in. Not taking responsibility for his actions and blaming others cost him his night job at the school and his part-time job at the Kroger grocery in Winchester.

"Shortly after this, Jimmy was wanted for questioning by the police. A young man had been killed during a gambling dispute, and Jimmy was suspected. He tried to convince me to leave Paris with him. He could have won an Academy Award for his performance; he was so convincing. I was at the Sweets when he pulled that stunt of trying to get me to leave with him. But Dottie knew Jimmy had done something terrible and told Katherine, who threatened him with a knife if he didn't leave her house. It was a terrifying scene when he hesitated to leave, but then he ran, was caught, and was later convicted of the crime. Because gambling was illegal, witnesses were afraid to talk, and with only circumstantial evidence, Jimmy was sentenced to fifteen years in prison.

"He wrote regularly, but I never replied. I pride myself on being a practical person, who weighs and measures most things, but in this, I failed. Naively, I thought Jimmy understood I'd ended it when I returned his letters unopened. I dreaded the day he was released because something told me that Jimmy would come for me. It was an intuition I just couldn't shake. But it was confirmed when word reached me that he bragged at a bar in Georgetown that he was going to Paris to get his 'teacher' wife. This was after being released on good behavior. However, he did something terrible to a woman that night. He was arrested for the crime and sentenced to another three to four years in jail. I've recently heard he was released from jail, again for good behavior, and is living in Louisville.

"I can never trust my heart again after making such a colossal mistake, which is why I've never married. The Sweets, aware of my misgivings and need to start a new life elsewhere, sent my references to contacts in Chicago. This is how I was accepted at the University of Chicago.

"But I have a sixth sense about Jimmy. I sensed him when I walked you, Linney, home that one night; it was the smell from the Jungle. It reminded me of when he worked part-time, loading meat at Kroger. Although Jimmy cleaned up as best he could before seeing me, like a fishmonger, the scent of animal blood never dissipated. Looking back on it now, it was unnatural for him to enjoy smelling like that. There was evil in it.

"The shame of almost marrying a man like that is my secret. I'm ashamed of it and what it would do to my reputation if anyone found out. I'd be barred from working anywhere with that stigma around my neck. I thought leaving before this school year began might be a better choice, but I'm not sure if the diversity program at the university will be ready in time. After today's events, however, it might be too little and far too late. I fear Jimmy's back."

It was here that Miss Virginia ended her story. "I am *so sorry* to mislead you, but I hope you have a better understanding," she said. "I'm not a coward, but I'll never pretend to be brave. I do fear for my safety. There are some things you can't fight, and I know when I'm beaten."

"Yes, ma'am. I promise not to say anything," I said. She seemed sad and relieved at the same time. I knew keeping her secret would be the best thing I could do.

"Thank you for making my story your special secret," Miss Virginia said. "I wouldn't want to be the talk of this small town if he finds me, so I have to leave without anyone knowing, especially him."

Miss Virginia stayed with the sisters, promising to retrieve their groceries, while I walked home with the memory of the day's events swirling in my head. The rain gradually changed to a drizzle and fine mist, making everything seem drab and gloomy, causing the evening to come early. I stood behind the windowpanes of our locked front door and peered out at the Jungle, thinking about the mysteries held within. What had the trees seen and couldn't tell? I thought about that dark green place and didn't know if I should keep my mouth shut about the possible dangers I was just told about.

Until that moment, I'd never been afraid of death. It was an odd part of life that Reverend Avery preached during Sunday service with a heavy dose of hellfire and damnation. It never occurred to me that, even if I tripped and fell, I might die and never breathe again. Or, if I got old, I would never see another sunrise. Life for me didn't hold the thought of never waking.

Nor did it occur to me that someone else could take my life and how horrible it might be to fight to keep it. All I knew about death was from watching television westerns or *Dr. Kildare*, which I knew wasn't real, or when it happened to Angela's kitty. We were all sad, but then she got another one, and all was right with the world again. However, Miss Virginia told me something beyond that. A finality on a level I had never considered before. I couldn't picture how hard it must be for her to decide to leave people she had grown to love over the horrible idea of it.

I turned the lights on in every room of the house and waited for Mom to come home. But the longer I waited, the harder it was to decide if I *should* tell. I told myself to stay safe and wait for events to unfold, though maybe I could drop hints that would suggest something without telling? But I promised, so what to do or say? I didn't know.

When Mom finally came home, I ran into her arms and cried like a baby.

# CHAPTER 14

## *The Warehouse*

————⚬⚬⚬————

S LIM HATED WORKING in the rain, and this massive storm, making jackhammer noises on the Warehouse's roof made him jumpy. As he stood inside the dock bay doors, the rain fell so hard he couldn't see five feet in front of his face. Sloppy work was not his thing, and waiting was a pet peeve. In his opinion, if you had to wait, one minute was too long. Waiting for ten minutes was an eternity. He didn't know why Stooly wanted to meet at this place anyway; it was wet and humid outside, dank and dark inside. It was a small, empty concrete warehouse, set back from the road with two dock bays: not well lit, but solid and dry. But a vacant warehouse building was better than none for shelter in weather like this, which didn't show signs of easing up soon.

Slim knew Stooly needed a warehouse as a front for the business. But way out in no-man's-land on Winchester Road? There had to be a reason for choosing this location. There was nothing but weeds and grass as far as he could see, and if you had to hide shipments, why this place out in the middle of nowhere, in an open field? Well, who was he to question? All he had to do was rake in the moola after all the business was done and protect Stooly's ass.

Marijuana, aka weed, dope, reefer, herb, pot, Kentucky Green, Jamaican—Call it what you will, it was a hit moneymaker in Kentucky. Stiff drinks like whiskey, vodka, gin, and scotch were legitimate enterprises he could profit from, especially selling bootleg. But he knew going legit was out of the question for him. No liquor commissioner would give him a license to sell, and besides, Augie had the bootleg part of the business sewn up. So as far as Slim was concerned, fuck it. If drugs were king, then Stooly was the Duke of Earl, and Slim was the Prince of "Piece" because his .22 pistol ensured business always went as planned.

Slim had lived a rough life. Abandoned by his family, and growing up in an orphanage didn't give him the best start. He always had a menacing look, but being falsely accused of something he didn't do, then doing time for it, put the nail in his coffin, and life went downhill from there. Released from jail, strung out on booze, drinking every day, and living on the streets of Louisville, he was broke and busted. Clarence "Slim" Jeffries had seen it all, but he didn't know where he would be today if it weren't for Johnny "Stooly" Davies.

One Sunday before Thanksgiving, inching along in a soup line, he found himself behind a well-dressed young man also down on his luck, but Slim didn't give a shit. Sitting at a table to eat his meal of cranberries with sliced ham, green beans, and a piece of cornbread, Slim found himself being stared at by the young man who had deliberately sat across from him. When Slim pulled his plate closer, protecting it and eating with a fork prison-style, the young man introduced himself as another down-and-outer. He said he could see Slim had done time by the way he protected his food with his arm. He went on to say he could be of help if Slim would give a fellow inmate some of his time. Slim was skeptical but listened to what the guy had to say, all the while sizing him up, his clothes, his looks, and his way of speaking. He hardly tasted his food, intrigued by the stranger's offer. It all sounded good enough, but it wasn't until he introduced himself as Stooly that Slim decided they'd be friends. Slim liked the song "Tan Shoes and Pink Shoelaces." After that day, Slim's life changed, and he never looked back. But this rain was messing with his vibe, and Stooly's tardiness wasn't helping.

Through sheets of heavy rain, Slim could barely make out the big white truck lumbering up the road with a sign on its side that read "Caruso's Feed & Grain." *Where the fuck is Stooly?* he thought as the shipment got closer to the Warehouse. After the truck backed up to the Warehouse's dock, two men got out. They didn't talk much; they never did. Drug dealing was a serious business. Swarthy in the face, Mexican for sure. Not that Slim had an issue with Mexicans in general, but this bunch could be mean as striped snakes.

"¿Qué pasa, cabrón?" said the one with big biceps.

Slim ignored the insult, took the invoice clipboard, and started inspecting the goods.

Unlike the taped wrapped bags of loose-leaf, which could break and spill, most of the stash they received was vacuum-packed into brick form for easy transport. Slim took out a one-pound brick, and right off the bat, he could tell it was prime. It had the weight and off-gas smell of grade 'A' number one C-Bo, or Colombian Red marijuana, but he still had to be careful to make sure it wasn't padded with Kentucky bluegrass straight from your momma's front yard. He cut it open, careful not to spill any, then moved the stash around inside the brick with a probe to ensure it was all prime. But to make extra sure, he walked around to get another brick from inside the truck. *Damn, where is Stooly?* He cursed again, thinking, *No table or chairs to sit on or place to weigh this shit. Just me alone with these jerk-offs.*

"No good for you, vato?" The guy with big biceps grabbed Slim's arm, which was his first mistake. Slim didn't like to be touched, let alone grabbed, for that matter.

Slim jerked his arm out of Big Biceps's grip and eyed him up and down.

"I ain't your man, so don't touch me. Insult me again, be the *last* thing you do. You know the drill."

"*I* know the drill. It don't mean going through the whole load, Ese."

"If I have to go through the whole truck, I will. Then up your ass when I finish. I'll do that. What you wanna bet?"

"Well, what *have* we got here, a Mexican standoff?" Stooly asked. He had walked up the side steps of the Warehouse while fingering a toothpick in his mouth. He stopped and stood, toe-to-toe and eye to eye with Big Biceps.

"Nah, business as usual." Slim was relieved that Stooly was *finally* there to watch his back but didn't let it show. He continued looking through the open brick of marijuana and then handed it over to Stooly, who never took his eyes off Big Biceps, who, in turn, stared back at Stooly. Slim had to admire the man. Stooly never seemed bothered, always in control like now, barely wet from the rain. Even the toothpick in his mouth was dry.

"That right? You check the rest, at least two or three more?" asked Stooly.

"I was just about to." Slim walked past Big Biceps to grab a few more random samples, ignoring Big Biceps and Stooly, who continued to stare each other down. Finally, the rain eased up enough for the sun to shine through the raindrops. This phenomenon, called "the devil beating his wife," caused Slim to make a mental note to get in Stooly's ass for being late.

When Slim returned from the truck, he was surprised to see two dirty plastic crates turned upside down to sit and place the bricks for weighing. Thinking, *Where the fuck did Stooly get these?* Slim sat down on one crate and placed the bricks of marijuana on the other. He opened each brick, one at a time, and inspected the contents. Only then would he be satisfied that the shipment was good.

Big Biceps positioned his body on one side of the truck's open door while his driving partner occupied the other side, waiting for the nod. When Slim nodded in Big Biceps's direction to indicate all was well, the men began to unload the shipment. With the tension eased, Stooly went inside to determine the best placement for the shipment. Slim was not far behind.

"Tense few moments, but we're off to a good start," Stooly said.

"Where the hell you been, man? You know I been here a full hour *by myself* in the middle of nowhere, waiting on you?"

"Forty-five minutes, Slim, forty-five. Couldn't be helped, though. This damn rain makes for slow going. Wasn't sure if the boys would get here in time, let alone find the place. I had to meet them out on Paris Pike to show 'em how to get here."

"I didn't see you drive up. How'd you get here without being seen?" Slim asked.

Stooly wrapped one arm around Slim's neck. Slim didn't mind because Stooly usually did this when he was in a good mood and needed to explain a slick move or something beyond Slim's level of comprehension.

"That's the beauty of the place. Who's going to believe we got hooch in here, out in the open and in plain sight, huh? Lovely. You look around out back? There's a hidey-hole place out there where no car, *or you*, can be seen. When the rain lets up, I'll show you the mound of dirt and the culvert we can use as a tunnel."

Stooly found some light switches, which Slim hadn't bothered to look for, and lit the interior. This made the place seem more inviting. Spreading his arms out at his sides, Stooly tipped his head back and did a twirl inside the Warehouse, emphasizing the breadth and depth of the space. Appearing pleased with himself, Stooly told the men where he wanted the pallets placed. He figured in the middle of the floor, deep in the bowels of the Warehouse, would be best. Money quickly changed hands when all was unloaded and the invoices were gone through. And just as they came, the Mexicans were gone, taking their biceps with them.

"I sure hate when you late, man," Slim said.

"Will you stop acting like a bitch riding my ass? You my wife now?" Stooly asked.

Slim ignored this question by busying himself with the tarpaulin needed to cover the pallets. Slim knew he had annoyed Stooly by his tone of voice. He didn't want to spoil his mood with petty issues; Stooly had already explained himself, and he didn't like repeats.

Together they stretched the tarp over the many pallets of marijuana to keep it as dry as possible. Then Stooly made an announcement. "Hey, man, I know this rain got you uptight, but looka here, I heard from The Boss today. We got a new partner."

"Who's it this time?" Slim asked. "Hey, look. I ain't gonna waste my time messing with no rinky-dink nigga who don't know what they doing. Wasting my time trying to get *me* killed. Hell, I take all the risk! All I gotta say is, whoever it is, better know his shit."

"You worry too much. I got your back, always have, and you know that."

"I'm just saying, I don't need nobody monkeying around. What's this dude's name? Where'd he come from? He better be connected tight."

"Oh yeah, real tight. Name's Ajax from Louisville. This cat's supposed to be good at running liquor too. Elusive little fucker, though. I ain't met him. Been trying, but so far, nothing."

"Don't sound too buttoned-down to me. You sure he's tight?"

"Can't afford to second-guess The Boss, now can I?" Stooly said. "But I tell you what, I ain't no fool neither."

"I know that's right."

"Listen. Go over and make sure Augie knows this dude. If Augie's good, I'll rest easier. I'm supposed to deliver a few bags to this Ajax at The Hall, but I don't like turning anything over to someone I don't know, haven't met, or can't find for that matter."

"Smart man. Yeah, I'll check it out."

"Oh, and take your gun."

⇒◦◦◦⇐

Augustus Williams, or Augie, was a good Christian and attended church every Sunday, even if he smelled like a moonshine still from Saturday night. He always wanted to give thanks to the Lord for his blessings. That and not getting shot while conducting business behind his "blessings" the week before. Augie suspected the whole town knew he was a bootlegger and was secretly grateful for him.

His high-pitched voice, fast talk, round belly, and genteel manner were misleading. They hid his illegal activity well. Augie was a shrewd businessman and was crafty in not getting caught, which was why Stooly liked dealing with him.

Augie had been in business for ten years, selling bootleg liquor from the basement of his home. His clientele included some local establishments and individual patrons looking to buy booze on the cheap. Even local households in the neighborhood could be counted on to partake of his fine libations from time to time. His bestseller was the moonshine he got from hillbillies near Flemingsburg and Morehead. It didn't come in often, and when it did, the price was steep, but he didn't mind because the boys in the hills sure knew how to brew some shine. He assumed most liquor was bought legitimately but knew the rest was purchased through bootlegs like him, which kept the cost down and profits high. Aside from selling bootleg liquor inside his home, Augie oversaw selling drugs outside his home. This was conducted down the street and around the corner. He didn't want illegal substances inside his house; that was a bridge too far for a person like Augie.

When Slim showed up to ask about business and if all was well, they had the usual conversation. Augie liked Stooly but was afraid of Slim. Intimidated might be the better word.

"Got some info about increased activity coming your way," Slim said.

"Yeah? Glad to hear it, glad to hear it," Augie replied.

"I'm sure, man. Hey, listen. You know a cat named Ajax? Supposed to be a well-known shine runner. He's gonna be working for us now, pushing MJ. Experience like his is hard to come by, you dig?"

"Sure 'nough, doing both ain't easy. But I never *heard* of the dude! Ajax, you say?"

"That's his name."

"Hum. Nope, don't come to mind. I been doing this a long time, but can't say I heard that name. Be hard to forget if I had."

"All right then. Hey, you take care now."

Slim's departure was as swift as his arrival. Augie frowned, thinking, *Now, that ain't right.* Slim's reaction had him stumped. Slim didn't seem fazed by Augie's admission. No surprise. No more questions. Just up and left. In all the years he'd known Slim, he'd never been short with Augie.

On the contrary, Slim had a way of sidling up to a person, feel him out, and then slip into a conversation to get the person to admit something he never thought he knew. Having had this done to you several times would make anyone nervous around Slim. However, this was different, short, sweet, and to the point. Augie didn't want any trouble, so whoever Ajax was, Augie knew in his bulging gut that he wanted no part.

# CHAPTER 15

## *Mô Ségré/My Secret*

I HAD TO tell my momma. I suppose the strange events of that day caused the tears to spill down my face. But I couldn't bring myself to tell Mom everything. The warning Miss Dottie gave me, twice now, or what Miss Virginia said about the man she almost married, were absolute secrets. I knew that part must be mô ségré, my secret and mine alone. If I said more, it'd make things worse. I only told of Miss Dottie's fit in the rain and Miss Virginia's leaving to teach in Chicago.

Mom said how terrifying it must have been to see Miss Dottie in such a state, and hearing about Miss Virginia's leaving was interesting. She also felt bad she hadn't had the time to see the Sweets or visit the Tallys to ask about their new friend.

"I bet you that friend of Jackson's has something to do with this mess. Seems since he's arrived, all kind of mischief's in the air. I can't say it's connected, but all the same, I have to see Jess. At least find out who this man is."

"No, Mom. Please don't say anything. Miss Virginia's leaving is a secret, so please don't tell. Promise? It's no one's business but theirs."

"I can't, honey, not after this. You're more upset than I've seen you in a long time. I can't imagine how it could get worse. First, it was that strange man following you home, and now this business with Dorothy Sweet?" This was not a question. Then she began to pace the floor.

Usually, when Mom paced, it meant she was thinking a million and one thoughts. I was concerned she might think there was more to the story than I was telling, so I had to try begging again.

"Mom, promise me please. It's my secret, and they trust me. Please."

"I think I'll bake another pie and take it over to the Sweets this weekend," Mom said, ignoring my plea. "I want you to stay away from that Jungle across the street. Wherever else you go is fine, but not over there, you hear me? I never liked you playing over there anyway. It wasn't much of a concern with a bunch of you kids running around. Bad enough coming home with Indian burns or crying about wet willies and spiders, but this is serious, especially with this strange man running around. No telling what might happen. These summer goings-on are starting to scare me, so stay out of there. I mean it! It might be a good idea to keep you away from the sisters and their teacher friend until this settles down." Then she stopped pacing and looked at me hard. "Why do I feel you're not telling me everything? You sure there isn't more I need to know?"

"I told you all I can. Please don't say anything?"

"Uh-huh…. All right then. If it means that much, I promise to keep this between us." She lightly tapped the floor with her foot, eyeing me suspiciously. It was all I could do to keep from biting my bottom lip, which I did each time I told a fib. It came with relief when she changed the subject and suggested we pop some corn and watch a program on TV. I felt a little guilty for not telling more than I should have, but what was done was done. The popcorn was tasty, but cuddling up beside Mom to laugh at the shenanigans of *That Girl* was even better. The world felt right and safe again, if only for a little while.

⟞⟝

I spent most of my time away from the Missus Sweets' for the next few weeks, reading the latest book under a tree closer to home. I had finished *Lord of the Flies* and was now reading *To Kill a Mockingbird,* which gave me something to do instead of dwelling on the mysteries surrounding Miss Virginia and the Sweet sisters.

When Mom found the time, she and I talked. I told her briefly about fast dancing but didn't tell her what Doreen put me through at the Youth Center. It just didn't seem to matter when more important things were at stake.

"So what are you reading now? What's this book?" Mom asked as she snuggled down next to me on the couch after taking a break from her studies.

"*To Kill a Mockingbird,* by Harper Lee," I answered.

"Oh *really?* Linney, you amaze me, you know that? You really do. Do you know how significant this story is to what's happening today?"

"No'am, but kinda." Shrugging, I said, "I just think it's a good story. My favorite character is Scout."

"Well, I'm glad you're reading it because this book actually highlights the importance of justice and the push toward civil rights. How I wish this issue of race would just go away. We've made so many strides as a people. But this constant talk of differences brings out the worst in people... it's a wonder we've been able to hold on to the advancements we've fought so hard to obtain. I'm concerned."

"Really? Why?"

"Because it could be taken away someday. I just pray the NAACP will continue to fight for our rights, and with Reverend King as their spokesman, it's my one hope. The world and life, in general, can be a dangerous place for people of our race."

"But why is race such an issue? I don't get it. Everybody seems to talk about it, and it makes no sense. Why does everything have to be so hard?"

"Life is hard, honey. People can be judgmental about others who look very different from themselves."

"Yeah." I couldn't help but sigh, thinking about how I was treated because of my skin color. But that was just me being sensitive, wasn't it? I thought to myself.

"I'll never forget the turmoil during the time before you were born. Oh, it was awful!" Mom continued, "After President John Kennedy was shot, we thought we'd be sent back to Africa."

"I remember. Everyone was so scared and panicky. I was told Africa was far away and very hot. Then, when they told me very short African people, called Pygmies, shrank people to a doll size or smaller and would do the same to us, I believed it."

"Oh my goodness!" Mom chuckled.

"Yeah, that scared me more than anything, but I should've known better. Since then I feel stupid believing all that stuff." Turning serious, I said, "I've been listening to some racist talk, Mom. Especially from Brenda. Sometimes, it makes me think, what if it's *us* and not *them* causing a lot, but not all, of our racial problems? Maybe we're the ones keeping it going?"

"There are some very misguided souls walking around on both sides of that issue, let me tell you. That's the worry I spoke about earlier. Talk like that is harmful, and I don't like it. It keeps us thinking badly about each other. I say, leave talk of racial difference alone, and slowly, it will become a nonissue. Think of it like this: it would be a boring world if we all looked the same, now wouldn't it? Our differences are what make life interesting and us interested in it. We have trees, right?"

"Yeah?"

"Are they all the same? Of course not. Different varieties of oak, walnut, maple, and even then, the leaves are not all the same color during the change in the fall. Think of that? We enjoy the different colors; they're beautiful. That's how I look at life and people."

"I like that. Mom, Anne Frank wrote in her diary, 'I believe people are basically good at heart.' I believe that too. It's kinda easy figuring out who bad people are, so I just avoid them. Doing this keeps me safe, right?"

"Well, your thinking's kind of Pollyannaish, but I think you're on the right track."

"Standing up for what's right isn't always easy to do, especially for me." I let out a deep sigh.

"How so? Honey, you can tell me, you know?"

"Never mind. It's just not easy." I decided to keep my thoughts to myself and said no more. My feeble attempts to speak up at the Dairy Queen reminded me that I didn't do this well, nor would it help my confidence if I continued to try.

She looked at me for the longest time and then put her arm around me and rubbed my shoulder. Times were changing. I was changing. I decided to be mentally strong and live by Miss Virginia's principles. Maybe if I did that, I could be fair and honest about my feelings and thoughts. That's what I told myself.

<hr>

During this time, I hadn't heard from Doreen. Then out of the blue, she called and talked as if the events at the Youth Center hadn't happened. I pretended not to care about anything she had to say.

"I haven't seen you in a while. What you up to? You want to come over?" she asked.

"Unh-unh, I'm busy today. I have a lot to do."

"I don't care if you're busy or not. It can't be much. You can put it off for later, so come over anyway."

A loud click left me listening to the dial tone because Doreen had hung up on me. Miss Virginia's words about seeing life through another person's eyes didn't mean much at that moment. Right then, I decided to visit when I got good and ready and not before. The tart taste of a green apple and a book to read were better than seeing Doreen anyway. I grabbed them both and walked out the back door toward the nearest shade tree.

The morning heat of the first week in August hit me full in the face. The humidity was so thick it was hard to breathe. Sweat formed instantly on my neck and forehead and trickled down my back. *This'll be a three-bath day for sure,* I thought. I rounded the corner of the house and ran smack-dab into Miss Edna.

"Well, my, my! I haven't seen you in a while, Little Missy. Now, where you going? What you got there?" she asked.

"A book from the library," I said. *Is it my imagination, or is Miss Edna intentionally blocking my way?*

"'A book from the library,'" she mocked in a singsong voice. "You forget your manners all of a sudden? What's the *name* of the book?"

"No'am. It's just a book," I said. I didn't like her mocking and tried to ignore her by looking down at the grass, but she wouldn't budge or move an inch out of my way.

"I can see the title anyway, the way you holding it for *all* the world to see. I'm just trying to make conversation. Why you being all siditty, not letting on what you been up to, and keeping secrets to yourself?"

"If I told you they wouldn't be secrets, now would they?" I forgot myself in that instance, and my sass shocked me. I knew I was in for it, so I tried pleading, "Please let me by."

I was not about to tell Miss Edna anything because she was just plain evil and mean. At that moment, Miss Virginia's words about Miss Edna's desire to belong seemed ridiculous. Suddenly, Miss Edna reached out and snatched the book from my hand, then fanned the pages like a deck of cards.

"Gimme back my book! Give it back!" I jumped, reaching to grab the book from Miss Edna, but she held it high and twisted around, laughing at my attempt to regain possession.

"I would if you didn't have such a high-and-mighty attitude. You got to learn to be nicer to folks older than you. I thought you was a proper young lady." Miss Edna began shifting the book from hand to hand.

"Give it back, Miss Edna!" Fumbling around her waist, I couldn't help but hit other parts of her wide body, which was embarrassing. In the struggle, she managed to grab the apple too!

"What, you gonna do? Tell your mommy, huh?"

"Please, Miss Edna! Give me back my apple!"

"Oh, 'please, Miss Edna.' Well, that's more like it. Here you go, but before I give it, how about you tell me what you been up to over there with those old ladies White as you?"

"Why you want to know so bad? What business is it of yours? You know everybody's business. You just mad you don't know mine. Anyway, I don't have to tell you. Now give 'em back!"

"You getting mad at *me*?"

"Give 'em *back*!"

"I hear you got an earful from Virginia about her leaving for Chicago. I also hear Dottie had a fit in the rain and lucky you were there to save the day. Ain't you the little hero? What you think about that? Is it true? I bet she was slobbering all over the place, just like a dummy. Could you see the slobber in the rain?"

"You an evil old woman! If you know so much, why you trying to get it out of me?"

"What're you hiding, huh?"

"You don't know anything, so shut your mouth!"

"Oh, so it *is* true! Why I got to keep my mouth shut, Little Missy?"

*"Stop calling me 'Little Missy,' you nosy old bitch!"* Then I pushed Miss Edna as hard as I could. She fell to the ground, which knocked the book and apple from her hands. I rushed to grab the book, and that's when my grandma's voice cried out.

*"Lindsey Anne Hollis!"*

I turned and froze on the spot, staring into the horrified face of my grandmother. She had a key to the house and must have heard everything after I called Miss Edna an "evil old woman." The bad word and my action surprised her as much as they did me. Miss Edna could have hurt herself in the fall, and for that, I was instantly sorry. I played right into her hands, and by the smirk on her face, she knew it. My immediate thought was to point to Miss Edna and say out loud that she had started it, but that wouldn't do. Instead, I had to own up to it and say I was sorry.

"I'm sorry, Miss Edna. I'm so sorry. Are you okay? I hope I didn't hurt you." My anger was gone as quickly as it was to rise. I reached out my hand to help her stand, but she waved me off.

"I'm fine. How you doing, Edith? This young lady needs to learn how to respect her elders. She's only sorry 'cause she got caught," Miss Edna said.

"Sorry or not, I'd feel a lot better if you'd leave my granddaughter alone. Seems to me she might have a reason for acting out like that. In the meantime, I thank you to dust yourself off and leave her to me." She turned to me, "Now get in the house, young lady."

I picked my apple from the ground and walked toward the house. Miss Edna called out, "She got secrets that one! Yes, she *does*, and I aim to find out what they are before long. You mark my words."

"You'll do no such thing but mind your business!" My grandmother made a beeline toward Miss Edna, and, pointing a finger in her face, she continued, "I know more about you than you'll ever know, Edna Allen. Now go on home and never mind me and mine. You ought to be ashamed of yourself. Picking on someone younger and smaller than you. What's the matter with you? Go on home. Git!"

After waving Miss Edna away as if she were a fly, Grandma and I came into the kitchen, where I sat down and held tight to my book; I didn't care much for the apple after Miss Edna's paws were all over it. Grandma stood there for a while, letting the hot breeze blow in through the open back door before speaking.

"What's got into you?" Grandma asked.

"I don't know." I was concentrating with a frown and pouted as usual but continued, "Miss Edna had my book and wouldn't give it back unless I told her about my visits to the ladies across the street. She kept picking at me, but I wouldn't tell. Then she told me what I told Mom the other day. How did she know? It was our secret, so how could Miss Edna know?"

Sighing, my grandmother sat down at the kitchen table with me. She reached for my hand, and I slowly released the book and laid it on the table. There was a long pause before Grandma spoke.

"Honey, I don't know how she knows. Your mother's concerned and wants to make sure you're safe. It isn't like you to ignore Doreen when she asks you to come over, so I came here to see if you were all right. You love to visit, right?"

"But I told Mom not to tell—"

"Well, she told me, honey, she had to. She worries about her decision to have you visit the Sweets. She can't be around all the time, and what happened was enough to concern her. Getting you involved in grown folks' business ain't Christian if you ask me. Your mother's my child too, don't forget, and when she's concerned, I'm concerned."

"I'm sorry, Grandma—"

"I know you are, but it don't take away the fact that you pushed Edna! Calling her out of her name is bad enough. That's sticks and stones, but physically laying hands is a whole 'nother thing altogether. Lord have mercy. I'm glad I came when I did. Lord knows Edna Allen is a mean-spirited woman, but I can't have you go beating up on her either. Like I said, I don't know how she knows, but never mind that now." Changing the subject, she asked, "Are you *that* protective of them, the Sweets, I mean?"

"Yes, ma'am. I guess. They're really sweet, like their names. Miss Virginia is the kindest person, and her leaving was a secret. Now everyone'll know. Why can't I have something no one else has, something all my own, friends I don't have to share? This means everything, and they trust me. That's important, right? I'll protect them with my life if I have to!"

"That's a bit dramatic, don't you think? How about Doreen? Isn't she someone you want to protect? If you felt half as much about her as you do the Sweets and their friend, she'd be protected *for life*, not to mention a lifelong friend to boot." I wanted to scream that Doreen could take care of herself! Doreen always had, and why couldn't Grandma see that? But Doreen was her everything, so of course, Grandma couldn't or wouldn't see past that.

"It's different with us, Grandma." That's all I could bring myself to say.

"All I know is Doreen's growing up fast. With her boyfriends and all, she just wanted to reach out today and share what you two always tend to do when you're alone together. But you ignored her, and she can't understand why. Why would you hurt her feelings, Linney?"

My suspicions had become fact. It became clear that Grandma had blinders on like a horse being breezed around a racetrack. Grandma looked straight ahead when it came to Doreen's behavior and not to the side where danger might lie. She saw what she wanted, and no matter how hard I tried, she would always think Doreen was the victim, the saintly one.

"Why don't you put the book down and come with me? It would do Doreen a world of good to see you. Not to mention ease my mind for the day."

"Yes, ma'am," I said, surrendering with a sigh.

"That's my girl. Now come on with me."

Trudging to Grandma's house on that hot day, I couldn't shake the fact that my mother had betrayed my trust. *Who else did she tell?* It wouldn't take long to find out.

# CHAPTER 16

## *The Great Come to Jesus*

D OREEN WAS SITTING in the garden under the shade of the pear tree when I came through the back door of Grandma's house. It had been at least a month since the Very Personally Yours kit, and as she rose to meet me, I was shocked at the change. She walked toward me as if in slow motion, no longer a girl without hips and boobs. Now she had both! She seemed to glide, full-bodied with a tiny waist, hair glistening in the sun. The song "Pretty Ballerina" ran through my mind as she came close, and I tried to close my mouth, now open in awe. Then her voice, dripping with sweetness, reached me.

"Hi, Linney. I'm glad you finally came over."

*This* voice was different than the one from that morning. Seized with jealousy, I stepped back in my worn-out Keds. I thought, *What's going on here?* This Doreen was no longer the same age as me, no longer tomboyish; she was a lady, beautiful and serene. Her light brown complexion was blemish-free and made a striking contrast to her blue-black brows, eyelashes, and hair. She was casually dressed in a pair of belted culottes, a sleeveless white blouse, and sandals with little heels.

"It's rude to stare, so close your mouth and say something," she said.

"You look amazing! What happened? You changed almost overnight?"

"Let's go to my room. I've got something to tell."

Doreen grabbed me by the hand, and with me behind her, I watched as Grandma smiled and draped a tape measure around her neck. I was left thinking Grandma must have felt pleased with how she handled me that morning.

Doreen told me how it was when she got her period, which didn't hurt. Within a month, she noticed her clothes fit differently. Because Doreen's chest was sore, she thought something was wrong with her and said nothing out of fear. She had no idea her boobs had started to grow.

"See how it all looks? And look! Smell! It's called Shalimar. Daddy got it for me! He said I was a young lady now, and *this* was his gift to *me*."

She began showing off, twirling around and forcing the perfume bottle under my nose, only for me to inhale the most delightful fragrance I had ever smelled. It was hard to hold back the urge to tear her eyes out and mess up all her hair, cutesy looks, and twirls. *It's not fair!* I thought. It just wasn't fair that she got to be all grown-up, and I didn't. *When will I get to look like that, a young lady?* I listened while Doreen went on and on, talking about her glorious self. After a while, my jealousy quieted down a bit, if only because her conceit was nauseating. To keep my breakfast from rising, I accepted my shortcomings and held back the green-eyed monster by joining the compliment party.

"You changed all within a month? I can't believe it. You're so beautiful."

"I know!" Doreen squealed. "It's like it happened overnight. I woke up one day, and here I am. I'll be fifteen in a few months, so I guess it's to be expected. I'm sorry I didn't tell you before, but that's because I know how much you want this for yourself. Linney, it's so great, and I can't help feeling glad I made it before you. I feel so pretty."

She was as apologetic as a cold lizard on a hot rock. Her smugness was getting under my skin. My jealousy and resentment started to rise again, and I found myself saying things I wouldn't have said any other day.

"I thought you didn't call because I danced with Barry," I said. "You never called to apologize for embarrassing me after you danced with him. Why not? I think you meant to hurt me, just like when you call me means names and stuff."

"Who cares what I call you? It's not *my* fault you're so *sensitive and touchy*. I asked Barry to dance with you because someone bumped into me on the dance floor and hurt my boobs. I wanted to sit some dances out. You're the one always holding up the wall without looking at any of the boys—who can't wait to dance with you, by the way. So I asked Barry to ask you to dance. *I did that, Linney!*"

"Your boobs obviously didn't hurt *that* much because you danced anyway! *Show off!* You knew you could dance better than me and then had the nerve to rub it in my face. In front of *everybody*—!"

"*I did not*—!"

"*Yes, you did!*"

"It wasn't me who ran off after," Doreen said. "Why didn't you say I hurt your feelings right then—"

"If it wasn't so embarrassing, I *would've*! I hope Angie gave you a good telling-off! You know what I think? I think you knew *exactly* what you were doing, Doreen because you can't help yourself—"

"*I did not!*"

"What're you trying to prove now, huh? Showing off how much you've grown and trying to get under my skin just because I haven't? Acting all superior, like you *always* do, because *you're my auntie?* Well, who *cares?*" We were standing toe-to-toe, spitting words at each other.

"*I* care! I care a lot about you and what you're going through—"

"That's a *lie!* You don't care about me—"

"*Yes,* I do. I care a lot, but you—"

"And what's more, you don't know a thing about what I'm going through—"

"*Momma* told me your secret! *All* of it!" Doreen said.

The sting of her words hit me as if I had been slapped in the face. I looked at her with disbelief and confusion. I was referring to my feelings and how I felt inferior to her. But she wasn't listening and blurted out something else entirely. Did Doreen need to know everything? Did she always have to be one step ahead of me? Could I *ever* have anything of my own?

I couldn't say anything more and ran from her room. I banged out the front door and let it slam shut without saying goodbye to Grandma. The sense of unfairness overwhelmed me. Mom's betrayal made me so angry I could spit nails. I ran without feeling the road beneath my feet. I felt terrible and knew I had misbehaved, but I didn't care and didn't want to apologize for it either. No, not one little bit!

I couldn't share anything with anyone without everyone knowing about it. What's worse? I had betrayed the Sweet sisters and Miss Virginia's secret by telling my mother. I had control over nothing. At that moment, I missed my daddy.

As I ran, I was vaguely aware of the heat but still wondered if it couldn't get any *hotter* than it was that day. I felt no breeze on my skin as I ran without realizing who I passed or what they said in greeting. That is until I ran into Miss Tally. She must've called my name when she stepped in front of me, which caused me to stop abruptly.

"Lord have *mercy*! What's happened now?" She held both my shoulders and frowned with concern. "You wanna tell me why the hounds of hell are after you?"

"Ain't there *no one* in this town minding their own *business*?" I asked. "There're spies *everywhere* watching *everything* I do and go and say and touch and even sneeze at! *Leave me alone!*"

"Well, that's a fine howdy-do, young lady. Who you think you talking to? Now, just calm down."

"I don't *want* to calm down! I want to be left *alone*. Can't you understand? I'm ugly, I'm clumsy… I can't do anything right, I can't… even keep a secret…. Leave me alone… *please*, Miss Tally. I don't want to say something… bad… to you too. Let me… go… Please?"

And she did just that. I didn't move an inch past her but swayed instead. I tried to stand up straight, but instead, the world spun around my head. I felt hot, very hot, then cold and started to shake with chills. The sensation of falling was overwhelming before blackness closed in around me.

⬥⬥⬥

Muffled sounds swirled around as if in a foggy haze. As I gradually regained consciousness, the breeze from Miss Anne fanning my body felt nice while Miss Tally repositioned a cold rag on my forehead. Miss Loren sounded excited, saying she'd called Mom, who was on her way. I didn't want Mom to come home and said so but was shushed by Miss Tally, who told me to rest. The rag she used to wipe my arms and legs felt cool, so I took her advice without a fight and fell asleep. The feel of someone stroking my face was comforting. Then, as if in a dream, I heard Mom tell me she was there.

Then my dream became a nightmare. I squirmed away from the sound of a man's voice. I yelled, telling him to get away from me and not kill me. I kicked out at him while he struggled to keep me still. But his voice was kind, and I slowly relaxed. Confusion set in because I woke to see a White man feeling my forehead and putting a stethoscope on my chest. Speaking quietly, he told my mother I would be okay, that I had overheated and would recover soon. He said it was a good thing Miss Tally was there to bring me inside out of the sun. Cool water, not cold, would replace the fluid loss and get lots of rest. He had a kind, wise face and smiled when he realized I was no longer fighting him.

"Welcome back to the land of the living. You gave us a fright for a few minutes."

"Who are you? Where's my mom?"

"Your mother's right here. My name's Dr. Roberts. After all these years of your mother working in my office, I'm pleased to meet you. Now, how are you feeling?"

"My head hurts. I feel sick. Where's Mom?"

"I'm here, honey. Just let the doctor finish his examination," she said.

Speaking to Mom, Dr. Roberts said, "She'll have a headache for a few hours but should recover just fine. Give her two aspirin, some unsalted saltines for nausea, only a few, and lots of water. Try to keep her out of the heat for the next few days."

He had a comforting touch, and his probing blue eyes focused on my face. His dark brown hair, streaked with gray, matched a mustache above lips that pulled back with concern as he started to speak to me again.

"What were you doing running in this heat? Anything you want to share?"

I didn't answer but studied his face, the same as he had mine. Then Miss Tally made her feelings known.

"She was angry as a hellcat. I can tell you that! Not like her at all," Miss Tally said.

"You can tell me if you're up to it?" Dr. Roberts said. "For medical reasons, I need to rule out anything other than this heat causing your fainting."

With everyone in the room looking down at me, I didn't want to say anything. But he insisted I say something in an answer for myself.

"I just wanted to go home. I was mad, and now I feel silly," I said.

"You're thirteen, is that right, fourteen next year?" he asked.

"No, sir, fourteen in December *this* year," I said.

"Oh, I stand corrected." Then he chuckled and to my mom said, "I think I get the picture. Janie, I don't think you have anything to worry about here. No underlying issues that I can find at her age. By all accounts, whatever it was that spooked her, I'm sure it'll work itself out. Is she afraid of strangers? Has she had an incident of concern lately? By the sounds of it, she's afraid someone's out to hurt her."

"A strange man followed her home a month ago now. That scared her badly, but nothing came of it. We haven't seen any strangers around, so for all I know, that's passed. The neighbors are good lookouts and keep her safe when I'm not home," Mom said.

"I see," Dr. Roberts answered Mom and turned back to me. "Young lady, don't run in the sun at high noon, especially on hot days like this. You don't want to scare your mom or her friends again, do you? Did you know you're a great help to your mom while she studies for her license?" I shook my head no. Then he continued, "No? Well, you are, and that makes her proud of you, and I'm proud of her." Then, like Stooly, he winked at me.

---

It was late afternoon when Dr. Roberts left us. As I pulled the curtains back to watch him drive away, I noticed a crowd had gathered. If they wondered what was happening, well, that would be me lying on Miss Tally's living room couch.

"You know, it's not every day we have a doctor do house calls and a White doctor at that. God, how the neighbors will talk! I'm sure glad my house was clean," Miss Tally said as she left us alone to prepare her evening dinner.

"Tell me what happened, honey," Mom said. "I always think you can take care of yourself without much help from me, but this is not like you."

"I like him." I didn't want to answer right away, so I thought changing the subject would buy some time. "He's not like what others say about them, White people, I mean. I hear bad stuff, but I don't think it's all true. They can't be as bad as they say. Do their houses really smell like Clorox and lettuce? Does he like you, Mom?"

"Their homes smell like anyone else's, so don't believe everything you hear." Mom chuckled and then continued, "And no, not all White people are bad, just like not all Black people are bad. He likes me well enough, but he likes my drive and willingness to make our lives better a *whole* lot more. Dr. Roberts is married to a lady who is just as nice as he is kind. Maybe you'll meet her one day. Something to look forward to, huh? They have a son, a few years older than you, who attends Paris High."

At the mention of high school, the dam broke. This time the telling was easy. Once again, the events came out like water from a fountain. I told all about how Miss Edna grabbed my book and wouldn't let me have it until I told her about my visits with the Sweets. Then I told her the awful name I called Miss Edna and how I pushed her down into the grass. How Doreen was showing off her new figure while I was still flat everywhere. She was prettier than me but very mean lots of times. How Grandpa would never like me and even brought Doreen perfume called Salamander! How I felt so jealous. How I didn't care about hurting her feelings but should have. How I wanted to come home and be by myself, all without seeing anyone or feeling anything. Then I told how I felt about her telling my secret.

"Why did you tell Miss Edna and Grandma? Mom, you promised not to tell, and you did! It was important to me!"

"First off," Miss Tally said, "the fragrance is called Shalimar, not Salamander. Nice fragrance. You ever smelled it, Janie Mae? Your grandpa's got taste! Sounds to me like you had one of them come-to-Jesus meetings. We should have held a revival!" She tried to find humor in the situation while listening in as her pork chops fried on the stove. "Second, your mom didn't tell Miss Edna anything. She told *me*. A thing like that, you can't expect her to keep to herself, sweetheart. All those secrets and odd goings-on in that house? Even gave me the creeps. She didn't tell anything that shouldn't be told, young lady. It's not like she told Sandy Beaumont." Miss Tally chuckled. "Otherwise, it'd be all over town by now."

"No, that would be *Edna*, just for spite," Mom said. They both laughed at this. Then Mom continued talking to Miss Tally, "I doubt Sandy cares one way or the other about this stuff. Edna must've overheard us talking out on your front porch. What do you think, Jess?"

"That woman's a menace, and to *think* she treated your daughter the way she did today? I don't blame Linney for calling her a 'bitch,' though. She is one!" Turning to me, Miss Tally said, "Linney, don't use that language again. You can't, but I will. And

Janie Mae, I know Linney's your little girl and all, but she's thirteen, for God's sake. A teenager, practically grown. But that temper needs taming. Girl, I thought I had a tiger by the tail, wee Lordy!"

"It's that Creole temper, I tell you," Mom said. "I didn't think I'd ever *see* it come out in Linney." Mom turned to me again. "Honey, listen to me. I love you with all my heart, and so do my parents, including your grandpa. I think he's afraid you'll make the same mistakes I made growing up. I'm not saying all my decisions were mistakes, but all the same, he's just full of fear. That's all I'll say about that. As far as Doreen is concerned, I'm glad you stood up for yourself 'cause she sure had it coming. She has the best of everything, but she wants more, and that *more* is being who you are. I believe *she's* envious of *you*! I love her, but my goodness, I hate to see the day when something bad happens or when she can't get her way. I talk to Mother about it all the time, but she can't see it. She won't. What should be important is knowing you are prettier than you realize, kinder than you think, and wiser beyond your years. You are special, not only to me but to a lot of people who love you."

I reached out to hug Mom. I felt better after hearing her explanations and how she deeply felt about me. That rest about Doreen, I wasn't so sure about.

"Edna Allen, that lady, I swear!" Miss Tally said. "Let's just hope she'll keep it to herself and keep her mouth shut, thinking she's got something on y'all."

"By the way, I meant to ask you about this new friend of Jackson's. Where's he from?" Mom asked.

"Who, Mitch? Girl, he's some guy Jackson struck up with right before July. He just showed up one day at Jackson's job at Hansley Mills, down on his luck. Jackson felt sorry for him. You know how Jackson is, so he set him up at the A&P, loading meat part-time. Names Mitchell Duncan. He seems like a lost soul. He was here once, but I didn't like him slinking around like a roach hiding in corners. Wouldn't even come out to say 'boo' to Linney when she came by. But Lord have mercy, didn't he stink up the house something *awful!* I told Jackson not to *ever* invite that nasty man back into my house. Jackson's heart can be too soft, but I tell you what, Mitch hasn't been back since, and I don't expect him to either. I think he and Jackson had words that day."

"He doesn't sound like a person Jackson would have around," Mom said. "I'm glad you put your foot down. Stink like that speaks of a wicked soul. You say he showed up just before the end of June before the Fourth? The time Linney was followed home that night in July?"

"That's right! Anything smell funny to you the night you were followed, Linney?" Miss Tally asked.

"Not that night, but last time at the A&P, it did," I answered.

I didn't want to say more because I wanted to avoid discussing anything that might lead to Miss Virginia's fear and Miss Dottie's premonitions. Miss Dottie's fit during the rainstorm and Miss Virginia's leaving were all they needed to know. Anyway, whenever they talked as if I wasn't in the room, I kept quiet, hoping to learn something I wouldn't otherwise.

Mom turned to me again. "I didn't mean to break your heart or my promise. I hope you'll forgive me for sharing your secret. I know it was important, but you're more important to me. It won't go any further, okay? Cross my heart."

"But it did, Mom! Doreen blurted it out today, and who knows what she'll do with it or who she'll tell. That's why I had to get away from her before I did something that'd make things worse."

# CHAPTER 17

## *The Necessary Call*

—◈◈◈—

"COME AGAIN? HE don't know the dude? At all?" Stooly asked.

"No, sir. Not a wit, not a notion," Slim said as he sat casually across from Stooly. "I'm telling you, man, Augie ain't never heard of *Ajax*. Looka here, I don't know what this is, but it don't smell right. You sure The Boss met this guy, knows him… what?"

"I don't know, man, ain't nobody 'Jack' told me shit. Other than expecting him to work with us, I know nothing. The Boss tells me what to do, and it's done. Had a hunch to follow up, and glad I did."

"The Boss needs to know, though, man," Slim said. "There's something sketchy about this dude he wants to use to push weed. We're local suppliers, man, no more, no less. Neither one of us use this shit bought from Mexicans set up by The Boss. We just love the money. Looka here, even if Augie does or doesn't know Ajax, we got to keep tabs on him irregardless, you dig?"

Ignoring Slim's double-negative use of the word *regardless*, oh, Stooly dug it all right. When Slim started using or misusing million-dollar words in any sense, Stooly knew it was time to get worried. This was a "tell" of Slim's that Stooly had known for years but never let on he knew. Slim wasn't afraid of much, but this nervous tic always tipped Stooly off that Slim was onto something. Stooly had his suspicions; however, the fact he was dead-on-balls right was a revelation. Now, he needed more time to unravel this riddle.

"I need to think about catching a snake that bites first before it rattles," Stooly said.

"You still meeting that dude, Ajax, up at The Hall this weekend?" Slim asked.

"That's the plan. But can't say how I'm gonna do it now, not with the information you just gave me. I need to call Louisville before doing anything, man. You hold tight. I'll get with you later." Stooly had no intentions of handing anything over at this point.

Stooly's tone was slow and thoughtful as he said this. Contemplating his next move weighed heavily on his mind. Stooly and Slim were like brothers; if he needed Slim, he knew he'd be close by. Always close by.

⸺◦◦◦⸺

It was a whole week later before Stooly decided to do anything. And another week after that, before he made the call to The Boss. There was some commotion earlier on the hill, where the siditty Negroes lived. A small crowd had gathered at one of the houses, and a White man was seen leaving later. Situations like that made him jumpy. He was assured the man was no policeman, but still, he decided to wait a while. Stooly liked to take his time. Playing the long game was his strong suit.

The call Stooly had to make was necessary. It would be the most important call in his chosen profession. This situation with the so-called *Mr.* Ajax forced him to question the background of a man hired by The Boss, who could off him without thinking twice. This call was the lesser of two evils. His thoughts were either to make the call or take his chances with a sketchy motherfucker who could slip inside an operation, then call in the Feds if things started to go sideways.

Perfume filled the air, stinking it up like a French whorehouse, as his sister Bessie sashayed out into the hot and humid night, waving a dismissive goodbye to her brother. Pimping prostitutes was an option Stooly had given some thought to, but that was *if* he had to get out from supplying drugs. However, the idea of young women selling themselves for cheap thrills was something Stooly couldn't stomach for profit.

He loved women and hated seeing them mistreated, especially young ladies starting out in life. Bess was a grown woman who couldn't be reasoned with, so if this was how she wanted to live her life, who was he to argue? After all, her big brother was supplying drugs that could end up in the hands of young people. How was that for a moral compass? Skillet calling the kettle black was beneath his dignity to engage in argument. He did have his pride.

Stooly had little choice over the life he led. He never knew his dad, and his mother died shortly after his fourteenth birthday, leaving him to care for himself and his baby sister, Elishia, or Bessie, as she was called. At the age of sixteen, he had been an unruly young man known for his knife skills which landed him in juvenile detention.

He served his juvie time in Lexington while Bess lived in foster homes. In juvenile detention, he boned up on his education and obtained a general education degree, thinking he could make something of himself. But life had other plans. After his release at the age of eighteen, he tried to enroll in a trade or vocational school, thinking it would open doors to a well-paying job, thus putting his sister under his care. But because of his record, he was denied entry to any of these schools.

On a simple B and E at a liquor store, he was sentenced to prison for five years, the judge not caring that his gun was defective and used to scare and not kill. He was assigned to the prison library and took advantage of the education denied him on the outside. He was a quick learner. Smart. He decided to apply what he had learned about business management to prosper and game the system that had been so unfair to him. The prison hardened and almost broke him with its dark underbelly. It was there he discovered his sinister side. A dark side he kept hidden because it scared him, like his worst nightmares.

Stooly served three of his five years. He had a nose for business and knew his strengths and weaknesses. He was a hit with the ladies who took excellent care of him, giving him anything he needed. Their money allowed him to purchase clothes and cars and put food in his belly. But he needed to be his own man, and although he was flat broke, he had a plan. While casing the homeless food line on a cold Thanksgiving Day in Louisville, he found Slim, and life was never the same.

Stooly yawned and stretched his lean, toned body, feeling weary from all these thoughts. Now after many successful years of illegal gains, he wanted out. How he got out was something he had to consider carefully. Bessie was a handful, all right. Too many years of scrimping and living off scraps others didn't care to give had made her a hard woman. Her only resource was her body, and who could blame her? She was something to behold, gorgeous, in fact. The life Bessie chose for herself was not an easy one, but Stooly knew Bessie wouldn't have to sell her body if he could provide better for her. He could never shake the feeling that he had let her down. How could he possibly get out of this life of crime when he felt he owed her so much? He wasn't selfish; doing right by her was always uppermost in his mind. But his options were limited, and the stakes were high. The money he made was just too good to give up right now. He had to give more thought to his future for sure, but at the moment, Stooly had a problem. And its name was Ajax.

It wasn't Stooly's nature to reveal he had any business problems, but he had no choice in this. The voice on the other end of the phone was all business. Stooly spoke to The Boss in conciliatory tones, full of bullshit but necessary under the circumstances.

"You say no one knows him, so what?" The Boss said.

"You run this thing, and you pick who you pick. Who am I to argue?" Stooly asked. "I do what you want and deliver the goods. I don't want anyone messing that up for us. But I got to trust who works with me, so it's all clean. You don't have a problem with him; I don't either."

"Then we understand each other."

"On that, we do."

"I hear what you sayin' though. I'll call my sources to make sure it's all copacetic. You the best I got in this thing. I don't want to lose my best moneymaker, so tell you what. Hold off on the transfer till you get the go-ahead from me."

"You got it."

"And one more thing…. Don't call me about this bullshit again." The phone went dead.

Stooly was hamstrung by The Boss. Nothing in his bones told him Ajax was legit. If Stooly's hunch was correct, this Ajax was someone he either knew of or had contact with before. It was a matter of time before he revealed himself. All Stooly could do was wait.

# CHAPTER 18

## *Fast Dancing*

MISS EDNA RECEIVED all she was going to get from me in the way of an apology, which was as sincere and polite as I could make it. My mother, standing behind me, also apologized for my actions. It was all too much, with Miss Edna smirking the entire time. I don't think she appreciated what we said to her, and I'm sure she felt like the ultimate victim for the simple act of us doing so. She made no attempt to apologize to me. Then and there, I decided that I would *never* apologize to her again unless it was absolutely necessary. Mom might have felt better about my efforts with this nosy lady, but I didn't.

Now I had to make amends with Doreen, and I didn't have the faintest idea how. As hard as it was to apologize to Miss Edna, it would be worse to apologize to Doreen. Mom told me to stay away from the Sweet sisters until she could speak with them. Until then, I had to bide my time and think of how to apologize to Doreen.

Returning to school was just around the corner. At Western, *Slang Book*s were loose-leaf notebooks used as a way for students to write what they thought about someone without signing their names. The book was circulated right before the school year started, and I couldn't wait to see what had been written. Each person was given an entire page dedicated to them for comments. It was a surprise when Angela told me I had a whole page in the book. I'd never had one before.

Part of me didn't want to read what was written, but when Angela told me they were going to the Youth Center to read it, I had to go also. By inviting Doreen, it would give me a chance to apologize to her. Doreen listened as I poured it on thick, telling her how sincerely sorry I was for hurting her feelings. She accepted my apology without argument or pushback, which was odd because she usually gave me a hard time. Then she agreed to come along.

Instead of my usual shorts or pedal pushers, I decided to wear a skirt. I wanted to look grown-up and didn't want to embarrass anyone, especially Doreen, by wearing the same thing as usual. I even brushed my hair into a high ponytail, then braided it into a big fat plait, which I hoped wouldn't frizz before the night was through. I pulled on a white short-sleeved blouse that didn't need to be tucked inside the skirt and put away my faithful faded Keds, opting for worn-out penny loafers instead.

Doreen and I met up with Angela and Carolyn, who had been away visiting family in Ohio. There was a lot to catch up on, and Carolyn had lots to tell, the *Slang Book* all but forgotten. With squeals of laughter and rapidly talking over each other, I was floating on air to have my friends with me again. But that feeling faded when Angela and Carolyn went on and on about Doreen's transformation. Doreen was a beauty, and the local boys let her know with catcalls and wolf whistles.

The music playing through the open doors of the center on that late Friday afternoon pulled us in. There were so many people trying to get in that I didn't see Brenda and Karen standing by the door until we were practically on top of them. Once inside, I just about got lost in the crowded squeeze of the dance floor. The cool wall I leaned against felt good on my back while I caught my breath and thanked God I'd put my hair up. A tiny wisp of outside air through an open window felt cool on my skin, and I welcomed whatever breeze came in. Now I wished like anything to have a pair of sandals to wear instead of hot, sweaty penny loafers.

I was determined not to be a wallflower, and because of Doreen's harsh words a few days before, I decided to dance with whoever asked me. It was no surprise to see Barry flirting with Doreen whenever there was a lull in the music. Other times they were dancing up a storm, either together or apart. I amused myself wondering what kind of person Barry would be if there were no dance floor to show off on. Because I had practiced dancing with the refrigerator door handle for so long, I was dying to fast dance and waited for the right moment, song, or person to try my new skills.

From a slow dance song to a fast dance, the transition of music was not always smooth. We often stood in the middle of the floor in anticipation, waiting for the next song to cycle on the jukebox to decide what dance to do next. Only then did we continue to dance *or* find a bench to sit on or a wall to lean against. It was unusual for Barry to dance without knowing the next song in the queue or the kind of dance to do. So it was a complete surprise when he approached me for a dance. After the last time, I didn't think he would ever ask again. Besides, he *was* Doreen's boyfriend.

I hesitated and glanced around for Doreen, but she was nowhere in sight. I wanted her approval before accepting because we had just made up, and I didn't want to risk upsetting her again. It also didn't help to see Brenda nudge Karen, standing next to her on the opposite side of the floor, then point at us, mouthing the words, *look at White girl.* Carolyn and Angela stood alongside me, waiting to see if I would accept Barry's offer to dance. The beating of my heart was so loud that I thought everyone could hear it.

"Ain't Too Proud to Beg" by the Temptations began to play. I stood there with my feet glued to the floor, knowing I shouldn't dance with Barry without permission, but he insisted. Barry grabbed my hand, no longer waiting for an answer, then asked if I was okay. When I nodded yes, we began not just any dance but the fast dance.

No longer timid, I moved effortlessly from step to step and allowed him to twirl me around many times. Then at the emphasis of a particular lyric or drumbeat, we moved as one.

Pausing and anticipating his next move, I danced by his side and never lost a step. Then it came. The extra steps I had practiced at home fell into the movements perfectly. I laughed out loud in glee, enjoying the grace of our movements. I was so happy and proud of myself. I saw no one and cared about nothing, only felt the pulsing music with Barry leading the entire way. When the music stopped, I was breathless. Barry smiled and held one of my hands while I reached out to place the other on his shoulder.

"That was *great!* You been practicing?" he asked.

"Yeah, at home… yeah. Thank you so much. I didn't think I could do it."

"Those steps. Where'd you learn those?"

"They just came to me when I practiced. It's some changed-up hillbilly hard shoe. I think that's what it's called. My uncle taught me how a long time ago."

Standing not far away, Doreen glared at us. She stood with arms folded across her chest; Brenda and Karen were on either side. Behind them, Angela and Carolyn beamed with pride. Angela silently clapped very fast and grinned from ear to ear.

"I want to go again. You have to teach me, okay?" Barry asked.

Then the song "Bernadette" by the Four Tops began to play, and the floor filled with people. As Doreen made her way to us, Barry grabbed my hands a second time. I declined, but with Barry's back to Doreen, he started to dance with me anyway. I followed his steps, ignoring Doreen as she got close. We began again, and I added the extra steps this song was perfectly suited for. Barry was a quick learner and followed my steps well. Then he caught a glimpse of Doreen glaring at us.

"Don't look at her. Look at me," Barry said.

I did as he said and kept dancing, twirling half-in and half-out, then a full spin with arms lifted, and I held his hands while the extra steps I practiced stayed in sync. When the pause in the song came toward the end, most couples twirled their partners, but not Barry. We kept dancing through the pause, and all I heard were the angelic voices in the song and the synchronized clacking of our heels on the wooden floor. The sound of the extra steps as we fell in sync when the lyrics started up again was amazing! A cheer rose from the crowd of onlookers. All eyes were on us, on me. The joy I felt quickly faded when the song ended because the disgust and hatred on Doreen's face cut me to the bone.

Many people came over to us, asking where we learned to do what we did. I had no words. However, I didn't want Doreen to take this moment away from me with her anger, so I asked Barry to go to her. But Doreen slapped Barry's hands away when he reached for her.

"Oh my gosh, look at you! Did you see me grinning? I just couldn't stop?" Carolyn said.

"I know! How'd you learn to do that? You're so good!" Angela said.

"It's a long story, y'all, but check out Doreen. She looks mad," I said.

"Serves her right! Carolyn said. Unusual for her.

"Remember what she did to you last time?" Angela asked me. "I chewed her out real good, though, Carolyn. You should've seen it. Doreen was awful! But I bet she didn't see this coming."

"Yeah, I heard all about it. Linney came to my house right after. What a *sur*prise tonight, huh?" Carolyn said, not letting her glee fade away just because Doreen was angry.

"Girl, I didn't know you had it in you. Where'd you get the nerve to show Doreen up like that?" Angela asked.

"That's not what I wanted to do, Angie, gee whiz!" I said. "All I did was dance. I practiced all summer so I wouldn't be embarrassed again, that's all."

"I don't think Doreen sees it that way or that her friends liked it either," Angela said. "Look at them huddled together, just *plottin'*. Oh well, win some, lose some."

"We don't look any better y'all. Let's go outside. It's too hot in here," Carolyn said.

Brenda and Karen huddled around Doreen outside while Barry stood by himself, leaning against the building with his head down. It seemed as though win some, lose some was more like *win some, lonesome.* I felt terrible but decided to ignore them and keep a safe distance. I was the one who invited Doreen, and in hindsight, maybe I shouldn't have. I guess it could be said I got my revenge on Doreen, but I had a lot more to learn.

# CHAPTER 19

## *Jimmy, Mitchell, Ajax*

Y OUNG GIRLS THESE *days sure grow up fast,* so thought Jimmy Marx. He could feel their heat from where he stood, which aroused him. Leaning against an abandoned house across the street from the Youth Center, he watched them come and go as they swung their skirts and flicked their hair, all the while strutting their stuff on long, lean legs. They called each other by name, so he quickly learned who was who. Watching had become his favorite pastime, and hiding in plain sight was a perfect foil. Even though he thought of himself as invisible, he liked to be hidden; he liked the dark. They didn't seem to notice him, what with their interest in only themselves. He thought it remarkable that they didn't notice any of the young men standing around ogling them, but they managed. Watching the young perfections in front of him, he couldn't help but reflect on his life and past indiscretions.

Recently, Jimmy had developed a taste for young flesh. He got close to snatching a sweet young thing a few months ago. But she got away, running like a young filly into the safety of her neighborhood. He found a way to get in through the back of that mass of trees across from her house. There he hid to watch her, cursing his failed effort. Sometimes that foggy feeling overcame him, which he blamed for his failure that night. It got in the way. When he saw her again at the A&P, he stayed close without her knowing a thing. Later, he saw her talking to Jackson's wife, which encouraged him to sneak down to her house before having dinner with the Tallys. If it wasn't for Jackson, he'd still be after that sweet piece of meat everyone called Linney. *Damn Tally's time!*

Jimmy had misread his friendship because Jackson was no fool. Jackson Tally had his suspicions and confronted him. As Mitchell Duncan, Jimmy managed to play it off perfectly but didn't want to press his luck, so he backed off. If Jackson wanted to have the length of years God granted, he wouldn't act on his *suspicions* and keep his mouth shut.

Jimmy never considered himself a lunatic, at least not in the medical sense of the word. His definition didn't go that far. Never mind that psychiatrists in prison suspected him as more than full-blown bat-shit crazy. Jimmy thought himself simply a little off, slightly askew, or peculiar. *So what do doctors know anyway?* It wasn't his fault life had not given him a fair shake and owed him a thing or two. Jimmy felt his talents were not fully recognized. *People should be more appreciative.*

It wasn't his fault he had a unique talent for changing his personality, which could be as foul as a Louisiana swamp or shined up like a brand-new penny. That's what Ajax will do for you after becoming dirty, he often thought. Ajax is what he called *It*, that elusive foggy feeling that washed over him from time to time when he wasn't himself and became someone else. He never used the name in prison; that was his secret, the one thing they couldn't take away from him.

Giving in to *It* allowed him to use other names. Nowadays, he used his Christian name only with those he considered stupid or knew from birth, which was few and far between. Jimmy liked when he became Mitchell Duncan, casually getting over on people on a day-to-day basis. But when he did terrible things, when his switchblade was sharpest, and he felt invisible and invincible, the name Ajax was gloriously useful. Using his alias *Ajax*, he even convinced The Boss in Louisville of his usefulness, which led to his assignment to good ole Paris, Kentucky.

So when he turned up at the legendary American Legion Hall to meet Jackson Tally, smelling from a long day's work at the A&P, he was surprised to see Johnny Davies and Clarence Jefferies checking him out and acting like they owned the place. Jimmy meant no harm but should've known better than to arrive without washing up first. Apparently, stepping on Stooly's shoes was a capital offense. If it hadn't been for Jackson, things would have gone badly for Stooly. Jimmy rarely made mistakes but blew it on that bright Sunday afternoon at The Hall. Jimmy was not used to disappointments but got his feelings hurt that day.

He knew Stooly and Slim, respectively, from his prison days. He knew them right off because their reputations had preceded them. Their exploits were almost as legendary as his, but not quite. Not by a long shot. Why they bothered to make every effort to lie low in lockup seemed useless. New to the system, Stooly was a known lady's man; as sharp as a tack, he could swindle Fort Knox out of all their gold. *Now, there's a smart man.* Cool and methodical, Stooly would cut you quick and ask questions later. You never saw it coming. And slick Slim, who served long before Stooly arrived, was now Stooly's wingman? Now, there was a dude to steer clear of! Mean as a caged honey badger and suspected of the most heinous acts of cruelty. How they hooked up was anyone's guess. But that was then. This was now.

He loved the smell of blood. Always had since the days he courted Virginia Lee Morgan. *What a sweet piece of ass she was!* He should've known Virginia would desert him when he needed her most. That decision was as stupid as the man who came at him, thinking he could get stuck with his switchblade and live. He had to make her pay for turning her back on him.

Learning to cut and load meat had its advantages. He had unique skills with his blade, especially when *It* and Ajax became one. He had learned to finesse that simple tool early in life, moving swiftly and cutting deep in places that would bleed out. Jimmy played it cool. He was staying at the YMCA downtown and had even cased out Stooly and Slim's operation on Winchester Road. It was stupidity that caused Jimmy to get caught back in fifty-three. Mitchell Duncan would never get caught.

Jackson's friendship and working at the A&P gave him cover and credibility. But that friendship was over, sad to say. For the time being, all he could do was watch and wait for his chance to shake things up and get back at Virginia. Striking fear in this peaceful, sleepy town whose only claim to fame was Lylesville Street would be sweet revenge.

His penchant for changing into whomever the occasion called for presented itself again in the hot afternoon sun when he chose to be the voyeur of lovely things. As he watched the neighborhood and checked out the sweet young things at the Youth Center, Virginia was an afterthought but never far from his mind. Her image and how she made him feel would be forever burned in his memory, like the sweet babes before him. Although Linney was pretty as hell, the one they called Doreen was ripe and plump, ready for picking when the time was right.

Until then, all he could do was wait and watch Doreen. When he did, he couldn't help but touch and rub himself, breathing hard, aroused, and sweating more than the day's heat called for. *How dare she arouse me like this? How dare she turn me on like quickfire with her newly formed luscious body, firm and round in all the right places? Swinging her hips and smiling with lips that beckon. Who does she think she is anyway?* These were his thoughts during and after he was spent. *This is her fault, damn it!* He had to punish her for bringing out this weakness for young flesh, especially hers. It wasn't his fault Doreen strutted up and down the street, smiling and laughing in front of him while he hid, unnoticed and invisible, among the condemned houses across the street from the place she loved to be seen: the Youth Center.

# CHAPTER 20

*Blowing Smoke and Cigars*

A BAD FEELING had come over Slim. It was unusual for him, but there it was all the same, and he couldn't shake it. According to Stooly, it didn't take The Boss long to discover Ajax had lied about his experience. Worse, the rumor was Ajax bragged about raping a young lady in Georgetown when he was released from prison. The details were fuzzy as hell, and The Boss didn't like how it added up. In fact, nothing did. Whether it was a brag, true or not, the speculation was bad juju. Lying and raping women was not tolerated within the Organization. After that final call from The Boss, they clearly understood his directions and what was expected. Ajax had to be taken out. Now.

Stooly had instructed Slim to rearrange a few business dealings in order to accommodate the takedown. As usual, this left Slim apprehensive, but he knew better than to second-guess Stooly or doubt his hunches. The stress of the plan caused Slim to consider getting into a different line of work, especially with the flack he got from his wife nowadays. Slim wanted to live a long life when it came right down to it. He wasn't so sure about Stooly.

Now here they were at the Warehouse waiting for Ajax to show. A man they had yet to meet. Slim knew Stooly didn't like doing this kind of thing on a Saturday night. It was bad for business. But what could they do when The Boss had already sent word to be at the Warehouse that night? Trying to pin this down had taken the whole of July; now, they were into August, with September not far behind. Profits were low, and The Boss wasn't happy. Getting this Ajax business settled was paramount. And Ajax was late.

Augie had arrived unexpectedly, talking fast in his familiar high-pitched voice. "I just came by to pick up a brick or two in case this *Ajax person* runs out in the middle of selling a dime or a nickel bag, you know?"

But Slim knew better. Augie was being nosy. Stooly obliged by telling him only what he needed to know but no more. This only gave Augie more than a legitimate reason to stay, much to Slim's chagrin.

"Well, ain't this my lucky day? I can't wait to meet the man gonna be selling pot near my house," Augie said. Then he positioned himself and his round belly to stand inside the Warehouse behind Stooly, eyes almost bulging out of their sockets.

There were few lights along Winchester Road, and with the Warehouse situated well back, deep in a field with no other buildings around, it was hard to keep watch on all sides. The view at the front was clear enough, but the dimly lit surroundings made Slim more than a little nervous. To Slim's mind, the brightness inside the Warehouse, with all lights blazing and the darkness from outside, made them stand out like a sore thumb. Steely-eyed, standing by one of the dock's open bay doors, Stooly turned to address the living inside the vast, brightly lit space.

"Somebody dim the lights. It's bright as hell in here," he said.

Loudly, Slim thanked God and obliged. He nudged Augie to follow him, and they walked to the sidewalls and flipped switches to turn out a few lights, leaving the middle illuminated. When this was satisfactory, Slim had a few questions of concern for Stooly.

"Now what? This nigga ever gonna show?" Slim asked, his patience running thin.

"I hope he shows up soon. My wife's making beef stew tonight. What's taking so long?" Augie's stomach rumbled loudly. The wait was getting to him physically.

"Hold your horses," Stooly said.

"Hold your horse, slow your row, don't break too fast. My ass, man!" Slim said. "This is fucked up. We been here an hour and a half already. What we gonna do if he don't show?"

"He'll show." Stooly seemed unconcerned and calm, which had the effect of quieting Slim's rising anxiety, but only just. Something wasn't right, and Slim knew it.

On alert, they scanned the road. Finally, Stooly motioned them to move back into the shadows. Standing closer to the sidewalls was safest instead of the middle of the floor.

"You boys waiting for me?" asked an unfamiliar voice from the shadows in the back of the Warehouse.

Strolling out of the blackness in a wide-brimmed fedora and blowing smoke from a cigar came the man himself. How he had gotten by them and in through one of the back doors without them hearing the rusty hinges creak was anybody's guess. There wasn't a sound for miles around except for their own voices, which left them wondering how *he* got the drop on *them*.

"Where the fuck—" Slim said.

"Did I come from? Yeah, about that. You boys have a crack in your hidey-hole. The lights out back make it easy to see this place, but they cast shadows in the weeds behind. Anyone can drive up with their lights turned off. Slowly roll the car and park a few paces out, easy walking through the culvert to the back with unlocked doors. Not very secure as far as I can tell, sorry, Johnny." Turning to Slim, he said, "Clarence, I take it?"

"I'll be damned!" Slim exclaimed.

His surprise was *not* the ineffectiveness of their warehouse location and ease of access from the back but because he recognized the man.

"Nice to see you again, fellas," Ajax said.

"Uh-huh, Mitchell Duncan, is it?" Stooly asked. "Smelly son of a bitch, we met last month? I am impressed. You clean up real good."

"Like a brand-new penny. That's what Ajax'll do for you." Ajax smiled broadly, showing a set of dingy, brown-stained teeth in his effort to make a poor attempt at a joke.

As Ajax nodded and smiled at Stooly and Slim, they gave nothing back in return. Stooly didn't chuckle or smile, and for a split second, Slim thought Stooly might have to rethink his plan. Truth be told, he knew Stooly was more than a little impressed. Sneaky bastards like this wouldn't go down easy. Deceptions of this kind had an odd way of going sideways fast. He also knew Stooly didn't like playing cat and mouse, and as deceptions went, Ajax was a rare gem.

As Slim stepped away from the group to inspect the back door, Augie wasted no time with introductions. "I'm glad to finally meet you. I must say I didn't have a clue *who* I would be doing business with, but I'm glad to meet you all the same, yes, sir. My name's Augustus, but folks call me Augie, the bootleg." The wide-toothed grin on Augie's face showed his eagerness to meet the man. Then it was back to business. "These bricks seem good to me. I hope we can come to an agreement on how you'll conduct business."

Augie's eyebrows rose in surprise when he received a sharp dismissive reply. "Ajax to you." A dispassionate look said it all. Ajax was not impressed with Augie's introduction.

"Mitch, I mean *Ajax*, you come alone?" Slim asked after inspecting how Ajax had gotten in unnoticed and unimpeded.

"Why, yes, I did, as a matter of fact," Ajax said. "Let's make this quick, shall we, gentlemen? Can't allow the masses to wait any longer for this fine sampling here. It's been what, a month now?"

Ajax moved his hands over the pallets of marijuana, then picked up a hard-packed brick of weed to sample. As he began to smell the contents, Stooly took it from his hand and slowly placed it back with the rest.

"Let's not," Stooly said. "This is a surprise, sure 'nough, but let's hold off for a few minutes longer. You don't mind if we have a chat, do you?"

"Not at all," Ajax said, unfazed.

Stooly had managed to obtain a few simple wooden chairs with round seats for them to use. As Slim pulled a chair around to sit down, he noticed Ajax shift the weight of his right leg as he too sat down. Slim straddled his seat, then placed his arms on top of the rounded spindles that ran down the back of the chair. Augie sat close by while Stooly stood close to Ajax. Slim listened as Stooly began to speak in that calm, soft, strong voice of his. Then he watched as Stooly slowly walked around the seated Ajax, who continued to puff on his cigar.

"It seems we have a misunderstanding, Ajax," Stooly said.

"Is that so?" Ajax asked, mildly curious.

"Yeah. Your credentials don't quite hold up to snuff."

"You contact Louisville?"

"I did just that, my man, and come to find out, *you're* not who we thought you were," Stooly whispered the last in Ajax's ear. "We don't like being lied to. Makes us nervous. Twitchy."

"I don't know what you're talking about—"

"Oh, but I think you do. Running shine? You lied to The Boss. He don't like that," Stooly whispered again. "And I just told you where I stand. I don't need to spell it out, but I think you understand what needs to happen." Stooly completed his walk around Ajax and stood directly in front of him, a mere inches away from Ajax's groin.

Augie got up from his seat. "Now look, fellas, I'm here to pick up a few bricks of reefer. I'm not here for any trouble."

"Sit down!" Slim said, which Augie promptly did with a loud and heavy thump.

Stooly took two steps back from Ajax and continued, "A few days ago, I see a man who breezes into my town with *secrets*. You know me. I don't know you. That's insulting. In turn, we insult *you* for not being a gentleman and, above all things, smelling like shit warmed over. And the next thing *I* know, you're our new partner? Now, I can't afford mysteries in my line of work. I don't like it. And I don't like you."

"I meant no harm—"

"Is that right? I see it differently." Stooly was now leaning close to Ajax.

Ajax stared back without flinching, took a draw from his cigar, and blew smoke in Stooly's face. Slim knew Stooly didn't care for the man; now, it was obvious the feeling was mutual. This put Slim on high alert, and he was ready.

"Now, here I thought I was an asset to your operation," Ajax said. "I even came to present myself as such, but unfortunately, something's gone terribly wrong." Then Ajax flicked the ash from his cigar. "To hell with you fuckers."

The next happened so fast; Slim couldn't make sense of what he saw, if he saw it at all. Ajax made a sudden move to his right pant leg, but it took Stooly a split second to have Ajax on his back with a switchblade to his chin. Slim stood up, pulling his .22 from his left shoulder holster, aiming it at Ajax as Augie ran to the Warehouse's front door, screaming like a girl.

"You try to bring that blade out on me, man, it'll be the last thing you do! You think you slick? *Huh?* Lying to The Boss! Think you can come in here and pull a fast one over on *me*? In *my town*? I don't think so! Orders from Louisville have changed, my man. Your services are no longer needed. The next time you rape someone will be the last time you rape someone."

Then coldly and methodically, while holding the knife to Ajax's throat with one hand, Stooly reached for the still-lit cigar with his other—it had fallen to the floor in the scuffle—and put it out on Ajax's face. Ajax moaned, reaching up to his face as Stooly got up to step over him.

"This never happened," Stooly said. "That's a permanent souvenir as a reminder I climbed all over your monkey ass, *and* it's a mild warning from The Boss not to ever let him see your fucking face again. I don't want to see it either." Stooly slicked back his hair, shot his shirt cuffs, brushed down his slacks, and dusted off his shoes while he told Slim to make sure Ajax saw his way home and out of his sight.

Slim reached down, yanked Ajax off the floor, and more than helped him to the front of the Warehouse door. He watched as Ajax, holding his face, staggered down the steps on the side of the building to his car. Following Ajax a short way, Slim got off a few shots in the air to hasten him along, but oddly enough, that slowed him down. When Ajax got to his car, avoiding the dry culvert, Slim could swear Ajax sat inside the shadows of his car, staring back at him for an unnerving amount of time. Slowly Ajax backed his car out to the main road, then drove silently into the night with dead headlights.

"That's a creepy motherfucker! You right about the snake biting before he rattles, though. How'd you know he had a blade, man?" Slim asked.

"I watch. I observe. Saw the shift in his stance when he sat down. I didn't want to take any chances. Word is that man has a nasty rap, so I brought my blade just in case. I wouldn't have thought in a million years that that stinky bastard at The Hall was this *Ajax*. Now we know. Time to tell The Boss."

"I thought we were gonna take him out. Why didn't you let me hit him with a couple of rounds?"

"He's a coward. The easiest thing was to scare him off. Less messy that way."

"I don't think you're right about that. I mean, something *strange* about that dude. Walking him just now to his car, I swear that creep sat there, watching me watching him. I think he's more dangerous than you think. *I* think he even liked the burn you gave him. I'm dubiously about his intent, you dig?"

The daggers Stooly threw at Slim with his eyes told Slim he'd gotten Stooly's attention. Slim gave himself away by using poor English again and cursed himself. He couldn't help it. Ajax had spooked him more than he wanted to admit. Maybe in a microscopic way, they had missed something and underestimated Ajax.

# CHAPTER 21

## *The Visitors*

D OREEN NEVER RETURNED any of my calls since my dance with Barry. I tried to reach her for a talk, but I guess she didn't want to hear anything I had to say. In the meantime, it was easy to put my issue with Doreen aside because Mom had unfinished business with the sisters and Miss Virginia.

Mom kept her promise and visited the Sweets when Miss Virginia was there. She brought her delicious pecan pie and discussed what I told her. The sisters said it was unfortunate I had to see Miss Dottie's occasional breakdown but were grateful I was there to help. They also reassured Mom they had nothing to do with voodoo or any of that superstitious nonsense; they were Catholic Christians and loved the Lord. For Miss Virginia's part, her news of moving to Chicago was for information only. However, Mom disapproved of me visiting Miss Virginia because she lived farther away. Miss Virginia understood, but I think she was more disappointed than she let on.

So it was settled. I was finally allowed to see the Sweet sisters again. The rest of August was spent finishing chores, dancing at the Youth Center, afternoon teas, and early evening readings. Miss Katherine and Miss Virginia taught me so much about manners and table etiquette, proper ladylike behavior such as sitting and standing like a lady, holding my head high with shoulders back when walking, and not speaking too loudly. Miss

Virginia opened a whole new world for me in reading about old-world manners and customs. The Sweets' book cabinet was a treasure chest of wonderful books. Although a little advanced for me, it held works by authors such as Jane Austen, the Bronte sisters, and Louisa May Alcott. Last year, I had already read *Little Women* as a reading assignment, but I couldn't wait to learn even more.

The most important lesson was understanding that everyone deserved acceptance, no matter how different they might appear or the color of their skin. I was no different from anyone else. I just had to love myself as much or more than anyone else ever could. But the more I tried, the more something would happen to make me believe differently. Accepting myself was a constant battle. I still dealt with a few zits and humidity, which fought my attempts to tame the frizz on my head. Abandoning the effort to smooth my hair with water and a brush, I was left once again to braid it in the usual two pigtails and accept the fate of the fallen.

Miss Virginia and I occasionally played silly games when she visited the Sweets. We made funny faces in the mirror, played tag in the backyard, or turned the water hoses on each other, getting soaking wet. It was great seeing her like this instead of the English teacher at school. Sometimes we spent all day in the small flower garden in the Sweets' backyard. The sisters loved spending time in the garden under the shade of an umbrella tree. I liked digging in the dirt, pulling weeds, watering the begonias and impatiens, and preparing the beds for irises, which bloomed along the side of their house in the spring. Petunias were already in full bloom and placed in window boxes under their front porch windows. Even though the sisters stayed away from growing vegetables, tending their garden helped me appreciate my grandpa's love of gardening. I was even allowed to take zinnia cuttings home, which I put in two pots and placed on our front porch.

My visits to the Sweets became so frequent that I never bothered to knock. Miss Katherine often had something baking in her air-cooled kitchen. Gone was the idea that the sisters baked cookies to lure us in, only to eat us later. The house always smelled of cinnamon rolls or cookies. Walnut brownies were my favorite. I even looked forward to running errands or doing small chores. However, they still insisted on walking around town, which was good for Miss Dottie's health, much like for Grandma. She liked the outside air, which calmed her, making her feel less dependent than she did otherwise.

I tried to get Angela and Carolyn to meet the sisters. They *said* they were too busy to bother with visits of any kind, but I knew better. They would come around before long. One day, after finishing *To Kill a Mockingbird*, I ran up the stairs of the Sweet house to discuss the book with Miss Katherine. I was excited, but then I heard familiar voices inside. I thought Angela or Carolyn had finally come to visit, so I quickly opened the screen door to see Doreen and Miss Edna sitting inside.

"My, but we seem to have a full house today," Miss Katherine said.

I didn't know what to say. I just stood near the screen door, listening to the awkward silence while they looked down into their laps.

At last Miss Edna spoke.

"I was just saying if it wasn't for Doreen here, I might not have decided to be neighborly and pay a visit to you sweet ladies. With so much going on lately, I think it's awful we waited so long to meet all our neighbors."

Miss Katherine seemed amused. Miss Dottie was clearly agitated, but it seemed to calm her with me standing close by.

"All summer, I've wanted to visit, so this morning I decided to do just that." Doreen nodded. Then, looking directly at me, she continued, "I've always been curious about the ladies who live in this house. There's so much gossip going around about voodoo curses and witchery that I figured I'd come to find out for myself. After all, it's only Christian to look after the poor and two old ladies when I have nothing better to do."

*How rude! Why is she talking like that, all proper and stuff?* Doreen didn't fool me for one minute. I glanced over at Miss Katherine and, by her demeanor, immediately understood how she felt. She had crossed her arms across her chest, ready to put things right.

"Now I find that interesting," Miss Katherine said. "We've lived in this house for about twenty years. We've never met the neighbors except for that young lady standing over there and her mother. And I must say Lindsey's been a revelation and speaks very highly of you, Doreen dear. Yes, a kind and dear friend who should be appreciated more."

"Is that so?" Miss Edna asked. "I know she comes over often. I can see her every move, and I—"

"Please tell me again why you *both* decided to pay us this visit? Like I said, in all my years, you've never bothered to come around, so say again, Edna, if you please?"

"I-I-I just said it was neighborly and—" Miss Edna said.

"Yes, that's right, I remember now. Please forgive an *old* lady," Miss Katherine said. "The neighborly thing for you, if I'm not mistaken, is snooping? I appreciate your visit but try being *neighborly* when you're sincere. Bullying unsuspecting young ladies and then coming over here on the pretense of being neighborly should be beneath you. I've heard about the hard time you've been giving Lindsey about visiting me, Edna. Oh, don't worry, we won't use voodoo curses or boil you in oil if that's what you're thinking goes on here. At least not on your first time over."

"Well, I *never*—" Miss Edna raised her shoulders.

"And I *am* done!" Miss Katherine said. Turning her attention to Doreen. "And you, young lady, what's your excuse?" Doreen's eyes opened wide in shock. "It can't be you just happened to visit Edna today and suddenly decided to pay us a visit. I've had experience with insincere young ladies before, but you're something else altogether. For a full ten minutes, you've sat in that chair and talked about nothing but yourself. You never bothered to inquire about us, the 'two old ladies' you so wanted to grace with your presence and get to know better, especially when you had 'nothing better to do.' Is that how you put it?

"Now, it's not my nature to be rude, but I must state the obvious. You've been extremely rude to my sister and me. You could learn a thing or two from Lindsey. There's not an insincere bone in her body."

"I wasn't trying to be rude, ma'am." Doreen rose from her seat. "I was just trying—"

"Just you remember," Miss Edna interrupted. "I see everything, and I don't appreciate being talked to this way, *old* lady. They say you're a witch and practice all kinds of spells up here in this house. Well, I wanted to see if it was true, and I also wanted to see—"

"*You've* seen enough and said enough, by which I've *had* enough," Miss Katherine said sternly. "I don't need to explain anything to *anyone*. I feel sorry for you, Edna Allen. I really do. I don't think you mean to be hateful. Maybe something's lacking in your life. Something no one can give you. I know I sure can't."

I couldn't believe my ears. The air in the room changed to a coolness, which oddly caused sweat to rise on Doreen's and Miss Edna's foreheads.

Speaking to Doreen, Miss Katherine said, "That goes for you too, young lady. I am not obliged to have pretenders in my house any longer than necessary, so will you both kindly do me the neighborly favor of leaving my house? Please!"

With Miss Dottie's cane in her hand, Miss Katherine slammed its tip on the floor with such force that I swear the pictures on the walls shook. This startled all of us and made her message unmistakably clear. I'd never seen her so angry.

As they were leaving, Miss Dottie made that grunt of hers. She looked directly at Doreen and Miss Edna, who looked scared to death, eyes wide and clutching each other. I tried to say something comical to ease the tension.

"Be careful, or she'll eat you." Unfortunately, my attempt at humor was lost because no sooner had I said this than Miss Dottie rose from her rocker and pointed a finger directly at Doreen.

"Don't go in them woods, or you'll die. Stay away, or you'll never see another day, no you won't," Miss Dottie said.

Until then, Doreen's composure was intact, but she lost it with Miss Dottie's words. She turned a particular shade of green, clearly visible beneath her light brown complexion.

"I'm gonna tell Momma!" Doreen shouted. She bolted out the front door with Miss Edna close behind while Miss Katherine disappeared to the back of the house.

I eased Miss Dottie back into her rocker, and as usual, she began rocking while looking out the front window. If I didn't know any better, I'd say she was watching Doreen and Miss Edna hurry away, but I couldn't be sure. Leaving her, I found Miss Katherine in her bedroom, sitting on the edge of her bed with her hand on her chest.

"When you've lived long enough and seen as much as I have, you begin to develop a sense about people," she said. "I can smell a rat a mile away. I apologize for letting my temper get the better of me, darlin'. It's good for my heart to beat so in confrontation but bad for my blood pressure." She chuckled. "I'm feeling better now."

I offered to make tea to calm her nerves, which she accepted. By now, I knew what to do with the ever-warm silver teapot. While I prepared the service, I thought of Doreen and what would cause her to do such a thing. Doreen told me she'd talk with Miss Edna, but she went against me instead. Was it because I danced with Barry? If so, that would explain why she wouldn't return any of my calls. *What an underhanded trick.* And how did she manage to fool Miss Edna with her phony sweetness? The thought made my stomach turn to think she could sink so low.

Underneath it all, I couldn't shake the premonition Miss Dottie made to Doreen. Was it me, or were her warnings growing more severe? Miss Dottie seemed harmless most of the time, which was when I liked her best. However, I didn't like it when she made those weird noises and said strange things. *Maybe I should fear her instead.*

Before I left for the evening, Miss Dottie motioned me over and patted my hand. I don't know what it meant. Maybe to reassure or thank me? But whatever it was, I knew for certain Miss Dottie thought that danger was getting ever closer and closer.

# CHAPTER 22

## *Telling Momma*

EDITH MUNRO'S YOUNGEST daughter wasted no time telling her mother what had occurred at the Sweets. Edith was horrified to hear Doreen would go so far as to spy on Linney, and with Edna Allen of all people. Sitting in Doreen's pink-and-plum-colored bedroom, Edith listened as Doreen explained how she tried to talk to Edna, hoping she would back off Linney. After hearing so much of this explanation, her mother didn't buy it.

"What I don't understand is why you felt you, and *only you*, could convince that lady to leave Linney alone. It makes no sense. If I didn't know any better, I'd swear you wanted to get back at Linney for some reason. Am I right?"

"No'am! I really wanted to help."

Doreen put on the largest set of puppy dog eyes she could manage. Seeing this, Edith's anger eased up. Edith knew she had never been as strict with Doreen as she had her older children. She felt Doreen's friendship with Lindsey would round her out a little, causing them to balance each other as they grew up together. As the years passed, she accepted that Doreen had a stubborn nature, thinking far too much of herself than she should, which made a bond with Linney nearly impossible.

Edith blamed herself for spoiling Doreen but had felt her daughter would outgrow her selfishness in time. But Edith had allowed Doreen to run roughshod over Lindsey for far too long. Now she felt it was too late to do anything about it. She had heard of Doreen's shenanigans, but she'd let the incidents go as girlhood hijinks. This newest escapade was something she could not ignore.

"All right. If your intentions were good, why didn't you say what you had to say to Edna and then come home? Instead, you drag Edna along with you to visit the Sweets? In all your fourteen years, if you thought you could control the intentions of grown folks… well, I don't know what else to say. I don't understand you, Doreen. I really don't."

"But Momma, you should've seen how Miss Edna went on and on about those ladies! *She* convinced *me* they were evil and probably witches, casting spells on people—"

"Doreen Elizabeth Munro! I can't *believe* what I'm hearing—"

"Momma, it's true! She had me believing—"

"I'm *sure* she said those crazy things. What I don't get is why you *believed* them. And this was the reason you took—no—the *opportunity* you took to visit those ladies? *Witches,* for God's sake. And you want to use that as an excuse—"

"It was scary, Momma. If you'd just let me tell you what happened—"

"I don't want to hear any more! I can see it now. You went over there, parading around as a sweet young lady, which you *can* be, only to have them boot you out of their house. The both of you! All you've done is made matters worse. You need to learn to behave better, Doreen, or life will be very hard for you, and what's more, you won't be able to overcome any slight disappointments. Not by far."

"They told me I would die! The crazy one told me to stay out of the woods, or I would die!" Doreen cried.

Alarmed, Edith Munro took a breath and looked hard at her youngest daughter. Doreen began to cry into her pillow with uncontrollable sobs.

Edith pulled her into her arms. "Oh there, there now, hush. Who told you this, Doreen? Who made you feel that was a possibility?"

"The crazy one. And Linney… she laughed at us. She laughed at the curse, Momma. You just don't know… Linney can be so mean!" Doreen's sobs were long and loud.

Caught off guard, Edith never considered that Doreen was exaggerating more than just a little bit and her sobs were false. *This is getting out of hand,* she thought. She had to speak to Janie soon.

⟞⬥⬥⬥⟝

Janie Mae Hollis thought and worried about a lot of things. One worry she didn't have was that of her daughter. Linney was growing up, and Janie was so proud of the person her girl was turning out to be. In fact, she liked her a lot, which was more than most parents could say about their children. Janie knew her daughter loved her but hoped Linney liked her at least a little bit.

She often heard Linney tiptoe past her bedroom, trying not to disturb her while she studied. When Janie finished a grueling night of study long after Linney had gone to bed, she usually looked in on her daughter. Often, Linney kicked her bed covers off as she slept and snored like the dickens. Janie typically pulled the discarded cover around Linney and watched as she snuggled into it without waking.

She was a beautiful child. Janie was thankful Linney was unaware of this fact. Too many young girls grow up fast and loose nowadays, particularly those blessed with good looks. Linney had started to grow out of that coltish phase and was tall for her age, agile even, which was apparent when she'd played badminton last July. Unlike Doreen, who was shorter and curvier than Linney could ever hope to be, Linney looked to be right for her age. While sleeping, the wise look on her face made her seem older than she was, but she'd always be her little girl. Her shè Lin.

Janie picked clothes off the floor during these late-night vigils and hung them. She took special care to place Linney's beloved Keds under her bed. She knew Linney wanted to wear the latest fashions, but Janie couldn't afford those things. For now, Linney needed to take better care of what she had. Janie had a hunch that Linney innately understood their financial situation and supposed this was why she never complained or asked for much.

It was hard for Janie to watch the pain wash over Linney when faced with the harshness of life. It was also hard not to intervene when hurtful words were said or when her daughter struggled to speak up for herself. Janie hoped her decision to remain silent helped Linney grow from within. Sometimes the stones of maturing were hard to ward off when aimed directly at your child. This was the heartbreak of raising a sensitive and independent girl like Linney. However, her distance went only so far. Hell would have to freeze over before Janie allowed any irreparable harm to come to her girl.

*Was it just a few years ago Linney came into this world?* Holding the tiny life in her arms while her husband stood at her side, beaming with pride, Janie had been full of hope for a bright future, and life seemed perfect. Unfortunately, her mother-in-law, Marielle Laurant Hollis, had other ideas and wasn't thrilled to share her son with anyone.

Marielle never considered herself a Negro; she was Creole, which is how most Creoles thought of themselves, or so Janie was told. To Janie's mind, this might have been the reason for Marielle's disdain for her. However, this complication in family dynamics paled compared to Janie's own family's objection. Ernest Munro was none too happy and wished like hell his favorite daughter had not met Laurant Hollis, the half-caste Frenchman most called Larry. Janie knew she had let her parents down by getting married so soon out of high school, but what other choice did she have? She and Larry were in love, and nothing could stop their passion for each other. Lindsey was the result, which should have been the end of the disapproval, but it wasn't.

After Larry joined the Air Force, they moved to Chicago, where he was stationed at Chanute AFB. Living with Marielle in Chicago was no picnic. Janie had to immediately learn the Louisiana Creole French language to understand the words leveled at her from time to time. Tempers flared, and arguments became more frequent. Even though Larry came home on leave, he never stayed long, leaving her alone with a recalcitrant mother-in-law.

He would be gone again for months overseas, which sometimes turned into years. Transfers were frequent, and traveling from base to base was not for Janie. Military life was that way, and it became all too much with Marielle in tow. One day, her mother-in-law suggested she take a break from married life and move back to Paris. Marielle reasoned the separation would do them good and give Janie a chance to reconnect with her family. Of course the split would be on a trial basis, and in time, they might rediscover a stronger love for each other, absence making the heart grow fonder and all. Janie took that advice, but to her way of thinking, it was out of sight, out of mind because that was several years ago and she still waited for her husband to come home.

To say Janie missed her husband was an understatement. Many nights she doubted the wisdom of her actions and how hasty she'd been in taking Marielle's advice. She often thought about her mother-in-law's role in their separation but tried not to dwell on her choice. Instead, she threw herself into her work, studies, and raising her daughter. She knew in her heart that she could make a go of it in Paris and come out the other side better for her decision.

Now Linney was entering a new phase of life. Everyone seemed to have stories of how teenagers could be a challenge to raise, but Janie felt blessed. For the time being, Linney didn't give her any trouble. Studious, conscientious, and sensitive, Linney's timid ways always held her in good stead. The thought of giving her something to do that summer by visiting the Sweets was the best idea Janie had come up with. But lately, it came with a worry that Janie hoped would come to nothing. Janie found herself bolstering Linney's confidence more than usual. She had raised an independent child, sure enough, but felt Linney was suffering alone. Yet it wasn't until Linney bared her soul over her feelings about Doreen that Janie understood the gravity of Linney's pain—a pain Janie knew all too well from her experience dealing with Sandra Beaumont.

Janie and Sandy had grown up together, and both were studying to become nurses. Surprisingly, Janie discovered she was in a competitive race with Sandra, who worked in the same doctor's office. Such as the time when Janie left her study papers at the office. When she went back to retrieve them, they were gone. According to Sandy, she hadn't seen them, only to have them show up on Sandy's desk a few days later when Janie went in early to the office. Sandy denied knowing anything about it but managed to ace the exam despite having a modest understanding of the subject matter. After a few days of study, Janie managed to come in under the wire of passing, no thanks to Sandy's underhandedness. Sandy's sniping and petty jealousy were hard to ignore. Janie feared Linney and Doreen were headed down the same path and felt powerless to do anything about it.

Janie's level of worry rose steadily after Linney's fainting spell. In her heart of hearts, she knew that Linney was holding back, not telling her everything. Something else was troubling Linney more than her insecurity with Doreen. Whatever it was, she hoped Linney would share and soon.

# CHAPTER 23

## *Dirty Laundry*

B Y THE TIME Doreen was spilling her guts to her mother, Edna Allen was busy thinking of another way to satisfy her curiosity about recent events. Edna had to finagle her way to find out what was going on in and around the neighborhood. Strange things were occurring, and she didn't like the thoughts beginning to stir her mind.

It annoyed Edna that she couldn't get Linney to say anything about her visits across the street. *What a mess that whole thing turned out to be*, she thought. Racing over to visit the Sweets with young Doreen a few days earlier hadn't worked out well, either. In fact, the whole visit left her more spooked than anything. And *what* was going on a few weeks back when she saw a White man leaving the Tallys' house? She just knew all these strange events had to do with little miss Lindsey Hollis. But, no one was talking, especially about this wicked stranger in town, Tally's new "friend." Try as she might, the proverbial doors of gossip were shut tight against her. With few choices left, she decided to try catching Jess Tally unaware. Maybe she could get information out of Jess. Not knowing was driving her crazy.

Most neighbors hung wash on the same day, and living next door to Jess gave Edna an idea. Edna decided to lay her trap on that early Friday morning, two days after visiting the Sweets. After watching and waiting, she got her chance for an ambush.

As Jess came out of her back door with a load of laundry, Edna hurried out with hers, making her first calculated move.

"Good morning Jess! What a beautiful day."

"It's a bright morning, all right," Jess answered as she placed her basket of wet laundry on the ground.

"I'll say. Haven't seen you out lately. Sure has been a *busy* summer, hasn't it? Been a hot one too. Hotter than usual."

Jess looked up at the sky and reached for clothes to hang on the line. Just then, Jackson Tally walked out and gave his wife a kiss goodbye before heading off to work. He acknowledged Edna's presence with a casual, "Morning."

Edna flushed. Her dreams of him sweeping her off her feet, professing his undying love, and forsaking his wife had not diminished. Edna returned his greeting more breathlessly and seductively than she should have. She couldn't help herself.

However, Jess missed nothing. Shielding her eyes from the sun with her hand, she looked over at Edna who watched Tally walk away. Edna should've known Jess wouldn't let this kind of behavior go without some kind of dressing down.

"You feeling all right, Edna? 'Cause if not, I know a place be happy to help scratch that itch. It's on the corner of Lylesville and Eighth Avenue. You know the place, don't you? Where you can make a few dollars?"

"What you talking about? Why you say something like that to me?"

"Like you don't know," Jess said. This was not a question.

"Now look here, Jess Tally. I ain't done or said nothing that'd make you speak to me that way! In fact, you been high-and-mighty with me all summer. What makes you think I want *your* husband anyway?"

"Did I say you wanted him? All I did was recommend a place that'd help ease that itch down below, but instead of thanking me, you assume I think you want my man. I think you just told on yourself," Jess said.

She fumbled, trying to find words, but then shut up before making a *complete* fool of herself.

"What's the matter? Cat got your tongue?" Jess asked.

"You just trying to get under my skin. What'd I ever do to you?" Edna asked.

"Now, I ain't about to mince words here today," Jess said. "You been spoiling for a fight all summer, mostly because you can't figure out what's going on with the Sweets and Janie Mae's daughter. It's just driving you crazy, ain't it? Why you keep helping yourself to other people's business? Now you out here, and I bet the *only* reason is to try to get information out of me. Well, you ain't gonna!"

Edna was speechless as Jess continued, "And while I'm at it, if you *think* I'm gonna let you get away with gawking at my husband, you got another think coming. I know you the one behind rumors of Jackson cheating on me. Deny it all you want, but ain't nobody around here as *tacky* as you. If I wasn't a God-fearing woman, I'd lose my religion right here and now. Look at him like that again when I'm around, and I'll slap you blind!"

"Hold your horses now!" Edna said after finding her voice. "You know that ain't true. I'm out here like anybody else, minding my own business, trying to get my laundry dry. We just happen to be out here at the same time. Your husband's good-looking, sure enough, er'body know that! You got me all wrong."

"Oh, come *on* now! I can see right through you, Edna, and that's what you can't stand. And by the way, who are you to go around hassling Linney about her business with the Sweets? Then, when she won't tell, go running over there with Janie's sister, Doreen, to find out for yourself? I never heard of such a thing! You ought to be ashamed taking advantage of young people. I thought I'd lived long enough to see and hear everything, but that took the cake. You making things worse. You got to know that."

"So that's it? Well, it ain't my place to stand back and let bad things happen to people around here. Not if I can help it. There's something fishy going on, and I think that half-White girl, *little Miss Linney*, knows what it is. Doreen thinks so too—"

"Doreen don't know nothing," Jess said. "She's as spoiled as the day is long, probably looking for trouble, and you fell for it. All you do is snoop and gossip. That's not helping—"

"You watch your tongue now. All I want to do is make sure everybody's safe, and keeping an eye out is all I *can* do—"

"Then do *better*! I don't know what you call yourself doing, but that ain't it. Nobody likes gossipy busy-bodies, Edna. You lucky people don't spy on you. See what you been hiding. Givin' you back some of your own medicine would serve you right. Try being a help instead of looking like a *ridiculous* old woman."

Jess's words stung. This day was not turning out at all as Edna had planned. Edna never thought of how ridiculous her meddling might look to her neighbors. She always told herself that snooping allowed her to stay on top of unforeseen calamities. Even though Jess had tried to put her in her place, she also brought out Edna's dogged need to know if anyone— even Lindsey Hollis—was in danger. While Edna was lost in thought, Jess came close and pointed her finger in Edna's face.

"*And stop bullying, Lindsey Anne!* I mean it. She ain't done *nothing* to you. Why you hate her so bad? Because she looks different, you think it's okay to pick on her? It's not her fault, and you should know better. I'm glad she knocked you on your ass, not that I'm saying she should, but you had it coming. Stay away from her, Edna. You try to harass that girl one more time, and I'll hurt you sure 'nough."

"Is that a threat?" Edna asked.

"Does it *look* like I'm making threats?"

Jess's eyes had turned a color that wasn't of this earth. Then Jess picked up her laundry basket and walked back toward her house. Yet before Jess got to her back door, Edna called after her.

"Did they cast a spell on that Linney girl?" Edna said, surprised by the level of concern in her voice. "Was that her in your house when that White man was there? I know something about mean spirits, you know!"

"Well, *bless* your heart," Jess said. Her words trailed off as she slowly turned back to face Edna. Then she quickly closed the distance and returned to where Edna stood by the clothesline. "You just can't give up the ghost, can you? Who cast *what?*"

"I hear things about them sisters, scary things that sound evil," Edna said hurriedly. "Nobody knows what *really* goes on in that house. When I was there, they said things that curled my toes—"

"Well, curl *my* toes 'cause you're *scaring* me. What'd you hear?" Jess and Edna stood nose to nose, so close that Jess could smell Edna's breath.

Edna harrumphed. "Now it's *you* wanting information from me?" Backing up to put some distance between herself and Jess, she clutched at her chest. "I left as fast as I could, Lord have mercy! Was that Linney girl *cursed* by them women?" Her insistent questions caused Jess to lose her patience.

"*Don't* try me, Edna. I mean it," Jess said. "I don't know nothing about no curse, and since when do you care so much about Linney? Tell me what you know. *Now, woman!*"

"Was she in your house?" Edna demanded.

"What if she was? What's it to you? Why you so desperate for information anyhow? Tell me what you *saw* and *heard* or so help me—" Jess was about to raise her hand as if to strike when Edna interrupted.

"She told that Doreen girl not to go into the woods or she'd die!" Edna blurted.

"Say *what?*" The shocked look on Jess's face was priceless.

"Dottie Sweet, the 'flicted one!" Edna said. "She told Doreen not to go into those woods over there or she'd die. I heard her say that. She put a spell on Doreen. I just know it! When that White man came out of your house a while back, I knew for sure something must've happened to Linney. And since Linney's over there all the time, I'm afraid they might've done the same to her. Now. That's putting two and two together. So *is* she okay?"

"You crazy as a bat, Edna, much less able to add—"

*"I'm no crazier than what I heard and seen already!"* Edna yelled, standing her ground. "I know I said and did some stuff I shouldn't, but what's done is done! There's a strange man been lurking around too. Creeping around Janie's house, especially that day Lindsey came from the store after talking to you! Look, girl, I got to know what's *going on*, I just *got* to."

Squinting at Edna, Jess said quietly, "Linney's fine. But tell me, how does Dorothy Sweet say something like that? Last I heard, she don't speak, so how the *hell* could she possibly say something like that?"

"Well, she did. Sure as I'm standing here, and God's my witness. She got up from that rocking chair of hers and pointed her finger at Doreen, saying what she did, I'm telling you. She put a curse on that child and probably on Linney too, if I had my guess," Edna said.

"And this person you've seen around. When was that exactly?"

"I can't rightly say. All I know is he's been around and a friend of Jackson's."

Edna didn't get an answer; instead, Jess's tone changed. "If what you say is true, you got to keep it between us unless you want everyone to think you're crazier than they think you are. Give me a minute to figure this out before the whole town knows. You'll find out what's been going on in due time." Then Jess turned to leave.

Edna grabbed her arm. "That's not good enough. I want to know now—"

"You can't know now," Jess said through clenched teeth as she wrenched her arm from Edna's grasp. "I'm sure you know more than most about what goes on around here, but what you're thinking ain't it. The most you can do is keep watch, especially that tangle of trees across the street, by using those binoculars of yours. I'll do the rest."

"Is that the last word?" Edna asked.

"You've got to trust me on this, Edna. Don't make it worse by pressing," Jess said. "We've aired some dirty laundry today, and this news changes things. If you really want to help, let me know if you see anything or anyone doing something strange around here."

This satisfied Edna enough to part ways in a Christian manner, leaving her lost in thought.

⬥⬥⬥

After getting chewed out by Jess Tally, Edna Allen sat at her kitchen table and cried like never before. The tears fell silently at first, then in earnest. She wasn't sure if the outburst was from pent-up emotions due to frustration, embarrassment, or the fact that someone, a most unlikely someone, had asked her to be part of something important. Edna had prided herself on not letting words get to her, but the truth hurt. Jess had forced Edna to face a reality she had denied for so long. She wanted to be needed, and snooping made her feel less lonely. Edna never thought much about being disliked. Until now, she never considered how her actions might look to others. Now she had been given a job where her talent for being nosy could be of benefit. She vowed to live up to the trust Jess had given her. A trust she did not deserve but was willing to prove even more because of it being given.

This turn of events surprised Edna. Her admission of caring for Linney was the most surprising of all. She supposed it started to change after she visited the Sweets with Doreen. Edna felt ashamed, not just over her treatment of Linney but her contemptuous behavior toward her neighbors. *How could I've been such a misguided fool?* Jess was right. She had to do better, and changing her view about Linney was the first step. Wiping tears from her face with the back of her hands, she thought being a better neighbor could be a step in the right direction, and she prayed this would redeem her in the sight of God, if not her neighbors.

What Edna shared with Jess was not an exaggeration but the truth, and it scared her more than she wanted to admit. The day Dorothy Sweet stood up to speak, Edna knew that whatever evil there was, it surrounded the Munro girls.

Until that morning, Jess had considered Edna a moron. A nosy, petty, troublemaking busybody of a woman too trifling to concern herself with. Listening to the clock tick on her living room wall, Jess debated whether Edna was making up stories to get information or telling the truth. Jess was not easily fooled; street smarts told her not to trust Edna to keep her mouth shut.

It would be a cold day in hell before Jess apologized to Edna for anything, especially after the stunt she tried to pull to separate her from her husband. As much as she disliked the woman, Jess tried to put those feelings aside for the time being. Besides, the fact that Edna had made something of herself was an inspiration of sorts. What did anyone know of Edna, really? Everyone had a few skeletons in their closets; indeed, Edna had hers.

But there was something else: Edna's concern about Linney. Jess weighed Edna's words carefully and considered if Linney was told a premonition, not a curse. Could that be the reason for Linney's behavior with Dr. Roberts a few weeks ago? She could tell something was off. There were too many coincidences and drama pointing in one direction, the Munro girls. To Jess, it was long past time to expose what was being hidden. It was time to beat the bushes and drive out the snakes. And the devil be damned.

Jess didn't know why Edna's stripes had changed overnight. But what she did know was that Janie Mae had to be told, and soon.

# CHAPTER 24
## *No Time for Lies*

W HEN GRANDMA EDITH called through the house with her usual "Yoo-hoo, hello the house" greeting, I was in the middle of learning how to cut a whole chicken into parts. I had cut into the breast to expose the wishbone and squealed in amazement at how easy it was to extract.

I was eager to show Grandma what I had done, but the look on her face told me it would be unwise, which caused my mother to ask what was wrong. Grandma didn't answer. Instead, she asked if we could join her in the living room to talk that midafternoon. We quickly cleaned our hands, looked at each other with shrugs, and went to the front room.

"I had to think long and hard about coming to speak to you, Lindsey," Grandma said.

"Me?" I asked.

"Janie, do you know what's going on in that house over there?" Grandma asked with a nod in the direction of the Sweet house.

"What's this about, Mother?" Mom asked.

"Are you aware of Doreen and Edna Allen's visit and what Dorothy Sweet said to Doreen? I've never seen Doreen so afraid, all because of what you've allowed Lindsey to do. Visiting half-crazed women! I had no idea the stories about them were true. This has gone *way* too far, Janie."

Our mouths hung open. We had no idea how to respond. I had forgotten Doreen's threat to tell Grandma, and I should've known she wasn't bluffing and would blab.

"Mother, I don't know what you're talking about. Linney, do you know what your grandmother's talking about?"

"It's not what you think, Grandma. Doreen and Miss Edna were already there when I came over. Miss Katherine saw their visit for what it was, so she asked them to leave."

"Did Dottie Sweet put a curse on Doreen?" Grandma asked.

I took a deep breath, knowing I had to answer. But what could I say to save the sisters' reputations and keep their trust? How do you tell the truth without telling the *whole* truth? I had to think fast.

"I-I-I wouldn't call it a… curse," I said as I tried to dodge the question, but it didn't work.

"What would you call it, young lady?" Grandma asked.

"Will someone *please* tell me what's going on?" Mom asked.

"I'm trying to get at the truth, Janie. This is no time for lies."

Then Grandma told us what Doreen had said about her visit to the Sweets. She told us how disappointed she was in Doreen and blamed herself for Doreen's behavior. Grandma was a fair person; however, in her opinion, no matter how thinly you sliced the bread, there were always two sides. So before she passed judgment, she wanted to hear what I had to say.

"Now, I want to hear it from you, Lindsey. What happened over there?"

"Miss Dottie has premonitions. She always has and thinks something or someone will try to hurt us, Doreen and me."

"You too? Not just Doreen?" Grandma asked.

"Yes, ma'am. Miss Dottie said the same thing to me, but they told me not to tell, and I didn't because everybody thinks they're strange enough already. They're good people who don't want to cause trouble. Please don't think they're crazy or witches who cast spells on people. They don't, honest!"

"I had a feeling you weren't telling me everything about what happened during that rainstorm," Mom said. "Is *that* why you were so scared? Oh honey, don't you know something like this must be shared?"

"Something like this has to be told to the police!" Grandma said. "Child, why *in the world* didn't you think someone else might be in danger? Of course, you wouldn't because you're too young to think about those kinds of things."

"But now wait a minute," Mom said. "This is, after all, *just* a premonition. It could be nothing at all. No need to go alerting authorities over nothing."

"Just a premonition, my eye! It could be something worse, and now we know."

"What do we know?" Mom asked. "That an elderly disabled lady believes something bad's about to happen? When? It could be today, tomorrow, or ten years from now. I do know the effect it's had on two girls. One scared out of her wits trying to protect two ladies from malicious gossip, and the other… who knows with Doreen, but it's enough to give me pause."

It was dumb luck and bad timing for me when Miss Tally knocked on the screen door. Mom invited her in, and Miss Tally wasted no time telling her about Miss Dottie's premonition. After this, Miss Tally unloaded, telling us what had occurred between herself and Miss Edna.

"What I don't get is why Edna's so concerned," Miss Tally said. "Wee Lordy! I looked Edna *dead* in the face, and I tell you she's worried about something. She has a sense about things, you know. Why would the ravings of a crippled old lady spook her? Linney, you sure you told us everything?"

There it was. Leave it to Miss Tally to cut to the heart of the matter. I was hiding something, and they knew it. But I couldn't tell the rest of the Sweets' and Miss Virginia's secrets. I just couldn't. I didn't want to tell another lie either, so what else could I do but run from the room? That's when Miss Tally caught me in midstride.

"If you're trying to prove you're the smartest person in the room, go right ahead. I'll stand back and watch." Gripping my arms, she continued, "But you ain't gonna leave this room until you tell us what's going on. Now!"

"But it's *mô ségré*!" I cried out.

"Lindsey Anne, come sit over here by me," Mom said.

Just as when Grandma said my full name, I had to obey. But this time, I wanted more than ever to be in my room with the door locked or to run far away, taking my secrets with me. Reluctantly, I sat on the floor with my head down. I hated every minute of what I was about to say, knowing I would betray a trust left to me.

"I told Mom that Miss Dottie has premonitions and sees things sometimes." This came out so softly I didn't recognize my own voice. "That day in the rain, she cried and screamed, saying the devil was in Paris. She told me not to go into the Jungle at least three times already because something bad would happen, but not to worry because she would protect me. Then Miss Virginia told me how the sisters helped her once when she fell in love with a man who killed someone in Paris. Miss Virginia thinks he's returned for her. At least that's what *she* thinks. She doesn't want to stay around to find out. She's afraid if word got out that she almost married a man like that, it'd ruin how well people think of her and ruin her chance of being placed at the high school or starting a new life somewhere else. That's her secret. I couldn't tell it all, the visions I mean, because they might make the sisters look crazier than what y'all think already. I promised to keep those parts secret because I didn't want anything to happen to them. I only told the part about Miss Virginia leaving for Chicago and Miss Dottie's fit in the rain, not the rest. So there. That's all of it."

No one said a word for a long time after I stopped speaking. The silence in the room was deafening. I glanced around at their faces and was reminded of the mannequins in the shop windows at J.J. Newberry's. They stayed that way until Miss Tally broke the ice.

"Like they say, what doesn't come out in the wash surely comes out in the rain," she said.

"I know who Virginia Morgan is," Grandma said. "It sounds to me like she needs protection. So do Linney and Doreen, if not others."

"I'll make sure to watch out for Linney while you're at work Janie Mae," Miss Tally said. "I've already asked Edna to keep an eye on the woods over there. That's the least she can do, and it'll keep her from stirring up more trouble."

"I'm proud of you for telling us everything, Linney," Mom said. "But some secrets can't be kept forever, especially if it puts others in danger." She turned to Grandma. "Mother, do you think we should reach out to Virginia and encourage her to go to the police?"

"You can't do that to Miss Virginia!" I said. "I promised to keep her secret so she'd be safe! If they go looking, he'll know she knows he's here and hurt her for spite."

"Honey, we have to alert the authorities, someone who can help," Mom said. "Edna's already told Jess a strange man's been lurking around and at this house no less. Do you know this man's name? The man Virginia almost married? We have to try to see if he's in town at least. I promise, no one, except us, will know we've reached out to the police."

Once again, I found myself wishing I was in my bedroom with the door locked. Mom wanted me to trust her, and maybe this time I could. I was trying to recall the man's name when Grandma asked something incredible.

"Did you laugh at Doreen when they told her she would die, Linney? I need to know if it's true. Did you laugh?"

"*No!*" As the insult hit me, my words came out like a shot. "They were rude, Grandma! I made a *joke* trying to get them to *leave*! All I said was they would get eaten if they didn't leave. That's *all* I said! That's when Miss Dottie said what she said to Doreen. Doreen's a *dirty liar*, but you'll never see it because Doreen never does anything wrong, does she? You think she's a saint. Well, she ain't!"

"Show some respect, young lady!" Mom said.

She gave me a stern look, but I didn't care. They had forced me to betray the people I wanted to protect most, and it was all Doreen's and Miss Edna's faults! No, I didn't feel like being respectful. So I did the next best thing.

"His name's Jimmy Marx!" I shouted. Then I ran from the room to find relief from the stares.

This time no one stopped me. I wanted to be somewhere, anywhere far away. I didn't know where to go except to my favorite tree, where I read and daydreamed. I buried my face in the grass and cried bitter tears, thinking nothing of the snot running from my nose. That's where I stayed until late afternoon, hating Doreen for trying to get back at me with her big mouth. I ignored what Miss Virginia said about hating. How could Grandma think I would laugh at something so serious? Not everyone could take a joke, and obviously, I was terrible at making them. Doreen had anything a girl could want, while I had nothing. *Why does she have to ruin everything?* Doreen was a horrible person, and I didn't care if I ever spoke to her again.

No one came looking for me. I was grateful for the time alone and stayed there long after the clock tower bells chimed one cycle. By then, my anger had turned inward with a vengeance. It felt as though I couldn't do anything right. I failed at everything: friendships, keeping secrets and promises, doing the right thing when it counted, everything. I hated myself for giving in and losing my temper. How could I be so stupid? I also disliked myself for allowing hate to rise in my heart so quickly. I felt awful, confused, and more alone than ever.

# Chapter 25

## Something Ain't Right

S TOOLY COULDN'T QUITE shake the feeling that this Ajax business wasn't over. A sickening feeling overcame him each time he thought about the issue. Slim spooked him with talk of what he saw when Ajax was unpleasantly escorted out of their gathering at the Warehouse. In fact, Stooly hadn't seen or heard from Slim since that night, which worried him. After driving to all points north of Paris to check supply-and-demand options for marijuana, he needed to touch base with his buddy. If nothing else, to shoot the breeze and find out how brisk sales had been lately. But before reaching for the phone, he needed a talk with his kid sister.

Bess was dressing to go out on the town with this new fellow of hers. Stooly didn't care who she got her tricks from. What he did care about was her mouth. Bess knew what he did for a living, of course, and their agreement was that she keep quiet about it. Lately, she'd been getting sassier with him, and he didn't care for it at all; loose lips sink ships. The longer he lived, the clearer it became that common sense was rare. In Bessie's case, rare sense and common sense were lacking.

Leaving clichés out of his thoughts for a minute, he tossed his spent Lucky Strike into the kitchen sink, left the kitchen, crossed the living room to grab another cigarette and lighter, then went down the hall to her room to ask about her new beau.

He found her sitting at her dressing table, putting the final touches on her makeup. Her bedroom was decorated with trinkets from previous trysts. Burning patchouli incense filled the room, but mixed with the fragrance of a heavy dose of Shalimar, the smell was a bit nauseating.

"Early in the day for you to be going out, ain't it?" Stooly's face glowed from the butane flame as he lit his cigarette. "Who's this guy you seeing again? What's his name?"

"What do you care? You my momma now?" Bessie asked while looking at her reflection in her mirror.

"Just thought I'd *endeavor* to ask about your current trick."

"Endeavor? Now, ain't you something. You can use your fancy words on them other fools out there, but that don't work on me, honey. You know what I do is my business. Why you so interested all of a sudden?"

"No sudden. Watching paint dry's not my idea of keeping my mind busy. Just asking. You don't have to tell me if you don't want. I'll butt out."

"That's more like it. Stand back. You're in my light, sugar."

Not long ago, it seemed, Stooly never thought of Bessie as a beautiful woman; she was his kid sister. But to look at her now, the whole package comprising her frame was well put together. Everything fit from the shape of her perky nose and full lips to her round, Betty Boop eyes and hips. She was the epitome of a downright sexy and gorgeous woman. Elishia "Bessie" Mae Davies had nothing on Dorothy Dandridge, but she came close.

He watched as she removed the last pin curl and fluffed her hair. After doing this, she got up wearing only a slip, no bra and reached for a bright blue dress hanging in her closet. He watched as it effortlessly slid over her body. Casually she asked if he could help with her zipper. With his lit cigarette dangling from the corner of his mouth, Stooly came forward to zip her dress. While he did so, she began to answer some of his questions.

"His name's Jimmy, just so you know. Don't need to know the rest."

"Just Jimmy, not James, no last name?"

"Look, you getting too nosy. Getting about like that Edna Allen person up on that hill. Thanks for help with the dress." She slipped past him and into the hallway, where she began to look for her shoes in the living room.

"Why the hurry? We don't talk like we used to, not that we ever did much."

"I hate making people wait. You seen my purse?" She asked while reaching for her black patent leather stilettos from under the couch. After she found her purse and sat on the stool in front of the easy chair to put on her size five and a half shoes, she gave in to Stooly's need for communication. "We don't need to *make* conversation unless you got something important to tell me. You take care of your business, and I'll take care of mine. Don't worry. I know how to keep my mouth shut. He don't know nothing if that's what you worried about. Just 'cause you don't know him don't mean he's gonna know all *my* secrets."

Stooly slumped in a chair with his left hand up to his face, index finger between his upper lip and nose, implying he didn't trust her. He knew Bessie hated when he made this gesture. It usually made her tell him anything he needed to know. She always came through; he knew her too well.

She furtively glanced over at him, probably thinking he didn't deserve all the sass-mouthing she was giving him. Stooly didn't know what had gotten into her lately, except that man waiting for her. In fact, he was sure she'd let that guy get inside her as many times as he wanted. Quickly dismissing that visual from his mind, he watched Bessie smile to herself. Then she let the smile drop, hardened her jaw, and glared over at him with a frown, which didn't diminish her beauty one iota.

"His last name's Marx, James Marx to you." She quickly got up and out the door, which slammed shut with a loud bang.

Stooly heard the clack, clack, clacking sound her stilettos made when they hit the pavement as she ran, probably to a car waiting for her on the corner. *James Marx*, Stooly frowned in thought. Bessie usually came home with a lot of money, but nothing was coming in from these hookups now that she was with this guy. *Something ain't right.* Maybe he was just another fella Bessie needed to get her thrills from, but that didn't sound like Bessie. Was she falling for this guy and didn't care about taking his money? That didn't seem like her either. This *relationship*, if you could call it that, could be dangerous for obvious reasons. Was she being used to bring money *to* this James guy, turning tricks *for* him and him alone? Stooly's instincts went into high gear. *Who the hell is this guy?* Stooly didn't know anything other than his name, and in this instance, that wasn't good enough.

Not long after Bessie left the house, Stooly called Slim, figuring it was time to chase him down, but after trying a few times, he still couldn't get hold of the man. Now, though, he needed to bounce his suspicions about this guy, James Marx, off him too. Something didn't jive. Without Slim answering his phone, Stooly was stuck, so he cursed to himself and lit another cigarette. To soothe his soul and get his mind off his building anxiety, Stooly called one of his women. He wondered if Luella was working that night.

Later, while lying in bed with Luella curled warmly around his body, he heard Bessie come in. Early for her. Without saying a word to announce she was home, she muttered something about it being over her dead body before she shared her man with another woman, then went directly to her bedroom and slammed the door.

⟞⟝

It was late. Virginia was tired, and her mind was weary. Getting up to stretch, hearing the crack and creak in her joints, she could feel in her bones that she needed to get to bed soon. The next day would be challenging. Her reassignment to Paris High finally came through, but she had to speak with the school administrators about her acceptance to teach at the University of Chicago next year. After waiting so long, she never thought it would happen, but talk about bad timing! Just like that, she had to leave teaching eighth grade English at Western Elementary and set her mind to teaching ninth grade literature at Paris High.

Starting tomorrow, as a matter of fact. She hoped the administrators at the high school would be generous and allow her contract to be written for only one year. After that, she *had* to leave for Chicago.

She had been spooked the night she walked Linney home, ensuring the girl got there safely. But that smell from long ago brought back memories she didn't want to recall. Her gut tightened, and a feeling of dread engulfed her as if Jimmy had walked over her grave. Staying in Paris for another year was playing Russian roulette with her life. A few weeks had passed since then, and she was beginning to feel more relaxed and thanked God nothing had come of her fear, rational or otherwise. Now, this reassignment had caused her to rethink her decision.

As Virginia removed the last traces of cold cream from her face, she thought, *What am I doing?* Staring into the mirror at her reflection, Virginia realized she didn't want to leave Paris. She had come to love the town and its people. On the brink of young adulthood, the students at Western brought endless pleasure to her life; she even imagined them as children of her own. The girl, Lindsey Hollis, was a joy. Staying would surely afford her a chance to mentor Linney or have her visit every once in a while. Virginia was disappointed Linney hadn't had the opportunity to visit, and she wanted another go at the chance to fill her house with welcome company. Her four walls needed a boost of cheer, and after all the empty years, it was time to make a change for the better.

Well, that did it! Her mind was made up. The suddenness of the decision surprised her. She would rescind her acceptance at the University of Chicago and stay in Paris. She could obtain her Ph.D. through the University of Kentucky in Lexington. She wasn't going to let a little scare from a long-ago memory move her out of the place she treasured. She loved her house and her drapes. She'd made a life here, and it was here in Paris she would stay.

With her mind reasonably made up, she prepared for bed. She needed to be fresh for the first day of school and kicked herself for being up so late, going over material she already knew and absorbing nothing more. Thinking and rethinking her decision had been a waste of time.

Then a noise, a knock, she thought, came at her front door. It was faint and light. For some reason, she thought it might be Linney at this late hour. So her concern grew, thinking something must be wrong. Then the knock came again but more insistent. She felt something wasn't right, and that's when Virginia hurried to open the door.

# CHAPTER 26

## *Hitting Pay Dirt at The Hall*

S TOOLY FINALLY GOT hold of Slim the next day. It was the first week in September, and Stooly had received word from The Boss about replacements for Ajax. It was none too soon because Slim was having issues at home. Apparently, Slim's ole lady had been hassling him to do house chores before the weather turned, which kept him busy all weekend except for nights when he worked. Slim's wife was a good woman who had pulled Slim up when he needed it. Stooly knew Slim's home life meant everything to him, but business was everything to Stooly. He needed Slim when he was at his best, sharp and aware.

Slim agreed to meet Stooly in the parking lot in front of The Hall that afternoon. Stooly liked doing business this way because two men talking together in full view of others didn't give rise to suspicion. After Slim got out of his pink-and-white Cadillac DeVille convertible, he high-fived Stooly on the white-hand side and down low on the black-hand side.

"I've moved more weed, man, than you can count," Slim said. "A little more than two pallets left from the six we got. You go check if you want. Demand from Cynthiana and Winchester's been high, you dig, not to mention Carlisle and North Middletown. It's been hard with the wife breathing down my neck every minute, though, man. Why I got married, I'll never know. It's tough getting out and hustling, but business is good.

Can't complain. I know you been up north scouting, but what's the word on the new guys 'cause I can't keep this up on my own unless you want to help? Shit, it's been, what, a month now we got rid of Ajax?"

"Hey, man, at this pace, moving the rest before the end of the month shouldn't be a problem, so ease up, okay?" Stooly said. "Two new guys will be here tomorrow. The Boss made sure it's legit this time. They meet with Augie as soon as they arrive. Speaking of which, you heard from that dude? Augie, I mean?"

"Yeah, man, but he's skittish, you know. Keeps saying he sees that Ajax Negro around, but when he double-checks to see if he's seeing straight, the dude's gone… like a *ghost*. I don't know, man. This guy Ajax, something ain't right," Slim said.

Money, always converted to hundred-dollar bills for easy carry and pass, changed hands between Slim and Stooly as this conversation took place. It was already known how many bags of marijuana Slim had moved, so the cash equivalent was understood. Stooly expertly felt the weight of the Benjamins to ensure that fact, then quickly put the envelope of cash in his car's locked glove compartment. Now that business was done, Stooly leaned on Slim's car and lit a Lucky Strike. He lit another one for Slim and offered it over, which Slim accepted.

"I hear you. Augie's just spooked and seeing things," Stooly said as he blew smoke through his nose and then his mouth. "I mean, he was *not* happy to be in the middle of what went down at the Warehouse. Could be it still bothers him. Sure hope the new dudes show up as planned."

"I heard that! It's getting lame pulling this by myself, man," Slim lamented with a sigh.

"Man, this place sure looks different during the day, don't it?" Stooly asked, describing The Hall in the afternoon and hoping to shift the subject to the mundane.

"I don't know, man. Same day, different dollar to me."

Shooting the breeze was easy between them. Stooly didn't always wear hard edges, and he liked their exchanges when the pressure was off. Changing the subject was not unusual either.

Stooly was eager to get the issue of Bessie's new guy off his chest and needed Slim's take.

"Listen, you ever hear of a guy named James Marx, Jimmy Marx?" Stooly asked.

"Who? Can't say I have," Slim said. "Should I?"

"Nah, just wanted to know if the name rang a bell," Stooly said. "Bessie's seeing this cat, and she's acting funny. I don't think she'd betray us to this guy, but something's off. I got this hunch I can't shake. She's not bringing in money like she used to from this habit of hers. She usually hangs out with fellas who buy her things, something she can pawn later, or big wads of cash to hold us over for a while. You know the drill. But *this* guy, she got the hots for *bad*, and all I know is his name."

"Ah, give it time. You know Bessie. She'll get tired of him quick, then on to the next. I wouldn't worry if I was you." Then a thought occurred to him. "*Jimmy*, wait a minute. What's the name of that cat killed some dude; way back here in Paris? In the pen with us?"

"I don't know no one put in the pen for murdering somebody in Paris."

"Yeah, nigga served a few years and was let out long before I was released." Slim snapped his fingers. "You got to know that dude, man, mean reputation. He put a hurtin' on this Paris dude, fucked him up real bad. Stone-cold killed him like a *nightmare*. I never saw Jimmy face-to-face, but the word in the yard was that he was a real badass, schizoid motherfucker. Quick with a blade too, man. All I know his name was Jimmy, could be James Marx, maybe?"

"No shit? You sure?" Stooly mulled this over as he put his cigarette out on the ground with the heel of his shoe.

"I hope like hell that's not the dude Bessie's seeing, man. This guy ain't nothing to mess with. Cat's mean as a snake and will—"

"Bite first, then rattle later?" This sent chills up their backs, each knowing Stooly had used that phrase before when referring to Mitchell Duncan, Ajax.

"Wait a minute, wait a minute." Slim paused for a second, then said, "You don't think he's the same guy as *Ajax…* do you? What the fuck, Stooly, man?"

"That's crazy, right? But anything's *possible*. Jimmy could've changed his name."

"Now, why would he do that?" Slim cocked his head for an answer.

"Who the fuck you asking? I don't know!" Stooly held both arms in the air. "Your guess is as good as mine. Maybe hide who he really is *if* he's *the* Jimmy you knew of in prison."

"But Tally knows this dude, man. He vouched for him—"

"We don't know how *well* Tally knows him, do we? He vouched for Mitchell, *not* Ajax.."

"You know Tally's honest as the day is long. That nigga ain't for hot piss—"

"It's not like Tally to get mixed up in a thing like this, I know, but people can be funny," Stooly said. "Unless Tally always knew him as Mitch, how would he know from different? Nah, easy enough to go to prison then use another name on the outside."

"But records can't be forged, man—"

"With no ID and no social, who'd know?" Stooly asked. "Easy enough to get booked as James Marx. Sentences can be light for murder, especially for first-timers with no priors way back when. You say he's a badass? He's probably smart as hell *and* a pathological liar."

"Hiding out in Paris. In plain sight? Now that takes balls!"

"Nothing to that, man. We do it." Stooly stated the obvious. "Look at where the Warehouse is located and what we're doing now… in broad daylight, with no one suspecting a thing." Stooly paused to let that sink in. "Listen for a second. Let's play this out for shits and grins."

"I'm listening." Slim leaned comfortably against his Caddy with folded arms across his chest while Stooly positioned himself in front of Slim and punctuated the air to make his points as he spoke.

"When he got out, it'd be tough to get a job using his real name, so he used another, *Mitchell Duncan*," Stooly said. "Why would he, or better yet, why *did* he? In our business, *we* know him as Mitchell Duncan, *Ajax*. What you wanna bet Jimmy *is* who Mitch *is*? If my hunch is right, that's how Mitchell knew us in the slam, man. He knew us; we didn't know him. I played it low, did my time, and you did the same from what you told me. He watched us. He waited. I'm telling you! Got to be! Damn, Bessie!" By Stooly's analysis, the pieces were starting to fit.

"Okay, now hold down. Let me think this out some more." Slim counted the scenario on his fingers and used air quotes as he spoke. "His real name's 'James Marx,' now a friend of respectable Jackson Tally, but known as Mitchell Duncan. He uses the name 'Mitchell' to get over on people *or* for any job he applies for after prison. He walks around using the name 'Ajax' when he shines up like a brand-new penny. That means Bessie Mae, dating a James Marx, is *fucked*! Do I have that right?" Slim had hit pay dirt.

"Bingo!" Stooly pointed his finger at Slim for corroborating his suspicions.

"*Man, that's crazy!* That's about the craziest thing I've ever heard, and I've heard a lot of shit! But this... this? I don't know... see... what kind of diapolitical... what kind of depravitied—"

"Exactly! What kind of 'diabolical or depraved' mind would dream up such a thing?" Stooly asked. "That would be a crazy bastard like Ajax!"

"No, that'd be you, asshole!"

"Hear me out, man, hear me out," Stooly said, ignoring Slim's dig at him. "Okay. I've seen all kinds of crazy, and let me tell you, crazy people can be extremely smart *and* devious. That's how they get away with shit! Like I said, anything's possible, but the *probability*, now that's another thing. It makes sense, don't it? Am I crazy for thinking this way about that motherfucker?"

"Man, I don't know." Slim sounded exasperated and shook his head from side to side. "You seem to have it all figured out.

*How* I don't know, but yeah, could be right. Like you say, anything's possible. Just don't go jumping to collusions—"

"I don't want to jump to 'conclusions,' but it seems to fit," Stooly said. "That dangerous fucker came to our town for some reason *and* using my sister while he's at it! We need to move slow on this one. I need to consider the *probability* that we might be on to something."

"Yeah. This whole thing makes no sense *whatsoever!*"

"What I can't figure is why he's using another name. Why didn't he use the name 'Ajax' in prison? Now, *that's* a name to be known for, but he wasn't. Just Jimmy. What's the link?"

"Who knows why, man? That asshole's a crazy bastard, and Bessie's in a world of hurt, man. You know that, don't you?"

"That's why I said we have to move slow and carefully," Stooly said. "Don't want to tip him off. I got to get my sister out of this mess quick. I hope she's in a good mood. Judging from last night, I ain't too sure. I need to find out what she knows."

There were many burning questions. Reasoning this out better over a cold glass of beer sounded good to Stooly. But since The Hall was closed during the day, anything would do, so they headed to Stanley's grocery. The pieces didn't fit as well as he had hoped. There were many holes left in this puzzle.

When Stooly had talked to The Boss a month back, he'd verified that no one knew Ajax; they just knew *of* Ajax. There's a difference. For all Stooly knew, The Boss didn't know Ajax was Jimmy Marx or that he'd committed murder in Paris once upon a time. Or did he? Cool and calm under pressure would do in this line of business, not hotheads or schizoid Negroes. The kind of men The Boss surrounded himself with gloried in murder when they thought it fitting, especially if crossed. Jimmy hid his deeds behind a false name. There was no glory in that. It made Jimmy Marx a coward, the worst kind of person among thieving cohorts.

Stooly understood another fact. The Boss, and people like him, never let on all they knew. He had earned The Boss's respect, but to think The Boss would put a schizoid murderer under his nose just to fuck with him as a test of some kind made Stooly's blood boil. He wouldn't want to be a "made man" even in another life. He was his own man. If what he suspected was true, he, Stooly, was out. He would turn over his part of the business to Slim if he wanted it. Stooly would get out of Paris and try his luck in the neon lights of states west of Kentucky.

✦✦✦

When they left The Hall for Stanley's grocery that late afternoon, Stooly was unaware it was the first day of school. They had to wait for a soda amid scores of students lined up to buy snacks before heading home from school. The waiting was made worse by kids coming up to touch Slim's car, which Stooly considered amusing. He watched tall Slim, with too much bass in his voice, shoo them away before they left fingerprints on the paint job.

While Stooly watched Slim constantly wipe down his Caddy, he took a step back and stumbled into little Lindsey Hollis. Stooly thought it mildly amusing how she fumbled with her words and fidgeted. She had a sadness about her, which was a shame, so he offered comments to make her smile. She was polite and cute, the way he thought Bessie could've been if given half the chance. As Linney walked away, he knew in his soul she would be a heartbreaker one day. But there was something else, a caution he had to consider, and he frowned at the notion. What would happen if that crazy asshole got one of these girls? He immediately shook off the thought, which was much too ugly to contemplate.

The sun was blindingly hot as he and Slim sipped on their cans of soda and worked out a way to find out more about this so-called Jimmy Marx. In Stooly's mind, if the guy named Ajax was Mr. Marx, it would be easy to determine because Stooly had already branded the jerk. Easy enough to ask Bessie about any scars on his face.

# CHAPTER 27

## *High School Daze*

I T WAS THE first day of school, the last week in August, and Doreen was in her element. Paris High was not at all like Western, and she loved it. For one thing, the building was bigger, not to mention the spacious rooms, with wider corridors and sturdy doors that opened onto large classrooms full of students of all colors, backgrounds, and financial means. The smell was the same but somehow different with unmarred walls, as were the *new* books, far from not-so-gently used. Doreen was given instructions, a class schedule, and a locker assignment with a combination lock from an office staffer eager to provide guidance.

Like Western, the classes were regimented, but the business of homeroom attendance was new to her. At Western, all students went straight to their first-period class upon arrival. This was different at Paris High, where each student was assigned a homeroom to gather for the first thirty minutes of the morning. Once attendance was called, they were dismissed to attend their first class of the day. After the hustle and bustle of orientation, Doreen needed to find her homeroom location before the bell; she didn't want to be late.

Doreen knew she looked "hot," but without Linney around to boost her confidence, she needed Brenda for reassurance and support. Waiting for Brenda in the crowded hallway, Doreen felt awkward until she finally saw stuck-up Carolyn, who walked by her as if she weren't there. Doreen grabbed at Carolyn's sleeve to get her attention.

"Hey, girl. Where you going?" Doreen asked.

"I'm trying to find my homeroom. My class schedule is crazy. Will you look at that?" She shoved the schedule under her nose. Doreen couldn't care less, though. Clearly, Carolyn was on a different plane of awareness as she talked on and on about her course load.

"Well, look at you," Doreen said in mock amazement. She couldn't wait for Carolyn to tell her how great she looked. "You've got a load, all right. What do you think about how I—"

But then, Carolyn was bumped by a group of students and dropped her books to the floor.

"Oh, sorry there. Didn't mean to smash into you," one of the White boy students said. Doreen was surprised to see them help Carolyn pick up her books.

"Thanks so much, no problem." Carolyn graciously accepted the books handed to her from the floor. "Can you tell me where this room is? I've been looking forever, but it's so crowded in the halls that I can't find it." Carolyn frowned down at the paper.

"Room 108, that's just down the hall and around the corner to the left. Can't miss it," said another, who motioned with his arm and pointed left with his finger.

"Thanks again!" Carolyn was clearly thrilled and, with a squeal, hurried off.

Doreen blew a puff of air up through her bangs. Exasperated at being left alone again and with no compliments, idle thoughts of Linney began to form. Truth be told, Doreen liked how Linney idolized and admired her. Each time she humiliated Linney and saw the sad-sack look on her face, Doreen felt unique, elevated, and better. She liked seeing Linney's face light up whenever she was around, like a puppy wanting a belly rub. It was strange how that adoration eventually ended up annoying her. The hanging on and the need for approval every time she looked Linney's way were sometimes infuriating. Linney's incessant need to be liked gave Doreen power over her.

Doreen had considered Linney a coward and didn't think she would ever speak up for herself. At least, she thought this would always be the case, but *boy,* was she wrong. Linney finally got a backbone, told Doreen off, and didn't apologize for it either. After Linney danced with Barry, whom Doreen had broken up with before the start of school, she was now the talk of the neighborhood with her dancing skills. Doreen had to admit that she admired Linney in more ways than one. But if Doreen admitted that to anyone, she'd be exposed for the fraud she was, which simply would *not* do.

To Doreen, Linney was still the little niece she could kick around, not the seemingly self-aware young lady Linney was becoming. Convinced the change had everything to do with those Sweet sisters, Doreen bristled at the thought of them, Linney's *new* friends. They had embarrassed her terribly, which she didn't think she deserved! What got under her skin the most was Linney looking up to someone other than her and *that* Doreen couldn't let stand. She and Linney shared and confided in each other a lot when they were younger. Now Linney kept secrets from her. Whenever Doreen tried to humiliate Linney, she bounced back as if nothing bothered her at all, which was maddening! Doreen's efforts to discover what the sisters had done to bolster Linney's confidence were clumsy at best. Her visit to those old ladies hadn't gone well.

After the tongue-lashing she got from her mother, Doreen had to get some of hers back. Linney had to take some of the blame. *So what's a little white lie anyway?* But that too blew up in her face in a spectacular way. Her mother got to the bottom of what happened at the Sweets' house, and Doreen was grounded for two days, which was brutal. She didn't care if she ever spoke to Linney again for the rest of her life. But here she was at the start of the new school term, with thoughts of none other than Linney swirling around in her head.

Doreen had everything a girl could want, in things, status, and position, but she wasn't content with just that. If only she had Linney's features and fair yellow/white skin. If she was as tall as Linney and had her creative ability and intelligence, then Doreen Elizabeth Munro would have the world at her feet. Yes, they were close as little girls, but grown girls wanted more.

She fidgeted and looked around for Brenda to come into view. While waiting, she couldn't help but notice the Black and White boys. *So many choices*, she thought. The White boys wouldn't look twice at her because of her coloring, but for Linney, they would. *Stop this! Stop thinking about Linney.* Standing alone, she felt swallowed up within the unknown vastness of this new school. Oddly, Doreen missed Linney.

⫷⫷◈◈◈⫸⫸

Feeling ignored, Doreen finally gave up on Brenda and reluctantly studied her class schedule and homeroom location. She walked down the crowded corridor to her assigned locker to get a book she had forgotten. On her way, she promptly bumped into a White boy with baby blue eyes who stared at her for an uncomfortably long time. She was annoyed despite her earlier feelings, thinking, *This must be the day for people bumping!* After a while, she found her homeroom, room 115, and nervously slid into a seat near the back. Neither Brenda nor Karen were there, and the only other Black girls were ones Doreen knew casually. That didn't worry her; however, what did were the White kids. Of course she had seen White people before, but not like this. Up close, she had a chance to observe them as they did her, mainly that guy she bumped into near her locker. He said he'd accidentally stumbled into the wrong room, which she found interesting, then he left.

Surprisingly, the girls were more like her than she had thought. She felt appropriately dressed in her best pink-and-green floral-print skirt, a white short-sleeved blouse, and white socks with tassel loafers. In turn, they wore regular shoes or saddle oxfords with white socks but the same type of skirt and blouse as her. Most of them had blond or brown hair that was either curly or straight. Few had ink-black hair like hers, tied in her usual high ponytail. Even though their skin tone was lighter, she didn't mind their coloring. They weren't so white-white like a plate or saucer; most were pinkie-brown or pinkie-red. They nervously tapped on their desks with number two pencils, doodled on notepads, and talked with each other about general stuff, looking around to be noticed. Like her, they seemed like regular people.

But then there were the others, the horsey set. The very wealthy White kids who lived in beautiful mansions and seemed miles apart from any of them, Black or White. It was unnerving to be so close to this set of students, sitting quietly, listening as their names were called, and waiting for their turn to say "Present." Most of them had full names like Sarah Houghton Taylor, Jennifer Collier Beckman, Forest Randolph McAllister, and Suzanna Mary Jaspers-Forsythe. *Who are these people? Don't they have regular names like the rest of us?* But then, if Doreen Elizabeth Munro was good enough for her to answer to, who was she to question? After this day, she hoped only first and last names would be called because most of these names were mouthfuls.

Unlike the wooden desks at Western, the smaller metal desks were situated close together. Doreen took advantage of this and inconspicuously leaned in slightly to smell the girl in front of her. Yet she detected nothing but soap, Dial—or Ivory, maybe? With these observances, she lost some uneasiness and relaxed in her seat. She felt a tap on her shoulder from a girl with light brown hair sitting across from her. She had delicate features, bright white teeth, and freckles sprinkled across her nose.

"I like your hair. Hi, I'm Clarissa, actually Clarissa Hutchens Ferguson, to be exact."

"I'm Doreen, Doreen Elizabeth Munro, to be exact." Doreen found it surprisingly easy to joke with someone she didn't know but chalked it up to nerves. She was also surprised at how willing she was to learn more about these "others" than what Brenda had told her. It was nice to have someone to talk to, and Clarissa seemed more than eager to do the same.

"I'm new to this school. My parents thought it best I attend public school instead of the county school. My mother said it would offer a different perspective on how everyone else lived or something like that. So far, so good. How about you?"

"I'm new to this myself, but I'm glad to meet you." Doreen didn't know what she meant by "how everyone else lived" but didn't let it bother her, all things considered.

"My first class is algebra. It's too early in the morning to focus on numbers. I hate math. How about you? What's your first class?" Clarissa asked.

"I feel the same way. It's my first class too."

For the next few minutes, they talked more in this way. When the half hour was up, the bell rang for them to proceed to their first-period class, and Clarissa asked to walk with Doreen. As they exited the room together in a crush of students, Doreen thought she would have to get on Brenda about her stories of these people if all went well. They didn't seem at all like Brenda had described.

All thoughts of being ignored disappeared for Doreen those first few hours of her first day in the ninth grade at Paris High School. That was until she ran into Brenda right after English 1 on her way to chemistry. With Clarissa standing next to her, oblivious of any character differences between them, Brenda made it clear she was disgusted. Chewing gum with exploding pops and cracks, Doreen was embarrassed to hear the words Brenda uttered to Clarissa's face.

"Who's the White girl?"

"Hey, Brenda, where you been?" Doreen asked nervously as she tried to ignore the insult altogether out of embarrassment.

Doreen saw Clarissa lower her head in shame as she left to get lost in the crowd of passing students. When Doreen looked back at Brenda, she squinted, acutely aware that her challenges would indeed be many. One would be putting Brenda in her place.

Doreen grew an inch taller that day.

# CHAPTER 28
## *The If Onlys*

SEPTEMBER WAS UPON us, and another school year had begun. I was never told what had been done about the secrets I had given away. Every time I asked, Mom said she was thinking about it. She said we should all take a deep breath and calm down before doing something we'd regret. She didn't punish me for running out after the telling; however, it didn't stop her from canceling my visits to the Sweets.

Since then, I hadn't seen Miss Virginia either. I half hoped she had left for Chicago because facing her would be hard. By sharing what I did, it felt like a weight had been lifted from my shoulders. I still hadn't forgiven Doreen for her lie. The high-handed way she behaved during her visit to the Sweets was something I would never forget. All I knew was that Doreen had been grounded for *two whole days* because of the lie she told about me. It didn't seem enough to me, but that was Grandma Edith for you.

For one week before school started, I watched for the Sweets, hoping to get a glimpse of their comings and goings. I often waited outside to see if I could catch them walking by, at least to wave a greeting of hello, but I never saw them. I would even walk back and forth in front of their house, hoping to get an invitation to visit on the sly. But it never happened.

Even though Mom never let on, I slowly realized she might not have only canceled my visits but told them of such as well. This made me feel worse, and while I yearned to visit the Sweets and Miss Virginia, I tried to occupy myself with other things. Viewing the *Slang Book* came to mind.

Angela warned, "You got a page all right. I'm not sure you'll like what you read, but take it with a grain of salt, okay? Try not to be mad. Call me after you're done reading it?" I promised I would, but now that I'd read it, I wasn't sure I could.

Doreen had a page with comments written, like COOL, PRETTY, BEAUTIFUL, BEST FRIEND, LOVE HER, HOLY COW! and on it went, which was typical. On the other hand, comments about me, such as STUCK-UP, GOODY-TWO-SHOES, MISS KNOW-IT-ALL, BRIGHT LIGHT, NICE BUT DULL, TOO SHY, GREAT DANCER! and so on, I could take, but WHITE GIRL, written in big letters across the page over everything else, was the worst. *Who would write such a thing?* It was one thing to be teased about my skin color or asked, "What are you?" by other kids at school. But another to see these words written in black and white for the whole world to see! To keep from crying out, I bit down hard on the knuckle of my thumb. As the saying goes, these were sticks and stones, but that didn't make the shame any less.

I couldn't change my skin color. Mom and Dad made me, so why was I hated for it? I couldn't tell Mom about this because it would be like blaming her for making me. That's when the tears came. *If only I could be like Doreen.* Of all the books to read, the *Slang Book* was one I wish I had never read at all.

⟡

The words in the *Slang Book* haunted me as I walked alone that first day of school. My thoughts gradually drifted into thinking about Doreen and my anger at her. Miss Virginia said to try seeing things from others' points of view, but that wouldn't work because Doreen's "point of view" always seemed to point back toward herself. *Stop thinking of Doreen!* I told myself as I walked closer to Western.

Western was a three-story, worn, brown clapboard-and-stone building that had suffered from neglect since the school integration laws were passed. Because of a lack of funding affecting upkeep, its decline and school integration forced Western to face ultimate closure. At least that's what I heard Mom and her friends say. I felt as neglected as the brown clapboards looked and thought how wonderful it must be for Doreen, Carolyn, and Angela on their first day over the hill at Paris High. Brooding and feeling sorry for myself, I climbed the worn steps with feet as heavy as lead. The many concrete steps that led up to the enormous front door dipped in the middle from wear. The door opened onto a long and narrow corridor with classrooms on either side crammed with students.

The smells of the first day of school always gave a comforting welcome to the inner halls of learning. The smell of used books and the wooden desks, often etched with initials of those students who had gone before with old gum stuck underneath as souvenirs, were familiar. The smell of new pencils, notebooks, and new clothing each student wore and wanted to show off were the hallmarks of the beginning of a new school year. Cheryl had a new dress and Mary Jane shoes. Monica paraded around in a new reversible skirt and a frilly blouse. Yvonne wore a new skirt and knee-high socks in new penny loafers with shiny pennies inserted for luck. I wore the same faded blue dress as last year and slouchy ankle socks stuffed into brown Hush Puppies, opting out of the worn loafers used for dancing. If Mom had the money to buy new clothes for me, I might not have blended into the walls so well that first day.

Aside from my friends being gone, there were more changes I had to face as an eighth-grader, such as changing classrooms when the bell rang. This was different from sitting in one room all day, so moving from one classroom to another was exciting and made me feel grown-up. Eighth grade classes were on the school's second floor, so this floor was a new experience. Each hour that went by, I wished I had my friends around, if nothing else, to ease my insecurity and encourage learning new things, like dissecting a frog in biology.

The day went by uneventfully until lunchtime. I stood alone in the cafeteria with my food tray and looked around for a place to sit. When I saw faces looking back at me with blank expressions, I was reminded of what was written in that book about me and bit my lip to stop it from quivering. Embarrassed, I put my tray away and rushed to the gymnasium to hide my face, now warm with tears.

I sat high above the gym floor on a bank of bleachers, empty of anyone else but me. Hearing the hollow echo of my "hello" bounce off the walls didn't bring much comfort because no one was there to return the greeting. If only I was more like Doreen. If only.

⟞⟝⟞⟝

Relief came when the last bell rang at the end of the day. Alone, I thought of walking over the hill to Paris High to gaze up at the enormous redbrick building with large windows and four white columns that announced to the world it was a special place of learning. But high school wouldn't be out for another hour, and on second thought, staring up at it would make me look weird. Instead, I decided to duck into Stanley's Corner Store to get an orange soda and an oatmeal creme pie to tide me over until dinner.

Stanley's was a small mom 'n pop corner grocery on Williams and Seventh Street that sold pantry staples and snacks like assorted candy, chips, and soda. It also operated as a little deli for sandwiches of packaged meats like ham, turkey, and salami. It wasn't as big as Arno's or J.J. Newberry's and was certainly no A&P. The old wooden floors were warped and sagged in certain places and hadn't been waxed in ages. It sometimes smelled of dirty socks and moldy bread, but it was an excellent place to stop and kill some time. It was usually dark and cool inside, which felt nice on that hot sunny afternoon.

The sunlight temporarily blinded me as I stumbled out the door with my snacks. I couldn't see who was standing in front or behind me. Without paying much attention, I opened my soda and bumped into someone. From the sound of the voice, I knew right away that I had stumbled into Stooly. *Great, my day's getting better and better. Did I really have to bump into the very person who makes my knees weak?*

Squinting in the sun, I could see Stooly's buddy Slim leaning against a pink convertible Cadillac with white leather seats, talking urgently to some kids about something I couldn't quite make out. Stooly looked as handsome and tan as ever in an open-front shirt, while his friend Slim showed off his muscles in a sleeveless T-shirt. With his dark, almost blue-black complexion, Slim was as tall as Stooly but scarier in appearance. The scar down his face, which gave me the heebie-jeebies, didn't help matters. When he smiled, he showed a row of the straightest, whitest teeth I had ever seen, but contrasted with Stooly, their looks were miles apart.

"Oh, excuse me, young lady. I'm so very sorry. Hope I didn't make you spill your soda pop," Stooly said.

"No, no, it's fine. Thank you."

"Aren't you that little lady I saw outside the chicken window at The Hall that time? I think you owe me five dollars." Stooly gave me a wicked smile and continued, "Nah, I'm just kidding. You don't owe me nothing."

"Oh, okay. I wouldn't have anything for you today anyway. Thanks again for helping, though. I think I thanked you before, but thank you again." Embarrassed, I fumbled over the words and hoped they sounded right.

"Not to worry." Changing the subject, he asked, "This your first day of school? What, you didn't eat lunch or something?"

"No. I wasn't hungry… it's a long story. I just wanted to get something on my way home until dinner. It'll do in a pinch, though."

"I see. Well, you watch where you're going now. Wouldn't want a pretty thing like you to get hurt or run over."

Stooly's dismissal was so smooth. I couldn't help but blush because he said it in a sincere and concerning kind of way instead of in a dirty-old-man kind of way. I was mesmerized by the trick of it all, which didn't last long.

Slim looked up from the pavement, which he was more than a little interested in checking out while we were talking, and said, "Hey, you take care now."

Hearing the deep bass in Slim's voice caught me off guard. I was mildly surprised and thought it odd, but considering his appearance. It fit him.

"Thank you," I said.

Turning to leave, I overheard Stooly say I was a sweet kid. Walking home, I daydreamed about him. I could imagine us sitting side by side at the movies or, if I were older, him dancing with me at The Hall. I daydreamed of the kind of dancer he might be, gliding me over the dance floor, making his other girlfriends jealous. He even called me pretty. For the first time that day, I felt good about myself.

Nearing home, I waved to Miss Tally and Miss Loren, who sat outside on Miss Loren's front porch. As I got closer to home, I heard a rustling sound inside the Jungle and was surprised to see Miss Edna walk into the clearing and make her way toward the left side of the Sweet's house. I'd heard Miss Tally had given her a mission to watch the Jungle. It seemed she took it seriously.

"Hi, Miss Edna. What 'ya doing?" I asked.

"Never you mind, now go on inside." Miss Edna waved me away, but I walked over to that side of the street anyway.

"Something happen?" I asked cocking my head from side to side.

"I said for you to go on inside now. Your momma be home soon. I've got things to do, and I don't need no help."

It was clear Miss Edna didn't want me to come closer. *What a ding-dong!* Considering how my first day at school had been, I was in no mood to take on a dopey and mean Miss Edna, so I did as told.

Peeking out the front room window of our house, I watched as Miss Edna tiptoed around the back of the Sweet house and came back around with a shovel. *What's going on? Why is she taking a shovel into the Jungle?* I tried to continue watching, but she was in there longer than I cared to wait, and besides, Mom had just come home. Then the phone rang.

"That was Angela's mother," Mom said. "Virginia Morgan didn't show up today at Paris High. No call-in, no answer at her door, nothing. Besides her friendship with the Sweets, do you know if she had any other friends or family she visited?"

"No'am. I think she has family in Frankfort, though. That's right, she wasn't at school today." I was so lost in my own misery I hadn't thought of Miss Virginia at all until then.

"She didn't let on she'd be out of town or was bothered by anything, did she?"

"No, ma'am. Holy moly, did she get reassigned to Paris High? I bet so. No wonder!"

Then a heart-rending scream came from the Jungle.

# CHAPTER 29

## *Day of Contrition*

I F ONLY I had done this. If only I had done that. If only I had told someone sooner. These were the thoughts going through my mind on that terrible day in September. The "if onlys" wouldn't stop repeating in my head on this day of contrition.

People said Miss Edna would never be the same after her discovery with that shovel taken from the Sweets' back porch. Good thing they were not home at the time. Virginia Lee Morgan was found facedown under a pile of leaves and sticks, buried in a shallow grave Miss Edna Allen found while rummaging in the Jungle.

I overheard a lot as people talked in whispers about what was discovered. Aside from dirt on the shovel, there was blood and hair, which Miss Edna neglected to see. The police determined the shovel had been used to further mutilate Miss Virginia's body before she was buried.

The police asked questions, and answers were given to the best of anyone's ability and knowledge. They searched Miss Virginia's house and found it had been turned upside down and inside out as if there had been some sort of burglary and horrible fight, a struggle for sure. The police thought she had been killed there, and then her body was dumped in the Jungle.

Some said Miss Edna had promised to watch for suspicious activity but never did she ever think she would find something like that, a dead body in the woods. The story was Miss Edna couldn't sleep the night before and, to her amazement, saw a car pull up and stop at the Jungle entrance. It looked to her like a man had taken something inside that place. He was there for a long time. It was too dark to see much, so her binoculars were useless. When he came out, the man moved like a panther, pacing around his car, looking left and right, then slunk back into his car and drove away like a whisper in the night.

The next day was a busy one, so it took time for Miss Edna to get to the bottom of "what was what" in the Jungle. The sight of that poor woman lying in that way was something she would never be able to unsee. The shock to her system was too much. "Lord have mercy!" she kept repeating to herself. That and vowing she would never ever snoop again.

⚯

I was lost in grief over Miss Virginia's death. I could still smell her lavender perfume, see her wide smile and hear the hope in her voice, now silent, gone in the blink of an eye. The thought of never seeing Miss Virginia again racked me with pain. I blamed myself so much for her passing and wanted more than anything to see her face again. If only I hadn't kept her secret of being afraid of Mr. Marx, she might still be alive. At least I had the handkerchief she gave me that day on the porch of the Misses Sweet to remember her by.

I was sent to my bedroom to wait for questioning and, being anxious, peeked out through the crack of my door. I could see my mother speaking quietly with a few neighbors and Angela's mother, Miss Sandy Beaumont. Dr. Roberts had long gone with the coroner. Angela was standing against the door to the kitchen and seemed to look off in the middle distance. I tried to get her attention, but the effort was in vain. Giving up on Angela, I closed the door and continued to wait, consumed by guilt. If I had said something earlier, Miss Virginia might still be here and not lying on the cold ground. Would I go to jail for making everyone keep secrets? That thought and the idea of death terrified me now more than ever.

Anne Frank's view of people seemed almost silly to me now because her notion of people being good at heart was flawed. I began to view life and death differently, thinking if good people didn't speak up when bad things happened, then bad things would continue to happen. So weren't we just as bad for not saying anything? I made a vow never to remain silent again if it would help or be of benefit. Protecting someone from harm was something I failed at horribly, all for wanting to keep a secret.

The wait for the police seemed to take forever. I heard the front door open, and footsteps came closer to my bedroom. Grandma, and Doreen of all people, entered my room. As Grandma held me in her arms, a flood of emotions washed over me at the loss of a wonderful lady. Mom entered while Grandma gently rocked me to soothe my grief. Then Doreen left, leaving them to sit on either side of me.

"Grandma, I hurt so bad," I said, sobbing into her shoulder.

"I know, honey, I know—"

"I tried to do the right thing, but I didn't, did I? I should've said something and not kept secrets. Miss Dottie said it was us in danger, not her. Not Miss Virginia."

Then Grandma said something I hadn't considered.

"Listen to me now," she said. Holding me at arm's length, her steady gaze never wavered. "It's possible Dottie's premonitions were misplaced and meant for Virginia and not you and Doreen, but who can know for sure? Dottie could only warn based on the sense that something dreadful might come to pass, and maybe, in her mixed-up mind, they were meant for Virginia instead. Don't dwell on the shoulds and shouldn'ts. Virginia's gone, and nothing, not even your tears, can bring her back. It's horrible, but try to remember that, sweetheart."

However, I didn't feel completely relieved. Miss Virginia was scared for her life. How's that for a clue I missed?

"You did what you thought was best because of your love for Virginia," Mom said. "That's where your comfort should come from, çá çé vré. Komprenn?" Mom spoke Louisiana Creole French on rare occasions, particularly when she needed to reach me, like now, to shake me out of my grief.

"Wé, Mamm, mo komprenn. Mé wé, mô ségré was no secret after all. Will I go to jail for not telling anyway?" I asked.

"Shush now, mô shè!" Mom said. "Secrets are secrets for a reason. Virginia trusted you, and you did well to keep hers. You did nothing to be ashamed of, so don't think any more about something you had no control over, shè Lin. And no. You won't go to jail, I promise."

After a while, a tall man with red hair under a blue police cap smiled as he entered the room. He wore a dark blue long-sleeved shirt and pants, a shiny badge, and black shoes with a big gun on his hip. Another man in blue, slender and not as tall with a balding head, came in behind him, gun the same size. They darkened the bedroom, even with the lamps on.

I answered their questions in all truth and with much sincerity. But when it came to answering questions about the premonitions Miss Dottie spoke of, I froze. I told the policemen Miss Dottie was not a witch and didn't cast spells but sometimes had feelings and visions. I felt this was all I needed to say.

According to the police, my story was similar to the Misses Sweets. The sisters said they suspected Jimmy Marx had committed the crime, but no one knew where he was or if he was in Paris. The police had gathered as much crime scene evidence as possible, which was being sent to Lexington for analysis. All they knew was the crime seemed suspiciously personal in how it was committed. Someone knew her, someone had a grudge, and until they could find this Mr. Marx, we all had to be watchful and very, *very* careful.

By early morning, the pain of losing Miss Virginia became worse for me. My stomach ached at each memory. I didn't go to school for the rest of the week. Even Mom thought it best to let events die down before going back. Anyway, I wasn't ready to be surrounded by schoolmates who would stare and ask more questions. Forget about making new friends now.

Mom took it upon herself to make arrangements for Miss Virginia. I think the guilt of not alerting the police concerning Miss Virginia's suspicions about Mr. Marx drove her. Yet, by not doing anything, she was protecting me. Together, our guilt could move the moon out of orbit and turn the world upside down. My mother looked in on the Sweets every day, telling me it was all they could do to just get up in the morning. Miss Katherine told her how Miss Dottie began to scream the words *no* and *it's him* over and over that night of the murder without Miss Katherine being able to calm her for some time. When the sisters heard of Miss Virginia's death, they were inconsolable. I couldn't help but wonder how deeply Miss Dottie must have hurt, knowing her visions couldn't protect Miss Virginia. This was something none of us could have understood.

It seemed the whole neighborhood was in mourning. I visited Angela, who told me what she had experienced that night. She got a glimpse of Miss Virginia before the coroner took her away. I'd never seen Angela at a loss for words or truly afraid until then. Now it was my turn to bring her the strength she so often gave me as she cried long and bitter tears over the horror she saw that night.

Since not being allowed to visit the Sweets after Doreen's lie, I was eager to resume my visits. However, gone was the willingness to entertain with tea and biscuits. Letting light and air into their house was an afterthought for them. I tried to bring humor into our conversations or open the house to bring in fresh air and sunshine, but it had no effect. Miss Dottie was gloomier than ever, and her depression seemed to have gotten worse. When I read aloud, she didn't engage as before, no matter which book I read. She sat motionless and unfazed without humming or rocking. I felt more depressed when I left than when I came. There was a hole left in the soul of that house, and I didn't think anything could fill it again.

We buried Miss Virginia on a Saturday, almost two weeks after her death. The day was full of bright sunshine and the bluest sky I'd ever seen in Kentucky without a cloud in sight. It was the kind of day Miss Virginia would have loved, but this thought made the day even sadder for me. The funeral was attended by friends, teachers, administrators from the school, and a few of her family members. Her brother kept twitching in his seat, and a half sister chewed and cracked gum throughout the service. I avoided them as much as possible. My mother and I sat with the Misses Sweet, who made up the rest of the family group.

I wasn't sure if the coffin would be open, but everyone said Mr. Beaumont did an excellent job of making Miss Virginia look pretty; I agreed. I had one red rose, which I placed inside her coffin to take to heaven. She looked peaceful, and I silently cursed God for taking her away from us so soon and in such a horrible way. I held Miss Dottie's hand as she sat without viewing Miss Virginia. I watched the tears fall slowly onto her face and joined the weeping of those who grieved her loss.

# CHAPTER 30

## *Is It Racism or Not?*

AFTER MISS VIRGINIA'S funeral, many mourners gathered at our house for a funeral reception dinner. Many flowers from the funeral service were brought over to decorate our home in comfort. Seeing the Sweets sitting in our house was weird because I never thought I'd see the day. It made my heart glad to see the neighbors extend kindness to the sisters. Grandma helped Mom in the kitchen with preparations; there was so much food! The house was full of so many people that they spilled out onto the front and back yards. They spoke in quiet whispers about Miss Virginia and the terrible event of her death, still guessing and gossiping over who could have done such a thing. I suppose I was one of the few who knew the police were looking for a Mr. Marx, who still had not been found from all accounts.

Doreen and I sat on the cold concrete steps of our front porch, talking for the first time since the awful lie she told on me. To speak about the premonition mix-up of Miss Dottie's seemed useless at this point. In typical Doreen fashion, she went on and on about herself and her adventures at school.

"Fact is, life's so full of interesting things, Linney, so much I never knew."

"Like what? What's different than now?"

"Everything! The White kids are not *at all* what I thought or what Brenda told us. They're like us in lots of ways. There's so much to learn and unlearn. It's not even funny."

I almost laughed, thinking she might even pick up a book and read it for discussion later. However, one revelation took me out of low spirits like a sudden jerk, her new friendship with a classmate named Clarissa Ferguson.

"She's White?" I asked.

"Yes, but that don't matter. Brenda doesn't like Clarissa, though. I had to tell her about herself because she embarrassed me!"

"Embarrassed you how?"

"She doesn't like me hanging out with Clarissa, but Clarissa's so nice. We have algebra together, of all things math *and* English. But there I was, enjoying myself, thinking I was cute and everything 'cause everybody was looking at me. But anyway, I was walking out of English class with Clarissa, and then Brenda came up to us and asked who the 'White girl' was. I was *so pissed* and could have slapped her down for that."

"Or snatched her bald-headed!"

"Who you telling?" We laughed so hard it hurt. Of course, this was inappropriate considering the circumstances, so we moved over to a secluded grassy area out of earshot of others. Caught up in the emotional roller coaster of events, it didn't occur to us that Doreen had called me "White girl" many times, which she didn't consider offensive or hurtful. Not to mention what was written in the *Slang Book*, so I quickly put it out of my mind and listened as Doreen continued, "But you know what? When Clarissa walked away, that's when I told Brenda off! I told her not to talk to me like that in front of White people, especially at school. It wasn't nice."

*That's all? Does Doreen think she did something?* If that was the best she could do in "telling Brenda off," she might have left well enough alone and not said anything for all the good it did. She should've treated it for what it was: Brenda was rude and racist.

"That's racist, you know? You couldn't defend Clarissa better than that?"

"They're the ones hateful toward us, not us toward them, so Brenda can't be prejudiced." Doreen was annoyed. "Oh, you're just too young to understand."

"Am not! Geez Louise, just listen to yourself! Yes, she's a *racist*. She's causing you to think you can't have a friend like Clarissa *just* 'cause she's White. It's almost like saying you're better than *them* and how dare you associate with *them*. You know how Brenda talks."

"They *all* think they're better than us, Linney!" Doreen said. "Brenda's trying to protect me, so she had a right to pull my horse in, but she didn't have the right to embarrass me."

"Embarrass you? What about Clarissa?… I'm surprised y'all still friends." I said dismissively while turning my head away from Doreen. "Didn't you just say they're not at all like Brenda says? So are they racist or not?"

"They ain't *better* than us if that's what you want me to say. Most of them think they are but ain't. Not Clarissa anyway."

"Then I think that's what you should build on. The sameness, instead of letting Brenda make you think *they're something you're* not. Who cares what color she is? I wish people would stop talking about color and look at people for who they are. Ain't that what Dr. King keeps saying? Talking about the character of the person or something? Look at the Misses Sweet and me. If we weren't friends, I wouldn't know anything about how wonderful they are, how kind and wise. Even though one is 'flicted, it makes no difference. She can't help how she is. She's the sweetest person, and they see the good in people. They're people with good hearts, just like Clarissa sounds to be."

"Mm-hmm. Those sisters can see *through* people, too, remember? Don't think I forgot the last time I paid them a visit. I haven't!"

"Well, you had it coming."

Being able to say anything back to Doreen was freeing. She ignored my comeback and continued talking about her friendship with Clarissa without getting angry. *Is it wrong to have too many friends?* Given half the chance, I wouldn't hesitate to jump at the opportunity of friendship with one of them.

It slowly occurred to me that Doreen seemed to regard Clarissa's feelings more than mine, not even bothering to apologize for the times she made fun of me. But then again, Doreen was more upset about *being* embarrassed than embarrassing Clarissa. I secretly hoped Doreen didn't come face-to-face with being viewed as different. I didn't think she could stand it if she did. Lost in these thoughts for a minute, biting at the cuticle on my finger, I returned my focus to Doreen's talk about Clarissa.

"All I know is Clarissa didn't seem bothered by what Brenda said. In fact, we even talked about me coming to her house for dinner."

"Going to Clarissa's house for dinner? You sure about that?" I narrowed my eyes in disbelief.

"Yeah, I'm sure! We even hang out in homeroom and other classes together, I'll have you know."

"How about lunch and in that study hall you told me about? Ever see her then?"

"No, but that's because I hang out with Brenda and Karen at those times. Sometimes Carolyn and Angela hang out with us too."

"I don't get it. I think you should include Clarissa when you hang out with them. Ever read *To Kill a Mockingbird?*"

"Girl, you know I don't have time to read! I'm too busy getting to know my way around high school and making new friends."

"Well, it has a lot to teach about life and differences between races and justice and stuff." I was starting to feel sorry for Clarissa because I knew how it felt to be ignored and left out. I was also annoyed and thought we were headed straight into an argument. It seemed Doreen was missing every point I was trying to make. I had to lighten the mood, so changing the subject, I asked, "So tell me more about high school, the teachers, the classes. What's it like inside?"

"You read and daydream too much! Life ain't like books, and I already said I don't have time for reading just for reading's sake." Doreen was clearly irritated. I could tell. She hadn't heard a word I said until, to my relief, she said, "Anyway, the boys are so fine, *girl*, I can hardly stand myself."

Doreen gabbed on and on about this while I listened. Sitting in the cool grass, I mentally compared high school to middle school and what I experienced on my first day. I didn't notice Stooly and Slim until they were upon us. I didn't expect to see them and watched as they stepped somberly inside to pay their respects.

# CHAPTER 31

## *Cat-and-Mouse Games*

LIKE MOST TRAGEDIES, Miss Virginia's death brought a lot of curiosity and sadness. I shouldn't have been surprised to see Stooly and Slim, but I was. After all, they weren't the usual visitors a person like Miss Virginia would attract.

As Doreen rambled on, Angela and Carolyn came over to us. Angela seemed to have recovered somewhat from the shock of seeing Miss Virginia's lifeless body because all she could talk about was the food. Unusual for her. She asked if we had tried Miss Loren's macaroni and cheese. Then she began discussing other food items brought to the occasion, like how good the country ham was, how delicious the sausage casserole and how Miss Virginia would have liked all this fuss just for her. I started to feel sad again and made an excuse to go inside to get something to drink. Standing, I walked toward the crowded house, curious to see how others reacted to Stooly and Slim.

I tried to find them while weaving in and out of people, careful not to upset the food others held on paper plates. *Where did they go?* Soon I gave up the search and decided to get some air outside, but with so many people filling every room of the house, I barely managed to squeeze through. This time I went out the back door, where fewer people were scattered around the yard, and out onto the common green. Then I saw them.

In the fading light of day, I could make out Stooly and Slim talking to someone near the barren softball field. It didn't seem to be a friendly conversation by the way they were gesturing at each other. Leaning against a clothesline post, I could tell they didn't notice me there. Their voices rose, but I couldn't understand what they were actually saying, no matter how hard I tried. The strange man suddenly ran away from them and down the steps to the street below. Stooly reached out and grabbed Slim, who had started to go after the man. Slim jerked his arm out of Stooly's grasp, and Stooly said something like, "It's not worth it," and that's when they slowly turned to walk back toward the house in my direction.

I didn't want them to see me, but I had to know more. At the corner of our house, I crouched at the edge to eavesdrop and spy on them further. I was in luck because instead of going back into the house, they stood close to where I was and began to talk in urgent whispers.

"You think that son of a bitch did this thing, man? What do you think?" Slim asked.

"I wish I knew. One thing's for sure. He fucked up today," Stooly said.

"You know it's him, man, you know it! We need to take care of this now!"

"Calm down, damn it! The world don't need to know—"

"To hell with that shit! That stinky son of a bitch ain't fit to spit on. You did that once, and that cold bastard didn't even flinch. Burned his face too! I think that asshole enjoyed it. He's not right in the head, and now this lady's dead! Ain't you concerned for Bessie?"

"You funny now? What do you think?" I heard the distinct sound of a cigarette lighter being lit, then heard Stooly offer a cigarette to Slim, who refused. Stooly continued, "Should've done what The Boss said and offed that fucker when I had the chance. That's my first mistake. Why's he here, at this place?"

"Back at the scene of the crime. Lurking in the shadows as usual. Who's next, huh?"

"But we don't know for sure he *did this* thing!" Stooly said. "Evil's out there running the streets, sure 'nough, and you don't think I want to go after him—"

"Goddamn it, we got to do *something*, Stooly, man—"

"We can't do *nothing* without calling attention to ourselves!"

The muffled, urgent, angry sound Stooly made when saying this was as if it was said through gritted teeth. *I can't believe Stooly's smoking!* I peeped around just in time to see Stooly's jaw unclench and hear his voice soften.

"Tried this shakedown. It didn't work. He ran. If the police catch him, that asshole will sing like hell. And then *we'll* be fucked. Gotta be smart about this, man. Can't go acting on a 'maybe,' but I tell you what—I'm getting tired of playing cat and mouse with that funky crazy bastard."

"Well, look who I found?" The soft voice of a lady came into the conversation. I recognized it as Miss Mabel Cox's, which was a signal I should leave and count myself lucky they didn't see me.

"Hey, Mabel, baby! How you doing sweet thing?" Stooly asked.

"I'm fine, real fine now that I see you two. Clarence, how's the wife?"

"She's doing just fine, considering."

I slowly slunk away, trying not to make a sound as I tiptoed my way to the front of the house. The long shadows of the day were closing in, and the evening caused a quiet to come down all around while the light faded into darkness. Many had started to say their goodbyes, some in hushed voices and others with warm hugs. I did the same with my friends and neighbors, absentmindedly lost in thought about what I had seen and overheard at the corner of my house.

Stooly and Slim suspected someone of Miss Virginia's death, and their suspicions had to do with that strange man. More troubling to me was that Stooly had a mean streak which was downright scary! Slim's behavior was not a surprise, judging by his appearance and that deep voice of his. He was a tough person from the mean side of the streets, all right! But Stooly, with his looks, was not someone I wanted to cross on my worst day. It sounded as if Slim wanted the stranger gone, but what Stooly wanted to do was far worse. *Who are these guys?* I realized I had no idea.

Crouching down to eavesdrop reminded me of Miss Edna's snooping. Grandma liked to say, "Eavesdroppers never hear anything good about themselves." Hearing this other side of Stooly shook me to the core. It served me right to overhear something I shouldn't have. Who was the strange man? Then it dawned on me, *the stranger from July? No, it couldn't be, could it?*

I didn't have time to think more about my suspicion because Mom called me to make sure the Sweets got home safely and wanted me to walk them over, then hurry back to help clean up. All the same, it was a mystery, and I hoped I could figure it out before anything worse happened.

———◦◦◦———

Jimmy Marx was not in a pleasant mood. His plans for viewing the goings-on at Virginia's funeral reception dinner were interrupted, and he didn't like that one little bit. Jimmy wanted to see the chaos he had caused, the sadness, the crying, and the pain he had inflicted. He lurked in the shadows of the event, creeping around the corner of the nearest house. In his haste to see the aftermath of his actions, he didn't shine like a brand-new penny.

"I can smell you a mile away. You know that, don't you?" Stooly said as he and Slim came upon Jimmy, unaware and away from the earshot of others. As Mitchell did so well, Jimmy remained calm while he listened to their accusations.

"So is it Jimmy Marx, Mitchell Duncan, Ajax, what? Who the fuck is you, man?" Slim asked.

"Word is you're the same Jimmy Marx who spent time in Kentucky State Reform up in Frankfort," Stooly said matter-of-factly. "KSR inmates don't forget murderers of young men from back in the day. Done in *this* very town. We laid low. Did our time. You knew us. We didn't know you. Now you back in my town. Who does that shit?"

Jimmy remained silent as Stooly continued to ask questions he didn't care to answer.

"That would be crazy motherfuckers like you. Wouldn't it?" Stooly moved his head from side to side, sizing him up as if he'd never seen him before. "Same cat who raped a *young* lady after being released from prison? Yeah. The same James Marx—or Jimmy, as it were—who wasn't known as *Ajax* in lockup. Now, why was that?"

A slight breeze moved between them; still, Jimmy didn't move an inch. He was invisible, and his head was starting to hurt. That fog was rolling in, but he held it back as Stooly rambled on.

"*You* knew Virginia Morgan. She's dead. You after my sister Bessie now? *I* don't approve. No one fucks over my sister without answering for it." Stooly narrowed his eyes with a piercing stare as cold as frosted glass. Jimmy liked the game Stooly was playing.

If he had known Bessie was Stooly's sister, he would have made her pay for the privilege of knowing him. Because of his ignorance, she was spared Virginia's fate. *Lucky bitch!*

"Who's the real Ajax, asshole?" Slim asked, jumping in before Stooly could say more and cutting to the heart of the matter. "More impertinently, how deep is your level of crazy, fool?"

"Yeah. How 'important' is all these fucking names? Mitchell, Jimmy, Ajax… who else?" Stooly asked. "What's going on in that *fucked up* head of yours? Let's hear it. I'll wait."

"Cat got his motherfucking tongue." Slim's tone was cutting, with no humor at all.

As they stared each other down, the cold steel that ran through Jimmy's veins was red hot. But he stood his ground and held his tongue, staring at them under heavy brows without blinking. *So what if I am James Marx?* What would they do, and more importantly, what could they prove?

"More to the point… why you still here?" Stooly paused to let this question sink in, but Jimmy didn't give two shits about answering. Then Stooly said something that got under his skin.

"Well, will you look at that? Gave you a warning you seem to be wearing well. How's that burn on your face?" Jimmy reached up to touch the wound, slightly narrowing his eyes at Stooly.

"*Fuck* this shit, man!" Slim lost his patience. "Say *something*, motherfucker!"

Pissing Slim off gave Jimmy a perverse sense of satisfaction. When Jimmy smirked,  Slim moved in to strike. That's when Jimmy ran. Stooly thought he knew everything. Stooly didn't know shit. He didn't know Jimmy at all.

⋙◈◈◈⋘

*It's not my fault that bitch Virginia didn't go down easy*, Jimmy thought. Neither was it his fault Bessie found out who his heart belonged to. It wasn't her. It also wasn't his fault that he burned to have Virginia's body next to his when blood ran hot in his veins. Bessie was a good lay, but she wasn't Virginia. He also fought against the feelings sweet Doreen awakened in him. Watching those young things at the Youth Center got his blood up. He thought Bessie Davies would calm that drive in him, but she only made it worse by causing him to want more. If not that sweet piece of meat named Doreen, it had to be Virginia.

Late that night, Bessie made it known she wanted more from him. He had to confess he wanted something more as well, but not from her. It wasn't the first time he'd been slapped, but it was the first time he'd been hit on the place he was burned by his own cigar. Stooly's burn had left a mark, which Bess was quick to pepper with kisses to make it better, but this only inflamed his anger and desire. Bessie was a stupid slut who felt her body solved everything. That night it didn't.

Funny how the head fog never rolled in when he was with Bessie. But that night, it did. He hit her hard and then banged her head against the dashboard of his car. She screamed obscenities that bounced off him with no effect. He dragged her from his car and left her on the side of the road near Winchester. His desire and urge to see Virginia surged in his veins as he watched Bessie, in his rearview mirror, throw her purse at his car, which was now moving farther away.

Of course, he knew where Virginia lived and made no attempt at hiding his arrival with a sudden stop at her doorstep. She was up late, *probably getting ready for something special*, he thought while knocking on her door. He knew her well, and as expected, she opened it innocently, probably thinking someone needed help, not that evil was on the other side. As her eyes opened wide, she exclaimed, "Jimmy!"

Ajax overtook him then. That foggy feeling overcame his actions as he let Ajax take full control. He forced his way into her house, slammed the door behind him, and wasted no time satisfying his need. She fought hard, scratching, screaming, running, and throwing various items at him. But he didn't stop. She begged him to stop, but he didn't stop. She smelled good and felt soft and warm; her tears only enhanced her beauty, and still, he didn't stop.

He had his way over and over again. Afterward, she begged and pleaded for him to go, but how could he? It wasn't his fault she caused this feeling in him. He buried his face in her neck, telling her so, but she wouldn't listen. He tried to make her listen, but she wouldn't. He got furious because she didn't understand, wouldn't understand, and hit her hard across the face because she couldn't understand, and he didn't stop hitting her. Only when he felt himself sway in ecstasy, covered in her blood, did he stop. His hands ached from the force of what he had done. *Serves her right*, he thought, as he stood over her lifeless body. She paid the price for what he had become. She paid the price for satisfying his need. She paid for causing him to lose control and making him do this to her.

Not bothering to clean up after himself, he wrapped her in towels he had found in the bathroom, rolled her body inside the kitchen rug she lay on, and carried her to his car. He gingerly laid her in the back seat where he and Bessie had been only hours before. Thinking about the lateness of the hour, he figured no one would see as he drove to that place the locals called the Jungle. There he laid her facedown in the dirt, and as her torn nightgown came up around her waist, he felt himself become aroused again. Taking his time, he did to her what he had never done to a woman before.

When he discovered Virginia had been found by Edna Allen, he thought she was a blessing in disguise. Still dark in the early-morning hours, he was unaware that Edna had been watching. He was satisfied and glad *she* had found Virginia and that *she* knew what he had done and what he could do again. He was pleased that this little town, *Stooly's town*, was now terrified knowing he was on the prowl and in their midst.

# CHAPTER 32

## *Genius in the Details*

I F PARIS'S FINEST thought they could find Jimmy, they had another think coming. Police patrols were everywhere; few escaped their scrutiny. The city was on edge, and officials were doing what they could to calm fears. The net result affected Stooly's profits, which made The Boss unhappy. The pressure to increase sales was the last thing he needed to worry about now.

Stooly had learned a lot before confronting Jimmy at Virginia's funeral dinner a week earlier. Many unanswered questions had come to light, but some remained. With so many thoughts racing through his mind, Stooly was beside himself on what to do next. Bessie was in a pissy mood because she hadn't seen Jimmy for a while, which was no skin off Stooly's nose. She could do much better. Bessie finally fessed up about her fight with Jimmy. She'd been wearing the gift of a goose egg on her forehead and a bruise on her cheek. All after kissing a burn on Jimmy's face. That burn was a dead giveaway, a gift Stooly was proud to have bestowed. But disfiguring his sister's face was something else altogether different. Jimmy ran before Stooly could climb his frame about that bullshit. In Stooly's mind, Jimmy's day would come sooner rather than later.

Whether Bessie knew it or not, she had served a purpose by naming her Jimmy *the* infamous James Jimmy Marx. Stooly couldn't prove it, but he would bet dollars to doughnuts that Jimmy was Virginia Morgan's killer. The crazed look in his eyes, that maniacal stare, the silence, and the lurking. It all added up. What didn't add up was motive. Stooly was no psychiatrist, but he knew Jimmy wouldn't stop. Not by a long shot.

As it turned out, Slim was right about the man. After some digging, Stooly discovered that Jimmy had been booked for killing someone in Paris named Calvin Manning back in 1953. The Mannings were good and honest-to-God, hard-working people. It was even said Calvin's nephew Bernard, or Barry as he was known, would go far. It was a vicious killing over a game of craps and one a town like Paris had never seen before. You had your usual rows from time to time, where someone might get stuck with a blade or shot at, sure. But those were minor compared to Calvin's murder. It was the kind of murder that was talked about in whispers, like a dreaded disease no one wanted to mention out loud for fear of catching it themselves.

At that time, Jimmy lived in Winchester, worked at the Kroger supermarket, then as a night janitor at Western, where his teacher girlfriend worked. It didn't take long for Stooly to find out that this girlfriend was none other than Virginia Lee Morgan. When Calvin was killed, those ladies named Sweet dropped a dime on ole James, so it was easy for the police to find him hiding under the ball field benches in Garrard Park. Jimmy got off with a light sentence because of no priors, but murder was murder.

As far as Stooly was concerned, Jimmy didn't deserve to be referred to by any other name than his Christian one; "Jimmy" would do just fine. To Stooly, cutting through the nonsense of name changing was the only way to deal with that asshole, to say nothing of saving his sanity. Showing up at The Hall in broad daylight in July took balls of brass but was reckless as hell. Showing up at Virginia's funeral dinner showed Stooly how brazen Jimmy could be, which was worse. That crazy fucker was making careless mistakes, as arrogant criminals who often pride themselves on thinking they were smarter than the average person do. They also spilled the beans when cornered.

Unlike Slim, waiting was a game Stooly played well. But this time, he knew letting the situation chill was out of the question, especially if Jimmy did something worse or started to squeal when squeezed. Stooly had to get rid of that worthless son of a whore without calling attention to himself or the business. If he managed it right, he would eliminate the scourge of Paris, thereby safeguarding the town, bringing his business back up to snuff, and satisfying The Boss. Getting rid of Jimmy would kill so many birds with a single stone that the thought made him giddy. But that was easier *thought* than done.

The irony of being sent to the slam for killing someone who deserved it caused him sleepless nights. Stooly didn't get this far without seeing and doing a few things. Some were too unpleasant to recall but enough to call his favorite girl du jour to keep him company on nights the memories wouldn't allow him to sleep.

Stooly wouldn't be able to stand himself if he let this slide any longer and cursed himself for not killing Jimmy when he had the chance. He couldn't have The Boss and his goons take care of this problem, either, especially now that it'd gone this far. That could get messy. The Boss liked neat and clean. So did Stooly. *If I only knew for sure Jimmy killed Virginia, I'd feel better about what I have to do.*

As usual, Stooly called Slim.

⚬⚬⚬

Slim didn't like sitting next to this fidgety asshole. It was about too much for him to take. He liked Augie, but it was clear he wasn't cut out for this kind of work. *What's Stooly thinking involving Augie, anyway?*

"I don't like waiting in here," Augie said with eyes wide, looking over his shoulder at every sound made in the place, his voice higher than usual. "Sitting in The Hall is not my idea of a pleasant afternoon. You know I don't want *nothing* to do with those folks over in Louisville, right? That night at the Warehouse was enough for me. I'll stick with bootleg liquor and moonshine, thank you very much."

"Take it easy, Augie, man. Stooly wants us here for a reason, so hold down."

"All's I got to say is I'll *leave* if it means some ugly business is about to go down. Whatever it is, I'll scoot sure 'nough."

*Fuck it*, thought Slim. "What's your problem? I said, hold down—"

"You think I like sitting alone with *you?*" Augie didn't expect an answer. "There, I said it. You make me nervous, you know? No offense, but this whole thing makes me nervous. The smell of that fried chicken is making me hungry too. I'd rather be home."

Slim chuckled at the sound of Augie's stomach growling. *Damn! All this over sitting next to me at The Hall?* The issuance of a fart from Augie's backside took Slim's mind off his own brooding. He sure as shit hoped Stooly showed up soon.

Slim thought it was an excellent call not to meet out at the Warehouse. There was too much heat in town with the recent death of that lady Virginia, so it was a good idea to lie low and not call attention to the goings-on out at that place.

*The Louisville boys sure picked the wrong time to roll into town.* Paris's finest were frisking every Black person in the city who even looked sideways at them, including Slim. Even though he let it roll off his back, it was a hassle he could do without. Thanks to the clean records The Boss kept, the Louisville boys were questioned and released. Now Slim sweated about what The Boss would think when the Louisville boys returned. Since then, Slim hadn't heard anything and hoped this meetup with Stooly would give him information about that.

As usual, Stooly came breezing in as if he didn't have a care in the world. *That's Stooly for you*, thought Slim as he shook his head. Augie sighed with relief and stood to greet the man with all the sincerity he could muster while Stooly slid into a chair at their table, not bothering to shake Augie's hand.

"Sit down, sit down," Stooly said to Augie.

"About time, man! I was about to give up on you," Slim said.

"Lot of ground to cover in this state. Business," Stooly said.

"What's going on, man? Talk quick 'cause I think Augie has to leave."

"I have to get back to the wife, you know," Augie said. "It's about dinnertime—"

"Slow down, Augie. I got your back," Stooly said. "You'll be out of here soon enough."

"Looka here, this town's buzzing, you dig? On edge about that Virginia lady," Slim said. "We can't do nothing without being watched. People pointing fingers left and right and some right at us! I don't like it, man."

"Which is why I want to talk to both y'all," Stooly said. "Augustus, conduct your bootleg business as usual. But don't expect anybody selling at the corner for the next few weeks."

"But I—" Augie was interrupted by Stooly, who seemed eager to make his point.

"I know you watch out for sales, but there won't be any for a while. Don't ask questions, just do as I say. Lay low. I'll tell you when to get up from that mattress again."

"Now," Augie started again. "I'm not gonna be part of any funny business—"

"Augie, will you *shut* the fuck up?" Stooly said sternly, much to Augie's visible surprise. "Mind your business and *only* your business from now on until you're told differently. You don't know *nothing*! You dig?"

"I-I-I think so," Augie managed to say.

"We're cool, all right. Now get out of here." With that said, Augie stood, shook Stooly's hand goodbye, and nodded at Slim, leaving a vortex of wind in his wake.

"What the hell, Stooly man?" Slim asked.

Stooly studied Slim for a long time, longer than usual, as if sizing him up and trying to think what to say. When Stooly spoke, he carefully crafted his words so that Slim understood the weight of what he was about to ask of him. Stooly told of his conversation with The Boss and what he wanted done, but he respected Stooly's decision on *how* to do it. Slim listened as Stooly told him his thoughts on right and wrong.

Soon the conversation shifted. Stooly had a lot to get off his chest in raw honesty. Slim was a willing listener as Stooly told of secrets kept from Bessie and who he was deep down, of which Slim knew nothing. Stooly told of what he hated, what and whom he had loved. He told of what he knew of books, learnings, and his flaws. Stooly told of all the things he tried to do but couldn't and spoke philosophically about life and moving on. He told of his need to end this way of life and what Slim meant to him. He talked of his dreams and hopes, and if he were asking for absolution, then yes, Stooly was asking for God's forgiveness.

When he was done, Slim took a long deep breath. He had refrained from ordering anything earlier, but now he felt the need to drink from the coldest glass of beer known to man as a chaser after a shot of scotch. A long drag from a cigarette wouldn't hurt, either. Slim watched as Stooly tapped an unknown rhythm on the table until Slim decided to say something.

"You know…" Slim paused for effect. "There are snakes you shouldn't fuck with. Timing's everything." He narrowed his eyes at Stooly as he waited for a reply.

"I want to send that man to the basement of hell." Stooly's response was cold and soulless.

"Tell me the plan before we go knuckling up." Slim was all in as he listened to how Stooly planned to catch the worst kind of snake.

Leaning close, Stooly spoke in Slim's ear. The words flowed smoothly, and the thoughts were clear. Slim offered objections when appropriate but admired the genius of the plan and its details. When Stooly was done, Slim sat back and said the one thing that came to mind.

"As they say, it's pretty when it's played right, but hell if you miss that note."

Stooly's only choice was to agree.

# CHAPTER 33
## *Culture Clash*

DOREEN WAS TOLD not to stray and come *straight* home from school. She found this annoying because Miss Virginia had been gone three weeks now, and it was almost October. *For God's sake, why all the fuss?* Miss Virginia's death did not affect Doreen the way it had Linney. It was a terrible way for someone to die, but it wasn't her, so what did she care? All she cared about was getting through each day at school. That and navigating the waters of her friendship between Brenda and Clarissa. One an innocent White girl and one a vindictive and scarred Black girl.

Doreen thought long and hard about her conversation with Linney at Miss Virginia's funeral reception dinner. Linney had sparked a curiosity in Doreen that she hadn't considered until that day. The idea of celebrating sameness was a suggestion Doreen hadn't thought of but now wanted to try. Each school day provided more opportunities for discovery, so Doreen would test Linney's belief that racism was just a notion and not a real issue. She was determined to find common ground in all areas of her new friendship.

Doreen and Brenda were longtime friends, and to her mind, Brenda had a right to be bitter. Brenda's life had not been easy with an alcoholic mother, a constant visitor at the local bars, and who knows where else; her father's identity was anyone's guess. There was a time for civility, but Brenda had none for any White students at school, especially Clarissa. Brenda, the bully, was having a hard time in school and making a bad name for herself.

Lunchtime was Doreen's favorite time of day. She often sat with Brenda and Karen to gossip about the day or current events. Sometimes Angela and Carolyn joined them, but Doreen got the feeling they wanted to be elsewhere. Doreen couldn't care less and could do without their judgments, anyway. It was enough to contend with Brenda's.

Lately, because of her developing friendship with Clarissa, she'd felt pressured to please Brenda. After an exhausting three weeks of trying to find a truce between the two, Doreen had had enough. She was being squeezed at both ends and felt she had to choose. Brenda was wrong, and Doreen felt that if this clash of cultures could be bridged, she would be the one to do it.

"Hey, y'all. How's it going?" Doreen asked. Sitting next to Karen and across from Brenda, she felt the tension already building.

"You tell me. How's the class load?" Brenda asked.

"It's okay. Math's kicking my butt though."

"Really? Your new friend ain't helping out?"

"What're you talking about? You get the craziest ideas sometimes, Brenda."

"Not as crazy as trying to be friends with them White people."

"You have *got* to give up fighting all the time."

"Obviously, I have to knock some sense into *your* head. They ain't interested in being your *friend*. You might think so, but that ain't the case. Them honkies don't care about you."

"Keep your voice down! They can hear you," Karen said. Brenda wasn't the quietest person in the world.

"I don't care! I'll say it again. *Louder!*"

"*Don't* say that ugly word again; you ain't cute!" Doreen said, clearly irritated. "*You* just jealous I'm friends with Clarissa. I keep telling you she's nice, and they ain't like what you think, but you won't believe me. So believe what you want and grow up already."

"Like you can make me? I'll say whatever I want."

"I mean it, Brenda, *stop it!*"

"Or what? What you gonna do, huh? Say 'much,'" Brenda said.

"Brenda, I'm not playing. Always trying to psych me out. Why you acting like this? It bother you *that* much I'm friends with a White person?" Doreen asked.

"*Honky!*" Brenda yelled.

The word echoed and bounced off the ceiling and walls amid the clatter of utensils, and lunch trays, even over the din of student voices. The room went deathly quiet. Doreen could feel her heart pounding as adrenaline rushed through her body from the anger and frustration.

"What's the *matter* with you?" she asked.

"You said 'much,'" Brenda said as she sat back in her chair and smirked, not at all fazed by the effect her comment had on everyone within earshot.

Doreen narrowed her eyes at Brenda, took a deep breath to calm herself, and carefully chose her words for maximum effect.

"Trying to embarrass me only makes you look worse. You're a *horrible* little person. You could get expelled for saying that, and I hope you—"

"No, what *bothers* me is you believe things have changed. Going around telling everybody you're such *good* friends with that girl—"

"Her name's Clarissa—"

"You really think *Clarissa's* gonna invite you to her house like you been saying? *I* don't think so. She got you thinking she's your friend. Well, she ain't and you can't see it. That's what bothers me, *dumbass.*"

"What did you call me?!"

"Dumbass! That's what I said. Got your head all *up* in her ass!"

"Come on, y'all!" Karen said as she tried to calm the escalating tension.

Doreen ignored Karen, who would have had better luck talking to the man on the moon for what it was worth. Not bothering to say anything more, Karen took her lunch tray and left them alone to battle it out.

"Take it back!" Doreen said through gritted teeth.

"You think you so smart, but you ain't nothing but *stupid*, sniffing after her all day long."

"I mean it, Brenda, take it back!" Doreen got up and stood across from Brenda.

"Or *what*? I'm waiting for you to do something!"

Doreen leaned in and quietly said, "*Kiss my ass and get glad*, you ignorant bitch!" It was as if she had slapped Brenda without raising a hand. Then she walked off, letting the full weight of her words sink in.

"Yeah, walk off, *dumbass* chicken! See if I care, *honky lover*!" Brenda yelled out after Doreen.

On Doreen's way out, she passed Angela, who stared at her with a questioning expression, and Carolyn, who looked more than a little curious about what had just happened. Doreen turned just in time to see a teacher approach the table where Brenda sat alone. Doreen hoped Brenda got what she deserved and didn't care. She also didn't care that Brenda made clucking noises like a chicken as she exited through the cafeteria doors.

⤙◈◈◈⤚

As she walked to her locker, Doreen felt satisfied with herself. It was high time she told Brenda where to get off and good riddance. Pigs would have to fly before she forgave Brenda, that is if she ever spoke to her again, and that was a *big* if. Pushing past other students on her way to her locker, Doreen saw Clarissa waiting for her.

"Hey there! You will *not* believe what just happened in the lunchroom. I told Brenda off, and I mean *good*! I hope she gets expelled for what she said. I'm so stupid, wasting my time on her when she's nothing more than a… what's wrong?" Doreen asked.

"I have bad news. I've been thinking all day about how to tell you. I'm so upset. I can't eat or think at all."

"Why? What's going on? Just tell me."

"You can't come to my house," Clarissa blurted. "I'm so sorry, Doreen, but Mom says it's okay to be friends with the Colored, but I can't bring them home to eat, hang out, or anything. Oh, I feel so awful I don't know what to say! We can still be friends, though. We'll always be friends no matter what, right?"

The sensation of blood rushing from Doreen's head to her feet was unmistakable. She didn't hear anything after, "You can't come to my house." It was as though she'd been punched in the gut and couldn't breathe. Doreen fell back against her locker, staring at the set of lockers across the hall, not listening as Clarissa rambled on and on. All she could think was that Brenda was right. She was indeed a dumbass.

Turning to her locker, Doreen ignored Clarissa, who continued to talk, pleading with her to listen. Doreen couldn't recall the combination to her lock and cursed softly at herself, "Damn it to hell, stupid bitch."

Before Doreen could explain the expletive was not meant for her, Clarissa quickly walked away, clutching her books close to her chest. She blended into the crowd of students with her head down until she was out of sight, the same as she had done that first day of school when Brenda called her "White girl."

Doreen fought back the tears threatening to spill and continued her attempt at the combination lock. Until that time, she had trusted her judgment. Now it had been shattered in a matter of minutes. Brenda was right; things had not changed. She was wrong to doubt Brenda's warnings and felt foolish about the fight in the cafeteria.

Doreen had grown fond of Clarissa and often wondered how their lives would've been if skin color was not an issue and she was considered someone other than what her coloring said about her. She saw the differences as something to build on, a foundation of solid stones that had now been rocked to the core by Clarissa's parents, who had other ideas. What right did they have to treat her this way? "Other than" is precisely how she felt, making her angry to feel so inferior and insignificant.

She had bragged to anyone who would listen that she was special to have a White friend. Now reality hit her between the eyes, telling her she wasn't. Heat rose to her face as if she had been slapped. However, she couldn't let her shameful hurt show. She couldn't let them know they had gotten to her. Tears slipped down her face, and as she felt their warmth, she slowly wiped them away, closed her locker door, and took a deep breath.

Lunchtime was over. Dreams of better days were over. *To hell with Linney and her funky ideas!* Doreen held her head high, and with her shoulders back, she walked to her class with thoughts of getting even on her mind. Doreen had no idea she was being watched by the same guy with the baby blues who gawked at her that first day by her locker and most days since.

After school, Doreen sought out Brenda and told her about Clarissa's disinvite. Groveling was not Doreen's style. Neither was swallowing her pride. It was hard to admit she was wrong, but she did. She took every word back and apologized to Brenda, who lorded over the fact that Doreen had gotten her just desserts. Doreen took Brenda's dressing down in silence, accepting the sticks and stones she hurled, which met their mark.

Brenda never understood the meaning of whispering, and this loud conversation was overheard by many students, particularly Reverend Avery's only child, Carolyn.

# CHAPTER 34
## *A Not-so-Simple Plan*

B Y THE TIME the first week of October rolled around, Doreen had rejected every effort Clarissa had made to reconcile with her. For a solid two weeks, whenever Clarissa called out to Doreen, she ignored her as if she weren't there. Doreen saw Clarissa waiting outside her classes but passed by or square-shouldered her in the school hallway. Once, Clarissa brought chocolates in a vintage blue tin container for Doreen to enjoy. Doreen promptly brushed them aside when placed on her desk. Whenever Clarissa braved sitting at the lunch table with Doreen and Brenda, they instantly got up and moved to another one, leaving Clarissa alone and laughed at by the other students, both Black and White. Doreen was mean and enjoyed leaving Clarissa with no idea what would come next. And had Clarissa known, she probably wouldn't have ever given Doreen the time of day if asked.

The plan was simple. The school's recent building add-on created a back stairwell leading, through double glass-pane doors, to the cafeteria and new classrooms. Brenda and Doreen would wait along the back stairwell, one behind each glass door. Because Doreen knew Clarissa's class schedule, she knew when Clarissa would pass through. Doreen was to stand on the landing at the top of the stairs behind one side of the glass doors. She would hold it open for students as they walked through on their way to class while Brenda held open the other door on the other side, standing against the wall. Clarissa, eager to befriend Doreen again, could be counted on to come around to greet Doreen behind one of the doors. Brenda would come from behind the other door and trip Clarissa when she did, causing her to fall down the stairs. Brenda could visualize Clarissa's skirt over her head, underwear showing while all the students laughed. This would cause Clarissa enormous embarrassment, which was the payback Doreen needed and the humiliation Clarissa deserved.

Doreen was all in until she overheard Clarissa defending her to other White students. Doreen had tried to humiliate Clarissa in every possible way, but there Clarissa was, defending her in much the same way as Doreen had done with Brenda that day in the school cafeteria.

Clarissa told her friends to back off and let her handle her business. She said Blacks were just like other people, and to keep saying mean stuff about them was hurting her ears. She told them Doreen was a good person whose feelings were hurt and didn't mean to be cruel, and she would always be Doreen's friend no matter what. Doreen couldn't figure out why Clarissa would put herself in a position to defend her like that, especially when she wouldn't stand up to her own parents for Doreen's sake. To Doreen's dismay, she started questioning her own selfish motives and slowly realized she might have been hasty in her judgment of Clarissa, the girl herself.

⟢✦✦✦⟣

Ever since she overheard Doreen sniveling to Brenda and begging for forgiveness, Carolyn was concerned and ever watchful of what Doreen and Brenda were up to. She was at the right place at the right time to overhear their plan, whispered not so quietly in the school library. With their heads close together, they didn't notice Carolyn sitting one table over with her back to them, head down in a book. Listening inconspicuously as possible, Carolyn thought it was God's grace that allowed her to hear the horrible plan. Disgusted, she tried to figure out how she could help avoid a catastrophe that was bound to befall her friend Doreen and the good-natured soul of Clarissa. Then an idea came to her and keeping her fingers crossed, she hoped she might prevent it.

Carolyn felt bad for Clarissa, as well as Linney. Both were treated badly because of skin color, and now Doreen had fallen victim as well. Carolyn had to drive home that bigotry came in all forms, and Doreen's treatment of Linney was no different. It had to be pointed out with finesse, but she had to move quickly. This dangerous prank could *not* be allowed to happen.

Lunch was scheduled from eleven o'clock to twelve with one-hour intervals for each class section: freshmen and sophomores at eleven, then juniors and seniors at twelve. At eleven on the nose, Carolyn took advantage of Doreen's being alone. She saw Doreen walk toward the cafeteria, holding her books close to her chest, frowning, and looking at the floor. As Carolyn came up from behind, she knew this was the time to make her move.

"Hey, how's it going?" Carolyn asked.

"Gosh, Carolyn, you scared me!" Doreen clutched her books tighter to her chest. "I haven't seen you around. How's it going, girl?"

"I asked you first. What you up to these days? Still mad at Brenda?"

"No, that's over. I'm just going through some stuff."

"Like what?"

"Just… stuff. You wouldn't understand."

"Have anything to do with Clarissa?" Carolyn asked.

Doreen snapped her head up and stopped walking to look at Carolyn.

"It might. What'd you know about it?" Doreen asked.

"I know that two wrongs don't make right. Whatever you're up to won't make you the better person." Doreen stared at Carolyn in disbelief as she continued, "I know about the disinvite because there're whispers. I also know that Clarissa's done everything she can to make it up to you, but you keep being mean and ignoring her. That's gotta hurt a lot more than she's hurt you."

"I don't know what you're talking about—"

"Don't you? I can't imagine the amount of courage it must take to be kicked in the shins and still come up smiling. Like Linney, Clarissa even fights for you with her friends. Did you know that?"

"Yeah…?" Doreen said, letting her thoughts pause in the air. Sighing, she had to admit this because she'd overheard it only a few minutes before. "What's that about Linney?"

"I don't know about you, but that kind of friendship's worth fighting for, a lot more than what you have with Brenda. Question is, are you worthy of Clarissa's friendship, or Linney's, for that matter? Think about it for a sec. I'm telling you this for your own good. Wise up. Don't do something stupid." With that, Carolyn walked off to catch up with others heading into the lunchroom's dining hall.

⎯⎯◦◈◦⎯⎯

Doreen was left alone with her thoughts over what Carolyn had said. She didn't have an answer for Carolyn's question but was struck by a profound realization that the kind of friendship from Clarissa, who showed as much loyalty to her as Linney, surely might be worth holding on to. Then like a thunderbolt, she got the reference about Linney. How could she be so stupid? She had even written WHITE GIRL in big letters in the *Slang Book* about Linney, not thinking *once* that this was a form of racism and possible jealousy. It never occurred to her that the same words she had hurled at Linney were racist against her own niece. Doreen was a racist bully. How could she not have seen the error of her ways? *Linney, I'm so sorry!* The shame was acute. Linney had given more than Doreen had ever given back. More poignantly, so had Clarissa. Doreen had personally felt the sting of racism and learned a valuable lesson. A desire started to grow in her to make every effort to improve her attitude about others different from herself, starting with her niece Lindsey.

⎯⎯◦◈◦⎯⎯

Doreen and Brenda stood looking across at each other from behind the glass doors that Friday morning, the first week of October. Doreen couldn't stop thinking about Carolyn's words from the previous day while she waited on the landing at the top of the back stairs. On the other hand, Brenda was gleefully lying in wait and seemed pleased with herself while waiting for Clarissa to appear. Students filed through in quick succession, laughing and talking, utterly unaware of the calamity that was about to unfold. Doreen saw Clarissa, and their eyes met. Clarissa seemed so glad to have an acknowledgment from Doreen that she gave a brilliant white-toothed goofy grin.

As she came through the open doors, Doreen reached out and grabbed Clarissa's arm and pulled her to stand on the platform behind the glass door on Doreen's side, just as Brenda's foot went out, meeting nothing but air. Clarissa looked confused about what was happening and turned to see Brenda step out from behind the other glass door, yelling at Doreen.

"What'd you do that for?"

"She could've broken her neck!" Doreen said in protest.

"And you think I care?" Brenda's hands were on her hips, threatening.

"No, you don't care. I *know* you don't. But I do, and I'm not going to let you hurt her."

Comprehension slowly dawned on Clarissa's face, as it did with other students who slowed their movements on the stairs to listen and watch. However, this didn't stop Brenda, who continued spewing hatred with angry words and accusations while pointing her finger at Doreen.

"You a stupid heifer, you know that? I knew you'd punk out on me! Who the fuck cares about this little honky other than you? Huh?"

"*Go to hell,*" Doreen said through gritted teeth as she moved close to Brenda's face. "You're a racist, Brenda. It's not right. *You're* not right."

Then out of nowhere, Doreen found herself looking into the concerned baby blues of the same boy who had been watching her all year. His deep voice asked after her welfare.

"Is she bothering you?" he asked. Doreen knew he was talking to her, but she ignored him for a while, looking past him to glare at Brenda.

"No, she has a class to get to…. Don't you?" Doreen's eyes flashed at Brenda. Then the dark-haired boy with blue eyes instantly took command of the situation.

"All right! Show's over, folks! Go on to class." He then turned his attention to Brenda. "Girl, I don't know you or what this is about, but I suggest you move on before I report you to the front office."

Doreen watched as Brenda stepped away from them and walked in the opposite direction to the school's front corridor, glaring back at her.

<hr>

As Mark Roberts watched Brenda walk away, Clarissa quietly introduced him to Doreen. This allowed him to say they had known each other since grade school. He didn't let on that he knew of Clarissa's attempt to befriend Doreen after the family snub and wanted to do something to turn the tide of misunderstanding between the two. He saw his chance that day as providence.

Although Mark would never describe himself as bashful, when Doreen smiled at him, he felt himself slightly blushing. He couldn't help but think how beautiful she was up close, and now that he was, he couldn't take his eyes off her. Mark was surprised to find himself unsteady on his feet in her presence. After all, he was a junior, an upperclassman, and a brainiac who prided himself on keeping his wits about him. From the first day he saw Doreen at her locker, he had watched her. He couldn't help but find himself drawn to this intangible mystery she had about herself. He felt he could probably spend the rest of his life trying to find out just what that mystery was.

He hoped Clarissa didn't see the effect Doreen had on him. But by the way Clarissa basked in the idea of Doreen being her friend again, he doubted she saw much of anything. He listened as Doreen talked as if no time had passed between her and Clarissa at all. Sighing, he accepted being ignored by them, which allowed him to ponder if inclusion and tolerance would ever overcome racism in most, if not all, of its forms. *Maybe one day.*

# CHAPTER 35

## *Sandra Beaumont*

T HE LAST WEEK in September, three weeks after Virginia's death, Sandra Beaumont was having an epiphany of her own. While sipping tea in her darkened sitting room, she couldn't shake the shock and vision of seeing Virginia Lee's body on the cold steel table in the funeral home's basement, waiting for her husband's ministrations. She couldn't ignore the thought of what Virginia had done to die in such a fashion. Virginia, who was said to have had a promising future, should not be lying there.

Her husband was the only Black undertaker and funeral home director in Paris, and Sandra knew the business was taking a toll on him. She also knew her husband felt duty bound to do justice to the body and give it as much dignity after death as it led in life. The emotional toll was heavy indeed. They tried to keep the unpleasant business of death from Angela as best they could. Unfortunately, Angela was privy to Virginia's body in a way that might scar her profoundly. After many discussions and late-night nightmares, Angela seemed to be coping better than expected, for now.

Sandra had been brought up in comfort with prominent parents in Lexington: the Lelands. But her father decided his funeral business, known simply as Leland's Mortuary, was needed more in Paris than in Lexington. She hated Paris and its down-home feel and resented that she had to leave her friends and adapt to this small-town way of life.

Sandra didn't need to befriend Janie Mae Munro but did so because she was new in town. To her way of thinking, the Munros were poor lower class and not on her level. Sandra believed Janie's mother had overindulged her and deluded Janie into thinking she had "class" of some sort. However, they were miles apart in that department. Because of Janie's friendly demeanor and beauty, Sandra often complimented Janie with sugary sweetness to show they were the best of friends. Yet, much to her dismay, Sandra realized she was not and would not be the belle of the ball in this small town. No, that distinction belonged to Janie Munro. Because of this, she secretly loathed the woman.

In time, Janie's behavior confirmed to Sandy that she was uncouth and stupid. Many times she watched Janie's clumsiness and eagerness to please. Who else would giggle at herself over the dumb and stupid things she did sometimes and mock herself in front of others? Most people thought this was an endearing trait, but Sandra thought it was just plain gauche and further marked Janie as classless. She managed to convince herself of this, so much so that it came as a shock when Janie had to go and marry Larry Hollis. How she captured that tall drink of water and pulled his attention away from Sandra was anybody's guess.

Soon after her father's death, Sandra married Clevedon Beaumont, who became the proprietor of the renamed Beaumont Funeral Home, taking up the business her father left behind. They were considered upper class along with the Averys, Crawfords, and Randalls. She loved the position. The unfortunate stigma of living next door to a funeral home had given her a distinctive aloofness from her neighbors. Few people ever bothered to visit, even on the odd occasion when she hosted a dinner party, and in due time, she resolved not to care. She reasoned that what the community thought of her was of no consequence. They would ultimately need her more than she needed them or their approval.

Janie's daughter, Lindsey, sometimes drove her up a wall with her seeming sense of self-entitlement. Angela, her angel, was an easygoing person who was kind, compassionate, and intelligent. Sandra never got involved with Angela's social life and viewed her friendship with Lindsey as her daughter's way of caring for a stray puppy, which was admirable. To her surprise, that friendship deepened, which caused endless frustrations for Sandra in her campaign to dislike Janie Mae. It was bad enough Janie's mother lived across the street where Sandra often saw Janie's younger sister, Doreen, sashaying about the neighborhood. No class or couth at all, that one.

Her part-time work at Dr. Roberts's office provided an outlet from the boredom of being a funeral home concierge when business was slow. Sharing office space with Janie and seeing her dedication to becoming a nurse caused a subconscious need to become one herself. The competition to excel in this endeavor overshadowed the realization that Sandra's heart was not in it as much as Janie's.

That was their history, but things had changed. Now they had this criminal problem, and the drive for superiority over Janie had shifted. Sandra could not dismiss the kind and gentle nature of the Misses Sweet. She knew little of them, yet there must be more to learn. There they were, sitting in Janie's house, no less; she had to ask herself why. Although Dottie had her challenges, Katherine's manners and comportment were the behaviors she had been taught to appreciate. But for some reason, Janie and her daughter Linney were the recipients of their attention. It was unusual.

Her previous attitude toward her neighbors had grown cold, distant, and calculated, to be sure. The realization of life's finality had profoundly touched her. After all, she wasn't immune to death's effects on a family and community. As she sipped her tea, Sandra contemplated how to elevate herself in the eyes of her neighbors and be a more productive member instead of holding on to petty grudges no one cared about but her. The Averys did what they could with the ministry. The Crawfords were active in housing—the Randalls in social endeavors, like sponsoring the Youth Center and contributing to the YMCA. She had to do more.

In the end, Sandra told herself that she would adopt a conciliatory approach in this time of need, and her first step would be to pay a visit to the Sweet sisters. Maybe it was time to quit her job with Dr. Roberts and devote time to doing good works. This sounded like a great idea because, in fact, Janie couldn't possibly do better in that regard. When it came to that thought, Sandra couldn't help herself.

<hr>

A few days after her epiphany and getting Angela off to school on a bright Monday morning, Sandra packed a basket. It was full of biscuits, her favorite homemade jam, packets of tea, and a bunch of flowers kept on hand at the funeral home for special occasions. She then headed out the door to visit the Sweet sisters.

Pulling the collar of her coat up around her ears as she walked along, she inhaled the freshness of the crisp air. She felt renewed on this gorgeous first weekday in October. The leaves on the trees had turned the unique hues that heralded the beginning of fall. She hoped the ice storms would not come earlier than expected and hinder her visits to the needy and infirm.

She had called to resign at Dr. Roberts's office, which was received without fuss. Sandra felt invigorated in doing what she felt was best for herself and her community. This thought quickened her steps as she walked the quiet streets that early autumn morning.

As she neared the place where poor unfortunate Virginia was found, she was surprised to see Lindsey Hollis walking out from behind the sawhorse barricade, which was still in place at the entrance.

"Is that you, Lindsey?" Sandra asked. The look on Lindsey's face reminded her of a startled deer.

"I know I'm not supposed to be here, but I can't help it. Please don't tell."

"Honey, what *are* you doing in there?"

"I don't know. We used to play here all day. I always thought it was safe, except for a few spiders and garden snakes, but… you can still see the tree house we made and the places we used to hide when we played hide and seek. The forts we built are still there, way in the back. No one comes anymore though, after… you know. They say it's haunted, but I don't think so. I don't blame them for thinking that anyway. Do you believe in ghosts? Do you think they'll cut it down, all the trees and stuff, I mean? I can't believe Miss Virginia's gone and was found… in there."

Sandra noticed the halting phrases as Linney tried to explain herself. Instinct told her that Linney needed more than just someone to talk to at this time. She seemed to be the loneliest person in the world, not at all the entitled young lady she thought her to be.

"Shouldn't you be in school? Why are you playing hooky and walking around on a cold morning like this?"

"I don't like school this year. I can't seem to make new friends, and now everyone stares at me and thinks I'm weird. At least that's what I think they think. So I thought I'd come to this place and maybe feel Miss Virginia's spirit or something. I don't know."

"Well, come on out of there. I'm on my way to see the Misses Sweet. You want to come with me?"

"I don't think that's a good idea. Miss Katherine might be disappointed I'm not at school, so I don't want her to know."

"By the thinness of the trees, she might have seen you already, don't you think? Come on, take a walk with me." This was a stern command for Linney to follow.

A sense of warmth flooded through Sandy's body, and it felt good knowing that finally, she was doing something worthwhile.

# CHAPTER 36

## *The Sun Always Shines*

IF I COULD only hear Miss Virginia's voice or feel her presence. Those were my thoughts as I hunched down to feel the ground she was found in. This time of year, Kentucky's weather could be fickle. One day cold and frosty, the next cool and sunny. But today, the frosty, cold feel of the dirt and rough nettles matched what I felt in my bones. I stood to make sure the buttons on my coat were clasped tight against the crisp air of the morning and dug my hands in the deep front pockets to keep them warm. Being kept at home for a whole week after the funeral didn't prepare me for returning to school. Word spread quickly of me keeping Miss Virginia's secret. It was hard to face another day of stares and whispers from my classmates, all of them saying things like I could've saved Miss Virginia if I'd opened my mouth and said something. I felt awful.

I still hadn't figured out the mysterious conversation between Stooly and Slim at the funeral reception dinner. Thinking about that gave me the idea to look for clues in the Jungle, some hint of what Stooly and Slim might be trying to put together, but all I found were memories of my girlhood. I knew the police barricade would prevent anyone from coming in, but I never thought someone would see me coming out. That would be Angela's mom, Miss Sandra.

Miss Katherine was just leaving her house dressed in a woolen coat with a scarf around her head when Miss Sandy and I arrived at the bottom of her steps.

"Good Monday morning Miss Sweet. I'm Sandra Beaumont. How nice to meet you."

"I don't know you, but same to you, good morning. I'm Katherine Sweet." Then turning to me, she asked, "What are you doing over there in those woods, young lady? I was just coming to get you out from over there. You know your mother would be very upset if anything happened to you. Why aren't you in school?"

"It might be better if we answered your questions inside, out of the cold," Miss Sandra suggested. "That is if you don't mind. I brought some biscuits and tea for us to enjoy, and I hope you like these flowers."

Straightening to her full height, Miss Katherine sized Miss Sandy up and down and peered at her basket of goodies. "Lord, don't let me forget my manners," Miss Katherine said. "Yes, come on inside and visit out from this cold air."

The warmth within the house was a welcome change. The gloom that had settled over the house after Miss Virginia's death seemed to be gone. Miss Dottie rocked in her chair and hummed a quiet tune. She paid little attention to her early-morning visitors but nodded when we came in. We took off our light coats and placed them on pegs in the wall while Miss Katherine busied herself in the kitchen with Miss Sandy not far behind. I searched for a vase to place the flowers in and prayed no one would press me about playing hooky from school.

Miss Sandy explained the reason for her visit and apologized for not visiting sooner than now. It seemed to me Miss Katherine was eager to get to know this lady. In their presence, there was a familiarity I hadn't felt since Miss Virginia's death. There was an ease in their conversation that was nice to hear, but soon the discussion turned to me. God did not hear my prayer.

"And why aren't you in school again?" Miss Katherine asked.

"I don't like being there after what happened to Miss Virginia," I said. "I don't have many friends, and nowadays, my classmates treat me funny and whisper mean things. I wanted to be where Miss Virginia was last, but I didn't think anyone would see me."

"Well, I did. If it wasn't for Miss Beaumont here, you'd probably still be there, am I right?" Miss Katherine asked, but I could say nothing in answer for myself.

"Sit up straight, child, as I taught you. You're in the presence of a lady, just like your mother." I did as she said but noticed Miss Sandy's back stiffening; then she quickly settled back in her chair. Miss Katherine glanced sideways at her as she sipped her tea but said nothing more. I looked from Miss Katherine to Miss Sandy, feeling an awkwardness come over the room. So I decided to say something if no one else would.

"Miss Virginia used to talk to me about accepting who I was and not worry about what others thought of me. She made it sound easy. It's not. Like taking one step forward and two back. The more I try, the more something will remind me I'm less than ordinary."

"Now, that's just pitiful," Miss Katherine said. "You know the truth of it, so never mind them. You just keep being the sweet girl you are. You'll be surprised how people will come around in no time. The sun always shines on the morrow, don't forget. Even if you don't see it, it's shining just the same."

"We have a *Slang Book* that us kids write in. We mostly write funny things about each other. This year is the first time I've been included. It was awful what they wrote about me."

"Lindsey, I wish you could see the wonderful spirit you possess inside. You're like your mother in that way. It shines through to your very soul, yes it does. Even Dottie there relaxes a lot more when you're around than not." Miss Katherine looked sideways at Miss Sandy again. I think she said this on purpose for some odd reason. "I suspect one day, you'll be called on to set things straight with an inner strength you never knew you had, and on that day, the choice you make will be the right one. Regardless of what others think."

"I think this awful crime not only happened to Virginia but to all of us," Miss Sandy said, then sighed. "We have each other, which should be good enough to get us through until that villain is found. A warm fire with friends can go a long way to feeling better." She turned to me, "So tomorrow, you'll go back to school, hold your head high, and get your education with a smile and a carefree attitude. This will blow over soon."

How odd. Miss Sandy seemed similar to Miss Virginia in giving advice. The tone of the conversation shifted between us, and soon I felt comfortable enough to look for a book to read. I carefully took out a book by Jane Austen titled *Emma*, which I had begun before Miss Virginia's death. For me, the challenge of understanding the stories and properly inflecting the language written inside was both educational and fun. If I had questions, Miss Katherine would always put the story into meaning and explain the importance of the language used at that time long ago.

Until the loss of Miss Virginia, the readings always soothed Miss Dottie. I wasn't sure if she would welcome another read. But I wanted to try, given what Miss Katherine just said about my effect on her. Once I sat in front of her chair, Miss Dottie leaned her head in her usual position, giving me the signal to begin. As I entered the world of Emma Woodhouse and her misadventures at matchmaking, I was comforted by the conversation between Miss Katherine and Miss Sandy.

"These biscuits are delicious. Did you make them yourself?" Miss Katherine asked.

"Fresh from the A&P," she joked. "But the marmalade jam is homemade."

"You don't say? You know I've got a garden out back. I love gardening with flowers. The ones you brought are lovely. You wouldn't mind if I called you Sandra now, would you?"

After a while, I forgot all about finding clues to connect the dots between Stooly and Slim's conversation. If they had any idea that man was responsible for Miss Virginia's death, I was sure they would have notified the police. Or would they?

As I lost myself in the reading, hearing the friendly hum of conversation between Miss Sandy and Miss Katherine, Miss Dottie spoke quietly but loud enough for me to hear.

"Virginia Lee's come home, yes she has."

<h1 style="text-align:center">CHAPTER 37</h1>

Stooly and Me

I'VE HEARD SOME say when God closes one door, He opens another. That's the way it happened for me and Miss Sandy. It felt as if the spirit of Miss Virginia was with us and would always be, if not in the presence of Miss Sandy, then in all the other Miss Virginias in my life.

I was allowed to spend the day with the sisters and Miss Sandy until it was time for Mom to come home. They left it up to me to tell Mom about my ditch, which I promised to do. Miss Katherine was excited to share her knitting and crocheting techniques, and when I was done reading a few pages of *Emma* to Miss Dottie, I shared some of the stitches I had learned. I was happy to see Miss Katherine back to her old self as she talked again of deportment and how young ladies should handle themselves in polite company.

As promised, I returned to school, but I couldn't keep the promise of telling Mom about playing hooky. I continued eating lunch by myself until Amy Cox's pointy chin and big forehead sat down across from me and dared to say, "Hi!" This was all I needed to make an effort to befriend my classmates. She had slightly wide-set eyes and three freckles on one side of her face, a small mouth that moved sideways when she spoke. She was funny and loved to talk—all the time, saying whatever came to mind. As it turned out, I was the one who held back because of my older friends, not them. Although my pinkish coloring stood out, it wasn't enough to make them not want to befriend me outright. This was a revelation, and in hindsight, being alone at Western had opened a whole new world of friends for me. I learned many things; growing up and reaching out to others was just the start. I liked that.

After Miss Virginia's death, many changes occurred in the neighborhood. I hoped Miss Sandy would become a regular visitor, especially after Angela and Carolyn finally said they'd come by, which made me happy. After she discovered Miss Virginia's body, the change in Miss Edna was evident. I overheard Mom say Miss Edna had invited Miss Evans—whom Mom and Miss Tally helped find safety and counseling—over for coffee. Next on Miss Edna's list was Mr. Johnson. She hoped to get him out of that darkened house. Mom wished her good luck with that one.

I never told anyone my other reason for skipping school when Miss Sandy found me. As hard as I tried, I couldn't forget the conversation I overheard between Stooly and Slim. Maybe it was the shock of hearing Stooly speak in such a way that scared me. It was hard to accept that he could be a bad man. Miss Virginia once said some things are better left alone, but I ignored her teaching once again. It was a bright Saturday afternoon, the first week in October when I decided to visit Stooly.

⋘⊙⊙⊙⋙

No one really knew the kind of work Stooly did for a living. There was just talk, but what I overheard didn't seem right. Because of that, I instinctively knew to be careful. I had no idea what I would say to him, but deep inside, I knew the words would come.

From the rise where our row of houses sat, I could look down at the row of houses where Stooly lived. Our section was considered the place where the better of us lived. Stooly's units were questionable at best and not as well kept. As I used the cut-across to descend the steps to his section of units, I looked over my shoulder, hoping that no one saw me, especially Miss Edna. The closer I got, the more my knees started to knock together. *Just put one foot in front of the other. You can do this.*

I had to guess which house was his and took a gamble, particularly on one with jazz music playing quietly behind the locked screen door. After I knocked, there was no answer; however, when I turned to leave, Stooly appeared at the door. The surprise on his face quickly turned to suspicion, so I rushed in with an explanation.

"Hi, Mr. Stooly. I don't know if you remember me from the store, but I wanted to ask you something. See, I shouldn't have snooped, but I did and heard you and your friend talk about that strange man when you were out back of our house at Miss Virginia's funeral dinner."

"Yeah?"

"Well… I heard you say something about hurting him and Mr. Stooly; you just can't do that. I know it's none of my business, but because I didn't say anything before Miss Virginia died, I just can't *not* say anything now. I just can't. Please, Mr. Stooly, *you* just can't."

He stood behind his screen door and studied me for what seemed like an eternity. I instinctively looked down at my Keds, wishing I could disappear, resisting the urge to bite at my fingers. Then he did the unthinkable.

"You want to come inside?" Stooly asked.

"No! I mean, I shouldn't 'cause I don't know you that well."

After a pause, he said, "Come on inside."

He pushed the screen door open, and once again, my knees, no longer knocking, were like jelly. There he was, open-shirted on a cool fall day, showing his smooth skin and muscles. I felt more embarrassed than afraid. He beckoned. I couldn't resist. I stood just inside the door, then started to lose my nerve, but that changed when he offered me a glass of water. I refused but shouldn't have because my mouth went dry all of a sudden. I swallowed hard and then focused on why I was there.

"No, thank you. I have something to say and want to get it out before I lose my nerve, even more than I have already… so will you let me speak?" I asked, trying to sound brave.

"I haven't stopped you so far, have I?"

He said this with all the softness and complex tones he was known for. But also, there was a presence about him that commanded cautious attention, which could not be denied. So I continued on as bravely as I could.

"No, sir, but well… is it true? Are you going to kill that guy because you think he killed Miss Virginia? Because if you are, it's not right! You could go to jail! That wouldn't help anybody, least of all Miss Virginia. You can't do it. You just can't, Mr. Stooly."

"You keep saying that. Sit down over there and listen to me a minute."

Stooly motioned to a chair and sat on the couch opposite me. He didn't say anything for a while. He just studied me, cupping his face with his left hand, then placing his index finger above his top lip. I noticed the little things. The faint smell of cigarette smoke in the air, how nice his hands were, the lull of jazz music playing quietly in the background, and his smell, clean and fresh, the way he sat relaxed and curious. When he spoke, he dropped his hand, and I focused on his mouth and how it moved. It was as if I was being charmed by a deadly snake, mesmerized, helpless, and drawn ever closer before it struck.

"There's no benefit in snooping. But you know that already. Even so, there *are* things you don't know and some you won't understand. I appreciate you wanting to keep me out of jail and all, *but*…" he paused for effect before continuing, "what you overheard was just me talking. Just talk, nothing serious."

"Well, it sounded serious and—"

"That, it might have. I don't like that man, and neither does my friend," Stooly said. "It's a shame you heard what you did, and I apologize. But I don't want you to go thinking I'm someone I'm not. You're a sweet kid. I'm sure it took a lot of courage to come say what you did. So I'll tell you this, and only this… I don't make a habit of going to jail."

"If anything happened to you, it would be awful. If anything happened to that man, it would be bad too, but worse for all of us," I said.

"Anyone see you come down here?" he asked, then got up to check his front window. His movements were as smooth as he was, no hitches, just glide.

"I don't think so." Now that I was there, I secretly hoped someone had seen me. I could kick myself, thinking I could do this, but it was too late to turn back now. *Be brave! He won't hurt you.* "But was it just talk? I mean, can I trust that's the truth, and you're not making fun of a 'sweet kid'? I'm almost fourteen, you know."

"I didn't know. I stand corrected." He took a deep breath, stretched, and then let out a long sigh. "Seems folks around here like to think the worst of people. What they don't know won't hurt 'em, and what you hear, you can't always believe. There's hidden meaning in almost everything. If you listen closely enough, you'll learn a thing or two." Leaning closer to me with both arms on his knees, he crossed them and said, "I hope you're listening 'cause I am. What's this about not speaking up before Virginia Morgan died?"

Instantly my face felt hot, and it must have turned beet red. I tried to swallow, but my mouth went dry again. *Holy moly, I've done it now!* I spilled the beans on myself and didn't see it coming. I had to find a way out.

"Mr. Stooly, it was a secret. Miss Virginia was scared and asked me not to tell, and because I didn't, she's dead. I'll only tell if it helps, but there's no benefit in *you* knowing. So don't make me tell. I just can't." I said hurriedly.

"And you don't want to share just a *little* bit of that secret with me because you don't know me very well, is that it? Yet you come here to warn me not to kill someone. Seems to me you think you know me pretty well." He paused and watched me with a steady gaze, then said, "I'll make it easy on you. Let's play a guessing game, huh? It won't hurt. I promise."

Stooly saying it slow and easy like that caused me not to do or say anything other than nod my head and wait for the questions. It seemed the air had changed to a fog that enveloped me. Now he was matter-of-fact and no-nonsense. I let my guard down, and that wasn't good. I guess it's true that some snakes withdraw their fangs for reasons unknown just before they strike.

"Does it have to do with a man," Stooly asked, "maybe someone Virginia knew might kill her?"

"Uh-huh."

"Someone you think you saw me talking to that day at the funeral dinner?"

"Yeah. But that's just me guessing, so don't go thinking I know for sure."

"His name James Marx?"

A chill went down my spine. Stooly said nothing more but continued staring me down, studying my reaction while I bit my lip and gnawed on my cuticle. If I nodded anything at all, it was unknown to me. What I did know was that a quiet understanding had passed between the two of us. Then he smiled and winked at me, reminiscent of the wink he gave at The Hall that day in July. In an instant, the spell was broken.

"I like you. I like your spunk," Stooly finally said. "Now, if you'll excuse me, I have some business to attend to if it's all the same to you."

As I rose to leave, I wasn't convinced, so I made one more plea, "Promise you won't do anything bad. I don't want to see any more trouble, and geez Louise, if you go to jail, I don't know how I could stand myself."

Chuckling, he put an arm around my shoulders and walked me to his open door. This embrace was the closest I had ever been to Stooly. He gave me a gentle squeeze, then said, "Now see, *I* thought you were listening. What was said today and what you overheard stays between us, understand?" He dropped his smile, and the twinkle left his eyes, becoming a steely gaze.

When he asked if I "understood," his squeeze tightened, becoming not so gentle but firm and stiff as a vise, almost hurting. His eyes, cold as glass, hardened more than just a little bit. Now I understood, more clearly than he could have guessed, and nodded in agreement. His squeeze eased up, and he opened the screen door for me to exit.

"When I said you were a sweet kid, I meant that, so don't you worry. Don't ever change your ways. You're gonna be a heartbreaker one day. I just know it. Keep your nose clean, and watch out for dirty old men. I won't let anything happen to you without me answering for it. That's my thanks for thinking about ole Stooly. You take care now." The sparkle was back in his eyes when he smiled, and he watched as I stumbled down the steps in my worn-out Keds.

They say there's honor among thieves, but I didn't trust that Stooly was telling the whole truth. But whatever passed between us that day was special. I made a silent vow that if anything happened and Stooly was involved, I would protect him with all I had.

# Chapter 38

## *Sassy Ain't Classy*

MORE THAN A month had passed after Miss Virginia's death, and people still whispered and spoke quietly about what was being done to find her killer. By mid-October, daylight hours were getting shorter. Because Mom didn't want me at home alone, I went to Grandma's after school. To my surprise, Grandpa was eager to talk to me, and it was during this time I got to know him better.

I used to think he was getting too old to be a journeyman, traveling to wherever the work was needed. But, according to him, he was sought after for his knowledge and skill. Even though he wasn't licensed, he had years of experience and was well known and trusted. If he slowed down, the job offers would dry up, and that they couldn't afford.

His humor drew us closer than I ever dreamed. One day, I asked what he thought of my dad. He said he didn't think much of Daddy because if he turned sideways, he'd disappear. He didn't think Mom could put enough weight on him to keep him from falling over in the slightest breeze, even walking sideways. The vision of my dad walking in that way made me laugh so hard it hurt.

We learned a lot about each other, and listening to him talk about his boyhood days and how shy and naïve he used to be growing up in the hills of Kentucky was fascinating. I learned how studious he was in school and how hard life was for a poor mixed-Indian kid. Then he met and fell in love with my grandma, and life was never the same. He told me how he had to prove worthy of her and fought to win favor with my great-grandfather. Through hard work and determination, he eventually won her hand. Grandma was the light of his life. Without apologizing for how he was with my mother, I knew his attention to me was his way of apologizing to us both.

During this time, I never saw Doreen. Even my grandparents didn't seem concerned that she wasn't home much. Occasionally, I talked with her on the phone. She told me she was dating but never said who. Because of what happened with Barry, I thought this was her way of keeping me out.

As for my friends, Carolyn enjoyed her studies and experiences at school. She was still fun but more serious these days, and because of this, my time with Amy and Angela became more frequent. Angela was back to her old self, food no longer an intense interest but gossiping as usual. While doing homework at Amy's house and waiting for our parents to pick us up, Angela went in on Doreen.

"Doreen's a mess! The way she acts at school, preening around as if she's the Queen of Sheba. Don't she know sassy ain't classy?" Angela asked.

"That's typical," Amy said.

"Yeah, but the White kids don't like it, especially some of the horsey set. She's been spending a lot of time being palsy-walsy with Clarissa Ferguson."

"Doreen told me about her. I wonder what she's like and—"

"Let me tell you though!" Angela jumped in. "Doreen and Brenda got into a huge fight in the cafeteria over Clarissa, and she hauled off and told Brenda where to go! Doreen walked away, leaving Brenda in the lurch—you know how she does, all superior and stuff. The whole school was talking about it, but no one got in trouble. Not that day anyway."

"About time!" I said.

"What do you mean, 'not that day anyway'?" Amy asked.

"Wait, let me tell y'all. It gets worse! Clarissa disinvited Doreen to that dinner she's been bragging about."

"Really?" Amy and I asked in unison. "Doreen never tells me anything anymore," I said.

"I guess we're not allowed in their houses for dinner or anything! Doreen got her feelings hurt, and this came right after she told Brenda off."

"I don't believe that!" Amy said.

"Well, it's true, Amy," Angela insisted.

"They really don't want us in their houses for visits and stuff?" I asked.

"Apparently not!" Angela rolled her eyes. "It's a shame Doreen just couldn't keep her big mouth shut, bragging all over the place about the invite. It was embarrassing. Clarissa did all she could to make up for it, but Doreen wouldn't listen. Anytime Clarissa did something nice, Doreen would embarrass her out of spite, just to be mean. I felt bad for Clarissa."

"I do too, but I feel worse for Doreen," I said.

"I *don't!* Don't get mad, okay?" Angela said.

"I'm *not* mad," I said.

"You know what? Clarissa shouldn't be held to account for how her parents feel. That's not fair," Amy said.

Angela continued, "Doreen had to eat her words and beg for Brenda's forgiveness after that disinvite."

"Nooo!" Amy and I said in unison again.

"Yes. But then Brenda planned to do this dirty trick on Clarissa. Tried to trip her on the stairs and failed *big* time. Carolyn told me Brenda was suspended from school and won't be back until *after* the holidays for that stunt," Angela clarified. "I'm so glad she got caught!"

"Serves her right! Oooh, there is a God!" I said. We giggled over this news with a shared dislike for Brenda. Then Angela's mood changed.

"Don't be mad, Linney. You know Doreen's been staying after school to walk home alone, or so we thought. Doreen's seeing an older boy named Mark Roberts, a *White boy*," she whispered. "He's also been driving her home from school!"

"Nah-uh! You trying to psych me out or something?" I asked while Amy's eyes seemed to bulge out of their sockets at this news.

"I didn't believe it until I saw it for myself." In a singsong voice, Angela added, "They were playing touchy-feely with their fingers under the desks in study hall, so there!" Then she got serious and continued, "I told Doreen she was playing with fire, and she asked me to keep it quiet. I told her I couldn't make that promise because it wasn't cool. I wanted to tell you because you got to talk some sense into her!"

"*Me?* Geez Louise, Angie!" I exclaimed. "What makes you think she'll listen to me?"

"You have to try, at least. Okay?" Angela asked. "Just think about what I said. Somebody has to say something. Make her see reason."

"Oooh, yeah, you gotta do something," Amy piped in.

"Y'all!" I yelled, looking sternly at them both.

So many thoughts ran through my mind. My assumption of Doreen's lack of communication with me had nothing to do with Barry but everything to do with Mark Roberts? *Roberts. Is that Dr. Roberts's son? I wonder if my grandparents know.* I didn't tell Angela these thoughts. I shared a lot with her, and the gossip was fun. But family was family, and blood was thicker than water—or mud in Angela's case.

I only knew of one case of race-mixing and never understood the harm. Our heritage was even brought about by those long-ago circumstances. But it was clear it wasn't accepted in Paris. After being disinvited to Clarissa's house, what was Doreen thinking? Did she think she couldn't get hurt? And there was a killer on the loose, and she didn't seem to care. What if Mark couldn't drive her home after school, breaking her heart and leaving her open to danger? The more I thought about it, the more I felt I had to try.

I didn't look forward to seeing Doreen that weekend, but what else could I do? The thought of talking to her about anything caused my hands to sweat. We weren't all that close these days, so discussing Mark Roberts might not have been the best idea. I'd lose count on my fingers naming the reckless things Doreen had done. Even so, this behavior had consequences that I didn't want to see her pay. I'd never forget pinkie swearing that we would always be friends, promising never to leave each other's side, no matter what. Now we were further apart than ever.

Grandma always seemed to expect me to show up, and once again, chaos reigned at her house. "Well, *there* you are." She smiled. "Come help me with this mess. I swear that man is worthless when he knows I have work to do. Setting a path to the garden with bricks lined with rail ties just tracks dirt all over the house. Inside *and out!*" she yelled out the door in Grandpa's direction.

"Who, Grandpa?"

"Just look at him out there. He needs to rest, but he won't. Maybe if you help him, he'll finish up soon and leave my floor cleaner than it is now."

"Okay, but first, I need to talk to Doreen."

"You just missed her. She didn't say where she was going, but I'm sure she'll be back soon. You're more than welcome to wait. You know today's her birthday?! While you wait, please go help your grandpa. I swear! All this mess is causing me to fuss at him more than I want to. Ruining my special plans for Doreen."

*That's just great!* I forgot this was Doreen's birthday. Talking to her about Mark today, of all days, was out of the question now. My only choice was to help rescue my grandpa from Grandma's wrath.

After I'd helped Grandpa in the garden, my capris and Keds were too dirty to sit in the house, so I decided to go home to change. I promised to return to celebrate Doreen's birthday. My grandmother continued to sweep endlessly at the dirt as I left, which never seemed to depart from her kitchen floor.

It felt good to walk under a clear blue sky. It would be Halloween in a few weeks. All thoughts of danger and Doreen's recklessness left my mind like a shot as I tilted my head back to feel the sun's warmth on my face. As the cool autumn air warmed around me, I thought of nothing else except what to wear later for Doreen's special day. But when I neared the Jungle, I heard muffled screams coming from inside. I stopped outside the entrance where someone had left a brown paper bag on the ground, and just when I began to peek inside the bag, the scream came again, this time more shrill and impossible to ignore. I slowly stepped inside.

My footsteps were loud on crisp leaves that had fallen from the massive trees as I hurried along among the twisted, fallen sticks and twigs. So loud was I that whoever was screaming surely could hear me and call out for help. But no call came as I crept forward without calling out myself. I looked up through the bare branches of trees, then passed the brick fort the neighborhood boys had built with some loose red bricks still lying around. I gazed up at the old tree house that should have come down long ago. I passed a pile of big sticks and twigs we used to support the mounds of dirt and grass needed to hide from our imagined foes or for places to hide in a game of hide and seek. I passed the spot where large tree branches had fallen over, which we used as places to sit when making up stories about monsters and ghosts that would scare us late at night.

As I walked deeper into the woods, I could see movement but couldn't make out what or who it was. I was coming close to where Miss Virginia was found, still marked with remnants of yellow tape tied on branches here and there. Then the figures became plain; someone was struggling on the ground. It was female, but there was another voice too. Getting closer, I knew who was screaming.

It was there that I saw what no one at thirteen should see.

# CHAPTER 39

## *The Jungle*

T HE DAY WAS unusually warm for mid-October, and the sky was as blue as the day of Miss Virginia's funeral. Wearing a light sweater around her shoulders, Doreen was positively giddy as she left the house in her new Saturday dress and tennis shoes to visit Linney. Today was her fifteenth birthday! So many thoughts were running through her mind she couldn't possibly concentrate on more than one thing at a time. As Doreen walked out the door, she reminded herself to go to Stanley's to buy something for her and Linney to eat. She told her parents she was going out but didn't tell them where. Forgetting to tell her parents where she was going was not acceptable either. *Who does that?* She then berated herself for being so absentminded lately. *Oh well,* she thought to herself. All she could think about was handsome, gorgeous Mark Jeremy Holden Roberts. One day, she would be Mrs. Roberts, and what a fabulous day that would be. To see everyone at her wedding, envious, no doubt, and how lovely their life would be together, happily ever after.

She and Mark promised to be discreet, but Doreen could not contain herself. Her mother had seen her driven in Mark's car and suspected the truth, and to Doreen's delight, she didn't seem to care. Her mom was the only one who knew, and if her mother decided to spill the beans, let her; at least it wasn't

Doreen who let the cat out of the bag. It had been ages since she talked to Linney, not since Miss Virginia's death anyway, and she just had to share the news, especially before her birthday party.

Doreen wanted to tell what he whispered in her ear and how he made her feel. She couldn't wait to share how nice he was, never mind that he was White and who cared these days anyway? Negro people had come so far in the past decade. They were not called Colored or Negro anymore, for that matter, but Black. That put them on an even footing with White people, didn't it? Plus she liked the term *Black*. After all, she wasn't so black, and he wasn't so white in color. Race didn't matter when they were together; surprisingly, they weren't that different.

They talked for hours about their plans and dreams. Mark told Doreen of his fights with his dad and controlling mother, but it wasn't that bad. He loved them both and knew the arguments were an effort, at least on his father's part, to get him to focus on his studies and future. He even volunteered at the hospital from time to time, helping where he could. He let her into his world of social manners and Southern gentlemanly behavior. She let him into her world of loving parents whom she felt would deny her nothing.

Doreen never wanted to lose her heart too quickly, but it was hard not to because Mark was so easy to love. He was intelligent, funny, and handsome and didn't care what people thought about his actions. Mark was his own person who wasn't afraid to push boundaries. He was sensitive and considerate to most people but didn't suffer fools. She felt protected in his presence, and when he listened to her, she felt she was the only one that mattered. He was a caring, trusting soul, and because of his kind nature, she could count on him to be there whenever she needed him, which made her feel secure and safe. He was there during the time of uncertainty between herself and Clarissa. Eventually, she and Clarissa mended fences; if it were not for that friendship, she wouldn't have known Mark. It was karma, it was fate, and she was glad. She didn't think anything could go wrong in her life from that point on.

She realized that she had not been the kind of friend she should've been to Linney. For that, she desperately wanted to apologize, especially for being jealous of her friendship with the Sweet sisters. The 'flicted sister had even cursed Doreen, but so far, nothing had happened. Doreen thought the saying must be true about curses working only if you believe them. Well, she didn't, but all the same, she should've known better than to one-up Linney. Reluctantly but graciously accepting defeat, Doreen had to give Linney her respect.

As these thoughts ran through her mind, Doreen took her sweet time strolling through the street to Stanley's grocery. Though she had taken the long way around and would have to double back to get to Linney's, she didn't care. She enjoyed seeing the dappled sunlight glinting through the trees on multicolored leaves, still clinging to their branches. She enjoyed hearing the swish, whoosh sound of neighbors raking the fallen ones into piles for later burning or discarding. *Linney'd know every leaf and tree. Linney's smart that way, what with all that reading she does all the time.* Learning came easy to Doreen, but Mark had sparked an interest in her to become more studious instead of reading fashion magazines all day. She was sure Linney could help. Doreen needed Linney more than she ever thought.

Outside Stanley's sat a man Doreen had never seen before. He was filthy, wearing a bloodstained apron with a barely visible white background. He stood, lowered his head, and nodded in her direction. She ignored him and hurried inside. Because she was the only customer, she took her time browsing for some tasty treats. She settled on the Little Debbie Creme Pies that Linney liked so much. She also ordered two ham-and-swiss sandwiches and two coke-colas. While she waited for the sandwich meats to be sliced and wrapped, she could see through the glass of the wood-framed door and watched as the stranger stood outside, staring at the front of the store. Doreen looked over at Mr. Stanley to see if he noticed, but he didn't seem bothered. Mr. Stanley only focused on the sandwiches and put everything in a brown paper bag.

"That'll be one dollar and twenty-five cents please." She thought about saying something about the creepy man but chose not to instead. She had a bad feeling but tried to ignore it as she nervously reached for her allowance money. Mr. Stanley took no notice of her trembling hands, thanked her, and bid her good day.

Doreen ignored the stranger as she exited the store, held her head high, and pretended he wasn't there. *If he tries anything, I'll scream my head off.* She picked up her pace and hurried along, thinking she couldn't get to Linney's fast enough.

When Doreen got to Linney's door, no one answered. Frustrated, she sat on the front porch to wait. *Where could they be? Linney's got to come home soon.* While waiting, she couldn't help but see the barricade crossing the Jungle entrance across the street. The sawhorse barriers, which were meant to keep people out, were still in place, but Doreen never thought for an instant that it pertained to her. In the back of her mind, the warning from Miss Dottie Sweet echoed. *What does that silly old lady know anyway?* She walked across the street, put down her bag of goodies at the entrance, and wandered in.

In her mind's eye, she could see herself and Linney playing games, gathering sticks and twigs to build fires that burned out as soon as they were built because the kindling was damp. Here they gathered mud after a hard rain and made mud pies, thinking they could be eaten after hardening in the sun. This went on until Doreen got an Easy-Bake Oven, where she baked real pies with a single light bulb; now, that was cool. The simple pleasures of catching lightning bugs and putting them in jars or catching June bugs that couldn't get away as they flew straight out from the string they'd tied to their bodies. This brought a smile to her face. She passed the Red Fort and gazed up at the tree house they all built to get away from the spiders and snakes on the ground, not realizing those critters could climb as well as crawl. She was amazed that the tree house was still there and had not collapsed by now.

Then she came to the place where Miss Virginia had been found. She knelt beside this area and reached to feel the ground where her body had lain. She knew Miss Virginia in eighth grade English and felt bad she'd been taken so soon. Doreen stayed there for a while and then got up to venture farther back into the Jungle. She didn't want to go any farther than necessary, but with the sun so high and the trees bare of leaves, she could see deeper inside, more so than usual. Maybe she could find the back entrance she'd heard of. But here, the branches scratched at her legs where they were not bent back by the comings and goings of kids from the neighborhood. There were so many thick branches that Doreen figured it was useless to continue and decided to turn back. That's when she saw him.

The man from Stanley's grocery was there, stooped down and hidden deep among the twisted branches of tree limbs and sticks. He was surrounded by the darkness of the Jungle branches with eyes visible as black burning coals. She was never more afraid than at that moment, so much so that she was frozen in place, staring back at him.

He rose, calling to her "Doreen, sweet Doreen," over and over again as he came closer to her. Turning, she ran, not caring about the sting of cuts to her legs and arms as she hurried blindly back through the brush. She was amazed that the entrance was not as close as she thought and questioned how he ever knew her name! She felt him clutch the back of her dress. Then he spun her around and grabbed her arms, tripping her as they fell together.

She screamed, and with her knees bent, she kicked at his chest, knocking him backward. But he was quick to recover, crawling forward like a spider. He bent over her and hit her in the face with his fist. She screamed out in pain and scratched at his face. She fought as hard as she could to get away from him. *I've got to get him off me… He smells so bad… Who is this horrible man… What will Mark think if he ever finds out? Oh God! Oh God! This can't be happening! This has to be a nightmare!* She reasoned that, yes, she was still asleep; she was dreaming. But the pain she felt when he hit her across the face again made it real enough. This was no dream.

As he tore at her dress and panties, his intentions were clear. But exhausted, she was overpowered and entirely at his mercy. She begged, she pleaded to be let go, but all he said was her name repeatedly. She could do nothing but scream. He tried to muffle her cries with his smelly hands and unzip his pants at the same time. He lowered into her so violently that the pain came as a shock with an intake of breath. Then her screams renewed to an intensity that mimicked the pain she felt between her legs. It hurt so badly at first. Then her mind went numb.

She had the sensation of being outside her body, as if floating and looking down at the incredibly terrible scene. She no longer felt the dirt underneath her and the small stabs of nettles and rocks pressing into her naked backside. She no longer heard the rustle of leaves as she scraped at the dirt, trying to release her arms to strike at the creature. She felt nothing but knew she needed help. She needed someone, but no one was there except them. She thought of Linney and the Very Personally Yours kit. It wasn't supposed to be like this, not like this! She instinctively called out to Linney, despite knowing Linney wasn't there.

No one would hear or help. No one at all.

# CHAPTER 40

## *Loose Bricks and Sticks*

AT THIRTEEN, YOU don't have a full concept of evil. At thirteen, you don't think about death. At thirteen, you think you'll live forever. At thirteen, you tell yourself that the boogeyman is not real. I will never forget what I experienced that day at the age of thirteen.

Lying very near where Miss Virginia had been found, Doreen was face up, beating wildly at someone on top of her. Her dress was torn and drawn up around her waist. She was trying desperately to free an arm pinned down by a man with a smell so foul that I almost threw up. If it wasn't for Doreen being attacked so violently by him, I would have. Her face was filthy and bloody. Her hair was barely recognizable as black in color because of the dirt caked there. Her legs were exposed up to her thighs as he unzipped his pants quickly, and as I watched, he did it with such a swift motion that I could hardly tell he had done it. I stood frozen as he quickly lowered his body onto hers, and terrified, I watched as she let out a scream of such pain, so intense, it seemed the trees above parted to let out the sound.

I ran. I ran back to the Jungle entrance with legs and dirty Keds flying. I ran away from the horror while trying to erase it from my mind. I ran, and as I did, memories flooded back in a nanosecond of my bond with Doreen. The pinkie promises, the put-downs, the insults, the fights, the hope and helplessness of wanting to be her or her me, the fun times, the bad times, the secret talks we had, the way she laughed, smiled, frowned, and the future we planned growing up together with our own families. The special memory of picking flowering clover stems for braiding into laurel wreaths on a bright spring morning all came flooding back. It can't end here; this can't be the end of that promise. And in that nanosecond, hearing her call my name in a plaintive plea over and over, "Linney… Linney… " My mission became crystal clear. She couldn't have known I was there. She didn't see me. She called my name because she needed me. So I ran back… to her.

It happened so fast. I'll never know how I knew what to do, how I did it, or why. I ran back, and the faster I ran, the farther away the jungle trees receded from me. As if in a bad dream, the trees kept getting farther and farther away; the sensation was as if I couldn't get there fast enough or would never get there. At all. But somehow, I got closer and moved stealthily. I quickly picked up two loose bricks from the Red Fort, one in each hand. I ran without hearing my footfalls on the crisp, dry leaves, my focus intense and measured. So vivid were the details of every little thing, sharp and clear, so brilliant were the colors, the feel of the air on my skin, so sensitive I could feel it prick at the hairs on my arms as they stood on end. I didn't hear anything. It was eerily quiet and still around me, no birds, no crack of sticks and twigs, nothing, just my breathing. I cared about nothing, not even caring if I had to kill.

He didn't hear me. He never stopped thrusting at Doreen's body, moving strangely in that way, moaning over and over above her. He was tearing her body apart. He didn't hear or see me as I came up fast beside him.

I struck him hard in the back of the head with one brick and hit him on the side of his face with the other. He rolled over and off Doreen. It was then that I looked the devil full in the face. This was personal. I will never forget the look of hatred mixed with anger and his snarl. Stunned, he seemed bewildered over how I came to be there, then became enraged.

I stood over that foul-smelling creature and, without saying a word, brandished the same brick I quickly picked up after it fell, threatening to hit him again. Daring him to come at me. Without moving, I stared down the monster with a horrible scar on his face and protected Doreen with legs that straddled her body. He was caught, and he knew it.

Suddenly, he howled like an animal, turned around, and scuttle-crawled away, deeper into the woods. The sound he made, like nothing I had heard before or since, had every hair on my body standing on end. It was as if he were speaking in tongues mixed with animal cries. It chilled me to the bone. I stood there, catching my breath for a few minutes, and waited for him to return while Doreen writhed in pain beneath me. I dropped the brick and looked down at her. She needed help right away.

—◦◦◦—

The horror was real. She was severely hurt. She clung to me as I struggled to lift her from the dirt. She was afraid but didn't cry. She was in shock; we both were. We stared straight ahead, and she occasionally looked up at me, seemingly surprised I was there. She looked around, wild-eyed, shaking, and clinging to me, almost ripping my shirt, reminding me of that lady who saw the devil once upon a time.

Her face and arms were cut and bruised. She was bleeding from several places and from one place I didn't want to think about. Everything moved as if in slow motion. I wanted help for her. The cuts and scrapes to my body stung, but I didn't care about those, only hers.

People were coming to us. Grown people helped us out of the maze of trees, some I recognized, and others I didn't. There was wailing and cries from a lady I knew, one who had warned of dangers in the Jungle. She warned us, didn't she? But wasn't that for the other lady who died? I felt sorry for the lady because she *had* warned us, and we didn't listen. We were stupid to ignore the lady.

I looked over at her again, she who clung to me, and I pointed to the others because she needed help. Then she collapsed, and for a crazy instant, I thought she had died. I insanely thought about what to peel off my skin if she had done. There was crying, but I could no longer hear the sobs.

The sounds that were muffled at first grew intense. I stared at their mouths, watching as words formed on their lips. I tried to understand what was being asked as their voices grew louder. I looked down at the ground because the sound was too loud for me to see clearly: screeching and vibrating sounds running together, too many voices, too much noise, and too much to answer for answers I didn't have.

I placed my hands over my ears to quiet the sound and that of my own screams. I screamed so they would shut up. I screamed because I had run away. I screamed because I was scared and a coward. I screamed at what I saw and did without thought or reason. I screamed for her and the hurt she had suffered. I screamed because they couldn't help me. I screamed because I didn't understand why I couldn't *stop* screaming.

# CHAPTER 41

## *First, Do No Harm*

D R. DAVID ROBERTS was in the emergency room hallway, casually checking the list of patients admitted that day for treatment. It was a slow day, slower than usual. Then a call came in of an ambulance arriving from Greenfield. Two young girls needed medical assistance. Nurses and interns hurried to receive the ambulance as it careened around the corner to the emergency room entrance of County Memorial Hospital.

"I'll take it from here," Dr. Roberts said and barked orders to the staff, "Admit them immediately to the second floor, east wing." His instructions were met with stares, and he knew what that meant. His instincts told him this would not be good, and he was right.

"But Doctor," the first nurse said, "the east wing is intended for—"

"It's intended for patients in need," Dr. Roberts said.

An EMP met Dr. Roberts as he ran up to the ambulance and gave him an update on the conditions of the girls. Dr. Roberts looked at Lindsey and, after checking her vitals, instructed that she be taken in first. His focus and concern then turned to Doreen, who was more critical, and he gave instructions that she be taken to the operating room, STAT! He spoke no more.

After Lindsey's vitals were rechecked and deemed stable, she was sedated, bandaged, and placed in the hallway to await transport to the east wing. Within a few hours, Dr. Roberts emerged from the OR, exhausted after administering to Doreen. He then instructed the interns and nurses on handling and processing the samples for lab analysis. To see Lindsey lying in the hospital corridor, still waiting for a room, enraged him.

"What's this?" he asked.

"I think there's a mix-up in the orders, Doctor. This says to admit her to the east wing of the hospital. Shouldn't it say west wing? We decided to hold her here for clarification," a resident intern said.

"There's no mistake. The orders are clear, so do as instructed," Dr. Roberts said.

"But Doctor, there's no protocol for it. She *can't* be placed in the east wing. Neither can the other one. You know why," the insistent intern said. He was trying to make a good argument, and in doing so, others gathered around as orderlies watched, awaiting what to do.

"Why are my orders being questioned?" Dr. Roberts asked. "Do I have to remind you of my position here? Take them up now, and—"

"But Doctor." The first nurse spoke up. "This sets a dangerous precedent for us to—"

"Dangerous for *whom*?" he asked.

"For us, the hospital, and Paris as a whole. We can't allow Negroes on the same floor as Whites. Besides, the west wing is empty of patients, which is where they belong," a second nurse said.

"Finally, someone's had the nerve to say it out loud," Dr. Roberts said. "Are you trying to tell me that in this day and age, a patient's race takes precedence over what side of the building they should reside in for medical care? That, for some reason, the health and well-being of anyone seeking medical attention should first be assessed with the archaic practice of race in mind?"

"No, sir," the second nurse responded, "but I think you should consider—"

"What? The consequence of my actions?" he asked.

"But they're niggers, sir! They carry diseases that could infect us all. We have to treat them differently," the earnest intern said.

"How you made it this far with that backward thinking I'll never understand," Dr. Roberts said. "What *are* they teaching in medical school these days? Don't answer that… I simply can*not* fathom it."

The first nurse chimed in. "He's right, Doctor. We can't allow them to be admitted to the east wing. There simply is no precedent—"

"There is now!" Dr. Roberts said. "I shouldn't have to remind you of the oath we take as physicians. *Take them up now!* I'll resign my position as chief of staff or the devil take me first before I allow these young ladies, *innocents*, to fall victim to another attack from an unknown assailant because of lack of oversight, *on my watch*, due to negligence from a racist staff! You do it now, or so help me God!"

With that, he stormed away and instructed another nurse of his choosing to follow him. Together they went directly to the admissions desk. Then he admitted Lindsey Anne Hollis and Doreen Elizabeth Munro to room 215 on the second floor of the east wing at County Memorial, posthaste. With the stroke of a pen and under his auspices, David Fitzgerald Roberts, MD, chief of staff at County Memorial Hospital, made history, and segregation at that hospital for medical treatment due to race was shattered. Nurse Goodall was the one he had chosen and instructed to be directly responsible for the care of the Munro girls. She smiled, delighted at the assignment and being a part of history.

In Dr. Roberts's mind, if race was such an abhorrence to proper medical care and protection, why then would police and reporters give two cents about two Negro girls, Black or purple? If authorities were so racist, they wouldn't bother to investigate, bring ambulances or gather reporters for a news story. They would just let Blacks kill themselves and never raise an eyebrow.

*But look at them standing around waiting for information*, he thought. Was it because they really cared about the community or the girls themselves? In any case, he reasoned that this whole business of racism belonged to the ridiculous backward thinking of Neanderthals. With that, he walked over to the reporters, waiting for his medical report. Dr. Roberts was unaware that his son, Mark, had seen and overheard the entire exchange.

⸻◦◦◦⸻

I awoke in a bed of white sheets with a light gray coverlet. The clean white walls surrounded windows crowded with flowers on the sill. My arms and legs were bandaged, and I suspected my cuts were coated with more Merthiolate than Mom had at home. Doreen slept next to me in a bed closest to the door. She had the same kind of machines as me, but more of them with lines stuck in her arms. I got the impression she was dreaming peacefully in the white sheets with her black hair spilled out over the pillows. There was a boy there also; I didn't know him. One of his hands rested on Doreen's. She slept soundly as little beeps from the machine kept pace with her breathing.

I stared at him without moving, trying to make sense of where I was and why. I must have moaned because he came over to me.

"I'm glad you're awake. I'll call the nurse."

"Wait," I croaked. "Where am I? Why am I here?"

"You're at the county hospital. You had quite a shock, so they brought you here for observation along with Doreen. She's hurt bad, but she'll be okay, considering."

"Who are you?"

"Oh, I'm sorry. We haven't met. I'm Mark, Dr. Roberts's son, Doreen's friend?"

"Hi. Linney, her niece."

"I know, but nice to meet you all the same. Listen … I want to thank you for being there. You're quite the hero, you know."

"No. I'm not… I didn't… you don't get it… I couldn't.…" The hoarse and raspy voice that came out of my mouth sounded strange.

"Yes, you did, and you are." Mark reached for a pitcher of water, poured some into a cup, and handed it to me with a straw he'd placed inside. "Here, drink this." After helping me drink from the cup, he said, "Lie still, okay? And rest. I'll be right back."

"I was so scared. I ran so fast…. I only came back because…." But I was overly ambitious. I sank back into the pillow, pulled the sheet closer, and tried to tell the horror of it while choking back tears Mark said were healthy to cry.

Soon Dr. Roberts and a nurse named Goodall came to check in on us. "I'm glad you're awake. How are you feeling?" he asked while shining a light into my eyes. "I'd say a  shock like the one you suffered *would* have you spend a few days here with me, huh? If I didn't know any better, I'd say you, young lady, are conspiring to keep your mother out of my office. I'm lost without her, you know. First heat exhaustion. Now, you've graduated to very courageous acts *and* bringing excitement to my hospital. What, no smile?" He chuckled. "Well, I see I have to work on my bedside humor." He patted my hands and smiled warmly. "You're going to be just fine. I want you to know that none of this is your fault. What you did was very brave. I, for one, am glad to know you." He frowned. "Some folks outside want to have a little chat, but only when you're ready and your mother returns from taking a break. Not before, understand? You're safe here with a few officers stationed outside for protection, which would not be provided if you were in the Colored west wing."

I didn't know what that meant and dismissed it, thinking Dr. Roberts was right; I had graduated from bad to worst things. All the while, Mark remained at the foot of the hospital bed, listening. He moved to Doreen's bed and asked, "Dad, is there anything I can do?"

"I appreciate your attention to these young ladies, Mark. As a volunteer, you've devoted much of your *time* here with these girls. And for reasons I don't understand, can't quite make out why." He said. Looking up from his clipboard of notes, he continued, "There's nothing more you can do, so thank you, son. I'm sure your mother can use your services at home."

Mark hesitated, then stepped aside to allow my mother and grandparents to enter the room. My tears spilled out again at the sight of my mother's face.

I was unafraid when the policemen came in with pads and pencils. They listened and wrote down as much as I could tell them. Dr. Roberts attended, standing with his hands crossed either below his waist or shifted behind his back. After a while, the good doctor stopped the questioning. As he escorted the officers out, one asked, "Are you sure she's thirteen, not older?"

Then Nurse Goodall injected something in the line to the solution bag attached to my arm. She had a kind face. "Sleep now. You did well."

# CHAPTER 42

## *Healing Starts in the Heart*

IT'S STRANGE HOW circumstances change quickly as time moves slowly. The events of that fall had drawn attention to Paris from as far away as Louisville. It was vital to protect the citizens of the Commonwealth, so reporters from Paris and Lexington were eager to get as much of the story as possible. According to Nurse Goodall, there were more flowers than the day before, and cards were piling up at the nurses' station. Because we were the first Blacks to stay in the Whites-only wing of the hospital, it would be talked about for a long time.

I retold the events at least a million times over and found it interesting to work with an artist who drew the man's description. The sight of the man, on paper this time, made me feel sick at the memory. I could never forget his appearance, especially the scar on his face. But I also had a secret. The conversation I overheard between Stooly and Slim made me wonder if the man who did this to Doreen was one and the same.

They talked about a burn on his face, which was more than a coincidence. The stranger had a facial scar, too, like a burn. I didn't let on that Stooly might know this man; I wouldn't squeal on him. I was a snoop the day of the funeral dinner, and as the saying goes, believe half of what you see and none of what you hear. After talking with Stooly, who promised he wouldn't do anything, I understood the code of silence. But with this attack on Doreen, my instincts told me there would be a reckoning, and somehow Stooly would be the deliverer. His statement of not letting anything happen to me without him answering ran through my mind many times. I made a vow to protect him. This would be the one secret, mô un ségré, I just had to keep to myself, for Stooly's sake.

The police officers were still outside the hospital room door the following day when Miss Sandy and Angela visited with Reverend Avery and Carolyn. While there, Miss Edna came with Miss Tally to give Mom a break. Miss Edna was unusually kind and sweet to me.

As Miss Edna laid her hands on my arms, she kissed my forehead and said, "I want you to know you're more than welcome to order as much chicken at my window whenever you want, no charge." I could see tears welling in her eyes. Without saying more, I knew it was her way of apologizing for her treatment of me. Turning to others, she continued, "Well, now, am I the only one going to give good wishes? Come on now!" That's when everyone spoke at once, which was comical.

Shortly after everyone had gone, Doreen woke in tremendous pain. I pushed past Nurse Goodall and went to her. Drowsy, with more sedation injected into her veins, Doreen held on to my hand and wouldn't let go. Nurse Goodall allowed me to curl up beside Doreen, and she stayed, watching as we fell into a deep sleep.

I woke to my mother whispering my name as she stroked my hair, calling me her brave little girl. I didn't feel brave or little anymore. I felt more grown than ever.

"I've never been more proud of you than I am now," Mom said. "But I have to tell you something important. I'm so sorry, honey. Miss Dottie Sweet passed away last night."

Nothing and no one could prepare me for the shock of this news, which was like a punch in the gut. Miss Dottie died quietly in her sleep. Per Dr. Roberts, the shock of what happened to us, coupled with her age, declining health, and mental condition, was too much for her to withstand. Miss Katherine was staying with Mom until arrangements could be made.

Mom said the whole neighborhood, even Miss Sandy, was pitching in and grieving these latest events. Even Mr. Sauerkraut had come by to offer help. His actual name was Oslo Gunther whose family had enjoyed living in the neighborhood for two generations. For any of his *kleine kinder*, as he called us, to suffer pain was something he felt personally. He wanted more than anything to help somehow. He took command that day of the horror as he passed by on his way to his farm, and it was he who caught Doreen when she fainted. He was a godsend. Afterward, he helped wherever he could, running errands and bringing fresh vegetables from his recent harvest. He even made wassail and brought strudel and baked pears for anyone who felt up to eating.

As much as I wanted to stay with Doreen, I also wanted to be with Miss Katherine. Dr. Roberts already arranged my discharge, as long as counseling was provided on an as-needed basis. Despite a whopping headache, I prepared to leave the hospital, and while waiting for Mom, a knock came at the door. I shouldn't have been surprised to see Mark Roberts, but I was when he slowly entered and sat in a chair next to Doreen's bed.

"So you're being discharged?"

"Yeah. A good friend passed away."

"You're quite the do-gooder, huh? I'm sorry. I didn't mean it that way. I don't know why I said it like that, though. What I mean is you have a big heart. Better than most even."

"What are you doing here? I mean, what are you *doing* with Doreen?"

"I know how it looks, but I can't help myself." Then he sighed and put his head in his hands. He was handsome, no doubt, with his dark hair cascading down over his head through long fingers. Like his dad, his deep-set eyes and heavy brows looked soft in expression. Mark's tall and slender frame seemed small in the chair as he spoke in whispers so as not to disturb Doreen, and I followed his lead.

"I sneak out of the house most days to come here. Dad's so busy with his practice and hospital rounds I'm hardly noticed. Mom's socially engaged most days and misses me only when she needs something. So it's easy."

"Easy? This is *crazy*. You don't know the half if they find out about you two. All that trouble coming down on your heads. I won't let you break her heart. I just won't. How d'ya like my big heart now?"

"You do have one, you know."

"Holy moly, can't you see how this might look to other people? Your dad's even started to ask questions. You're going to make things worse—"

"Not if I can help it. I know the kind of times we live in. Love just doesn't know color." Mark gestured with his hands more than was necessary. "This is more of a surprise to me than anyone. I didn't expect this to happen, but it did. She's old enough to know what she wants, and even though I'm two grades ahead of her, we both know what we feel—"

"All I want is for Doreen to be happy." Softening, I said, "I sure hope you know what you're doing."

"I'm going with my feelings, and my feeling is that she is my life, my future."

"You know this is kinda reckless, right?"

"Yeah, it is, I know. Foolhardy even. But I can't stay away from her. If anything worse had happened to her, I don't know what I would've done. I owe you everything."

"You owe me nothing, okay?" I said. "I'm not as old as y'all, so I don't know a lot about this stuff, but I know her. She's full of herself and expects the best. Anything short of that might break her heart. If you can't take on the world, then I say don't waste her time. That's what I think anyhow. She needs to heal, and that starts in the heart, right?"

"You're older than you think and wiser too." He looked at me without wavering. "I dig what you're trying to say, though. In the meantime, I'm going to be here, waiting. You might not like it—heck, maybe no one will—but that won't make me budge from her side."

"I understand," I said with a sigh, knowing this was the best I could do while being defeated by love.

"I'm glad. Thank you for loving Doreen as much as I do." Mark smiled at me for the first time. He had a nice smile.

"You're welcome." At this, I think I blushed just a little. "You should go before someone sees you here again."

He bent over, kissed Doreen on the forehead, then stroked her arm and left. I started to see what Doreen saw in Mark, and I approved of her choice. Even though I was still concerned about her future with him, I decided right then and there that I would support whatever choice she made, even if it was Mark Roberts.

When Mom and my grandmother came, I hugged a sleeping Doreen and said goodbye to Grandma, who would stay on. I walked from the hospital room humbled, knowing that this was a brand-new day for integration. My life had changed, and I hoped Doreen would be able to walk with humility and her head held high after all this. Even though Black and some White employees smiled and waved goodbye, the stares from some other hospital staff were piercing as I bravely walked down the hospital corridor, out the front doors, and into Mom's car with news reporters and police all around.

⸺◦◦◦⸺

Doreen numbly waited for Dr. Roberts to finish his examination. She was told of the damage she had suffered but would heal. They could not know if she'd be able to bear children; only time would tell. At her age, the prognosis was favorable, but nothing was guaranteed. Tears fell silently down her face at the news the doctor delivered. She had no idea how fulfilling having her own children would be, but she wanted that experience with Mark. She had known nothing about sex, but she wanted nothing more of it if it was anything like what she had experienced. Her tears were for that thought and grieving for her and Mark's sake.

Doreen was told that no one could know the psychological effect her experience would ultimately have on her psyche, so counseling was recommended. Her friends used the word *psych* all the time when fooling around or faking someone with the truth, but this was nothing to joke about. Subconsciously she knew that her outlook on life, and life in general, was forever changed.

She had many visitors. Karen, and Brenda of all people, came to visit as if nothing had happened between them. Brenda even threatened to kill whoever did this to her. Angie and Carolyn, with her father Reverend Avery, came to pray for her recovery. He also prayed for the damnation of the soul of that lowlife who had attacked her so viciously. Doreen thought it mildly amusing that the reverend prayed for the damnation of his soul. Shouldn't he pray for the salvation of the wicked soul of the man instead?

However, she had not received a visit from Clarissa or Mark. How could she face him anyway? She felt dirty, unclean, and ruined. How could he want her now? Their secret love was sweet and full of promise. Now it was lost.

Doreen sat silently, listening to the others talk with a look of disconnected curiosity. She didn't see the humor in anything and rarely smiled or laughed. They had all seen the artist's drawing of the man Linney had provided the police. Doreen couldn't stand to look at it for long. Her visitors talked of someone named Jimmy or James Marx, but no one would say if he was or was not the man who did this to her, they just whispered suspicions among themselves.

Amazingly Doreen didn't blame herself, nor should she have. She didn't think her actions caused the rape; instead, she thought life was cruel and unfair. Realistically she knew that life was that way in equal measure, but overall, it had been incredibly unfair to her. Life had turned its back on her, and she could no longer trust it. Now she couldn't think past tomorrow. If she could think past today, that would be a miracle.

She thought Linney was the lucky one. She had escaped Doreen's fate, but where was Linney now? Doreen knew of Miss

Dottie's passing but felt nothing, only that she wouldn't have the chance to ask how she knew her fate. Was Miss Dottie more important to Linney? That was selfish thinking, but couldn't Linney come to visit, at least for a little while?

When she was finally up to it, she read Linney's account of events in the newspaper. Doreen's memory of that day was hazy, and like snapshots in her head, events didn't flow smoothly. When she read Linney had run away when she first came upon the scene, Doreen was stunned. How could Linney leave her like that? How could she run when Doreen needed her in the worst way?

Not only had life betrayed her, but Linney had betrayed her the most.

# CHAPTER 43

## The Snake Charmer

W HEN STOOLY AND Slim learned what had happened to the Munro girls, they wasted no time putting Stooly's plan into action. Stooly had already let a whole month slide; in this sense, he blamed himself for what happened to the girls. Even though Slim tried to convince him otherwise, Stooly's guilt didn't budge.

Stooly thought long and hard about the day Lindsey confronted him regarding his plans to kill Jimmy. She nailed Jimmy Marx as Virginia Morgan's killer by sharing that secret she kept for Virginia's sake. Relieved, he finally had his proof and knew what he had to do. But little Lindsey had touched his heart that day, and he held back. He promised to protect her and not cause harm to that bastard. Well, one of those promises he had no intention of keeping. Because of him, that sweet girl shouldn't have had to go through what she did. But her courage in doing *what* she did had spurred Stooly to do what he must. Now, it was time to charm a snake.

The artist's drawing in the papers caught Bessie unaware, and she exclaimed aloud to Stooly, "That's Jimmy!" Stooly already knew but didn't let on. Bessie was devastated. She had fallen hard for the man, and he suspected she would be heartbroken for years to come. His fervent wish was that Jimmy would become a distant memory of a love Bessie thought would bring her happiness but didn't.

Stooly set his house in order, leaving enough money in the bank to care for Bessie and settling his accounts with his lenders. He had already spoken to Slim about his genius plan, and Slim was more than ready to do what had to be done. Good ole Augie had waited, and when the word came to lie low, Augie did just that. The Boss had given his blessing a while back to do what was necessary. But The Boss didn't suspect anything of what was about to go down, which was good for now. Stooly would square his account with The Boss later. What mattered was what he had to do.

The first thing was to find and catch Jimmy without anyone knowing. The element of surprise was on their side. When it happened, it would happen fast.

❧

Jimmy had moved out of the YMCA in Paris and lying low in a motel on the outskirts of Winchester. Coincidentally, very close to the Warehouse of Stooly's operation. His job at the A&P in Paris was done; he didn't dare go there again. The money given to him from Bessie was enough to hold him over for a while. From time to time, he would drive to Paris late at night and creep along the streets with dead headlights. He'd park his car on a darkened street and walk to the back of that place he had taken Virginia and ravished sweet Doreen. Jimmy *had* to visit his old haunts; he couldn't help himself. If it wasn't the Jungle or the house across from the Youth Center where he lurked, it was the American Legion Hall. He could be found in one of these places—that is, *if* you were looking.

Oh, how he *hated* that girl who stopped him in midthrust, interrupting his fun with Doreen. The glow created by the sun behind her prevented him from seeing clearly. It was as if she descended from on high, and in the shadow of the sun, he thought an angel had come to tell him it wasn't the right time to take Doreen. It even struck him with a brick to get his attention. He ran away as quickly as possible to avoid divine judgment. His quick recovery was another sign that an angel from God had delivered him, never mind the tremendous headaches that had affected him since that day. Then he saw the drawing in the papers. That girl was no angel! She was the same filly who got away that muggy night in July. Lindsey Hollis.

On this night, his plans for Lindsey would be completed. Feeling invisible, Jimmy would let Ajax out and lurk in the darkness to wait. With his fedora's wide brim tipped to one side to hide what he could of the scar on his face, Jimmy snuck into The Hall's back door. In for a quick night's drink, then on to Greenfield. Jimmy made his plan, and Lindsey was the prey.

<hr>

When Jimmy walked through the door that gave access to The Hall's back stairs, Slim was standing on the other side. As Ajax said of himself from time to time, Jimmy was *shining like a brand-new penny*, thought Slim. The stage was set.

"Well, lookie, lookie who I just found," Slim said. As he slid back to avoid the harsh light from the open doorway of the back-hall stair, he chuckled at a startled Jimmy, or whoever the hell the man was calling himself these days. *Looking at him, no one would ever know the psychopathic thoughts that ran through this man's mind*, thought Slim. The sight of Jimmy's wide-brimmed fedora cocked to one side made Slim curious about whether he'd ever thought to himself, *Standing in front of me is a man who'd reach down my throat and yank out my liver before I ever knew it was gone*. Not a chance. Time to charm the snake and go along with the ruse of name shifting.

"You trying to find me for some reason?" Jimmy asked.

"Yeah, you can say that." Given their last encounter at Virginia's funeral reception, Slim was surprised Jimmy spoke. Maybe catching him off guard did this, so Slim took full advantage of the ambush.

"What's the reason?" Jimmy asked again, clearly curious but guarded.

"You just the man I'm looking for. I got a job for you if you're interested."

"*You* got a job for me?"

"You gonna start repeating what I say? Yeah, man, I got a job for you."

"Thought you worked with Stooly. If he's part of it, I ain't interested."

"You don't get it, my man. *I* have a job for you, Ajax. This ain't got nothing to do with Stooly, man, so hear me out. Have a seat."

"Yeah, okay. I'll play." With that, Jimmy sat down to listen.

Slim told Jimmy that he had parted ways with Stooly. He apologized profusely for the dustup between them a few weeks back and the months before. No skin off his nose if he was Ajax or whomever. No hard feelings would be appreciated. No offense taken, Jimmy assured him.

"Stooly getting too big for his britches, thinking he can't get 'got.' Well, everybody can get *got*." Slim continued, "Tired of being Stooly's *flunky* and feeling like a pigeon for the man anyhow. We been tight for a long time, but it's time to cut ties, you dig? I can't do this alone. I need help, and you just the man I had in mind. Smart. Quick. That's you, ain't it, Ajax?"

"You think?" Jimmy asked after Slim clearly stroked his ego.

"Look, I got this thing set up, and Stooly won't suspect nothing, man. I'm done pushing weed and LSD. Pushing real drugs like cocaine, heroin, and methamphetamines is where the big money at. Don't believe me? Here's half that amount, all for one night's work."

At this point, Slim gave Jimmy a brown envelope full of more hundred-dollar bills than he cared to count in a day.

"You know this sounds too good to be true, don't ya? But I ain't about to look a gift horse in the mouth, if you know what I mean."

"You can keep that, just for accepting. Call it a show of trust. And looka here," Slim said, showing a packet of pills. "These are the real deal."

Slim further stroked his ego by commiserating with him, sinking the hooks in deep. "Look, man, I know the law must be after you, what with that drawing in the papers and all. Damn, if it didn't look *just like* you! To hell with that Munro girl."

Jimmy said nothing in response. Slim continued.

"Stuck-up bitches going to that White school should be taught a lesson, and good for whoever gave that tease what she had coming," Slim said, faking his disdain for Doreen. "It must have been ordained by God. Speaking of which, it's *by* the grace of God I ran into you tonight."

What Jimmy said next confirmed that his arrogance was in full force. Jimmy didn't disappoint.

"Then you understand," Jimmy said, sounding relieved. "You do what you got to do. They had it coming, you know. Teachers and young bitches, they all the same. Next is that Lindsey girl. I have plans for her tonight. I had her dead in my sights back in July, but that little bitch outran me. But. Listening to this business venture of yours, I think I can bide my time on that sweet piece of meat. At least for a little while."

"Fuck 'em if they can't take a joke." Slim took a hard swallow on the bile rising in his throat, tightened his jaw, then continued, "You know… Slim paused to clear his throat, "We can stake out your plan for that little bitch now and deal with this shit later."

"Now, why would *we* do that? Like I *said*, that bit of business can wait. Where you got this stashed, anyway?" Jimmy asked, referring to the packet of pills. "Can't be in Paris, no way. It's too hot."

"You right," Slim said matter-of-factly. "Meet me out at the Warehouse site. Give me time to get everything laid out. We'll discuss details then."

"Sure thing," Jimmy agreed.

After a few more exchanges, Jimmy slipped down the back stairs with Slim as a lookout to make sure he wasn't seen. Afterward, Slim wasted no time calling Stooly to tell him the fish had taken the bait. Stooly had to move fast.

Tonight, it took all Slim had to play the game and not let Jimmy get next to him. He was amazed at how easy it was to not trip over his words. Slim's twisting of words was an adrenaline rush getting the better of him. Holding back caused the rush to need somewhere to go, often coming out as gibberish, mainly big words or thoughts. That nervous energy had gotten him into trouble once upon a time, which had taken years to control. So out of respect for the man who brought him off the streets and the wife who kept him grounded, he held back. However, he knew he'd need that adrenaline to deal with this twisted bastard. He didn't think Stooly would mind.

They say God never makes mistakes. Well, as far as Slim was concerned, it was up to man to correct *if* the Almighty had done. *It's nearly Sunday morning*, thought Slim.

A fitting night to make that right.

⊰◎◎◎⊱

Jimmy wasn't fooled easily. It didn't escape him that Slim never smiled the entire time he talked. Not once. Slim had known Stooly for a long time; it was unlikely the worm had turned overnight. The more Jimmy thought about it, the more he suspected Stooly had to be part of this, and maybe, just maybe, it was a trick. He would meet Slim, yes indeedy, but he would bide his time to see if Stooly showed up. If so, they would see what Jimmy was made of, and Stooly would finally get what he deserved. Yes, sir, the time was ripe for easy pickings. After he finished with them, he would get rid of that stupid girl, Lindsey, and then finish up with sweet Doreen without interruptions this time. He turned his attention to the heavens above, and in the night sky, he saw blood on the moon.

*How fitting.*

# CHAPTER 44

## *Blood in the Moonlight*

———◦◦◦———

J IMMY HALF EXPECTED to see Stooly at the Warehouse, but he
was nowhere in sight. Jimmy had kept his eyes peeled for
Stooly's car or a show of his presence somewhere, but there was
none.

"Let's see what you got, Black man," he said.

"Come on up around here. I got it all set up," Slim said.

As Slim ushered him into the Warehouse, Jimmy began to
relax a little, thinking Slim might have, in fact, cut ties with
Stooly after all. Like at The Hall, Slim kept referring to him as
Ajax, which suited Jimmy just fine. Pallets of marijuana were still
on the floor, but much less than the last time he had seen the
stash. Memories of that evening faded when he saw the table full
of drug paraphernalia. Slim began to point out the different
kinds of pills, tablets, and powders, then defined the effects each
had on the taker. Slim talked about profits, what each "take"
would be, how it could be distributed, and so on.

Jimmy asked questions, and Slim answered expertly, too expertly.
As Slim blathered on and on, Jimmy grew suspicious. He couldn't
put his finger on it, but something wasn't right. Maybe it was his
imagination, but he didn't think Slim was that savvy or had thought
this through to polish; it sounded too easy, too smooth. Slim was
slick but not smooth. There was a difference.

Then another thought hit him, just like that brick thrown by that girl. Slim was lying. Jimmy knew this in his bones, but the *why* eluded him. Slim was good, but Stooly was better, and this had Stooly's name written all over it. Jimmy couldn't figure it out, but no matter, he had made up his mind to damn the consequences. He'd take the money and drugs, then finish the mission he'd planned for Lindsey. Jimmy decided to end this funky charade. He had better things to do.

He had stopped listening to Slim a long time ago. As they laughed and joked about profits, Jimmy thought Slim was just another stupid jigaboo, and thought of something to catch Slim by surprise. A death Slim had long in coming was at hand. The head fog was rolling in. It was time to allow Ajax to take full control. Slim needed to see the invincible devil in the moonlight.

"I thought you said we were alone," Jimmy said, pretending to see someone in the back recesses of the Warehouse.

"We are, man. What's your problem?" Slim asked.

"There's someone back there, so what the *fuck*?"

"Who?" Slim stopped fingering the pills on the table to look deep into the Warehouse's darkness but didn't see anyone. Jimmy instinctively knew Slim had no idea what was about to happen to him.

"Her, goddammit! Hell, man! Look at her!" Jimmy even managed to convince himself that gorgeous Virginia Morgan was walking toward him, beckoning. He was more than convincing.

<hr style="width:30%" />

Slim made sure to lock the back doors of the Warehouse after Jimmy slipped in the last time, so someone hiding in the back was perplexing. Confused, Slim stepped around to Jimmy's left to get a better look, peering into the gloomy darkness. Too late, Slim heard a click and felt the switchblade graze the right side of his chest, then, just as quickly, cut across his right thigh. Slim wasn't standing close enough to get the full force of the automatic blade to his side, but the cut to his thigh was significant.

He grabbed at his side, stumbled on his injured leg, and turned to face a crazed Jimmy Marx snarling like a caged animal. Bending at the waist, Jimmy moved with arms open wide, giving himself enough room to leverage his next move. Excruciating pain coursed through Slim as Jimmy twirled the switchblade in his fingers, demonstrating he had skills Slim might not be able to outmaneuver. Slim cursed himself for not being better prepared. He and Stooly had agreed not to make unnecessary noises, so Slim had left his .22 in the car. That was a mistake. The sudden change in circumstances was alarming, and he instinctively knew Jimmy smelled blood in the water.

"Ooh, woo, hoo, hoo, you just met Ajax! Missed your side but got your leg, though."

A chill went down Slim's spine as he watched the full manifestation of Jimmy's psychotic episode unfold. Jimmy's cold black eyes were wild with derangement. Referring to his switchblade as "Ajax" and hooting like an owl was clearly Jimmy's way of saying he was no longer there. Jimmy got the jump on Slim, and for the first time in his life, Slim felt real fear; and Stooly was late.

"There's blood on the moon tonight. Red blood shows black in the moonlight." Jimmy continued, "Did you know that? You think you can get over on me with bullshit? You think I can forgive and forget when money's on the line? That money looks *so-weet*! Jimmy wants it *all* and Ajax? He's gonna do all the dirty work."

"So it *is* Jimmy Marx, I presume. Or is it Ajax, you crazy son of a bitch!" Now that the ruse was off, Slim couldn't let fear overtake him. He knew he had to have the presence of mind to be up for the fight of his life. He was in the snake's pit.

"No, no, I'm not crazy, but Jimmy's glad to meet you all the same! Jimmy's only crazy when he's Ajax, and tonight is your lucky night 'cause you get to meet 'em both. Nice to meet ya! You and Stooly had fun. Now it's my turn. You try to fool me, make fun of me, *burn* me! Don't you know when you do that, I got six ways from Sunday to get back at ya?"

"That leaves all day Sunday to snatch your ass. So let's dance." Slim was ready.

They had been circling each other up to this point, with Jimmy making fake lunges while Slim nursed his right leg, slightly dragging it, making sad scraping noises along the concrete floor. Jimmy threatened with his switchblade while he hooted, twirling his blade, also named Ajax, between his fingers and throwing it from hand to hand. Then Jimmy made the sound of a caged animal and charged at Slim with the knife.

Ignoring the pain in his leg, Slim parried and turned, grabbed Jimmy's lunging right arm, then spun around. This placed his back on Jimmy's chest, and he slammed them both to the ground with his weight. Slim banged Jimmy's knifed hand on the Warehouse floor with all his strength, but to no avail while Jimmy hit Slim in the kidneys with his left fist.

"*Motherfucker!*" Slim yelled out in frustration and pain as Jimmy kept hitting him in his kidneys. Jimmy fought like a crazed cat, hitting, spitting, and wiggling furiously to get from underneath Slim.

After making the last volley to Slim's kidneys, Jimmy finally slid from under Slim's right side, with the knife cutting Slim under his right armpit. Slim yelled from yet another excruciatingly painful cut.

With the tables turned and a swift move, Jimmy straddled Slim, who was now flat on his back. But Slim was not to be outdone and put a well-placed left into Jimmy's groin, which loosened Jimmy's grip on his switchblade. Jimmy buckled from the blow and rolled over and off Slim. Slim was up and kicked the knife from Jimmy's hand, then kicked Jimmy in his kidneys, back, and sides and kept on kicking him about the head. Blood spilled out of Slim's right underarm, and as he was reaching to stanch the blood, Jimmy knocked Slim's injured right leg out from under him.

They rolled on the floor, Slim punching Jimmy as hard as he could, with Jimmy grinning with every hit, punching at Slim's bleeding arm, head, and ribs. Slim had managed to roll Jimmy onto his back again. It was at this time Jimmy focused on something other than Slim. Jimmy growled at the sight and began to cower and cover his face.

Lost in the frenzy of his struggle, it seemed to Slim that Jimmy's mind had slipped even more than before. Slim paused his assault to stare at a stricken Jimmy, who looked up from the floor beyond Slim. As the Warehouse lights shone behind the approaching figure, Jimmy said, "The Angel of God has come. The blood of Christ."

⚬⚬⚬

Dressed in faded blue bib overalls, the bib fastened on one side, shirtless, showing his smooth bare skin and wearing black lace-up boots, Stooly strolled toward the two men as if in slow motion. Slim slowly rose and watched as Stooly moved in long strides to the idiot, writhing on the floor in a fetal position. Without ceremony, and in one smooth motion, Stooly picked up the switchblade Slim had kicked away earlier and straddled Jimmy's body. The glare from the overhead warehouse lights glowed behind Stooly as he grabbed a tuft of hair at the front of Jimmy's forehead and, in one swift motion, scalped him from the front of his forehead to the top back of his head. To Slim, Jimmy's scream must have been louder than anything Doreen or Virginia could have made. But that night, no one gave a shit, especially Stooly.

Stooly didn't stop there. He began to skin Jimmy, cutting the burn scar off his face, then his lips, ears, and nose. He plunged the knife into his abdomen many times and, each time, twisted the blade, so the wound wouldn't heal. Slim knew this was Stooly's way of killing when the attack was as personal as this one was. Slim turned his head and let Stooly do his thing, not wanting to watch as Stooly plunged the knife in again and again. When the screaming stopped, it did because Stooly had plunged the knife into Jimmy's heart, again twisting as it went in.

Stooly was covered in blood as he dropped the switchblade on Jimmy's lifeless body and began to stand. The overalls, which covered his skin, were no longer light blue but glistened with sweat and Jimmy's blood. Stooly didn't say a word as he stood. He and Slim looked at each other for what seemed like an eternity and then silently walked together, as planned, to hose Stooly off at the side of the building.

After Stooly washed as best he could, he changed into clothes hidden in Slim's car while Slim did the same. Stooly studied the cuts on Slim's body, particularly the wound on his leg and under his arm.

"You a lucky son of a bitch, you know that? You cut up bad, but the one under your arm missed a major artery."

"No shit?" Slim asked in obvious pain that before now didn't seem much.

"Yeah, the gash on your belly don't look so deep. You'll live, but it's your leg I'm worried about."

"I'm sorry I left my gun in the car, man. That was a dumb-fuck move. I'm better with a piece than a blade, man. You got me on that skill."

"No need to apologize, Slim. I was the one late to this party. Glad I didn't have to use my own blade; Jimmy supplied that. After what you told me of his plans for Linney plus the admission of raping Doreen *and* killing Virginia Lee, that schizoid bastard had to die."

"I found out something," Slim said as he winced under Stooly's ministrations with the iodine and bandages Slim's wife kept in the car for emergencies.

"Hold still, now. What's that?"

"Jimmy's blade is named Ajax. Ain't that some shit? Jimmy even used that name for himself from time to time."

"Huh." Stooly paused to let the thought sink in. "That's why he never used the name Ajax in prison? I guess there was no need to until he was out and on his own. Twisted fuck!"

They bandaged Slim as best they could under the circumstances. Then Slim joked, "You know my wife'll do a better job. I'll have to lie about how I *got* these cuts, but she'll know better. She's smarter than I give her credit for, I'll say that."

"You got a good life with her, man. Don't fuck it up."

Together they carefully wrapped Jimmy in a plastic tarp and put the body in the trunk of Jimmy's car. Then they hosed down the Warehouse floor and sprinkled sawdust to dry the remaining blood and water. The crushed aspirin Slim had used to trick Jimmy as cocaine was swept to the floor, and the table full of sleeping pills used as fake barbiturates was packaged up and given to Slim to put back in his medicine cabinet. The envelope of money given to Jimmy earlier was in the glove compartment of Jimmy's car, just as they thought.

It would be a long night of driving Jimmy's car to Louisville, but that was the plan. Stooly's car was Bessie's now. It was she who drove him to a certain point on Winchester Road. Without asking any questions, she hugged her brother and journeyed to points unknown. The walk from there had taken Stooly longer than expected, but if he had to do it all again, he wouldn't change a thing. Despite his injuries, Slim wouldn't have it any other way.

All was in order, and Stooly shook Slim's hand for the last time. Stooly was Slim's ace boon coon, and Slim was Stooly's. Stooly and Slim agreed that young Lindsey would never know of this night; it was Stooly's way. It was understood. The gallons of gasoline cans were lined up, waiting for Slim. As he watched Stooly drive off, Slim turned to the cans and began his final act of the evening.

As the Warehouse lit up the early-morning sky with flames, Slim felt his sins being washed away. Stooly had done his thing. Yes, sir, Slim thought. *That beautiful son of a bitch did his thing.*

# CHAPTER 45

## *Facing the Music*

T HE TIMID AND shy young girl of thirteen was gone. I felt I'd already lived the life of a much older person. My posture improved, and my thoughts became clear. I even moved and spoke differently. A certain amount of maturity comes with knowledge, I suppose. It was as if I'd matured overnight, and people noticed. Everyone said I was more athletic than most, but now courage was added because of the Jungle incident. I wasn't so sure. However these comments were meant, I didn't dwell. More thoughtful and serious, maybe, but I was no hero, no matter how courageous or athletic people thought me to be.

Nightmares were a constant companion, and most mornings, it wasn't unusual for Mom to find me next to her when she awoke. Sometimes, a glass of cold water from the refrigerator helped when I couldn't sleep. Using that refrigerator door handle to learn fast dancing seemed an immature act to me now. What did that handle know about anything? If I had to face something like what happened to Doreen, would I know what to do? Could I defend myself or cry out for help? Would anyone come to rescue me? These thoughts, and moments like these, kept me awake at night.

Per Miss Dottie's wish, she was cremated shortly after death. There was a small memorial service held in her honor. After her passing, I had no more tears to shed, just strength of purpose and knowledge. For me, Miss Dottie was heaven-sent, and I missed her. I was wrong to believe her premonitions were meant only for Miss Virginia. Now I know they *were* meant for Doreen and me. Maybe Miss Dottie had a blind spot where Miss Virginia was concerned. I don't know for sure, but that would explain the profound grief she felt when Miss Virginia died. Miss Dottie knew what would happen to us, and I never got the chance to thank her for the warning or apologize for doubting her vision.

I visited Miss Katherine often and took time to reminisce about Miss Dottie during the quiet of my visits. It was just the two of us, with an occasional visit from Miss Sandy, Miss Tally, and Mom. Miss Katherine allowed me to read any of the books in her book cabinet, and over time, we gradually moved into our old routine. Miss Katherine listened as I read while she knitted or crocheted, ready to discuss what I didn't understand from what I read.

Guilt settled in on me from time to time, caused mainly by the knowledge that I didn't push hard enough to prevent what happened to Doreen. Instead, I tried to uncover mysteries that were none of my business. The fact that I ran immediately instead of staying to help Doreen didn't ease the guilt either. I didn't know how to face her, and because of this, I avoided her out of shame. My mother admonished me for staying away, but I needed more time to think and gather myself.

According to Angie, Doreen was not the same. She was more depressed than anyone she had ever seen and not cheerful at all. After she got home from the hospital, her night terrors increased. Once, Doreen had to be sedated, and some nights my grandparents had to leave the lights on all night long. This news made me feel worse, which caused me to further distance myself from her.

However, I was called to task during a visit with Miss Katherine. While she sat quietly knitting, she asked after Doreen. Because of the horrible impression Doreen made the day of her visit, I didn't think Miss Katherine would care so much.

"I haven't seen her since I left the hospital," I said.

"I can't believe it's been, what, at least two or three weeks ago, hasn't it? Now we're into November, and you haven't bothered to see her? Why?"

Her tone sounded like she was making fun of me. I responded with an explanation as serious as her questioning sounded false.

"I can't." I sighed, then confessed. "I'm ashamed of what I didn't do at first. You know, on that day, and also what I thought of Miss Dottie's warnings."

"What do you mean, child?"

"Well, after Miss Virginia was found in the Jungle, I thought Miss Dottie got her visions confused. I thought the warnings were really meant for Miss Virginia and not us. I should've realized Miss Dottie's visions were true. I was so stupid."

"That does *not* sound like the caring young lady I've come to know and love."

"I just know Doreen will act all mad at me like she usually does. It's my fault she suffers. I don't think I can face her anger."

"You'll have to face it sometime—"

"But I ran away—"

"You *ran* because you were scared! You were afraid of what you'd seen and ran to save your own life. A shock like that and no one, I tell you *no one*, would blame you for fleeing when you did. But you came back, and that's what matters. As for Dottie's visions, well, they were what they were. You can't go blaming yourself for believing what you did."

"Maybe. But I can't help it. I'm trying to forget, but… at night, it comes back."

"Bashing that man over the head and, who knows, even saving that girl's life at your own risk is what counts. I knew that pent-up anger of yours would come in handy, and it did that day. You didn't hold back and made the right decision. Doreen didn't end up like poor Virginia; God rest her soul, so you have nothing to feel bad about. Doreen ought to be grateful."

I was silent, thinking about her words. Everyone said I was wrong to stay away, but having Miss Katherine say the same thing, affected me differently. Then Miss Katherine began pointing her knitting needles at me.

"You need to stop this foolishness! If I didn't know any better, I'd say you're being selfish! Yes, just pure-de selfish, thinking only about yourself and your feelings. What about Doreen's feelings? Ever think of what that poor thing must be going through, or are you going to disappoint me by saying you haven't even thought about it?"

I was stunned into silence. Miss Katherine had never spoken to me in this way, and because I didn't have an answer, I had no choice but to sit and hear her out.

"I'm not going to tiptoe around you now. The composed young lady I see before me today is partly due to that horrible experience you went through. As bad as it was, you learned a thing or two about yourself. Don't abandon Doreen when she needs you most, Linney, honey. Don't do that to her or yourself. Believe me, you'll regret it later. I know. Believe me, I know."

"But what if she's angry and doesn't want to see me?"

"Do it anyway!" Miss Katherine said, standing her ground. "When you see her, steel yourself for accusations, but hold firm to the knowledge that you did the best you could. God doesn't ask more of His angels when He knows they've done their very best, darlin'. You did your best, and that has to be good enough."

She was right. They were all right, my mother, grandparents, and friends. I had abandoned Doreen, just as I had done that day in the Jungle. Why did I come back for her, only to leave her now? Doreen made a poor impression on Miss Katherine, and even she had more compassion for Doreen than I was showing. I was acting like a jerk. I had to make it right, so I rose from the floor and placed the book back in the cabinet. I gave Miss Katherine a long tight hug and kissed her forehead.

"Thank you. I haven't been a good friend. Only you could make me see that. I'll let you know how it goes."

Right then and there, I rushed out the door to my grandma's house to see Doreen, hoping for the best. It was time to face the music.

# CHAPTER 46

## *The Sorry Dance*

A S I KICKED through a pile of fallen leaves that had blown together in front of me, it calmed my nerves to think of facing Doreen's verbal assault. It was full-on autumn, and as I walked to Grandma's house, I couldn't help but think of the last time I made this journey. After helping Grandpa in the garden, I never thought my life would've changed so much that day.

Slowly reaching for the gate, which opened to steps leading up to the house, I half hoped an invisible barrier would stop me from going farther. But there was none. I stood there with half a mind to go across the street to Angela's house, but I told myself, *Don't be a coward. Now is not the time to be a weenie. Be brave. Be strong. You can do it.* I took a deep breath, bravely soldiered up the steps to the front porch, and knocked on the door.

Grandpa Ernst opened the large door and, without saying a word, nodded his head to the floor and motioned me to come inside. I gave him a hug and a kiss on the cheek while he pointed to the stairs leading up to Doreen's bedroom.

"She's been waiting for you. We all have," he said. "Good luck."

Gathering courage, I took another deep breath and marched up the stairs with legs that felt like cement blocks. When I knocked on her closed bedroom door, she said, "Come in."

Doreen was lying across the bed, reading a *Seventeen* magazine. An open page of *Look* magazine lay on the pillow, and the magazine, *Life,* had been tossed to the floor. She didn't say anything as I walked into the room and sat on the edge of the bed, trying my best not to slip off its side. The bedroom lamp was on as she casually turned the pages, not reading but looking at the pictures. I cocked my head sideways to view a photo of a model wearing shiny white go-go boots and what could only be described as a short cape of drapery that might have come from a fancy living room window.

"Would you wear that?" I asked.

"No, I don't think so. Where would I wear it anyway?"

"I don't know, maybe on a date or something?" *How could I say something so careless?* I thought after the words left my mouth.

She reached for my hand and squeezed it tight without lifting her head. *This is the moment she'll let me have it. She'll give me the full weight of her anger right here on her flowery bedspread.* But what she said next surprised me.

"All I ever wanted was to be better than you." Her words sounded soft and wistful. "All I ever thought was one day, I'd be so far above y'all and live far away from here and never look back. Now, I can't see my future. I thought I was cute, even pretty. I look at the pictures in this magazine, and I don't see myself. I look in the mirror and don't recognize my face because I've changed. Inside, I mean, and that should show on my face, shouldn't it?"

After all Doreen had been through, her level of conceit hadn't changed. Did she know what she was saying? She had been staring into space as she spoke but then looked directly at me when she asked that question. I suppose she didn't want an answer because she continued.

"I mean, shouldn't I be scarred on the outside, ugly and dirty? Shouldn't I be someone who no one wants to see? I can't go to school on Monday. They say it's time, but I can't do it. I can't be like you, all strong and independent. You don't seem to need anyone but yourself. I wish I could be like that, but I can't. I can't go out and let people see my face, who I am, really. I used to be unafraid. I used to be sure of myself and who I was, and now I don't know. You know everything, and I know nothing."

While I sat listening to Doreen feel sorry for herself and listing her faults, I began to feel that shame again. I didn't know how to respond, so I said nothing. I listened and held her hand while she continued to ramble.

"I've made mistakes I can't take back. You know that? I thought I had the world at my feet. I was so naïve, thinking nothing bad would ever happen to me. I followed Brenda around and allowed her to lead the way. Now, I don't even want to hear her voice. At one time, I thought she was smarter. Being mean and nasty to people, always the one with the answers, was the way to go, but then I met Clarissa, and life changed. All I thought I knew—I didn't."

"But you didn't know—"

"Let me finish!" Doreen insisted. "I met people in high school, White people, who treated me like they treat each other. They didn't treat me differently, at least not at all like we thought. Then I realized *we* were the mean ones, especially Brenda. People like her are closed-minded, distrusting, intolerant bigots, so there! Another think I had coming, huh? I thought I'd figured it out. Then it all changed. Clarissa wasn't who I thought she was, or at least who *she* thought she was. That's when I realized I knew nothing of the world at all. How could I have been so wrong? Right now, I feel so lost, Linney, I could *die*." Then she let go of my hand.

*Was Doreen suffering from a broken heart? Maybe.* Her world had crashed around her, and she had no idea how to cope. Doreen felt her conceitedness and narrow view of life had let her down. But instead, she'd let herself down. She had put her friends in one basket without realizing that people are complicated and different. Friends come in all shapes and sizes, some better than most. Miss Virginia taught me that, but sadly no one had taught Doreen. Being caught unprepared for this kind of pity party, I tried to say the obvious.

"If it helps… I'm still here."

"You're still here? But where've you been?" This time her tone was more accusatory. It came on suddenly, and I was not ready. "*I've* been here, Linney, not you! *I* was left in the Jungle while *you* ran away! You weren't in the dirt and sticks fighting for your life! You weren't the one screaming for help. *I* was! I called out for you, but you ran away and left me there by myself. *How could you?*"

The turn was dramatic. Doreen hadn't forgotten anything, just left it in the dirt she found herself in that day until she could drag it out to scratch me with it. Then I faced her with the sad, uncomfortable truth. I stood up to my full height and didn't hold back.

"It's true! I left. I ran as fast as I could because I was scared and didn't know what to do. I ran to get help for *you*! But I was the *only one* who could help, so *I. Ran. Back.* I didn't leave you. I came *back*! You and I faced that man together, and I beat him back… for *you*—!"

"Get out!" she yelled almost as loudly as that day in Jungle. "Get out of here and run like you always do! Run back to your mommy!" Doreen was up like a shot, fist tight after throwing a pillow at me, which I managed to dodge.

"I'm not going anywhere! I'm sorry. I'm *so sorry* I left you, but I'm not leaving—"

"I said get *out*!" She pushed me in the chest and threw a magazine at me. I didn't push back but stood my ground against the door while she threw another pillow and then another, which I caught in midair and held tightly.

"Unh-unh, I told you no! I'm not leaving, and you can't make me! I said I was sorry for leaving, but you know what? When I came back, I was not afraid. You know why? Because I heard you call my name *and* because you needed me. I hit him with all I had. I wasn't afraid of him, and I'm *not* afraid of *you*!"

"I hate you! *Get out!*"

"Go ahead! Hate me, call me names, *I don't care*!"

Then Doreen came at me with everything she had, punching, slapping, and clawing at me while I tried to dodge the blows. I was able to turn her away from me and hold her tightly from behind. I didn't hit back but let her punch out all her fears and pain, not letting go, no matter how much she squirmed. I held her because I wanted her to feel better and come out of this feel-sorry-for-me place in her head. I held her because I wanted Doreen back—not the sassy Doreen I knew and wanted to emulate, but a better Doreen who recognized that life can be cruel, but we don't have to be cruel in it. I held her for me and my hope of becoming a better person without resentment and jealousy. I held her because she was my friend, and I no longer wanted to be mean toward her despite her conceited belief in herself. I held her for healing's sake and shared love. I kept saying to myself, *Healing starts in the heart* as I held her while she struck out, not at me but at life and the world, with hands and arms that swung wildly at the air.

Eventually she calmed and stopped swinging, then began to cry. She cried mournful tears of relief and regret. The emotion shook her shoulders so violently that holding her tightly became difficult. I was exhausted. As we slid down the closed door of her bedroom to the floor, she found her voice.

"I tried to fight him… I had to. I fought so hard. And it hurt. He hurt me so bad. How could he do that to me? *Oh*, Linney! How could he do that to me?" Quietly I tried to shush her as she choked on words and sobbed out the pain held inside for so long. "I'll never be the same again. Who will love me now?"

"Hush now, hush. There'll be brighter days, you'll see," I said. Her tears continued, and as we cried together, we hugged each other, slowly rocking together to soothe our souls. All this time, she had no idea how much words and being treated differently could hurt until it happened to her. She was so ashamed and asked for my forgiveness. While I understood that this was true, I also knew the tide had turned. This was our sorry dance.

After the crying subsided, someone pushed the door to her bedroom open. My grandparents stood looking down at us on the magazine and pillow-strewn floor.

"You girls done throwing fits?" Grandpa asked with a concerned look.

We both giggled, shamefaced, which was when Grandma handed over tissues and warm cloths to clean our faces, saying, "It took all I had not to come in here, but Ernst held me back. We were standing close by, listening. That is, until we heard a knock at the door. Clean up 'cause Doreen has company waiting for her downstairs. Hurry up now, you two."

I could hear voices and laughter coming from downstairs, but I didn't recognize who it might be. However, Doreen knew and turned wide-eyed to look at me.

# CHAPTER 47

## *The Turning Point*

THE LONGER I live, the more I know that I know nothing. This sentiment echoed over and over in my head as the day faded into evening. In the living room of my grandparents' house sat Clarissa and her mother, Mrs. Lora Woodbridge Ferguson. At least, that was how she introduced herself.

This was the first time my grandmother tried to put on airs. She was so undone by the visit that she didn't know what to do with herself. It turned out to be unnecessary because, despite her name, Miss Ferguson could not have been more friendly. She made conversation easily and was happy to meet the girl Clarissa had spoken of so highly and had *persuaded* her to meet. The "persuaded her to meet" part was expertly handled by my grandmother who said she was equally pleased to have put aside hard work to entertain someone who'd come to her home unannounced, causing her to possibly lose a day's pay, but never mind that.

Miss Ferguson tried to make up for the comment. She told us that she had been distressed to learn of Doreen's misfortune, which *persuaded* her to rethink her position and extend a personal apology. She considered it beneath her upbringing to behave the way she did in dis-inviting Doreen and sincerely apologized for the pain and humiliation she had caused. In fact, Miss Ferguson wanted to make up for the rudeness Doreen had suffered at her hands by personally inviting her to visit with them—that is, when or if she felt up to it.

This was a turning point. Doreen was happy to accept once my grandparents approved, which they did, however, hesitantly. On the other hand, I was wary about Doreen moving within the horsey set circle so soon and hoped she could keep her feet on the ground. If this was a step in the right direction, I sure hoped Miss Ferguson knew what she was doing.

As my grandmother served coffee and shortbread cookies, my grandfather comfortably smoked a cigar, squinting through the smoke to watch Miss Ferguson. Clarissa and her mother were spitting images of each other; both had light brown hair, delicate facial features, and hands. Clarissa had kind, expressive eyes, and I suppose she had to be a gentle soul, giggling and smiling a lot, seemingly pleased that she could score a victory with her mother. I was glad to finally meet Clarissa for many reasons. But more so because she was the first White girl I had spoken to in a friendship kind of way. She fit in and seemed comfortable talking about all sorts of things without hesitation.

Most of our neighbors would be stunned when they got wind of their visit. I couldn't wait to gloat to Angela. Then I thought my first impressions might have been too harsh. After all, it couldn't have been easy for Miss Ferguson to come all this way to apologize. If the Woodbridge-Fergusons of the world were any sign, these people were nothing like the pretentious snobs we'd believed them to be. I hoped she got the same impression of us. However, I wasn't so naïve to think that all people were as accepting or friendly as this; far from it. But that day, Miss Ferguson set an example I hoped we could all live by.

Before they left, Miss Ferguson told us she would send an invitation in the mail and to watch for it. After they drove away, we stood looking at each other with our mouths open. Doreen let out a squeal I hadn't heard since our girlhood days playing with our Barbie dolls. I knew Clarissa's visit had given her the validation she needed: she hadn't been so wrong about people after all. For the time being, it seemed Doreen was on sound footing, secure in the knowledge that the acceptance she longed for always lay within herself and embracing others without judgment. This made me smile because I felt the same way.

I wish I could say Doreen snapped out of the terrors that visited her dreams from time to time, but I can't. She continued to suffer, and frequent bouts of insecurities plagued her but faded as soon as they came. I have since learned that trauma is slow to heal, and only time allows us the luxury of coping with pain, which lessens with time. I was the one who knew the scars remained unseen and unbidden until something came along to remind us of the old horror. It took a few more weeks for Doreen to blossom again, slowly embracing the whole of life, beginning with friends who loved and supported her.

⟶◈◈◈⟵

For me, returning to school had not been an easy adjustment; however, Doreen, having received her full share of attention, had adjusted reasonably well. She became a more gracious and humble person, still conceited but more genteel. Such as asking me if she looked pretty just before she left for her visit to the Fergusons. When I told her, "Yes," her reply was, "Of course I do," and with a wink, a smile, and a flip of her hair, she departed out the door.

Doreen talked about her visit for days after, and I didn't think I would ever hear the end. How grand the whole affair had been and how she hoped to live like that one day, high on a hill, surrounded by tall maple, birch, and strong oak trees and acres of grass with white fencing all around the grounds. Everyone was comfortable with each other, and not once did they mention her race or treat her differently. Doreen told me *everything* and confided what she could about her continued affection for none other than Mark Roberts.

Doreen told me, "I saw Mark! Clarissa arranged the whole thing. We were a threesome, with Clarissa acting as chaperone, walking down the long avenue of hickory trees. I didn't care how cold and frosty that morning was because Mark was with me. We were left alone for the most part, watching the

Thoroughbreds and their behavior. You should see them up close, Linney. They sure are beautiful, regal, and magnificent animals. Mark told me how hurt he was for me over what had happened. He stayed by my side the whole time in recovery. But of course, you know that because he talked with you. He said you gave him the courage to see us through. He told me nothing had changed for him. I feel the same. I just love him, Linney. He was so thoughtful, telling me he'll wait for me until all the pain is gone, if it ever is. He wants me to trust his judgment and move slowly. We have to be discreet until the time is right. I agree." This declaration of love was a foundation for a long-lasting relationship, which was the most special kind. I hoped one day to be so lucky.

We still went to the Youth Center, but it was more needed to normalize our lives than to socialize. I was always watchful for any humiliation from Doreen, but it never came. Old habits died hard, I supposed. But while she was sincere in her apology, I was still left with the scars of insecurity. I often thought how difficult it must be to live with the terror Doreen faced that day in the Jungle and come out the other side a more appreciative person, full of introspection and grace. I admired her bravery and resilience, and I think she admired mine. If she could come through *that*, then so could I.

Doreen began relying on me more and more, asking my opinion and taking my advice. I'm not sure why, but I took it for what it was; she respected me. She also began to read literature, not just fashion magazines. I was happy to share my knowledge of all things, literary or poetic. Doreen, Carolyn, Angela, and even Amy made a pact to meet every Wednesday, sometimes at Miss Katherine's tiny house, to discuss the latest novel each of us read. I couldn't wait to discuss the characters' lives and uncover the meaning of the written word. I loved our meetings, which we called The Wednesday Club.

<hr>

All this happened before and after Thanksgiving. Before I knew it, my birthday had come and gone. Now I was fourteen, and

Christmas was upon us. Because of occasional arthritis flare-ups in her hands, Miss Katherine couldn't knit or crochet as often but sat in Miss Dottie's rocking chair, quietly rocking and reminiscing about her days in Kentucky. It was these quiet moments, listening to her speak while the fire burned in the old fireplace, that were most special for me.

One evening, after helping decorate her house with the few Christmas ornaments she had put away, she fell silent, looking at one that held an apparent special meaning for her. She sighed while looking at the old figurine, exquisitely made with delicate cuts and flourishes in the dress and small details in the face. I had never seen anything like it and watched her fingers caress it lovingly.

"So much history in a person's life, I suppose I should share it—" Miss Katherine said.

"What is that?" I asked.

"It's my first ever real present from a special someone long ago."

"It looks special."

"So it is. It feels like only yesterday when I received this gift. It was the best day of my life, or so I thought. It's funny how you can forget meaningful moments. Moments you think you'll hold on to forever. Seeing this reminded me of how much I had forgotten, and then it all floods back."

"It's beautiful. The figure looks sad but regal. Hmm… who gave it to you?"

"It's old history that shouldn't go to waste in the telling, no it won't. I think you'll appreciate the history and the story, which I would like to share now. Set it up there on the shelf so I can look at it while I say. We all have secrets and mysteries that a lifetime of living will give. As you grow older, you'll have many of your own, I imagine."

It began to snow as I set the figurine on the shelf. All was perfectly quiet. As the fire burned and smoke rose through the chimney, I sat at her feet and listened as Miss Katherine began her story.

As if reading from a book, her voice took on a melodic tone and wove a story about the sisters DuBois.

# CHAPTER 48

## *The Sisters DuBois*

ELOISE DUBOIS WAS the toast of the town in 1920s Chicago. She was the belle of all the belles in Hyde Park and loved every minute of the adoration she received at the debutante coming-out parties. She was one of a pair of sisters whose father was a prominent White physician and whose mother was a quadroon from New Orleans and taught at the University of Chicago.

Her parents were members of the near-do-wells at the height of the Gilded Age of 1900 Chicago. When Eloise and her fraternal twin sister Beatrix were born in 1901, the Gilded Age had reached its zenith, and their parents had prospered in glorious wealth. They enjoyed many of the privileges money could buy and the pretentiousness that went along with their riches. The twins were spoiled beyond what was considered decent.

Eloise was the youngest by two minutes, and most considered her the prettiest of the twins. She had the delicate features most octoroons of her lineage possessed, with pink, rosy cheeks mixed with her barely perceptible café au lait complexion. She and her mother, Louisa Evelyn DuBois, née Devereaux, had no problem with membership in the Blue Vein Society.

On the other hand, Beatrix was pretty in her own right, slightly plump with a roundish face, a few inches shorter than her sister, and whose café au lait complexion had no hint of pink and more of the olive undertones of her heritage. Most of the time, she "pinked up" only when embarrassed or angry, so her skin undertones were not always apparent. As the eldest, Beatrix never understood why Eloise received so much attention; after all, her Southern accent, mimicking their mother's, was annoying.

In 1912, at the age of eleven, they lost their father on the ill-fated Titanic. Traveling home from a symposium in France, Devlin Merchant DuBois had boarded the Titanic in Cherbourg at the last minute. The shock of their father's death affected them tremendously, but the loss was devastating for their mother, who shut herself away with grief in her bedroom for weeks, which eventually turned into months and then years. Eloise missed her father's praise while Beatrix the constant reassurance of his love.

After a year of mourning, Louisa slowly resumed her social engagements but did not return to teaching. She rarely saw her twins except on the odd occasion when she inquired after their studies. Being absent a mother and losing a doting father, the twins were left to their own devices, much to the detriment of their upbringing. Squabbles and fights were constant, and jealousy ran rampant on both sides. The twins would not have had the luxury of continuing to live the life they were accustomed to if it weren't for the extensive financial trust set up by their father. With the tutors and the housekeeping help this afforded, they grew up cloistered but without much in the way of parental love.

By the time they were sixteen, their mother had reemerged in their lives and, with astounding vigor, resumed the responsibility of raising her daughters to ensure their future introduction to society would be a resounding success. It was vital for them to marry well because the money for the privileges they enjoyed was quickly running out. Of this fact, her daughters were blithely unaware. So a successful coming-out for her seventeen-year-old daughters was crucial. Beatrix didn't appreciate the attention their mother thrust upon them after years of disinterest, but Eloise was beside herself with glee. During the debutante balls, Eloise's butterfly curtsy was the talk of the town. Their coming-out came and went with success and aplomb, much to the chagrin of Beatrix.

Beatrix was annoyed with the whole business of being a debutante and felt it more than unfair that she was overlooked by the season's suitors. But Eloise was not. On the contrary, Eloise had received many proposals and was conflicted over which one to accept. After two years, Eloise was still considered quite the catch, and flirtation became an art for her.

Eventually while visiting relatives in New York, she decided to accept the proposal of Mr. Archibald Vanderhaven of the New York Vanderhavens, steel magnate partners of Carnegie's US Steel. Because of the Titanic tragedy, Mr. Vanderhaven knew of Eloise's father but little of her racial makeup or background. He loved her coloring and considered her an exotic beauty, naturally tinged with a slight hint of cocoa. Archibald saw what he wanted to see, ergo for what he wanted to hear. He only heard about her mother and sister through Eloise, who distorted the truth more than somewhat.

In 1920s New York society, the lack of references was a significant issue. However, because they were a well-respected family whose name had grown in popularity after the death of their father, the facts of Eloise's heritage were easily ignored. For Archibald to nab one of the infamous sisters was a heady prospect indeed. Eloise's dowry was substantial, which was considered a good match with Archibald's ever-growing wealth.

Beatrix, however, didn't see it this way. She thought Archibald was too high-minded and the worst kind of society snob. She felt sure Eloise would have a miserable life as his wife, especially when they traveled abroad to Europe, which Archibald would need to do to attend to Mr. Carnegie's steel business holdings. Beatrix knew Eloise would be bored to sobs. She also pondered whether their union would be received respectfully or if Eloise would be considered more a paramour than a wife. How long would it be before Archibald uncovered the truth and tire of defending the demanding and pretty Eloise or her honor? Taking Eloise from Chicago's bourgeoisie society to the rarified air of New York's upper crust, akin to an aristocracy, would be an easy enough adjustment. But secrets could be kept for only so long and, once discovered, were bound to end in tragedy. As with some society gentlemen, Archibald had a wandering eye for the ladies, and a person like Eloise was reluctant to share anything, least of all her husband.

Beatrix tried to get her mother to see reason and resist the match, but her mother wouldn't hear of it.

"Eloise has to accept that men will eventually tire and seek pleasures elsewhere," Louisa said. "By the time any improprieties are known, Eloise will be blessed with at least a child or two and well established as the grand dame of Chicago and New York's upper crust. All our money worries will be over. What will it matter if Archibald turns out to be a cad in the end?"

"Oh, good grief, Mother!"

"Now, you listen to me!" Louisa said sharply. "You keep your mouth *shut*! If Archibald knew the truth of Eloise's race, all our hopes for a secure financial future would be destroyed! Enduring his infidelities is a trade-off against this one little lie."

"An *outlandish* lie! Shame on you, Mother," Beatrix said, turning on her heels in disgust.

Never shy to speak her opinion, Beatrix hinted at this issue to Eloise. But Eloise would not hear any negativity concerning Archibald that might spoil her upcoming nuptials. Beatrix's warnings fell on deaf ears.

Before her wedding, Eloise did all she could to distance herself from the Colored citizens of Bronzeville and insulated herself in her Hyde Park neighborhood manse. She was embarrassed to have Archibald know more about her less-than-White relatives and friends. Eloise was instrumental in creating a reason for not inviting them to the wedding or reception, which might expose her true heritage. What was worse? She lied about Beatrix, secretly telling Archibald that Beatrix was a cherished friend who lived with them and that her twin was abroad, and with sad regrets, was unable to attend the wedding. When this was discovered, Beatrix's heart was crushed, and all were forced to go along with the ruse.

In 1923, with no formal announcements in the newspapers, let alone the society column, their wedding was a small private affair at home with a few discreet Chicago White elites in attendance. Eloise worked the ruse flawlessly. But Beatrix had taken all she could stand and refused to go along with the ruse any longer. She threatened to tell the truth or burn in hell! This was when Beatrix and Eloise had their last horrendous fight.

"You're just *ashamed*," Beatrix started, "of being a Neg—"

"Don't you say that! I am *not* ashamed!" Eloise said. "You're just jealous, yes, just *green* with envy! I hope I *never* see you again! Thank God, I'll finally be part of the White race."

That's when Beatrix slapped her. "You go to *hell!*"

Without flinching and rising to her full height, Eloise said coldly, "I'll do that gladly."

On the way down the long staircase of their home, with just a few guests waiting at the bottom and Beatrix following close behind, Eloise tripped and fell, twisting her ankle badly. In the commotion, Eloise blamed Beatrix for pushing her, which Beatrix had not done. Melodramatically, Eloise pleaded with Archibald to take her away quickly.

Beatrix was fuming at the top of the staircase landing, listening to Eloise's horrible accusation. She could only watch as Archibald helped his bride off the stone floor, who then limped to the limousine, waiting for their departure to New York. Beatrix was blamed for pushing Eloise and could do nothing to absolve herself from this egregious lie. She lived the rest of her days with the guilt that she had slapped her sister. Pushing Eloise down the stairs was something Beatrix only wished she had done but could never do.

⊸◈◈◈⊷

Eloise lived a full-throated life within New York's high society as time went on. Eventually, Archibald became increasingly inattentive to Eloise, and as Beatrix predicted, his infidelities became too many to name. He often left Eloise alone to fend for herself, wrestle with the household staff, and struggle with New York's social elite snobs. They never fully accepted her no matter how hard she tried or how lavish her dinner parties were. She lived in constant fear that they would or had guessed her true racial and ethnic identity and, as a result, found herself trying too hard to prove otherwise. Her ankle never healed properly, and ironically, she never sought medical help for it but kept her deformity as a way to get attention and sympathy from Archibald. But it never worked. Instead, a walking cane became her constant companion. While keeping up public appearances as the perfect high-society couple, behind closed doors, she had become a nag and constant complainer whose need for attention was ignored by her husband.

Many years passed, and the children never came. Eloise spent money on extravagances and cocooned herself with luxuries, which soothed her loneliness for a short time. World War II kept them abroad far longer than expected, and in doing so, she began to long for the sight of the Statue of Liberty on the eastern shores of America. She missed her home in Chicago. As Archibald busied himself with ensuring the delivery of much-needed munitions and artillery using US Steel, Eloise had seen enough of the countryside of Italy, Britain, and France. After all those years, she missed her sister Beatrix and regretted their fight on her wedding day.

---

Eloise loved to browse the shops on the streets of Paris. In 1946, France was slow to recover from the ravages of war. Eloise often passed a shop or two, rebuilding as best it could. Their meager efforts were heartbreaking, and Eloise wished to do more to help. While walking down Avenue Montaigne during Christmas and mindful of stepping carefully on her twisted ankle among the fallen bricks leftover from bombing raids, she passed a small shop full of ornaments and figurines in the window.

This shop had survived the blitz of war. A lone ornament, so beautifully made, looked out at her in the window. Eloise was astonished at its fine workmanship. She had her share of art deco figurines by Chiparus, Philippe, and Preiss inspired by Erté's *Harpers Bizarre* cover illustrations. A beautiful and lone Fabergé egg, given as a wedding gift from her husband, was something to behold. Her home in New York, and their enormous Christmas tree, were elaborately decorated each year. But never had she seen anything like this. A figurine so skillfully crafted, she thought the thing would speak. So delicately made, the intricate detail of the bronze figure's garments fell in folds around her arms and limbs to suggest they moved of their own accord. With arms outstretched in supplication, it seemed to be reaching out for answers, which she knew would never come. Eloise had to have it.

The ornament was surprisingly cheap but full of meaning for her. She paid the shop owner three times its worth. If for nothing else, it might help with the effort to rebuild their business or buy food, at least for a few days. Once home, she immediately thought of her sister Beatrix. The figurine would be a gift to atone for what happened between them, and she hoped forgiveness would be her reward.

She instantly began making plans to travel home for Christmas. She didn't care if Archibald accompanied her. In fact, she hoped he wouldn't. She had seen more than enough of the torture and suffering innocent people had endured in their homelands. With these ardent thoughts, Eloise began preparations for her return home with abandon.

⇒◦◦◦⇐

Eloise's homecoming was not met with fanfare as when she left after marriage. The mansion now seemed drab and small, unlike the large, expansive mansion of her youth. Looking up at it, she smiled, thinking it was the best manse in all of Chicago's Hyde Park when she was a girl. Even so, it couldn't compare to the cold vastness of any of her estates. Eloise couldn't wait to feel the cozy warmth of its interior and to see Beatrix.

Martha, the housemaid, met Eloise and gave her a warm welcome. Eloise stood in the open foyer with its stone floor covered in an expensive oriental rug. How bare it had been during her fall down the stairs many years before, but this was the only change to the house she could see thus far. The furnishings were still covered in rich brocades, and the rooms were still wrapped in the décor of Victorian traditions. It seemed time had stood still in this comfortable old home.

Her mother was seated in a rocking chair in the sitting room to the right of the foyer. Louisa anxiously peered around to see who had come to call while she sat cozy by a blazing fire. As Eloise walked toward her mother on unsteady legs, the familiar sounds of welcome reached her daughter's ears.

Eloise was shocked at her mother's aged appearance and felt terrible she had not corresponded during her long years away. Louisa admired Eloise's svelte figure but was concerned that she walked with a pronounced limp and questioned if it would get worse. "Tosh, tosh" was Eloise's comment in an attempt to set her mother's mind at ease. Louisa had ordered Eloise's bags taken up to her old bedroom, and tea was brought in while Eloise made herself at home. Louisa insisted her daughter sit in her rocking chair, but Eloise refused and sat near the hearth, thinking how good it felt to be home.

⟶◦◦◦⟵

Beatrix had been doing her share of Christmas shopping after volunteering at the Salvation Army soup kitchen when Eloise arrived. Weary and tired, she longed to sit with her mother to tell of her day. Beatrix had never married, not because she didn't want to, but because suitors were few, and those she met never moved her to accept their proposals. In the years that followed, she spent most of her time volunteering for charities, giving dinner parties, knitting or crocheting doilies for rest homes, and caring for her needy mother. She often thought of Eloise and the life she must be living. But sadly, she knew she would never see nor hear from her again since their fight many years ago. So it came as a total and pleasant surprise to see her beautiful sister, Eloise, sitting with their mother that pre-Christmas evening.

At first, Beatrix thought she was looking at a ghost. It couldn't be Eloise, but it was, with her beautiful beaming smile, standing with open arms to greet her. They embraced and stood at arm's length, looking at each other. Eloise asked after Beatrix's health and Beatrix of Eloise. Eloise also marveled that Beatrix had lost some, if not all, of her plumpness. Beatrix was alarmed to see Eloise walk with the help of a cane, and she questioned why she had allowed her ankle to heal in such a manner. Once again, Eloise refused to discuss her ankle and insisted on hearing about Beatrix and her mother's daily lives since she had been gone.

Eloise was alarmed to hear of their financial struggles. She was told that Archibald's stipend had not been delivered on a timely basis and, when it was, was far less than promised. Eloise said that she never bothered with finances. As with most women in her position, this was always left to the husband to manage. She was his wife and conducted her wifely duties, but delving into financial concerns was not one of them. Hearing of their hardship, Eloise blamed herself for not looking after her sister and mother better and promised to inquire about this as soon as possible. Beatrix assured Eloise that their position was secure, but they had no idea how long.

<hr>

Christmas Eve was a festive affair with meats and fruits of every assortment and plenty of eggnog to go around. Now that Eloise was home, family friends stopped by in more than their usual numbers. The staff had decorated the house with holly and boughs of fragrant greenery. Bowls of fruit and nuts were set about within easy reach. The punch with a pineapple ring, spiked with a bit of cognac, was served in the best crystal Louisa had on hand with an assortment of shortbreads, cookies, and tiny unpowdered beignets.

They observed the evening tradition of each person opening *only* one gift. Eloise had received a set of intricately crocheted handmade doilies from Beatrix, which were lovely. However, the stunned look on Beatrix's face at the gift she received from Eloise was priceless. Tears stung Beatrix's eyes as she touched the figurine's outstretched arms and looked over at Eloise, understanding its meaning. Hugging Eloise, she told her how sorry she was for the harm she had inflicted long ago and how much she loved her twin. For Eloise, this was all she needed to know. She had been forgiven for the hurt she had caused Beatrix and her family. The previous slights and loneliness faded as they sat with their guests to reminisce about the glory of days gone by, far too soon. The night passed with well-wishes and joy that continued into the New Year.

At the end of the New Year's Eve celebration, the DuBois sisters were the happiest they had been in a long time. All past recriminations had been forgiven as they enjoyed a whole week of family togetherness. Eloise even promised to see a foot specialist for her ankle. As so often happens, though, these feelings of joy crashed around them seemingly in an instant.

One evening as Beatrix helped Eloise up the stairs to prepare for bed, an insistent knocking came at the door.

"Don't open the door, Beatrix, please don't! Something terrible's on the other side. I can feel it!"

"Oh, it's probably just one of our guests. Probably forgot something."

Beatrix needed to pry her sister's fingers from her arm as she struggled to pull herself away. When she opened the door, she was unprepared to see Mr. Archibald Vanderhaven waiting to be admitted.

Mistaking her for the housemaid, Archibald was quick to make the intent of his visit known. "Pardon me, I'm Mr. Vanderhaven here to collect my wife. We're leaving for New York this evening, and I have no time to waste. Do be so kind as to call her down, girl."

Beatrix did no such thing. She found it intolerable to be ordered about and in her own home, no less! Instead, she said, "My *sister* is home for the holidays. She'll remain here until her visit is through."

Archibald seemed insulted at this affront and yelled through the house and up the stairs for Eloise. Eloise stood at the top of the staircase and looked down at him. In a calm voice, she said, "I can hear you. You don't have to shout."

Beatrix watched as her sister painfully descended the staircase holding her cane in one hand while she held on to the ornate banister with the other. Beatrix thought *The once beautiful and elegant Eloise, my sister, has been reduced to this pathetic creature dominated by this elite social reprobate. How dare he!*

As Beatrix made her way to assist her sister, Archibald stepped in her way, barring access to Eloise. As they briefly jostled, she recalled raising her hand once but regretted it since that day. The desire to do so again and to Archibald no less was intense, but she stood silent.

Then Beatrix glanced up to see her mother at the head of the stairs, who said, "Beatrix! Stand aside."

Obediently Beatrix moved to the side but gave Archibald too much of a wide berth, as it turned out. She watched as Eloise limped up to Mr. Archibald Vanderhaven, then promptly asked him to leave. When he refused and reached for her arm, Eloise stumbled back and away from him.

"I intend to divorce you, Archie. The grounds should be clear. But how *dare* you hold back financial help to my family? How could you do such a thing and then have the temerity to come here and demand I go with you after ignoring me for most of our marriage!"

"You little strumpet!" Archibald seemed to enjoy this moment as he moved close to Eloise and spoke softly through gritted teeth. "You're too *lame* to take out in public and too *spoilt* to be around. I'm tired of making excuses for you and *lying* to everyone about what and *who* you *really* are. Your heritage is an *embarrassment!* I only married you for your *name* and the money you brought to this sham of a marriage. That money is *long gone.* You're living off *my* fortunes. Your *family* ought to be *grateful.*"

Eloise was incensed. She struck out at him with her walking cane, but Archibald was quick. Before anyone could react, he grabbed the cane and hit her on the side of the head with it. The blow was swift, brutal, and violent. She fell to the very floor he had lifted her from years ago, but this time he made no attempt to pick her up or offer an iota of concern. He cursed at her instead.

Beatrix rushed to her sister, "Martha, call the authorities before I *kill* this man myself!" Beatrix stared at Archie from the floor, transfixed, as her sister lay on the floor, shouting.

"I can't see! God help me. I can't see, help me, please! Where is everyone? Beatrix, I can't see anyone! Jesus! Jesus!"

The maid ran to call for an ambulance and the police while Mr. Archibald Vanderhaven ran from the foyer and out the front door to his waiting car.

The Vanderhaven scandal was immense. The DuBois Hyde Park mansion was reported as cursed because this was not the first time Miss Eloise had been maimed, and the tragedy of the loss of their father was more proof of it being so. The Chicago and New York newspapers were full of inaccurate facts about the events of that day. Eloise Vanderhaven would have partial sight restored after the temporary blindness; the papers falsely reported that she was forever blinded from an unfortunate accident at the DuBois residence, her childhood manse. The truth was Eloise Vanderhaven would not have full use of her right foot; the papers stated that she would never walk again due to an unfortunate fall she sustained while on her honeymoon on the Greek island of Caicos. The newspapers surmised a great many things. Eloise Devereaux DuBois Vanderhaven, the social climber who had passed for White, was now a societal outcast.

The divorce and its settlement were the talk of the town. Mr. Vanderhaven was more than generous in his alimony payments to Eloise while also providing for her sister and mother for life. For her part, Eloise never let the papers know of Archibald's infidelity and cruelty. This held her in good stead, which was, after all, the done thing. Let the papers print what they may; in polite society, the truth was never spoken aloud. The money given in the settlement was a thank-you for Eloise's discretion.

The scandal had shaken the DuBois greatly. Louisa Devereaux DuBois suffered a fatal stroke shortly after the divorce terms were finalized. She was buried next to the memorial site of her beloved husband, leaving Beatrix alone to care for her invalid sister.

The blow to Eloise's head was a far more significant injury, which the papers had not exploited with lies if they had known. While it was true Eloise had lost a great deal of her eyesight, she had been hit in just the right temporal spot, which caused a lack of muscle control, affecting her ability to swallow, walk properly, or speak as before. Over time, she lost all hope of improvement as her health deteriorated with each passing year. Beatrix did all she could to help Eloise improve, but it was no use as the depression regarding her condition took its toll.

Eloise was forever changed as these symptoms worsened, to the point that she could only drag her foot as she walked, using her cane to navigate around and sit drooling in her mother's favorite rocking chair.

# CHAPTER 49

## *Surprise Revelations*

M ISS KATHERINE LOOKED down at me, knowing I must have guessed the truth. I gazed at the fire, now glowing embers, while dark shadows grew tall around the room in the dying light.

"Miss Eloise is Miss Dottie?"

"Wé."

"You're Miss Beatrix?"

"Ça cé korèk. Èskizé e paddonné mô ségré, shè. The scandal was too much for us after Eloise's injury. The papers had done their damage. The shame Eloise felt, passing for White and all, didn't do much for us in the community. Besides, Bronzeville had lost its prominence by then, so there was no need to stay. The age in which we had grown up had long since vanished. It was a struggle to keep our position in society after those events. Archibald made his fortune, which helped us prosper in Chicago, but not for long. We had to stretch our finances and live elsewhere. Live in a place where no one knew us. We could disappear, living peacefully without anyone knowing our shame, keeping our secrets guarded. We came South and resided in Lexington for a little while. But in 1950, it was here in Paris we decided to settle.

"It was my turn to call on strength I never had before. I learned to hold my head high and not let the sting of gossip and the stigma of those events break me down. It's second nature to me now. I do it still today!"

"But your last name's Sweet, and you never speak Creole. Kòfè pa?" I asked while getting up to turn on a lamp or two to light the room. Miss Katherine was eager to explain events as I watched her, seemingly relieved to tell the tale.

"If we spoke our Louisiana Creole French, we couldn't hide as well now, sé nou? It was easy to change our names to something less pretentious than DuBois. Eloise began to have those visions of hers not long after her injury. Actually, I think they began *before* her warning about not opening that door. I ignored that warning, but never again. Over time, they increased in frequency. I trusted her visions and realized they should be heeded and never questioned.

"After we moved to Paris, I saw an improvement in Eloise. Then one day, I don't quite understand how or why, but it just happened. One morning, she sat up in bed and said, 'Dorothy, sweetie? Is that you?'

"That's how it came to be. I started referring to her as Dottie, and she would respond. She never responded to the name *Eloise* after that and hasn't spoken much since. I chose Katherine for myself. We bought this house outright with cash, and no one questioned us at all. Who's going to question two spinster ladies like us anyway? The deed was signed with the last name 'Sweet,' which is who we've been ever since." Miss Katherine settled back into her chair.

"I see the connection now, you and Miss Dottie, me and Doreen," I said as realization hit me. "No wonder you wanted us to make up and kept pushing me to do better. All this time, I knew there was a mystery about y'all, but I never knew it was anything like this."

"It's bittersweet. We had the bitter, now we have the sweet, don't you see?"

"I do. It all makes sense."

"I lacked the courage to strike back at Archibald once he hit Eloise or even protect her before it got that far. I've often asked myself why I didn't move faster or stand my ground against that man. Or was it because I subconsciously thought it served her right? I was transfixed at the horror of it and did nothing but stare up at him from that floor. I tell myself it was the times we lived in that caused me to be still, but who was I fooling? I've regretted all my life not doing anything to protect her when it mattered, which is why I applaud your courage. I admire who you are and your ability to see clearly and do what's right."

Then she asked me to hand her the figurine. I watched as she caressed it and waited for her to continue. "This means more to me than you can imagine. Family is precious, and life is short. I hope you've gotten something out of knowing us. I know we've been blessed by knowing you."

"Remember what you told me about God not asking more of his angels?" I asked. "You could only do so much. No one should judge when you've done your very best. I know you loved each other, I could tell. Your secret's safe with me."

"As we say in Naglé, ohh, dat girl there, sure 'nough a Creole chile, she is."

⸻ ❧ ⸻

I felt lighter and less heavy on my feet when I left Miss Katherine. The mystery of the Sweet sisters had been solved. They were not the old hags and voodoo women we thought them to be but sweet, kind, and generous ladies who'd suffered tragedies just like the rest of us. Sweet was a fitting name. Now I understood what my mother meant when she said, many months ago, that "some people have a lot of secrets to hold on to." Mom must have known the secret these two ladies kept and knew I would benefit.

I was lucky to have good neighbors and teachers, family, and special friends like Miss Virginia and the Sweet sisters. I might not have had everything I wanted, like new clothes or sandals, but I had all I needed. There were more lessons to be learned from Miss Katherine's Christmas story, as I called it, and I had the rest of my life to discover what those might be. All I knew was I would never be embarrassed about my skin color again. I didn't want to be anyone else other than who God made me.

Walking home, thoughts swirled around me like the falling snow. It had deepened and fell softly on the twinkling Christmas lights, which I could see everywhere, in the windows of each house decorated for the season. Like looking through a shaken snow globe, the neighborhood took on a dreamy quality as I watched the snow fall. Miss Tally and Miss Edna had grown closer, and it showed seeing the glistening string of Christmas lights strewn across both porches. As I admired the scene, pulling my coat tighter around me, I couldn't help but think of kids like me waiting for Santa's arrival. Maybe one day, one of them might think of uncovering secrets. I hoped they would have someone to help guide their way, as I did.

I tilted my head to the sky and watched the snowflakes fall like stars onto my face. I stuck out my tongue to taste the flakes, catching as many as I could. They melted, of course, without any taste at all. After a while of doing this, I reluctantly continued my way home. As I kicked through the deepening snow, the headlights of a car came toward me. It came to a stop in front of my house. The lights stayed on me longer than I liked, which set off a warning in my head.

The search for the mystery man, James Marx, had ended. I know this because Miss Tally told Mom that Mr. Tally had given up trying to find his new friend a long time ago. He was still a wanted man, but the police had stopped actively looking for him. It was reported by the staff at the YMCA that Mr. Mitch was last seen with a burn scar on his face, much like my description of the man named James Marx. The guess was Mr. Mitch was the same man, and it was said he had used the name of Mitchell Duncan to disguise his identity. There were plenty of rumors and whispers of ghosts of the past as stories spread around town about the connection between Mitchell Duncan, James Marx, and a person named Ajax.

*Who's in the car?* If it was James Marx, I was sunk. My boots felt stuck to the ground, and I stood there with no one else in sight except me. How could I be so stupid to stay so long at Miss Katherine's and then walk home at night? I wished I had those bricks again. I wanted to run, but the snow was so thick around my ankles I knew I wouldn't get far. I could scream, and because the night was quiet, the sound would travel far, wouldn't it? Someone would surely hear me, wouldn't they?

The car lights dimmed as they turned off, and the car door opened on the driver's side. Then I heard my name called by a familiar voice, questioning at first. I didn't recognize the tall figure, but once I did, I ran full force into the waiting arms of my dad. Daddy had come home.

<hr>

I'll never forget the expression on my mother's face when she saw Daddy. It was a bit awkward to see them stare at each other for so long. She reached out her hand to touch him, and he met it with one of his, then they hugged each other warmly and close. I quietly left them alone to talk about matters only they knew and understood.

The days flew by as the festive Christmas season came and went. It was the happiest time of my life with so many gifts and holiday parties. My father got familiar with the neighbors, who brought him up to speed on the year's events. He reconnected with a few of his high school buddies and even visited Western Elementary to give a special Christmas talk about his military work. Daddy and I had long discussions about what I had experienced and learned that summer. He was a better listener than most, and I loved his advice.

When the New Year came, it was time for him to leave for his new job in Washington, DC. The plan was when Mom passed her final exams, we would move to DC. I didn't like the idea at all. Moving to a new place without knowing anyone right before high school was terrifying.

The effect this news had on Doreen was unexpected. The thought of me leaving her was something she couldn't accept.

Doreen had come to depend on me for a lot more than friendship, as it turns out. We shared an experience no one could understand, a deep connection on the order of a twinship, much like the Sweet/DuBois sisters. No one could agree on what to do until finally, my parents saw the wisdom of me staying with my grandparents to finish school while Mom left to live with Dad. It was settled.

In the early spring of 1968, I finally received a pair of sandals and a new Schwinn bike. As much as I wanted the sandals though, I would always wear my trusted Keds. They got me through the year before, helped rescue a lot of my pride, and kept me humble. They were with me when I helped cradle Miss Dottie and the courage to confront Stooly, and they were the ones that made me fly that day to save Doreen. For me, they would always be a constant companion for years to come. Before long, Mom thought it was time for a training bra and a Kimberly-Clark kit of my own; I had started to grow boobs!

Mom passed her exams with flying colors that summer and became an LPN, which made us, including Dr. Roberts, proud. Running the candy striper program took more of Nurse Goodall's time, so he hoped my mother would transition from being his front desk clerk to his head nurse, but it was not to be. I think it was sadder for Mom to say goodbye to him than to me. Dr. Roberts had become a special part of our family.

This is how I came to live the rest of my remaining school years with my grandparents and claim the blue bedroom as my very own. Staying with them helped ease the pain of not seeing my mother, who left that summer to be with my dad. My days were spent helping Grandpa in the garden while Doreen learned tailoring and clothing alterations from my grandmother.

Thanks to the lessons learned from Doreen's experience, I went on to high school and avoided the pitfalls that befell her. Thanks to a new English literature teacher, Miss Hansbry, I excelled in my studies and received honors, which gave me a new nickname from "Goody Two-shoes" to "Professor," but I didn't mind. I knew I was more than that.

To say I was the harbinger of change would be a stretch. I will say more change in the town was seen than felt. For instance, communities grew together, and people were nicer to each other. Segregation was starting to be a thing of the past. I think it would have happened in time anyway, whether I lived in Paris or not. I grew taller, unconcerned about my appearance or what people thought of me. The sisters and Miss Virginia taught me the value of being beautiful on the inside, if not the outside. I loved life and Jesus Christ as my savior and respected everyone, no matter where they came from or who they were. I was no longer jealous of Doreen; I liked me.

Boyfriends came and went, and surprisingly, also for Doreen. From the outside, she appeared unaffected by the tragedy of the past year, but I knew better. She held on to her deepest affections, not trusting her heart or body to anyone… save one. I watched as she gradually developed into the incredible creature she was destined to be, conceit and all. You just had to love her.

I never saw Stooly again after that day at his house. The rumor was Bessie had moved to Las Vegas, and Stooly might be with her, but who knew for sure. I imagined him wearing his best shiny shoes, teasing and flirting with the ladies, looking dapper and very handsome.

I did see Slim once during the fall of '68. He was standing by the side of that car of his outside Stanley's. As Doreen and I rode by on our bikes, he didn't smile, if he ever did, but nodded, asking how we were that fine day. He paid particular attention to asking after us if we were okay and being careful and such. The question of what Stooly might or might not have done to Jimmy nagged at me from time to time. I never told a soul about my conversation with Stooly or my suspicions. There were many things I wanted to hold on to. The memory of his promise and the special connection I felt that day was one.

Looking down at the ground, I happened to look up during a lull in Slim's conversation. When he and I locked eyes, I caught my breath when he said, "I won't let anything happen to you without me answering for it." In the instant chill down my spine,

I knew a reckoning had taken place. In that silent knowing of cool understanding, he and I, and only he and I, knew what could never be spoken; and it was good. Somewhere I've heard, the greatest trick the devil played was to convince us he didn't exist. But Slim and I knew better.

After a while, Doreen and I pedaled off. I turned back to see Slim looking after us. He tossed a cigarette to the ground, put one hand in his pocket, and with the other, waved.

In my seventeenth year, Miss Katherine passed away quietly while I read to her at the end of the day. Sitting in Miss Dottie's rocking chair, she seemed peaceful and serene as I crossed her hands over her body and wept. I could never refer to her as Miss Beatrix. For me, that was not who she was. Like Miss Virginia, she and her sister would forever be Miss Dottie and Miss Katherine Sweet.

My habit of walking up the hill to my favorite tree to think and read never failed me as the years marched on. I would often think of how our lives had changed, starting with the events of that summer in '67. Mainly how I had grown with the help of those ladies. In my mind, they would forever be so very dear.

# EPILOGUE

LOOKING BACK ON those days, I often wonder, what do we know of our neighbors? Do we really know ourselves and understand the reasoning behind our own motives? Will we ever know the many eyes that watch out for us? Guardian angels watch over us all. God is ever-present, and Jesus is always near. Life is full of mysteries, and some are better left unsolved, while some questions are best left unanswered. As the grass grows green, fragrant, and sweet along the path ever stretched before us to parts unknown, we are left fervently questioning our choices. Don't.

The late 1960s were turbulent. But just like a well-used bicycle, the wheels started to come off in 1968. The assassination of Martin Luther King Jr. and Robert Kennedy sparked riots and social unrest. The nation mourned the loss of the many advances we gained in fighting for civil rights. Many lost hope that it was all in vain. It wasn't. These changes, and more, were felt across the nation, the world, and even our small town. We weathered the storms of dissent and thrived.

The Youth Center gave way to Teen Square, where both races danced together as the music progressed to include rock and roll, and the continued wave of British band music swept the nation into the 1970s. As they say, Motown never blinked. Soul music proliferated and grew more popular, ever changing and influencing culture. "We're a Winner" by the Impressions was a favorite dance tune, and the words coupled with that of "O-o-h, Child" by the Five Stairsteps helped get us through the worst times. Unfortunately, the selling of marijuana transitioned into methamphetamine drugs as a viable trade in Louisville, Lexington, and the surrounding areas of Kentucky, including Paris.

No one heard from Stooly again, even though rumors of him abounded. Some say Slim was overheard saying The Boss forgave Stooly for leaving the drug trade in Paris to others. After all, Stooly was like them, a stand-up guy, and eventually respected for his actions. The Boss's men took Jimmy's body and dumped it in a shipping container of acid. It was buried deep in the ground on the Louisville, Kentucky side of the Ohio River. That's what they say. Even so, I doubt Slim would have divulged anything about Stooly. I warmed to him because of that loyalty and discovered he wasn't so bad after all.

Slim lived the rest of his life ever watchful and satisfying his wife and her honey-do list. He would always suffer weakness in his right arm and walk with a slight limp in his right leg. Despite this, he would retire after a life of repairing cars from a garage business of his own, known merely as Aces.

Augie continued to sell bootleg liquor from the basement of his house, blithely unaware of what happened to the man known to him as Ajax. Years later, shortly after his life was threatened by errant moonshiners for cheating on profits, he converted to serve Christ as an ardent deacon for Reverend Avery.

Mark Roberts, two years older than Doreen, attended Harvard to obtain a degree in medicine. Although they seemingly went their separate ways during high school, they would surprise us. When Doreen graduated high school, she joined him in Virginia, where Mark practiced medicine. There, their dreams came to fruition. I was their biggest supporter and fan, with many attending their beautiful wedding. Following in his father's footsteps, he practices medicine while she excels raising their children.

As new opportunities abounded for others, the Greenfield neighborhood saw many changes. Miss Edna never snooped again and became the beloved grand dame or highly favored person of the Greenfield neighborhood. She got to know Mr. Lonesome well, and at that late stage in life, was content. She continued cooking chicken at the American Legion Hall until 1983. Upon her passing, it was rumored that during World War II, her use of special herbs and spices was the model Colonel Sanders of Kentucky Fried Chicken fame used to perfect his famous recipes. God only knows the truth.

The Tallys moved to Chicago. They often visited my parents in Washington, D.C., as did I, swapping war stories and reminiscing about the old Greenfield neighborhood. Dad would eventually accept a position in Colorado Springs, retiring there, where my parents lived permanently under Colorado's brilliant blue skies.

Mrs. Sandra Beaumont continued her charitable endeavors with women's organizations, focusing on homelessness and domestic issues. Thanks to the endorsement received from Mrs. Woodhaven Ferguson, she was recognized for this work by the Daughters of the Revolution, Kentucky chapter. This was far and away from anything the Averys, Crawfords, or Randalls could boast.

Angela and Carolyn attended Morehead State University, studying business management and psychology, respectively. Clarissa went on to attend Wellesley College for political science. Mrs. Ferguson became a patron of the arts. She was welcomed to the Kentucky Board of Education as a prominent member, championing female education efforts for women of color and the disadvantaged. I was the benefactor of her position and actions, being granted a scholarship to attend college to study education. This was an absolute honor.

Barry and I became more than dancing partners. We wrote to each other daily while he attended Yale, with me at the University of Kentucky. Now, I dance with him every chance I get for the rest of my life, God willing. I cherish Miss Katherine's figurine, which was given to me upon her death and is often a topic of conversation; that and Miss Virginia's handkerchief, which the figurine sits upon.

The Jungle is still intact and considered hallowed ground. No one dare enter or bulldoze it because of what happened there. Rumors are of it being haunted. It is said a lady can be seen roaming between the trees, smelling of lavender, and singing softly, right before the rising of the morning dew.

## *The End*

# ACKNOWLEDGMENTS

There are so many people to thank for helping to make this book possible. I will try to name them all and hope I do not forget anyone.

I would like to thank the people of Paris, Kentucky, who graciously gave their time and attention to this project. They include but are not limited to many high school friends such as Ronnie Scott, who gave his time and support in helping to open doors for interviews and available resources for research. Delia Baldwin Sadler provided much-needed support and guided me toward other resources like Betty Ann Rice Allen, Director at Paris-Bourbon Kentucky Chamber of Commerce and Tourism. Betty Ann subsequently read and approved this book's Introduction page and pointed me toward Sharon Fields, Author, Educator, and Circulation Clerk at Paris-Bourbon County Library, for further accuracy. Many thanks to Betty Ann and Sharon for helping me fine-tune the front matter and for their valuable support.

Teachers such as Doris McFarland and particularly Mrs. Kenny Roseberry, whose insight into Paris's rich history and engaging interviews I could not have done without, thank you. I will always treasure the interview and autographed copies of *Paris and Bourbon County* and *Bourbon County 1860 – 1940* by notable authors Jeanine and Berkeley Scott. Thank you for your time and the history lessons. So good.

I must mention the treasure trove of historical information from recorded interviews with the citizens of Paris's African American community. Thank you to Sara Abdmishani Price, Collections Coordinator at the Louie B. Nunn Center for Oral History Special Collections at the University of Kentucky Libraries, for helping me obtain these interviewed recordings. The interviews, titled "Bourbon County and Kentucky African American Oral History Project," were conducted by Reinette Jones and Kellie Scott. The recordings are a remarkable testament to the lives and struggles of those who lived through the civil rights era in Paris, Kentucky. Again, my heartfelt thanks.

Many other resources, too many to name, were used in my research and provided valuable reference material. Most were obtained from the Paris-Bourbon County Library, the University of Kentucky Library, and the Kentucky State University Library database in Frankfort, Kentucky. These libraries provided a plethora of information about Paris's and Kentucky's history of slavery, the origin of slaves, culture, and people, particularly during the "segregation to integration" era of the civil rights movement.

My Creole heritage has been one of the many inspirations I drew on for my main character. Through her, I had to investigate other online data sources, such as the *Louisiana Creole Dictionary* website and "Khouri-Vini Louisiana Creole French," found on the *Memrise* website. This is the language and mother tongue of Relelia B. Davies (French pronunciation = Dáviès), or Momma Rei, my Creole grandmother. This seldom-spoken language is the original voice of the Louisiana Creole people and is represented in this book. Distinctively different from the fabulous Cajun French, I hope I haven't botched it too severely. I also hope that it sparks interest in further reviving the language of the French-speaking people of Creole descent (gens de couleur) of Louisiana.

Many thanks to the people who have put their eyes on this book. Apart from those already mentioned who gave sanctions to the Introduction, they include beta readers, book coaches, critique partners, editors, family members, and friends who endured my "kiss, cry, and heavy sigh" moments. You know who you are, and again, thank you very much.

A special thanks to my father, who never let me forget my Creole heritage, from food to language to culture, and the love of reading the many books in his private library. To my "one and only" son, I love you dearly. He has no idea what a blessing and inspiration he's been to me. To him, I say that nothing is out of reach if you believe in yourself. You can do it. Thank you to Mr. Allen Lewis for his encouragement and support throughout these many years. What a blessing to have him in my life, especially during those dark days of uncertainty. No one could ask for a better family friend. This I know for sure. A grateful thank you and much love to my mother, Nora Frances Harris. She has made many things possible, and I owe so much to her. I hope this makes her smile. The written stories and works from my other grandmother Jo Emma Harris have been invaluable, and I am so thankful to have had them passed down to me. I will always treasure her love of history and family recollections, along with those of my uncle Harry Lee Harris. I received my first book from him in 1967 and want to give a heavenly thank-you and say, "I have it still, and *I'm OK....*"

God has been with me throughout this journey. I give my ultimate thanks to Him.

# GLOSSARY



*(Not to be confused with Louisiana French, also spoken in Louisiana, known as Cajun French.)*

**çá çé** = this is
**e** = and
**èskizé** = excuse
**kòfè** = why
**komprenn** = understand
**korèk** = correct
**mamm** = mom
**mé, wé** = but yes
**mo** = I
**mò** = me
**mô** = my

**Naglé** = English
**Non** = no
**Nou** = we
**pa** = not
**paddonné** = forgive
**sé** = could
**ségré** = secret
**shè** = sweetheart/darling
**un/in** = one
**vré** = true
**wé** = yes

## Sentence translations used in novel

(**"Ça cé korèk. Èskizé e paddonné mô ségré, shè** = This is correct. Excuse and forgive my secret, darling.)

(**...çá çé vré. Komprenn?** = ...this is true. Understand?)

(**sé nou?** = could we?)

(**Kòfè pa?** = Why not?)

(**mô ségré** = my secret)

(**shè** = my darling)

(**"Shush now, mô shè!"** = Shush now, my sweetheart!)

(**mô un ségré**) = my one secret

(**Wé, Mamm, mo komprenn. Mé wé, mô ségré** = Yes, mom, I undertand. But yes, my secret...)

## Mexican Urban words and meaning
## (some Spanish)

**cabrón** = asshole/bastard/dumbass

**ese** = man, bro, homie

**qué** = what

**qué pasa** = what's going on (inflection is key, considered rude if said to someone unknown)

**vato** = dude/guy (bato = guy or dude, but vato = considered to be vulgar and offensive)

(**... .It don't mean going through the whole load, Ese."** = ... .It don't mean going through the whole load, man)

(**"¿Qué pasa, cabrón?"** = What's going on, asshole?)

(**"No good for you, vato?"** = Not good (enough) for you, man?)

## German words and meaning

**kinder** = children

**kleine** = young, small

(**For any of his *kleine kinder*, as he called us to suffer pain** = For any of his young children to suffer pain.)

# COLLOQUIAL EXPRESSIONS

*(definitions refer to how the words are used in the book and as the author understands them)*

**Ace Boon Coon** = is said to refer to a person as a very good and trusted friend. Usually used between two people of African American descent. Closer than a family member. A person of trust and dependability.

**Ain't got the sense God gave a goose** = which refers to a stupid person.

**As apologetic as a cold lizard on a hot rock** = refers to an insincere apology.

**Bad Juju** = not a good omen. Feeling of being cursed.

**Beholden** = used to denote owing someone, i.e., money, possession, or favor.

**Big Wally** = Enormous pimple.

**Black and White hand side** = a slap of hand palms in greeting (white hand side), or a slap of the back side of hands in greeting (black hand side). Usually used between two people of African American descent.

**Bless your heart** = is a common Southern expression. Usually, if the emphasis is placed on "bless," it is used to excuse someone for being stupid or foolish. If the emphasis is placed on "heart," it is used as an expression of endearment for doing something viewed as very sweet and pleasant or to pity someone who doesn't know any better due to a physical affliction or illness.

**Blinders** = a horse racing method used to fix blinders on the side of a horse's head so that no distractions are seen. The horse focuses on the track ahead of him.

**Boil you in oil** = is playfully said to describe scalding someone if they misbehave or have misbehaved.

**Break too fast** = in horse racing, it is imperative not to allow your horse to move before the pack at the beginning of a race. To 'break' is to start together. This euphemism can be applied to humans as well.

**Breezing** = a training technique used in thoroughbred horse racing. To build lung capacity in a horse by running around the track at a moderate speed without urging.

**Climb his frame** = to refer to a verbal assault given to someone for doing wrong. Used in much the same way as "chewed him out" or "cleaned his clock."

**Come again** = used when needing someone to repeat what they just said. Usually used to have someone repeat something outrageous.

**Common sense ain't all that common** = to refer to some as not having good reasoning skills.

**Doing this in chapters** = refers to doing something one step at a time. Breaking something into pieces.

**Fix (fixing to or fix me)** = preparing to do something or go somewhere, i.e., "I'm gonna fix me a bowl of cereal."

**Full of spit and vinegar** = refers to a hot-tempered person, i.e., "He's just full of spit and vinegar." An angry person who says vile and nasty things.

**Get in his ass** = to verbally tell someone, using explicit language, how they've botched something. To get "on his ass" connotes a gentler telling-off.

**Get in your britches** = to verbally tell someone (usually a child) that he might get a spanking.

**Getting some of yours back** = to get back the respect lost from an unwarranted attack. To get back what was taken. To get back *at* someone who has done you wrong.

**Give her a piece of my mind** (without literally doing so) = to tell someone how you really feel without concern for their feelings.

**Give a horse his head/give him his head** = a racing term to allow a horse to run full speed (full out) without urging. To run free at their own pace. Allow someone to do something without interference.

**Going back home** = refers to going home or traveling to your hometown.

**He's so thin; if he turned sideways, he'd disappear** = refers to a very thin person.

**High-handed** = refers to someone overtaking a situation to make it beneficial for themselves.

**High and mighty** = thinking more of yourself and/or intelligence than required.

**Hold your horses/hold up/hold down** = to slow down, wait or quiet your voice or action. Refers to someone assuming more than they should or moving ahead in thought or actions.

**Hot piss** = is typically said when wanting to hurt someone, such as the act of using hot urine to throw on someone you dislike, i.e., a pot of hot piss to throw on someone or to say, "Where's my pot of hot piss." A messy situation.

**Kentucky rain** = fine rain that creates a sizzling sound when it hits tree leaves.

**Knuckle up/knuckling** = a horse racing term used to roll knuckles into a horse's neck to urge him on. Used to refer to preparing for a fight (street slang).

**Let's play/dance** = to refer to an altercation or engage in a fun activity.

**Meaner than a striped snake** = refers to a very mean person.

**Mud Bugs/Crawdads** = Crayfish or Crawfish. Usually found dwelling in a river bank.

**No'am** = contraction for no ma'am, i.e., "No'am, I don't mind."

**Pull/Rein your horse in** = refers to an effort to control a person acting in such a way to cause possible harm to others or themselves either through actions or words.

**Proper speech/speak proper** = refers to speaking without any Southern inflection or accents.

**Psych** = is used as slang, unlike lying. Often used to refer to fooling or tricking someone into thinking one way when the opposite is true. Then confess the truth, i.e., "I psyched y'all out. You know I wouldn't do that."

**Scratch that itch** = refers to something that has to be severely scratched to ease irritation or a craving. A derogatory phrase that is sometimes used to refer to a need for sex.

**Siditty(Saditty)/Bougie(Bourgeois)/Uppity** = used to describe people who think they are better than others.

**Six ways from Sunday** = a phrase used to denote a desire to get back at a person in many ways.

**Slap you blind** = to strike someone so hard as to cause loss of sight.

**Slow your row or roll** = used to refer to someone who is pulling ahead of you in thought or action. "Row" was a vernacular used by fieldhands or enslaved people, referring to works moving too fast for others to keep pace. "Roll" has become a more popular derivation of this phrase.

**A snake that bites before it rattles** = refers to a person who will strike when you least expect it. It is expected, but unsure when it will occur.

Different from a "bitch slap" which is unexpected.

**Snatch her baldheaded** = to quickly pull the hair off the scalp, which results in baldness.

**Studying** = refers to someone watching without speaking, i.e., "She said nothing, just studied me for a long time." A way of learning something from a textbook or research.

**Tell her about herself** = to tell someone how badly they have insulted you by telling them their faults in hopes of correcting their behavior.

**Telling stories/Telling tales** = telling lies. Telling a story of fiction.

**The devil beating his wife** = a phenomenon that occurs when the sun shines through clouds and rains simultaneously.

**Thought up** = to get people riled up or to stir 'up' trouble through conversation.

**Wouldn't spit on him if he was on fire** = to dislike someone so much if they were on fire, you wouldn't bother to throw any amount of water on him to put out the flame.

**Y'all** = to refer to a group of people. A contraction of the phrase "you all."

# ABOUT THE AUTHOR

Donna Lawrence writes in the genre of women's fiction set in historical periods, even touching on coming-of-age in small-town America. *Miss Virginia and the Sweet Sisters* is her debut novel. She is working on her second novel and a collection of short stories and poems.

She is a poet with works published in a compilation and local newspapers. Two of her poems are featured on the 9/11 Memorial Museum website.

Donna Lawrence was born and raised in Kentucky but has been a longtime resident of Colorado. Both states hold special meaning and the many experiences she's had are ones she draws on in her writing.

She posts monthly on her personal blog.

Debut Novel: *Miss Virginia and the Sweet Sisters*, fiction.

Look for: *Looking In from Outside*, a collection of short stories and poems.

The 9/11 Memorial Museum Website Poems: "The Rain" and "The Heir."

# CONTACT

Crescent Hill Press
PO Box 200754
Denver, Colorado 80220

**Email:** donna@donnamarielawrence.com
**Website:** donnamarielawrence.com